The Open and Shut Case

Volume One of

The Case Books of Octavius Bear

Harry DeMaio

"Alternative Universe Mysteries for Adult Animal Lovers"

Paperback ISBN 978-1-78092-689-6
ePub ISBN 978-1-78092-690-2
PDF ISBN 978-1-78092-691-9

Published in the UK by MX Publishing
335 Princess Park Manor, Royal Drive,
London, N11 3GX
www.mxpublishing.co.uk
Cover design compiled www.staunch.com

Dedicated to GTP

A Most Extraordinary Bear

Acknowledgements

These books have evolved over a long period of time and under a wide range of influences and circumstances. I am indebted to many people for helping to bring Octavius and his cohorts to the printed page. Thanks most especially to my wife, Virginia, for her insights and clever suggestions as well as her unfailing enthusiasm for the project and patience with its author. To my sons, Mark and Andrew and their spouses, Cindy and Lorraine, for helping make these tomes more readable and audience friendly. To Cathy Hartnett, cheerleader-extraordinaire, for her eagerness to see this alternative universe take form. To some fellow authors, Richard Hoskin, Charlie Colman, Barry Raut and members of the Monday Morning Writers Group for their valuable observations and to friends like Dan Andriacco, Lisa and Pete Taylor, Joe Querciagrossa, Paul and Jeanne Bernish as well as Steve Appel for taking the time to read, comment and enthuse.

A special thank you to my editor and coach, Coleen (Ms. Comma-kaze) Armstrong for her critical support, excellent suggestions, enthusiasm and battlefield survival techniques for my punctuation and grammar. Kudos to Jim Effler, my illustrator, who so wonderfully made visible the characters I saw in my imagination. If, in spite of all this help, some errors or inconsistencies have crept through, the buck stops here. Needless to say, all of the characters, situations, and narratives are fictional.

The Players

The Good Guys:

Octavius Bear –Narcoleptic war hero; consulting detective, scientist, inventor; seeker of justice; mega-billionaire owner of Universal Ursine Industries; gourmet/gourmand; somewhat sedentary and grouchy just on general principles.

Mauritius (Maury) Meerkat – Part-time narrator; assistant to Octavius; African *émigré* with a French-Dutch background; clever with a shady history;

Inspector Bruce Wallaroo – Irrepressible but brilliant marsupial; an international law and order genius from Down Under; often calls on Octavius and Maury for support.

Bearoness Belinda Béarnaise Bruin (nee Black) – Romantic interest of Octavius; very rich widow of Bearon Byron Bruin living in Bearmoral Castle in the Shetlands; Owner-pilot of the last flying Concorde SST; Gorgeous polar superstar, with the Aquashow, "Some Like It Cold."

Bearyl and Bearnice – Belinda's stunning twin sidekicks; Actress and singer, respectively. Co-pilot and flight engineer of Belinda's SST.

Frau Schuylkill – Octavius' beautiful Swiss she-wolf housekeeper/cook/pilot with many other mysterious and military talents. She rescued Octavius from his dive off the Breakurbach Falls struggling with his nemesis, Imperius Drake.

Wyatt Where – Another wolf. Former military intelligence officer who had retired to a security post at the Bank of Lake Michigan in Chicago and then quit to join Octavius.

Howard Watt – A porcupine, high tech security authority who also left the bank with Wyatt to join Octavius. A laser and particle beam accelerator expert.

The Chicago Police Department – Irish Setters and Polish Retrievers all named Daley or Dzawlicza (pronounced Daley.)

The Bad Guys:

Imperius Drake – "Moriarty with wings." Arch-villain, Leader of the Black Quack gang; Brilliant but loony duck who has developed a serum to make the animal kingdom his slaves; Seeks vengeance for ridicule by the scientific community and the death of his beloved Lee-Li-Li.

Bigg Baboon – The major muscle in Black Quack; the archetypical dumb heavy

Chita - Imperius' clever, deadly and not always trusted associate; beautiful, fascinating, clever, sexy, immoral and highly independent feline who joins forces with Imperius but entirely on her own terms. Chita reappears in subsequent books as a principal character in her own right.

<u>Assorted Other Characters</u>: Montgomery Moose III, Chairmoose of the Bank of Lake Michigan and overstuffed jerk; **Bombey Megatunni,** Komodo Dragon, a Casino Security Chief; **Henry, Ozzie and Izzie**, Nevada Desert Patrol; **Win-Win**, Panda, Owner of the Golden Pagoda Casino.. **Ferrucio Ferreti,** genetics sleaze; *Il Professore* **Roberto Rabbito**, genetics phony.

The Development of Civilization — Part 1

Our Origins

(From "An Introduction to Faunapology" by Octavius Bear, Ph.D.)

"*About 100,000 years ago, according to scientific experts, a colossal solar flare blasted out from our Sun, creating gigantic magnetic storms here on Earth. These highly charged electrical tempests caused startling physical and psychological imbalances in the then population of our world. The complete nervous systems of some species were totally destroyed.*

For example, Homo Sapiens lost all mental and motor capabilities and rapidly became extinct. Less developed species exposed to the radiation were affected differently. Four-footed and finned mammals, birds, and reptiles suddenly found themselves capable of complex thought, enhanced emotions, self-awareness, social awareness, and the ability to communicate, sometimes orally, sometimes telepathically, often both. Both speech production and speech perception slowly progressed with the evolution of tongues, lips, vocal cords, and enhanced ear- to- brain connections. Many species developed opposable digits, fingers or claws, further accelerating civilized progress. Some others (most fish and underground dwellers) were shielded from the radiation and remained only as sentient as they were before the blast.

*This event is referred to as **The Big Shock**. It remains under intensive study.*"

Prologue

The Peacock, with art-deco tail

Spreads it out like a billowing sail.

The poor Peahen does not.

She can't share his proud lot.

Eyes unveil in the tail of the male.

"If that damn peacock shows his beak in here one more time, I'm going to nail his feathers to the wall and turn him into performance art."

Opening day of a new museum exhibit hardly qualifies for a World Peace and Tranquility Award. Opening day at the Loupe Museum in downtown Chicago showed early signs of re-starting the Great Inter-Species War.

The Director was sitting on top of his desk next to the phone, whiskers quivering, tail aloft and eyes glowing with righteous anger. It was 8:00 AM, two hours before opening time. He'd already gone through two pots of prairie coffee and had just called out to his secretary for a third.

"This museum has been managed by my family of pack rats for over a century and no damn art deco feather duster is going to tell me how to open a new show. That bird's squawk is enough to set off the burglar alarms. 'Docteur Loupe, the lights in Hall Three are too soft. Docteur Loupe, the gift shop doesn't have enough copies of my monograph. Docteur Loupe, the walls in the Deep Blue Sapphire Room create echoes. The room should be still and silent.' If he wants still and silent, he should swallow a sponge."

The speaker – Montebello Loupe Ph.D., *Director of the Loupe Museum for the Decorative Arts in Chicago.*

2

The target of his ire – Phillipe de Peacoq, *Parisian Curator Emeritus and Senior Fellow for Manifestations Artistiques from the Global Association of Exquisite Jewelers and Gemologists.*

The event – Day One of the blockbuster show – ***Jewels to Die For - Bijoux, Baubles and Blood*** – a traveling treasure trove of beauty and evil. Each gem in the collection bore its own unique curse. Each, it is said, had inflicted hideous mayhem on those who had crossed its glittering path. The public and the press ate it up. Between phone interviews, requests for private showings and the constant bitching of the peacock, Loupe was at the end of his ordinarily short temper.

The "star" of the show was the Deep Blue Sapphire, a magnificent 372 carat, faceted gem whose name didn't begin to describe the intensity of its unfathomable indigo depths. Males had killed for this stone and a few females had been caught up in the collateral damage. Legend has it that since its discovery two hundred and thirty five years ago, at least seven individuals lost their lives, all in "unusual" circumstances and all due to ownership or attempted ownership of the sapphire.

In all, there were thirty five "cursed" pieces in the show. Radiant emeralds; deep lustrous rubies; shimmering diamonds; pearls - large blacks, miniscule but perfect whites and every shade and size in between; a rainbow of sapphires – displayed either unset or in necklaces, bracelets, chokers, and enough earrings to adorn the lobes of a pack of poodles. No matter their gemological pedigrees, they all shared bizarre histories. Strangled tomb robbers, suicidal nobles, impaled jewel thieves, assassinated royalty, disappearing actresses, choking rock stars. Everything that makes death worth dying!

And in one hour and fifty minutes, the museum doors would open and the games would begin. There was a large and impatient crowd assembling outside the building. When they finally did stampede into the exhibits, with any luck, some oversized beast would trample that feathered test pattern underfoot. Oh, how he hated that pretentious, pompous Parisian.

Just as Dr. Loupe was settling down again, a horrendous screech came echoing down the halls. Who else? That damn peacock! This time the burglar alarms did go off ,and as the Director scrambled from his office he was knocked over by a black and orange freight train *(later identified as a cheetah)*. Guards and staff were running in all directions. The gift shop was a shambles and on top of all the other noises there was a god-awfully loud duck sounding off non-stop…"QUAAAACK, QUAAAACK, QUAAAACK, QUA…*(you get the idea)*

"Au secours, zut alors, sacre bleu! It is gone! C'est disparu!!!" And more of the same from the *Parisian Curator Emeritus*, as he spread his gorgeous fantail dramatically and fell over in a dead faint.

The dazed and bruised pack rat picked himself up from his collision and skittered down the hall past the recumbent bird and into the Deep Blue Room, where ungodly quacks were rattling every door, fixture, and display case.

"Shut that duck up!!" he shouted, "I can't hear myself curse! Who is that anyway? Shut him up, I said."

Over the din, a guard, trying to hold his ears, pointed to the floor in front of the Deep Blue Sapphire's display case and shouted, "It's not a duck. It's an egg!!!"

"A what?"

"An egg. See it?" He pointed at a shiny black ovoid the size of a puppy's football. The sound seemed to radiate from it.

"Get it out of here! Now! No! Wait! Better yet, get some of the shipping blankets off the show trolleys and cover it up. Don't move it yet!!"

He looked up for the first time at the side of the case. Stuck to the buffed aluminum of the Deep Blue's plinth was a sign. Written on vintage vellum in Olde English Script was the greeting, **"Salutations, Bear! Attention, Wallaroo! Now You See It, Now You Don't."**

4

Dr. Loupe jumped up on the Small Animals' Viewing Platform and stared into the empty case. The white velvet pedestal that had modestly borne the proud jewel was intact. The display top seemed firmly in place, but there was a distinct absence of jewelry. The sign said it all. The Deep Blue had been deep-sixed.

Running back to his office to call his chief of security and the police, he tripped over the supine peacock. He told his secretary, Aramantha, to revive the bird while he made his calls.

"Get me Inspector Wallaroo," he screamed into the phone. "Where is that hopped up Aussie?"

After a few seconds, Aramantha darted back into his office. An albino rat, it seemed impossible that she could be any paler than she usually was. She was! "Doctor Loupe," she stuttered, "I think the peacock is dead!"

Loupe dropped the phone and ran out into the hall to view the elegant fowl, tail in full array, artfully ensconced beneath a piece of Greco-Roman statuary – three piglets being nursed by a she-wolf. Rustling through the forest of feathers, he leaned over and listened for a heartbeat or a breath. Nothing! Aramantha was right. Phillipe de Peacoq, *Parisian Curator Emeritus and Senior Fellow for Manifestations Artistiques from the Global Association of Exquisite Jewelers and Gemologists* was no more. The Deep Blue Sapphire had claimed another victim.

Octavius

Chapter One

Do Bears give you a scare? Well, me too!

So I'll pass on this tactic to you.

You just fix that old Bear

With a cold, piercing stare.

But make sure that he's Winnie-the-Pooh!

"However!"

"However what?"

"Maury, every picture of meerkats I've ever seen shows you guys as watchful, vigilant and alert little creatures. Why don't you ever pay attention to me? For your exclusive and personal edification, I have just completed a brilliant exposition of my upcoming testimony on the accelerating incidence of white-collar crime throughout the known universe. I'm a witness at CCRIME.* I refuse to begin again."

I should tell you that Octavius Bear, my employer, mutual confidant and classic pain in the tail had just returned from another of his brief attacks of involuntary sleep *(narcolepsy, to the medically inclined)*. We were sitting *(he had been slumped)* in his oversized office. This in turn, was inside his opulent mansion located just far enough from Cincinnati and the Ohio River to maintain some level of secrecy. Not a lot, but some. More about geography, topography, architecture, and other such stuff shortly.

(Congressional Committee for the Restoration of Industrial and Marketplace Ethics)

Over half an hour had elapsed since I was last "exclusively and personally edified." As you may know, Octavius is a nine foot tall Kodiak bear, the largest of the ursine species, larger even than the male polar bear. Standing upright, with his jaws open, formidable teeth on total display, brown and black fur bristling, eyes locked in a fierce, unblinking stare and his Dolby 5.1 roar at full amplification, he presents a magnificent example of nature at its most powerful and horrible.

On the other paw, among his many talents and accomplishments, he is a brilliant, self-taught practitioner in biology, physics, ursinology *(bears)*, voodoo, chemistry, apiculture *(bees)*, and oenology *(wine, especially honey wine or mead)*. A self-made megabillionaire, he is also a first rate electrical, electronic, structural, weapons, aeronautical, marine, space, mechanical, and chemical engineer. A truly remarkable combination!

Early in his career, while he was dabbling in biology, he developed an antidote for the annoying *(for him)* need for bears to hibernate. This allowed him to dedicate himself year-round to his businesses, his studies and research, his personal avocations and especially his primary vocation – the protection and betterment of all animal-kind.

Much of this latter activity over the past few years has involved battling the ultra-criminal Imperius Drake and his two henchbeasts, Chita *(you guessed it)* and Bigg Baboon. Much more of them later!

Unfortunately, unknown *(or more likely, unaccepted or unadmitted)* by him to this day, the antidote for hibernation has a serious side effect. The Great Bear falls off

into periodic and often poorly timed narcoleptic sleep that can last from a few seconds to upwards of an hour.

Once he wakes up again, he blithely carries on as if nothing had happened. Every now and again, when it has resulted in a particularly dangerous or embarrassing situation *(cf. Octavius Bear and the Overflowing Bathtub)* I've tried to make him face up to his problem. Score so far: Bear 564 - Meerkat 0. But I digress.

"I don't suppose you'd believe me if I…"

"No," he roared, "I would not. Now pay attention. If the bleeding hearts insist on their ridiculous assertions that megabillionaires caught with their paws in the honey pot are simply victims of an oppressive society, I shall have to…"

We were interrupted by the soundless approach of Frau Schuylkill, Bear's housekeeper, cook, chief pilot, and security officer. Octavius had hired her from an old inn in Switzerland where she had nursed him back to health after his accident at Breakurbach Falls while pursuing the arch-fiend Imperius Drake. Not to put too sharp a claw on it, she is a wolf. A dangerous, good-looking wolf. In fact, a real fox.

And she is blindly devoted to the Bear. She glanced over at me with that hundred tooth grin that gave new meaning to the phrase, "wolf your food."

"Your pardon, Herr Bear," she rasped, "but Inspector Wallaroo has just arrived and must speak to you urgently."

"All right, Frau Schuylkill," sighed the Bear, "but make sure you and Maury get everything breakable out of his path."

"*Ja, mein Herr*" she growled, pausing to pick up several priceless and fragile antiques presented to Octavius by various and sundry crowned *(and uncrowned)* heads of state.

Inspector Bruce Wallaroo requires no introduction to crime aficionados. He has bounded his way through forests of felonies since he first emerged from joey-hood and is now one of the world's leading criminologists

– on a par – although Octavius would never admit it – with the Great Bear himself.

His career began as an obscure foot patrolman in Melbourne – bouncing along on his beat in the seamier parts of town – The Bounding Bobby, they called him. There weren't many marsupials on the force and even among them, he stood out, if for no other reason than his inability to stand or sit still. Morning formation was sheer torture for him. He ducked out of police parades because he couldn't stay in line. He wanted to leap to the front and wave a baton. Bruce was nothing if not patriotic. On ANZAC Day he covered himself with the flag and caromed off street corners, public buildings and rubbish bins singing *Advance Australia Fair* on the top of his lungs. He came dangerously close on several occasions to being mustered out by his superiors for being too energetic. This, of course, was anathema to any self-respecting policeman.

Then, one evening, Bruce's fortunes took a turn for the better, although it didn't seem so at the time. He was hopping along the street covering his beat when he suddenly heard screams for help. He turned into an alley and saw a pack of tough looking dingoes trying to assault a female emu. *(The national bird, for goodness sake!)* His senses of duty, patriotism and chivalry all rose up to supercharge his energy and he went to work battering and flattening the wild dogs. He got several severe bites for his trouble, but finally the snarling pack, licking their own wounds, retreated from the scene, howling menacingly as they slinked away.

He staggered over to the emu and said, "G'day mum, are you quite all right?"

Before she could answer, he passed out. Next morning, he woke up in a hospital bed with bandages scattered around his leathery hide. He had lost a little of his right ear in the bargain. A wombat nurse clumped into the room, carrying a stack of newspapers and said, "You're a bonzer hero, officer, look at these tabloids." There on page one of the Melbourne *Monitor*, the Sydney *Shout*, the Canberra *Clarion* and the Antipodean *Advance* sat a picture of Bruce, covered with blood and lying unconscious on his side. The headlines varied a little, but they all said essentially the same thing: "Hero Bobby Rescues Mayor's Daughter." The stories went on to tell how he had single pawedly held off a pack of thirty ravenous dingoes *(there were really six),* beat several of them to death by jumping on them *(he wounded one,)* and carried the hysterical emu to safety. *(He collapsed at her feet.)*

Obviously, the mayor's daughter had been somewhere she shouldn't have been, doing something she shouldn't have been doing with someone she shouldn't have been with. So she created a story making Bruce the biggest hero since Ned Kelly, the famous Australian bandicoot. He got the publicity. She got away with whatever she was trying to cover up.

Bruce read all the newspapers carefully and was ready for his superiors when they came for his report. He claimed he couldn't talk much – too weak from loss of blood and in some pain but essentially, the mayor's daughter's story was true. The press descended on him in his hospital bed and took more pictures of him, this time swathed in bandages. He was interviewed by two TV stations until his doctor, a Tasmanian Devil, bared his teeth and ordered everyone out of the room.

Next morning, the Mayor and Police Commissioner dropped by to thank him and to tell him he was being promoted to Sergeant in the plain clothes detective division. And thus it began. It turned out Bruce Wallaroo was a very fine, nay excellent, detective and he became a legend in his own mind. Promotion followed promotion as he cracked thefts, robberies, murders, drive-by embezzlements, art and jewel heists. He was called on by Interpol and began to spend more of his time on international assignments, now as a representative of the Australian National Police. He began undercover work, but discovered he hopped around too much to keep the covers on.

It was on one such assignment – an international peat moss smuggling ring – that he met Octavius Bear. Together, they caught the chief smuggler, a nasty Irish terrier, broke up the ring, got peat moss prices down once more to reasonable levels, and saved the industry from being shoveled under.

So, Wallaroo sprang up from obscurity Down Under and bounced to the very pinnacle of his profession. Together, he and Octavius have created legends that are studied worldwide in police colleges, intelligence training programs and even detective correspondence courses.

Yes, Inspector Wallaroo is a marsupial of the highest intelligence but he is also virtually unintelligible when he lapses into his heavy Strine accent. He can also reduce a room to rubble by the simple act of "pacing back and forth" – which in his case consists of springing from one vertical or horizontal surface to another with incredible speed and impact while his Aussie mind moves at warp nine.

Needless to say, we never allow Frau Schuylkill and Wallaroo to be alone in the same room. She would no doubt tear him apart in a moment, all the time snarling about his "big dirty feet all over my nice clean sofa." or "*Ach*, another broken end-table." Right then, I could hear her howling loudly in the kitchen – her standard reaction whenever Inspector Bruce Wallaroo arrived.

Between his bounding, his Strine and her baying, a casual conversation among friends/colleagues doesn't come easily. So in the interest of keeping you with me, I'll filter out the background noise and translate the foreground. Before I do, I'll give you a raw sample of Bruce's conversation, just so you know what an effort I'm making on your behalf.

"G'day Maury, G'day Ocko. Had another dust up with yer wolf. Oughta flick that sheila back of beyond and git a proper jillaroo (female hand). *She's a no-hoper. D'give her a gobful m'self, but she's a bitie, she is. Don't want nuther barney* (fight) *wither, I don't."*

You probably got the drift. Frau Schuylkill did not greet Bruce with anything near cordiality, and once again he's urging Octavius *(to no avail)* to get rid of the wolf and take on a more traditional housekeeper. He further states that like myself, he doesn't want to mix it up with Frau Schuylkill whose hundred or so teeth, silent approach, tenacious jaws, dumbfounding speed, and muscular weight would...well anyway.

With the exception of an occasional "Crikey," "G'day," "Shrimp on the Barbie," and other Qantas Airlines Strine to remind you of Wallaroo's origins, I'll present his dialog in Midwest U.S. English for the rest of this story. This is difficult for me, given my French-Dutch-African foreboers. At a later point, I'll tell you how a Meerkat ended up on the African offshore island of Mauritius, but obviously Inspector Wallaroo has a pressing need to confer with the Great Bear.

"Ocko," he blurted, "that damned Duck has done it again." Inspector Bruce Wallaroo was the only one permitted to call Octavius Bear "Ocko," and this only after long years of association.

"Calm yourself, Inspector," rumbled Octavius, "and come down off the piano. Would you like a drink?"

"Thanks, Beer, I'll have a bear, if you don't mind."

"Maury, beer for the Inspector! I'll have mead and get something for yourself. Now, Inspector, are you telling me that Imperius Drake has come out of his self-imposed retirement and is back to doing his dire and desperate deeds?"

"I am indeed, although I doubt he ever retired. I think he just went south for the winter."

"You're probably right," said Octavius. "It was too much to hope that his last defeat at our paws would have discouraged his criminal urges but...once a Duck, always a Duck."

Here, of course, the Bear was referring to the generally irascible nature of ducks as illustrated by the famous Daffy, Donald, and Scrooge. But Imperius Drake took irascibility to a much higher level. He was out and out nasty with major top notes of dastardliness. While other criminal minds had risen to challenge Wallaroo and Bear, none had created the same obsessive priority in their busy lives as had Imperius Drake.

13

"Rightcherare, Ocko, he's a bad bloke, but this crime beats all. I wouldn't have believed it was him if he hadn't left his signature at the scene."

"The Black Quack???"

"The same! It must be him. As far as I know, no one else can make the damned thing. And he's the only one who can handle it without going starkers."

The Black Quack was an apparently solid, ebony ovoid about the size of a duck's egg, made of some unidentifiable material that withstood all our efforts to analyze, dismantle or destroy it. Seemingly inert, it emitted an unbearably loud and constant quacking sound whenever it was approached or touched. No doubt it was Imperius' version of giving us the bird. The only way it could be handled or transported was with high-tech earplugs and soundproof containers.

"Well, Inspector," growled Octavius, "you've identified the culprit but so far Maury and I are totally in the dark as to what exactly our old nemesis has done."

"The Impossible! That's what he's done. The Impossible!"

"My dear Inspector Wallaroo, remember my first principle of detection. After eliminating the possibly improbable, whatever is left is probably impossible."

"Yeah, yeah, I know, Ocko. But this time he's done it. Made an irreplaceable jewel disappear into thin air."

"Oh, come, come, Inspector, not another trite jewelry theft. Maury, how many disappearing jewel tales do we have in my memoirs?"

I had returned with the drinks. Wallaroo chugged his beer, and Octavius sloshed his keg of mead as I pondered a moment over my mug of fermented coconut milk VSOP.

"At least a hundred," I replied.

"And how many of them were the Deep Blue Sapphire?" shouted the Inspector.

This stopped the conversation dead in its tracks. I had never before seen the Great Bear blanch, but he was certainly doing a good imitation.

"The Deep Blue? But we designed the security for that ourselves." he said. "It was impregnable!!"

"I thought so too but when I arrived on the scene and saw an empty case, a smart-ass sign addressed to you and me and the Black Quack! Well, Crikey! And on top of that, there's the dead peacock."

"Dead peacock? Imperius killed the show curator? He's never killed anyone before, although he did try to do me in once."

"Not sure. There's going to be an autopsy, but the medical examiner said she thought it was a heart attack, induced by the shock of the theft and the sound of the Black Quack."

"Sure sounds like Imperius! But how did he know we were involved? How did he do it? Why did he do it? There isn't a fence in the world that would touch that stone and unless he wants it for himself…but no, this kind of job is not his style. He's had plenty of opportunities in the past to steal major league valuables, but he preferred fraud or extortion or something else less physical and more fungible. Were Chita and Bigg Baboon mixed up in it?"

"Not sure about Bigg, but the museum Director said he was knocked over by a high speed, spotted cat running through the halls. Who else could that be?"

"*Messieurs*," I said slipping in and out of one of my three native languages. "Perhaps the jewel is meant to be symbolic. Maybe the way he pulled off the heist is a message of something bigger to come. The Duck's ego is titanic. He obviously found out you two designed the security. He can't resist pulling your tails and telling you he knows you are on the spot for the museum's security. Ruin the show! Embarrass the Bear and Wallaroo! Score one for the Duck. Previews of coming attractions! Who knows what's next?"

'Maury," burped the Bear from behind his mead keg, "there are times, albeit few, when I realize that behind that adorable twitchy-nosed face there is a formidable brain at work. You could be correct. All right, Inspector, the game is apaw. Let's hear your story from start to finish. And please stop jumping on the mantelpiece."

Just as Bruce was about to launch into a detailed exposition of the Chicago heist and associated death of the not-too-lamented peacock, there was a "thump" and a "slosh." Octavius had drifted off again, sending a spray of mead squirting onto the floor. Two "time-outs' in the last hour! Strange!! Maybe he's actually tired.

Chita

Chapter Two

Spotted Cheetah's breathtakingly swift.

It's a really remarkable gift.

From zero to fifty

In no time. How nifty!

And just think! Not one gear must she shift!

In Chicago, a few hours earlier, Chita had found herself deeply involved in a very high priority mission – running like hell, trying to escape capture and keeping her gorgeous hide intact. She had dashed through the museum creating chaos. She had run right over that poncy-looking pack rat and that squawking peacock. How could such a beautiful bird have such an ugly voice? Reminded her of some of the runway models she knew. She bounded down the stairs. Stay out of the elevators. They're traps!

She had a fake emerald necklace dangling around her ear and neck. After crashing into one of the gift shop showcases she had emerged bejeweled. She brushed it off. God, what crap they sell! Nothing but the real thing for Chita. Nothing but real diamonds for this cat, although this phony sapphire didn't look bad. She had it in a bag around her neck. She still couldn't figure out what went wrong with the heist. She was supposed to switch the stones, but there was no stone in the case to switch. She had slapped that stupid sign on the side of the case and had run like a demented…cheetah. Past a guard scratching his mane in bewilderment.

That quacking black egg should have had them all rolling in agony up on the third floor, and for that matter, maybe the whole museum. She could still hear it and feel it reverberating in spite of her electronic earplugs and the fact that she was finally at the front door. She tripped up another security guard and made it out into the street through the mob of animals waiting to see the exhibition. She ran up the block and hid in a doorway to catch her breath. Wind sprints, always wind sprints!

"Now, where do we go, Chita?" She was going to have trouble darting through the Chicago traffic.

After several years with Imperius and Bigg, she was acclimated to big cities *(New York, Mumbai, Paris, London, Milan)*. Lately she'd spent a lot of time in Manhattan but navigating there was easy. The streets were all numbered and the avenues either had famous names or numbers. Those she could keep straight. But here she was in Chi-Town with that silly river and lake and all those stupid street names. Plus, she wasn't sure where she was going. Dumb, dumb, dumb! Which way was the lake? Imperius had told her to home in on the lake. Too many damn buildings in the way! Dashing into the street in front of a set of screeching wheels, she looked over her shoulder. A landmark! The elevated train is that way, so the lake must be the other way. Go, Chita, go!

As she ran off, she heard a loud whistle and sirens behind her. Oh, rats, the police. The museum guards were faster on the panic button than she thought they'd be. All those security guards looked like they had been rented from a home for retired wagon horses. They were big, but they were slow. But now the canine cops were on her. This called for a bit of brain work. She could move a lot faster than a police car in and out of traffic, and she could dash through buildings, but they were also on foot. Retrievers weren't exactly slouches when it came to speed. On a straightaway she could leave them in her dust, but they knew these streets. She didn't. She would shortly be in deep catnip.

She ran into the lobby of a building and whirled through a coffee shop, knocking over a few urns in the process. Ouch, that stuff was hot. Out through a revolving door. Damn it, her tail was stuck. Back up and then out. Two amazed sheep panicked and dropped their packages. Which way, which way? She looked up at a street light. Signs, signs – No Parking – No Right Turn on Red – Vote for Mayor Daley – Navy Pier, Next Left. The Navy Pier, that's

19

what she wanted. She made a mental note to vote for Mayor Daley if she happened to ever get back to Chicago, and took off to the left.

Just then, she heard a louder police whistle, and she turned in time to see a Polish Retriever running right at her. He barked, "Stop or I'll shoot!" Pedestrians scattered, looking for cover. He sped after her, and she managed to run out in front of a bus. She missed it. The cop didn't! "Oh nuts!" she thought, "No one was supposed to get killed on this caper. Wait till I get my claws on that Duck."

Taking advantage of the accident she ran into the top floor of an underground parking structure and paused for minute to once again catch her breath. This whole thing was a mess. Imperius had a lot of explaining to do. With his majestic airs. "That's tactical, Cat, That's your job!" Well, right now, saving her rear end was job one. She started out again, working her way down the floors, jumping around the occasional car or a driver on foot.

The lowest floor was lake shore level, and she bounded out under the car barrier and into the open streets. Hotels and skyscrapers above. Cars and trucks down below, but there it was. The Navy Pier. They had walked along it last night after they'd moored the boat midway down the dock. A black hydroplane named Miss Lee-Li-Li. After Imperius' lost love. But why they had to use a hydroplane was beyond her. It was fast, sure, but it chewed fuel like a shark, and it stood out like a sore paw. To say nothing of the noise and that ridiculous rooster-tail wake it threw up at high speed. Stealth a la Imperius, the jerk. She tried to talk him into something less conspicuous but as usual, he would have none of it. *"Ego über alles!"* When they docked last night, they had hung a couple of signs on it advertising lake rides the next morning. Fifty Bucks! At least the other Pier denizens wouldn't get too suspicious. But who knows what the cops would think?

Speaking of the cops, she couldn't see any for the moment. It began to rain. Really rain! A deluge! Good! Lightning too! It might provide her with some cover. But, oh, how she hated to get wet. Damn that Duck!!! She spotted the boat in the distance and after sniffing and staring all around her,

20

made a break for it. Down the street, on to the boardwalk, around the attractions, restaurants and booths, off the Pier's edge and into the cabin.

"I made it," she shouted, "Let's go before the cops come! Bigg! Imperius! C'mon, we need to get moving." No answer! She was alone. It figured.

Now what the hell should she do? She went outside again, cast off the mooring ropes, and threw those stupid "Rides for Fifty Bucks" signs over the side. Soaking wet and increasingly unhappy, she started up the engines and let them idle. Get ready for a fast getaway whether her partners in crime were aboard or not. The rain was really rapping away at the deck and the windscreen. She wasn't crazy about going out on the lake in this stuff. On the other hand, she wasn't crazy about duking it out or worse with the Chicago Police Force.

Suddenly she heard a thump; she looked up and saw Imperius flattened out against the wind screen. He must have flown or tried to fly over from the museum roof. The gale had knocked him for a loop. How he'd made it to the boat at all was beyond her. She reached out the cabin door, grabbed his wing and slid him down the water-soaked plastic windshield until she could drag him inside. He landed on the cabin floor, shook his head and waddled into the storage locker under the wheel without saying a word. He stuck his head under his wing.

"Oh, you're quite welcome, Your Highness. Rescuing storm-battered drakes is all included in the warranty. Think nothing of it. We live to serve."

Now, where the hell is that dumb Baboon? She looked down the Pier and caught blue and red lights flashing. The cops! And they were heading this way. Those dogs could track her scent even in the rain. OK, decision time. Run or...ruin?

She looked again, trying to calculate how much longer she could sit there before they broke out the artillery. A shot bounced off the deck. Time's up!! One more scan for Bigg Baboon. Whoa! There he was on top of a concession stand! She kicked in the transmission and started to move down the edge of the Pier toward him. Bigg seemed panic-stricken. Looking one way and then the other! First at the cops and then at the moving boat. Finally, he jumped, caught a cable, and climbed hand over hand, swinging across the Pier using power wires and the concession stand bracing. If a lightning bolt hit one of those wires, sautéed Baboon. She gunned the engine, then idled again, trying to move up next to the stanchion supporting Bigg's run for the roses. As she drifted past the pole, she heard a thump on the rear deck. Not even checking to see whether he was alive or dead, or whether he was even on the boat, she poured on the power just as the police cars and foot dogs came racing at her. As a final gesture, she turned, gunned the engines again and slammed the cops with the hydroplane's rooster tail wake. She hoped they liked baths. "Now, oh swiftest animal afoot," she thought, "Let's see how fast you can move on the water." Water, she hated water.

Chapter Three

He's a beautiful dog to behold

With his long, vibrant coat of pure gold.

And his tail's quite a sight,

Swishing left and then right,

Spraying water so blithely and bold.

Four Chicago police cars stood in the heavy rain at the edge of the Navy Pier, lights flashing, radios crackling terse commands to no one. Their occupants, matted fur hanging in soggy strands, were standing together staring after the wake of the rocketing hydroplane as it swiftly faded among the churning waves. Lightning struck a stanchion at the far end of the Pier and the accompanying thunder rattled the windows in the nearby pavilions. *(To say nothing of a few nerves.)*

An unmarked fifth car had just joined the pack and the back seat occupant, an Irish Setter and Lieutenant of Chicago's finest, sprang out the door snarling. "Get the Coast Guard on them," he barked.

"Already have, Loot," said a grizzled old Sergeant *(also a setter),* "but CG doesn't have anything that can match the speed of that thing. I called in a helicopter but these squalls and thunderstorms have grounded everything till the storm cells pass by. The dispatcher said your buddy, Inspector Wallaroo, just got out ahead of this mess. Where is he going?"

"He's flying down to Cincinnati. He and Octavius Bear designed the security on those jewel cases, and it looks like they blew it. They're going back to the drawing boards. A bit late, but what the hell, they may discover something. OK, bring me up to date. What happened here?"

"Can we get back in the car?"

They shook themselves off, spraying everything and every dog in sight and jumped into the back seat. Two of the cruisers moved away. Not much more they could do. The chase through the Chicago streets had ended when the perps took off in the jet black hydroplane just a few nose lengths ahead of the pursuing police. Frustration!

The Sergeant rubbed his head against a towel hanging in back of the front seat and said, "As best we can tell, there were only three of them, but they all didn't arrive at the dock together. The museum guards chased the cat down the stairs and out into the street. We had two officers stationed at the doorway, and they took off after the cheetah. That cat is fast."

"Fastest thing on four feet," said the Lieutenant.

"I believe it! Anyway, it dashed across Michigan Avenue and almost got hit by a couple of cars. Caused at least two pileups that I saw. I was standing near the museum entrance and I called in several cars to pick up the chase after one of our dogs got hit by a bus trying to catch the cat. He's on his way to the hospital right now. The perp was running in and out of streets and alleys, around the hotels and office buildings, through the underground parking lots and then broke for the Navy Pier. This black hydroplane was tied up halfway down the Pier. It looked like it might have been there for a show or something."

"Anyway, just as we came rolling up, the cheetah took off down the Pier, jumped into the boat, started up the engines and started looking around frantically. We were about seventy yards away when the cat cast off. We fired a couple of warning shots, but I'm not even sure he or she heard them in this downpour. It looked for moment like a clean solo getaway, but suddenly, a black duck came flying out of the low lying storm clouds and flopped on the windscreen. The cheetah pulled him, her or it into the cabin. And then, instead of taking off onto the lake, that crazy cat started heading down the length of the Pier toward the shore. We had overshot, so we turned back and started to pursue the boat in the cars and on foot, when some kind of an ape carrying a long tube came swinging down from the top of one of the concession stands. Then, holding the tube in his feet, he went hand over hand across a bunch of hanging pennants toward the water. The boat stopped short, and the ape jumped off a swinging light stanchion and landed on its deck. We got there just in time to get hit with a plume of water as they turned, gunned the engines, and high-tailed it out onto the lake at full speed. They must be nuts. The rain was pelting. The lightning was zapping any target it could find, and the waves were huge and beating like crazy. They still are. If they don't flip that damned thing out there, I'll be amazed. For all I know they're on the bottom of the lake right now."

"I wouldn't bet on it," said the Lieutenant. "You just described Imperius Drake and the Black Quack Gang. The ape is Bigg Baboon, the muscle of the gang and the cat is Chita. She's a real menace. They're wanted by the law in just about any place where there's money. They've pulled off some pretty audacious stuff in the past and they haven't been caught yet. The police got close a few times but they always slipped away at the last minute. The cat must have at least 9^3 lives. And Imperius Drake is a crime wave with wings. As soon as this crap clears, make sure the choppers are up and running that boat down. A low slung black skimmer like that won't be easy to spot in this weather unless it's running at high speed and throwing up a rooster tail. And if it is, it's only a matter of time before it flips over. It's going to be even tougher to find if it capsized. I don't care about them, but that jewel is priceless. Tell the Coast Guard to start a search and rescue operation. I'm heading back to the museum."

*****

"Imperius, you owe me big time for this one! You know how much I hate water and this is the very worst example of water I can think of!" Chita, well on her way to being totally inundated by the walls of spray thundering on the cockpit from all directions, was screaming at the top of her lungs to overcome the shriek of the winds and the thumps of the waves slamming against the hull of the hydroplane. She was battling with the helm and the throttle, trying to keep the boat right side up, facing forward and moving in the general direction of northeast. Bigg was gripping a vent in the stern of the boat and being very profoundly seasick. Imperius looked up from the relative shelter of a storage locker forward of the wheel and quacked at her – in Chinese, a sure sign that his nerves were not at their best.

She had the craft running at medium speed, enough to ride with most of the waves ,but not enough to flip them unless they caught a really deadly roller. The freak storms were actually individual squalls. A look to starboard revealed a sunny sky and tranquil winds a mile or so away. But here and now, this was the flume ride to end all flume rides. She had struggled into a life jacket in case they capsized, but Imperius figured he could tough it out doing what ducks do naturally: flying away. Bigg looked like he had found a jacket, but Chita wasn't sure. She was half hoping that Imperius and Bigg would get blown overboard. She even considered helping them along.

She was too caught up in survival to think much about what had just gone down at the museum, but something was very, very wrong with this whole caper, and she was going to find out what it was. But first, oh crap, just what we need, lightning. Bigg was groaning and periodically depositing his previous two meals across the aft deck. Maybe he'd lean too far over the side and be swept away. Too much to ask!

They were supposed to take this floating flapjack all the way up to Lake Huron. The subject of refueling had been passed off by Imperius as a trivial tactical annoyance. "I'm sure you can handle it, Cat!" Right now, she needed enough fuel to fight off the roller coaster waves and get out of this perfect storm. Well, maybe not perfect, but close enough for government work. Imperius continued to prattle at her in his native Mandarin, of which she understood, thankfully, not one word.

Once they got out of the storm cells *(if they got out)*, it was going to be just a matter of time before a Coast Guard boat or chopper twigged onto them. Riding low in the water and sort of delta-shaped, she wasn't sure how much of a radar signature the hydroplane threw back. "Oh, Chita! What are you doing?" she screamed. "You should be lolling on satin sheets and lapping up champagne." She kept trying to turn shoreward, getting slapped back one degree for every two she turned. They should break out of this nonsense in a few minutes but then…but then.

Heading in for a fuel stop would just make capture that much more likely. Besides, where was a marina when you needed one? She had mapped several when, much against her better judgment, she was planning this run, but she had no idea where she was at the moment. The GPS was working but she couldn't get at the map plot and keep the helm steady at the same time– and Imperius, damn him, was no help. He was probably communing with his ancestors, or praying, or doing something equally unintelligible.

The wind and rain were dying down. They were moving out of the storm cell. It was almost like going through a door. On one side, all hell breaking loose, on the other…isn't it a lovely day for a sail on the lake. She throttled back for a moment and let the steel coils in her four legs relax. Her claws had dug deep gouges in the wheel and on top of all that, she looked a mess. "I hate water!" she screamed to everyone and no one.

Bigg raised his head a couple of inches from the hull, looked at her briefly and slumped back down. Imperius was staring at something. At what, she couldn't tell. Tough to figure out when a bird's eyes don't face forward. Then she realized. He was morphing back into his Mandarin Duck persona. "Nice timing, jerk. You'll be out of it for a while. Ah, well, a female's work is never done. So, where the hell are we?"

*****

"So where the hell are we?" The voice belonged to Captain Daley of the Chicago Police department. He was addressing a small crowd of uniformed police, plain clothes officers, museum security, Director Loupe, the Crime Scene team, and the Medical Examiner. They were standing in the hall between the Deep Blue Room and the spot where the body of Phillipe de Peacoq *(Parisian Curator Emeritus and Senior Fellow for Manifestations Artistiques from the Global Association of Exquisite Jewelers and Gemologists)* still lay. Every eye in his feathers seemed to be staring accusingly at the Captain.

27

For a moment no one spoke, and then a chorus of voices barked, grunted, squeaked and yapped. "All right, all right, one at a time. What have you got, Lieutenant?"

The Irish Setter, still dripping from his double dousing, shook his head *(damn near drowning the diminutive museum Director)* and growled. "It's what we don't have, sir. They got away." He proceeded to tell them the Navy Pier story in chapter, verse, paragraph, sub-paragraph, and footnote.

"Do you think they're still alive?" the Captain asked.

"We can't be sure until we find the boat, if we find the boat. That's a hell of lot of lake out there."

"They couldn't have gotten that far with the storm beating them up. But if that sapphire is sitting on the bottom of Lake Michigan, there's going to be hell to pay. Even if," he thought, "we also got rid of three of Crimeland's true elite."

"There's going to be hell to pay under any circumstances," squeaked the Director, whiskers at full attention. "All of the individuals and institutions who loaned us their gems will want them out of here immediately. The media, who incidentally are gathering in the main lobby, are going to turn this into a full scale soccer riot. And let us not forget the untimely death of one of the world's greatest gemological authorities, a true genius, loved and respected by all of his colleagues and the art community at large. Irreplaceable! A truly tragic loss!"

The Director's secretary, Aramantha, was standing at the perimeter of the group trying unsuccessfully to choke back her laughter. "The old fraud!" she thought, "An hour ago, he wanted to kill the peacock himself."

Mistaking her convulsions for incipient hysteria, the medical examiner led her back into the Director's office.

"OK," said the Captain, "Inspector Wallaroo is taking a quick round trip south to confer with Octavius Bear. Something is obviously wrong with the show's security system. If they can figure it out, you may be able to salvage the exhibit. In fact, if I know the public, they'll be breaking down the doors once the press splashes it all over the landscape. Doctor Loupe, you'd better get your PR people going on an official statement. I'm calling the Commissioner. We're going to have to come up with a story of our own and I'm going to have to tell him what our follow-up plans are. Does anyone know the condition of that officer who was hit by the bus?"

"A broken leg but he'll survive. Not sure he'll ever walk a beat again." This from one of the Sergeants.

"All right! Crime Scene, Medical Examiner! Let's get going. I hope that gang did survive. I want to get my paws on that Duck and that high-speed calico cat. Does anyone have any idea what that Baboon was doing while all this was going on?"

*****

At the moment, Bigg was staggering to his feet, his face a very unappetizing shade of green, the rocking of the boat threatening to send him into another paroxysm of upchucking. *(How much food would a Baboon chuck if a Baboon could chuck food? Sorry!)*

He crawled along the side of the streamlined cowling and stuck his head into the cockpit, staring at Chita. "Oh, God, Bigg, you stink! Here, help me push back the windscreens and get some air in here. I have the pumps going full speed to get the water out. Those waves pushed in a couple of the windows. Imperius is changing his personality again, so don't even bother trying to communicate with him. There's a marina about two miles up the shore where with any luck we can refuel before we get spotted. I'm going to change into my black panther outfit to confuse the gas jockeys, although how you pass off a jet black hydroplane named Miss Lee-Li-Li as just another pleasure boat is beyond me. There's probably an alarm out for this crate already. Imperius, why couldn't we use a dime-a-dozen speedboat?" No response.

"After we fuel up, I'm heading for this wooded inlet here on the map, where we can sit things out until dark. Then, as long as we keep to reasonable speed and mix in with other lake traffic, they may not be able to single us out on their radars. At least that's the plan, but so far nothing has gone according to plan. By the way, I still have the phony sapphire I was supposed to substitute. I assume one of you has the real thing."

Bigg gave her one of his hyper-vacuous stares and said, "I don't think so."

Imperius Drake

Chapter Four

Yes, the Duck is a talkative bird.

But his discourse is really absurd.

He just quacks all the day

In a garrulous way.

Yet he never pronounces a word.

Hi! Maury here! We're back in beautiful Ohio!

From long and somewhat sad experience both Inspector Wallaroo and I knew it was pointless to try to rouse the Great Bear out of his narcoleptic seizure. He'll come out of it soon enough, sometimes picking up the conversation in mid sentence.

And we'll know when he wakes up. As will our neighbors in the entire southwestern region of Ohio, Kentucky and Indiana. If I'm not immediately within his sensory range, he will call for me. Loudly! My name, 'Maury,' lends itself to a roar: "MRAUR-EEE!!!" It has been known to set off storm warnings and earthquake alarms throughout the area.

So, as Octavius Bear snores loudly and peacefully with his massive furry head perched atop his keg of mead, and Inspector Wallaroo ponders and paces *(i.e., springs, jumps and bounds)* around the den, reducing it to a shambles, and Frau Schuylkill continues to bay and howl from somewhere in the domestic quarters, let us move to a quieter spot – say, Octavius' lab – and I'll supply a little more back story on Imperius Drake and the Black Quack gang. But first, I'll give you a brief tour of the environment.

The Bear's lab, shops, and launch facilities are underground and about twenty times larger than the mansion that by itself would give Blenheim Castle a run for it. It is common knowledge that bears like to burrow, and Octavius does everything in grand style. In fact, the mansion itself is a fraud. He bought it in the last stages of decay from an Ohio River steamboat captain who was down in his luck, and then totally gutted and restructured the interior to fit the needs of a sedentary but nine foot tall *(standing erect)* 1,400 pound Kodiak tycoon. The exterior resembles a gigantic haunted house and has been used as a set for the smash-hit Midwest Mayhem Movies series.

The only things that suggest there may be more to the property than meets the eye are the missile silo and launch pad, disguised as an oriental pagoda and the Romanesque hangar where the Bear keeps his highly customized stealth C-5A Galaxy, *"Ursa Major."* The missile, missile silo, and control center were hangovers from the Great Inter-Species War, and Octavius decided to restore the system and make it operational. As far as I know, he has never fired it in anger. A little pique perhaps, but not anger.

The huge plane, a gift from the Air Force after one of Octavius' secret but highly successful missions for the government is, in fact, a flying headquarters, lab and if necessary, weapons platform. When needed, the entire contents of the Bear's subterranean lair can be loaded on the *Ursa Major* in less than an hour. In unencumbered tactical mode, we can be airborne in 45 seconds. The runway is cleverly disguised as an Interstate By-Pass that has been under construction for the past eight years. Complete with orange marker barrels, warning signs, and fake bulldozers, the runway has fooled the local populace and successive governments into believing it is just leisurely highway construction as usual.

But I have shamefully digressed. We're down here to discuss the Black Quack gang and its leader, Imperius Drake.

Imperius Drake alters the number and composition of his gangs to fit whatever dirty deed he is planning at the particular moment. And he always has an ample supply of willing contractors and mercenaries on every continent ready and waiting to do his bidding – yes, even in Antarctica where a well-organized group of Emperor Penguins have long terrorized the international weather stations and exploration parties.

By contrast, his core gang is very small – only three – Chita, Bigg, and Imperius himself.

"Imperius" is the nom-de-crime of Yu-Aul-Kum, a Mandarin Duck and former scientist at the Pan Asia Institute for Avian Advancement. A brilliant chemist, geneticist, physicist, biologist, and developmental psychiatrist, he devoted his early life to the genetic enhancement of bird brains, creating a serum that would create a race of "Super Anitidae" – the über ducks.

He made his experiments known in a series of papers delivered before the International Genetics Experts Society. He was roasted. The society chairman, *Il Professore* Roberto Rabbito, a self-important Italian white rabbit with Noble prizes on his brain, singled him out for scathing mockery.

"Doctor Yu. Can you tell this august body just how it is you propose to take a brain the size of a walnut and create a jumbo avian intellect without increasing its mass? Will all future birds have to carry their heads on their backs to handle the weight? It will upset their aerodynamics. Or will they have auxiliary heads fastened to their wingtips or ha, ha, their backsides? I don't think so, and I'm sure all my colleagues agree.

"Hear, Hear!"

"Perhaps, Doctor Yu, the only bird with the big head is you! *Basta!* You've been wasting our valuable time. Thank you, Yu!   Ha, ha, ha!"

Mocked by his fellow scientists worldwide, shunned by medical and professional journals and threatened by government functionaries, Yu-Aul-Kum fled to the highlands of Nepal with his adoring mate and fellow scientist, Lee-Li-Li. There, after long contemplation under the direction of the Dalai Duck, he began to work again. In desperation, he began performing experiments on himself.

The experiments showed promise. Every week, he re-tested his IQ, synapses and reflexes. He was getting smarter. He was quicker. His eyesight was enhanced. He could fly higher, longer and perform breathtaking aerobatics. In a power dive, he once chased a falcon to the ground, caught him and then…killed him.

Yes, killed him. A mild-mannered duck wiped out a fearsome bird of prey. He felt a surge of power building up in his body and psyche. He was becoming the Über-Duck Archetype.

He was also becoming a menace. Sometimes after an especially risky trial, he could feel his body change along with his mind. His beautifully hued feathers turned black. His crest flattened. His eyes took on a Piercing stare. His wings shook and trembled. His "quack" was sharp and rasping. He ate ravenously.

And…he frightened Lee-Li-Li. This was no longer the devoted mate she had loved. This wasn't the high-minded scientist she had so admired. No longer did she hear him discourse on the importance of bettering life for avians. He was turning into a loon.

Over and over, she tried to get him to abandon or at least redirect his work. The Duck would have none of it. "So close, so close! I'll show those unbelieving nitwits who has a big head. They'll come begging me to allow them to assist in my great work, and I will laugh at them as they laughed at me. I am almost there, Lee, almost there. Just a few more tweaks to the formula, and I'll be ready. We'll have to find some stray dodos to experiment with. If it works on them, it'll work on anyone."

Just when he believed he was finally going to achieve total success, Lee-Li-Li, fearful for his life and sanity, burned his lab notes and swallowed their entire supply of the serum, sacrificing herself to prevent his self-destruction. The serum worked, expanding her intelligence by a factor of 5000, but the overdose burned out her brain and she died in his wings while solving once and for all, Schrödinger's dilemma of quantum indeterminacy.

Maddened by his loss and swearing vengeance against all his foes, real and imagined, Yu-Aul-Kum has since reconstructed his notes and the serum and with each dose transforms himself into the scourge of modern civilization – Imperius Drake. The temporary reconstitution is astounding – not only does his intelligence rise well beyond the scale of any known animal including dolphins, but his vindictiveness and hatred are also without equal. The transformation is made complete by a stark change in his physical appearance, morphing from the multi-hued beauty of the Mandarin species to a somber, black, and ominous winged predator whose maniacal "quack" stirs panic in the hearts and souls of all who hear it.

But before he could reach this pinnacle of achievement, he needed a new start. Armed with super endurance and GPS, and reverting to his natural Mandarin guise, Yu-Aul-Kum flew to the North American continent to begin his campaign of global revenge. Here he knew he could find the facilities, money, and support he required. But he must be careful. Using yet another alias, he applied and was accepted at the Genetics Science unit of Octavius Bear's Universal Ursine Industries. There he amazed his colleagues and superiors with his knowledge, technique, and almost inexhaustible energy. They gave him more and more responsible projects, and he was soon able to gain all the access he needed to equipment and processes to support his dreams of conquest.

Then, for the first time, he encountered Octavius Bear. The Bear was on a routine personal audit of the Genetics Science facilities at UUI. Going through the work-in- progress reports, he discovered a massive development project for which no executive authorization existed. Octavius literally hit the ceiling. It was the Duck! Caught out in his nefarious deeds and transmuting into his evil counter-self, Imperius Drake attacked Octavius with a lab knife. Octavius had been attacked before, certainly, but never by a...duck (?) The two of them engaged in raucous thrust and parry. Imperius landed several major wounds on the Bear's legs and body. Octavius flailed wildly, and truth be told, it was he who wreaked the most extensive damage on the UUI labs. Fortunately, the Great Ursine just bearly survived the Duck's onslaught and threw the maddened canard through a plate glass window four stories up.

He fell over, taking a specimen table and a Doberman lab assistant with him. The crash could probably be heard in the next county. Two apes pulled the dog out from under the Bear and hauled him onto a gurney. They left Octavius lying on the floor, unconscious. All of the staff in the room combined couldn't lift him.

A call went out for the UUI Chief Physician, Dr. Chiti BingBang. Dr. BingBang was an orangutan from Borneo who had met Octavius in his travels through Malaysia and sprang at the Bear's offer to head up UUI's Medical Unit. He bounced into the room, dropped his bag on the end of the gurney, and ran his paws over the dog. The squashed assistant had several broken ribs. "Strap him up," he said, "He'll hurt for a while but he'll be OK."

He puffed his cheek and throat flaps at the Bear and jumped up and hung from a ceiling fixture, looking down at Octavius' huge bulk. "Hmmm, cuts, several bruises!" He dropped on top of the Bear, waking him up. *(Had he been unconscious or on another of his narcoleptic excursions?)* Octavius thrashed out, bearly missing the orang and shouted, "Where is that Duck? I'll kill him!"

"You may have already. You tossed him through the window four stories up. I doubt he survived it. Now settle down while I check for cuts, bruises, breaks, and possible concussion."

He probed and prodded, looked in Octavius' eyes, held up his fingers and asked, "How many?"

"Four, dammit!" shouted the bear, "Get me up out of here. I'm all right!"

"I'm afraid you're correct, Doctor Bear," said the physician. "I was hoping you'd be wounded a bit more so you would slow down for a while. No such luck!"

"Slow down?? I'm about as sedentary as they come."

"Yes, I know. You could use some serious exercise. Planned exercise, not Duck tossing! I'm talking about your mind and how you wear out your associates. Oh well, I'll want to see you next week when you come back from Las Vegas. We can discuss it then."

"How did you know about Las Vegas?"

"I read scientific journals, too." He turned to his assistant and said, "Clean up his cuts. None of them are very deep. He doesn't seem to have broken anything, but he'll ache for a few days. Somebody get a fork lift in here to get him on his feet again."

While Octavius was being bandaged up, a badly wounded Imperius sneaked back into the UUI building and into his office. He took his notes and serum and began to drag himself out through a little used passageway. As he limped along, he noticed a sign: High Security Area – No Unauthorized Admittance. Below it a complex electronic door lock glowed. That was more than he could resist. Throwing his enhanced brain into super high performance, he ran through several million code permutations in several seconds. The lock clicked, and the door opened, just as he knew it would. He shut it behind him. He looked around. No one there but up on an experiment table glimmered a long titanium tube with an imposing trigger housing and what looked like an advanced electronic sight. An experimental weapon! That's what he needed. A weapon! Tucking his notes and his serum into the nerd backpack he always wore in the lab as part of his disguise, he limped-waddled up to the table, swiped the notes lying next to the weapon along with several CDs in a nearby computer, and struggled to lift the gun from its base.

Unknown to him, his early attempts to open the door had set off a silent alarm. Just as he had managed to get the gun tucked under his wings, the door flew open and two armed guards raced in. "Hold it right there. Don't move, or I'll tase you."

The Duck charged them, swinging the weapon in front of him. The guard's taser missed. The other guard fired a gun at the Duck and the bullet caromed off the weapon's housing, smashing the sight. Enraged, Imperius struck one of them, doing further damage to the weapon. Knocking both of them over with his enhanced strength, he made it out of the lab and then out of the building, flying a wobbly course into the forest that surrounded UUI. Broken and dented, he had the weapon. It was broken and dented too.

When the guards reported to Octavius, they told him they were sure that the weapon had been destroyed in the fight. There were pieces of the housing and electronic sight left on the floor. The notes, however, were gone. Needless to say, the Bear was not pleased. Neither was the government when they found out. But fortunately the notes the Duck had stolen were from an early prototype that, while not a total failure, wasn't anywhere near what they were trying to build – a portable, high precision, endoatmospheric, charged particle beam projector.

Since that day, several years ago, Octavius and Imperius have been engaged in an ongoing life and death struggle that often affects the welfare of the known universe.

And yet, for all of his tremendous assets, Imperius Drake's clawed web-feet are not without their Achilles' heels. First of all, the serum's transformation is temporary, usually lasting a week, sometimes longer, sometimes less. After each cycle of transformation and return to his natural Mandarin state, Imperius/Yu-aul-Kum has to spend time recuperating from the extreme trials the serum places upon his resources. Reverting to his colorful but nerd-like state of mild mannered Mandarin scientist, Yu-Aul-Kum is at his most vulnerable until he recovers his strength and mental acuity. Several times in this transitional and debilitated state, he came close to being captured or eliminated by Octavius and Inspector Wallaroo. Close, but not close enough.

Lately, however, Imperius has shown signs of not transmuting his personality at all. In either persona, he is a complete madbird. Slowly but inexorably, he is being taken over by his fiendish discovery.

The other obvious liability that constrains the Demon Duck is his physical size. Yes, he has titanic brain power, but in the size and physical strength department, though enhanced, he is hardly the biggest kid on the block. And for this reason, he allied himself with two of the most physically fit, powerful and agile creatures he could find – Bigg and Chita. More on this anon.

Chapter Five

The Marsupials have to be seen.

In Australia, they're king and they're queen.

Kangaroos are quite tall,

While the Wallaby's small,

And the Wallaroo's right in between.

"MAURRRREE!!" As I stepped into the freight elevator to head back to the den, the lupine howling and wallaroo stomping were joined by an ursine sonic boom. "Where is that overstretched hamster?"

Octavius was awake. "Maury, can't you have the common decency to stay in the room while we're having a conversation? Inspector Wallaroo is giving us the details about Imperius Drake's latest escapade, and I must say that so far, they are typical Duck."

Wallaroo looked at me. I looked at him. We both shrugged. I poured him another beer, got another coconut milk for myself and checked to see if Octavius' mead keg was empty. It wasn't, but it would be soon. Back to the beehives and meadery!

"All right, Inspector, I must apologize for Mr. Meerkat's lack of social grace, but do go on."

"Well, Maury, as you know I'm on loan to the Interpol Fine Arts and Jewelry Protective Squad for an indefinite period. It's all the result of the three of us recovering that cache of paintings stolen from the estate of software magnate, Jimmy Doors."

"One of our better performances," burbled the Bear. I said nothing, for it was during the shootout with that gang of art thieves that I got the bullet wound in my backside. It still bothers me on cold winter nights, and I am all too often reminded of that unnecessary bit of gunplay brought on by Octavius falling asleep at exactly the wrong time. Another story for another day.

"Any road, Maury," said Wallaroo, "I was approached by the Global Association of Exquisite Jewelers to design and direct the security for their once-in-a-lifetime show of unique and precious gems at the Loupe Museum in downtown Chicago. The show curator was a poncy Parisian peacock, but who was I to argue the toss? If they wanted me, well, mate, there I was. It was a ripper of an honor."

"And so you two set up the program, hired the security, coordinated with law enforcement and managed the event." I said. For some reason, Octavius had never mentioned this assignment. Yet somehow Imperius Drake knew he was involved and I didn't. I felt a pout coming on.

"Actually, Maury, the Inspector just called me on a few design details, and we ran a few tests on the encryption systems here in the lab. It was entirely his show."

"Imperius didn't seem to think so!" The pout had arrived.

"Too right, but Ocko's got fair dinkum. *(Whatever that means.)* I designed and personally oversaw the construction of the most secure display cases the world has ever seen. Want a rundown?"

"I'm all ears, Inspector," I said. *(Hardly the truth.)*

"Well, for starters, for the really high value merchandise, which the Deep Blue Sapphire definitely is, the showcases had to be made of a heavy-duty, shatterproof, non-flammable, chemically inert, semi-ferrous, transparent alloy that could be firmly attached to a base that was so heavy that a small crane had to be used to move and lift each one into place. The attachment of the alloy case to the base was done with super magnets powered by redundant self-contained energy cells. No museum electricity was used in the cases at all. Each energy cell has a life expectancy of ten years and all had been tested and retested. As long as the cells and magnets were active, no force – animal or otherwise – could lift the top off the cases. All the oxygen had been pumped out of the case and the jewels sat in a near vacuum. They could burn the place down and the jewels would survive."

"Formidable!" I said.

"There's more. Here's where Ocko came in. Once activated, the energy cells could be turned off only by sending a 2048 bit encryption key to both of the duplicate processors controlling the power. The key was sent through a constantly shifting high frequency radio signal that matched up with a timed receiver in the case. Only two transmitters exist, and they have been under strong protection in the vaults at the Bank of Lake Michigan, one of the show's sponsors."

"Only I, the bank president and the Director of the Loupe Museum have access to the safe in the vault. I called over to the bank before I flew down here. They say the keys have not been disturbed. No unaccounted for fingerprints or DNA around the vault, no images on the surveillance tapes, and the interlocking lasers that protect the approach show no signs of interruption. I'm going to check myself first thing when I fly back."

"Wow," I said, "You've certainly outdone yourself this time, Bruce."

"I thought so too, Maury. Well, this morning just before the show opened, the museum guards surveyed every room and ran back the video tapes since last night's closing. Everything was fine. In fact, the Deep Blue is one of the Museum Director's favorites and he stopped by to look at it again two hours before the doors opened. There it was, big, blue and sparkling, and under the watchful eye of that crazy peacock."

"And then?" said the Bear, lifting his dripping muzzle out of his keg of mead.

"And then they struck. Actually, we only know for sure that the cheetah was there. No sign of the other two. She came running through the halls at top speed, knocking over staff members, the Museum Director, guards and gift shop items while dashing in and out of all the exhibits. As she ran through the Deep Blue Room, the guards gave pursuit. Hopeless!! No one came close to catching her. When they returned to the jewel room, the case holding the Deep Blue was empty. On one side of the case a sign in ornate script read, 'Salutations, Bear, Greetings, Wallaroo! Now You See it, Now You Don't,' and on the floor screaming away was that g'dawful Black Quack egg shattering eardrums. Out in the hall the peacock had fallen over dead. "

Obviously in an emotional state, Wallaroo hopped up on the Bear's desk and knocked over his mead keg. "It was that damned Duck," he yowled. "I'll have him skewered yet. My reputation's in the dunny, and I'm made to look a real dipstick. Yours may be too, Ocko. Worse yet, he's got that beautiful jewel, and who knows what he plans to do with it."

"I'm sure we'll find out shortly. The Demon Duck's ego will not be silent for long," said Octavius as he toweled off his fur. "Mead is sticky stuff. I'll have to go bathe."

"Sorry, Ocko," said Wallaroo.

"Not to worry, Inspector! Plenty more mead where that came from. The bees have been working overtime lately. Their new queen is a bit of a tyrant. Meanwhile, Maury, first get a replacement for this keg and then why don't you and the Inspector file a flight plan for Chicago and go see things firsthand and report back to me. Two observers are better than one. Talk to everyone involved. See if you can kill off this curse thing while you're about it. Funny, peacocks are usually sturdy birds. Many live to very old ages. Weak heart, do you think?" Shrugs!

Off goes Maury again into the field. As I mentioned, Octavius gives the term "sedentary" a new meaning. Not that he's lazy. It's just that he's gigantic and gets in his own way in confined spaces. He also suffers from several wounds he incurred while volunteering for Operation Ice Cube during which the dictatorship of the Arctic Circle was finally overthrown and a new democratic government installed.

So, our normal M.O. is for me *(along with Inspector Wallaroo if he's on the case)* to do the groundwork while the Great Bear intellectualizes his way through the problem. It looked like this was going to be one of those cases. He confirmed it when he pressed a button under his desk and slowly sank through the floor on his own personal elevator platform.

"I'm off to the showers," he rumbled as his large black nose dropped from behind the desk.

Inspector Wallaroo had commandeered a Chicago Police helicopter to make the trip down to the Cincinnati wilds. *(Why is the Great Bear's lair near Cincinnati? Why not?)* Bruce bounded out the door of the mansion and into the cockpit to call Ohio Air Traffic Control. This would take some time since Bruce's Strine was not recognized as aviation English, and some rather tortuous misunderstandings and repeat transmissions were inevitable. Meanwhile, the hangar crew was topping up the chopper's fuel tanks. I ran over to the hangar to get an ample supply of barf bags. I had flown with Inspector Wallaroo before.

When I returned, Frau Schuylkill had come back into the den to survey the damage and tidy up now that Bruce was gone. I asked her to get a fresh keg of mead before Octavius' return. Still gently baying and shaking her lupine head as she looked around the room, her uncanny ears suddenly perked up. "Herr Meerkat," she growled, "I hear a plane. Shall I inform Herr Bear?"

"Let's give it a couple of minutes and see what it does, Frau. It could just be passing over." *(I didn't believe that for a minute.)*

"Do you think it's that verdammte Duck? We should go on red alert." she snarled. The Frau had been in the military in her younger days and had flown jets for the Swiss Guard. It was she who piloted the *Ursa Major*. Octavius was too big to fit in the cockpit. I was too small to reach the controls, but she was just right. "Should I arm the anti-aircraft missiles?"

"It wouldn't hurt, I guess, but don't get trigger happy." We'd had several near miss situations when the wolf overreacted. Fortunately, we were able to pass them off as some pyrotechnic tests for July 4th and paid the potential victims handsomely to keep their mouths shut.

As she left for the war room, I stepped outside, heading for the chopper, when at the far end of the runway I spotted a sleek and high powered aircraft touch down and come hurtling toward the mansion, ***showing no sign of slowing down!!*** Thank the gods the runway was built for our own C-5A – a plane that doesn't get off the ground without some running room. The shrieking engines suddenly dropped a note or two, and the airplane slowed and executed a 90-degree turn to a stop just at the end of the concrete.

"Oh no!" I moaned. "I know that plane and I know that crazy landing." It wasn't the Duck, but in some respects, it might just as well have been.

Envision a Concorde SST – the last of its proud line. Envision the plane in pure white livery with racing polar bears painted behind the cockpit, and if you looked aft to the tail, a regal portrait of a white polar beauty complete with bearonial crown and the aircraft ID letters BBBB-NB. On each side beneath the windows in a blue and white art deco font – "*Aquabears.*" My day was now complete. Bearoness Belinda Béarnaise Bruin (nee Black) had arrived, and our hangar crew was rolling out the jetstairs to greet her. I, on the other hand, was all set to make my exit before she got out.

It's not that I dislike the Bearoness. Quite the contrary! She's fun! She's beautiful! She's quite a stunner in spite of her now *(deliberately)* indeterminate age. It's just that when she shows up, the world starts to spin in the other direction.

The prima water ballet, diving, and synchronized swimming star of the long running aquashow, "Some Like it Cold," and widow of the fabulously wealthy Bearon Byron Bear, Belinda combines all the coy *hauteur* of a super wealthy diva and the glitzy horsepower of the best of the showbiz superstars. She is a real piece of work. And, truth be told, Octavius is still nuts about her, even though they have sort of agreed to a platonic relationship. They first met in different times and climes. As soon as Bruce gets us airborne, I'll fill in you in and distract myself from his flying by telling you the story of Bel and Tavi.

"We're good to go, Maury," Inspector Wallaroo bellowed over the whine of the chopper's engine. "Watch the ragin' rotor."

Staying low to the ground and trying not to be blown away or sucked up by the whirling blades, I skitttered up the landing struts and into the passenger seat. Holding onto my barf bags for dear life, I struggled to close the passenger side door, before belting myself in. Meerkats and helicopters are not natural allies. Meerkats and police helicopters are even further along in the strained relations department. We started to move.

Before I pick up on the early romance of Bel and Tavi, I should take a moment to describe Bruce Wallaroo's flying technique. It will explain why my narrative will be interrupted by occasional shrieks and hopeless attempts to keep the contents of my stomach inside my body. To be brief, the Inspector flies an aircraft the way he moves on the ground – by leaps and bounds. "Straight and level flight" has no meaning for him. Unfortunately, the helicopter, with its roller coaster capabilities is an ideal fit for the flying Wallaroo. Marsupial and machine become one, and they bound all over the sky, swooping toward the earth and zooming around obstructions – trees, buildings, highway bridges, other aircraft – and then leaping heavenward again only to slip and slide above the landscape. Strangely, we have always gotten to our destination in one piece and in record time. But I would hardly describe it as the "friendly skies." The things I do for Octavius Bear.

Speaking of the Bear, let me now *(Whoops, hey Bruce, cut that out!)* tell you a bit of his early days and his short and unhappy romance. He told me this story one particularly depressing night when the weather was Cincinnati gray, and the wind howled unmercifully. Octavius, who certainly could hold his mead, had actually reached his limit that night. Sighing and slobbering a bit, he proceeded to tell me the short history of his dalliance with the then Belinda Black, youngest female member of the Churchill Black polar bears. "Black polar bears?" you query. No, white polar bears *named* Black. The name alone gives you a good picture of this family who considered themselves unique and distinctly superior to the other *Ursi Maritimi* who roamed the area of Hudson Bay in Canada. Actually, the name Black originated with a long lost ancestor who discovered that under all the white fur, polar bear skin is black. S'true! Honest! Look it up!

During the annual polar bear migration, young Belinda, in search of some entertainment went wandering away from her mother and siblings. Dad, as usual, had long since taken off. *(Watch the bridge, Bruce!)* Nosing around in the accumulated snow and abandoned outbuildings around Churchill, she made a startling discovery. One of the buildings was occupied....by a really large and macho-looking Kodiak bear. Taken aback *(she had only seen the well-built brown species before from a distance)* but overcome by her ursine curiosity, she carefully padded up to the side window to get a better look.

"Either come in or go away," said a booming voice that sounded absolutely dreamy to the young Belinda. "I see you out there, and there's no point trying to fade into the snowy background. Your black nose gives you away."

"How do you know I'm a Black, and what's wrong with my nose?" blurted Belinda before she even realized she *had* given herself away.

"Nothing," the voice responded, "Actually it's kinda cute. Of course, you're not a black bear. They all live farther south in the forests. You're about the palest polar I've ever seen."

"I am too a Black and proud of it. The Black name has lent itself to generations of the highest quality ursine families. I'm on my way to Winnipeg with my mother to be introduced to Polar society at the Bestiary Ball. I haven't made up my mind what animal I'll dress up as."

"Try a polar bear," said Octavius, who of course was the voice. "You look great just the way you are."

"Oh no, I couldn't go naked. Mother would have a cub," cried Belinda.

Octavius' laugh could be heard for miles and cracked a few ice floes in the bargain. Thus began the ill-starred romance.

The Great Bear was in Churchill finishing up a research project to get his Ph.D. in ursinology from Kodiak U. He was studying polar bear migrations, little knowing that he would learn more about the species than he really was prepared to deal with. Especially from a sylph-like beauty who tipped the scales at a mere 500 pounds, was six feet long and whose fur glowed an iridescent white.

Days went by, and Belinda kept returning to the Bear's research station. They took to roaming together over the pack ice that was just breaking up. Octavius was dumb-struck as he watched her frolicking in the icy water, executing slithering dives and pirouettes, plummeting into the depths and shooting out again, sometimes with a fish in her mouth. Belinda was not only a natural beauty; she was a natural swimming star and an accomplished flirt.

Then it happened. Mother Black came upon them one day and things came to a frigid halt.

"Belinda, what are you doing with this awful Kodiak, young lady?"

"But, Mother we're good friends…in fact, I think I'm in love with him."

"You are nothing of the kind, Belinda. How could you possibly be seen with a rough and uncouth bear like that? He's not a Black!"

"No, ma'am," said Octavius. "I'm brown but you're not black. You're white."

"He's not only brown. He's stupid. You come with me this instant, Belinda."

Octavius, who was a certified genius by anyone's measurement –with three university degrees to his name at the age of ten –took serious umbrage at this remark, lost his temper and growled, "I'm the most intelligent ursine north of the equator, lady. Don't you call me stupid, you white-haired old sow."

Belinda broke out crying as her mother pushed her back toward the aurora of polar bears that she had left. Octavius slumped by his station and brooded for days. It would be years before he saw Belinda again.

(Dammit, Bruce, we almost hit that TV tower. Pay attention, willya. I think I'm gonna be sick.)

Chapter Six

All raccoons are mysterious guys

With those scary black masks on their eyes.

They cause all kinds of grief.

Each excels as a thief.

Which is why they must wear a disguise.

Chita stared at Bigg in disbelief. He didn't have the sapphire? She was about to have a massive hissy fit when she heard the sound of a helicopter overhead. The cloud cover was pretty heavy, and a fog had started to rise off the lake. The storms had played massive games with the temperature. Maybe the helicopter hadn't spotted them. As the light faded, being in a jet black boat began to turn into an advantage. She shut down the engines and waited. The chopper didn't seem to be hovering or scouting. Maybe it was just a commercial or private craft making its way up the lake.

She looked at Imperius. He seemed to be coming out of his trance. He was still in his Mandarin mode, but he was no longer prattling Chinese. His eyes still seemed unfocused and he stuck his head under his wing. "OK, jerk, sleep it off. I hope that damn serum kills you before this whole relationship kills me."

She needed some time to figure out how to walk away from Black Quack. Enough was enough! Sure, she owed her current standard of living to Imperius and his hare-brained plots. Sure, many of his schemes worked, and the three of them were all worth a lot of money in banks all over the Caribbean. But money didn't seem to motivate the Duck. As a means to an end, of course. He kept ranting about cataclysmic revenge. But for its own sake, money meant little to him. Bigg, for all his stupidity, knew the value of

51

a buck, euro, yen, pound, and peso and was more than a little interested in acquiring the stuff and all it could buy.

Now she had enough of a taste for the good life and enough funds to pursue it, and she wanted out. It wasn't as if she hadn't supported the program. She hadn't let the team down. Most of Imperius' crazy intrigues would have blown up if she wasn't there to pull him back by his ebony tail feathers. And she was pretty good at a little larceny herself. But, as she said, enough is enough. She wanted to go back to her New York penthouse and sing with the grungy rockers. No matter how things turned out, this was it. No more Imperius insanity. Chita was getting out.

While this soliloquy was going on, she was also donning her panther outfit in order to fake out the service guys at the marina they were approaching. She started the engines but left them at idle and slipped with the current up against the fueling dock. Rocky's Refueling Center. Oh, boy! This should be fun. Bigg was sitting on the aft deck trying to find his stomach. Imperius was still out of it. Well, Chita, once again, it's your show.

A raccoon with a baseball cap slowly moved up to the hydroplane and the gas pumps. He looked at Chita and the other two. Not sure what to make of this, but wondering whether there was a profit to be made, and not just for the fuel. He tipped his cap and said, "Hello ma'am. What'll be?"

"Fill it up with hi-octane," said the Cat.

"This is quite a craft you've got here, ma'am. Miss Lee-Li-Li! Is that you?" he asked.

Yeah, that's me. I'm an oriental panther and I race with other hydroplanes. We're on our way to Canada for the World's Hydroplane Grand Prix. *(Lying in her teeth, of course.)*

The raccoon didn't believe her for a second. He was a boat racing maven, and there was no World's Hydroplane Grand Prix, especially in

Canada. He looked in the cabin as he was filling up the tanks. "Who's the duck?"

"He's my sponsor. A little strange, but good for the money, and before you ask, the Baboon on the aft deck is my mechanic."

Chita thought she saw a strange expression come over the raccoon. This guy knew something. He finished pumping and leaned over to polish the windscreen.

"Can I interest you folks in some refreshment?"

"No thanks, we still have a ways to go. What do we owe you?"

The raccoon reached for her credit card but instead saw her bringing out a wad of cash. Stranger and stranger. Nobody paid in cash. His larcenous brain kicked in. "There's something weird here. I want to get these three off the boat. Then I'll call the cops and they'll impound it. I'll claim salvage. I could sell this crate for *mucho dinero*. Me, with a record as long as my paw being a good citizen and reporting some suspected criminals. Now, there's a switch. Even if I'm wrong, they may be willing to pay me off so they can keep on going. Ok, let's give it a go."

He pulled the gun that he kept for protection. Some of these lake joyriders got pretty rough when they were drunk. "Look, lady, I don't know what you three are up to but I have a funny feeling that you're not who you say you are. Why don't you get off the boat while I make a call and see if you're wanted for something. Don't do anything silly. I'm a crack shot. I learned at my father's knee."

He was so mesmerized by the cat that he let his gaze fall away from the duck. Imperius was back in his full Black Quack mode and the moment he saw the raccoon's attention wander, he flew at him, claws extended, and grabbed the gun. Bigg tackled him and Chita gunned the engines and started to pull away from the dock, still holding on to the cash. The raccoon jumped on to the deck of the hydroplane and was trying to wrestle with Bigg. Stupid move! Bigg sat on him, and he hissed and growled at the Baboon.

Chita looked over at the squashed *Procyon lotor* and said, "I hope you can swim, friend, because we're going to dump you overboard as soon as we get out into the channel. You're lucky we didn't just bash your head in. But, a little bit of professional courtesy, crook to crook. Remember, you may not know where we are, but we can probably find you."

With that, she pushed the throttles forward and as they reached cruising speed, Bigg got up, grabbed the raccoon by the paws and tossed him into the lake.

"I can't believe that dope," said Chita. "He was going to try to turn us in but first he filled up the gas tanks. What a jerk! Still, I hope he learned the raccoon paddle at his father's knee. Imperius, are we still going to Pondscum, Michigan?"

The duck, obviously still recovering from his serum-induced transition and perhaps with a little sea sickness tossed in, nodded his head in the affirmative.

"When we get there, you guys have a lot of explaining to do." Taking full advantage of the poor visibility, she gunned the engines and shot northward on the lake. Full speed! If they hit something, they hit something. She was sick of water and just wanted to get back to dry land.

The Development of Civilization – Part 2

<u>Telepathy</u>

(From "An Introduction to Faunapology" by Octavius Bear, Ph.D.)

The onset and selective progression of telepathy among the species of the world remains an area with many dark corners and unknowns. It is not clear, for example, which animals first became aware of their telepathic abilities or how they were manifested. Some authorities believe that all beings have intrinsic telepathic powers but require some special conditions or events to trigger them. Telepathy can be passive, active or both. For thousands of years, animals that "heard voices" were considered insane. It is only in the last few hundred years that we have realized that many of them are victims of passive telepathy – receiving telepathic "broadcasts" with no way of turning them off..

Many animals broadcast unconsciously and only become aware of their questionable "gift" when someone else tells them what they have been thinking. This too is a highly dangerous condition, if for no other reason than making personal privacy impossible.

A relatively small portion of the population can deliberately and selectively practice passive and/or active telepathy. This condition is not restricted to one species, nor is any one species more susceptible to having the power. It has been found that even animals from the same litter may not share the same telepathic abilities.

One path of research seems to be bearing fruit, however. Some animals who are incapable of comprehensible speech seem to have compensated by practicing telepathy. A small group of scientists claim that telepathy can be activated and taught through exercises. Even surgical techniques have been proposed. Thus far, there have been no reported cases of non-telepaths developing the abilities through medical means.

It is also not clear how desirable the prospect is. Many members of religious sects, government, law enforcement and the military have proposed isolation of all individuals with telepathic talents. This has caused many of the "gifted" to hide their capabilities. Some, such as Imperius Drake, do not!

Chapter Seven

Lady Panther, her coat black as night

Seldom shows herself out in the light.

Her eyes glow sparkling gold.

Her demeanor is cold.

And she'll certainly give you a fright.

While Bruce is making sure he flies under every overpass on I-65, I shall fill in more of the back story on the Black Quackers.

To carry out his dreams of world domination, Imperius, an equal opportunity employer, used discrimination and diligence, searching the world for the assistance and support he required. He found them in South Africa, where he had once more fled after his set-to with Octavius at UUI.

Oddly, the candidates he found are by nature mortal enemies, each capable of destroying the other. Perhaps it may be this virtual impasse that motivated them to join forces and work with the Duck. On the other hand, perhaps they were bored silly and had nothing much else to do. We'll never know. At any rate, strange and mysterious as it may be, Bigg Baboon and Chita fell in with him and became the nucleus of the dreaded Black Quack Gang.

In Bigg's case, "fell" is the appropriate verb. As you probably know, Savannah Baboons live in small troops and spend the night in trees to avoid the few predators *(including cheetahs)* they fear. Bigg, a huge but exquisitely clumsy specimen, considered himself something of a ladies' ape. Never has an animal been so oblivious and so wrong about his own sex appeal. His real name is the almost unpronounceable African title – Mstbitruifyuseso – *(meaning one who falls down a lot)*.

He got his shorter name after his first attempt at romance with a decidedly uninterested female who shouted, "Get your paws off me, you Bigg Baboon." The name stuck. Bigg was a pariah with an unbroken series of non-starter romances. The rest is folklore.

Anyway, early one morning in the savannah, Bigg was snoozing comfortably among the branches when he felt a push. Dropping twenty feet to the ground, he hit his head on a rock. He was unconscious and taken for dead by his troop who had done the tossing. They had been trying for months to figure out how to rid themselves of this embarrassment. So he didn't see them sneaking frantically away to another part of the veldt.

When he awoke, he was dizzy, dazed, and desolate. Sitting there, trying to figure out which way was up, he heard the nearby bark of a cheetah. Alone and at first fearful, the age-old instincts of the species *Papio Ursinus* surged through his blood. He would withstand this potential assault or die trying. Backing up against a tree, picking up a stout branch and baring his claws and intimidating teeth, he awaited the arrival of his mortal foe.

The female cheetah is a solitary predator, who *(unless she has a cub)* spends almost all of her adult life alone, skillfully fading in and out of her surroundings in spite of her unique mottled coloring. Using her intense speed (0-60 in less than 5 seconds) this fastest animal on four legs can appear from nowhere, bring down her prey with her relatively small but highly effective jaws, and drag her meal into seclusion, where she can dine undisturbed.

Chita is a female cheetah with all the aforementioned characteristics and no cub. She had been living on her own around the same savannah, picking off prey, lazing in the sun, and wondering how she could break into the big time, whatever that meant. There was a gnawing discontent inside her that she couldn't quite define. All she knew was it annoyed her, and she couldn't scratch at it.

At this moment she was wandering within a few hundred yards of Bigg. She sensed his presence, sniffed the air, gave a sharp bark and prepared for her extermination run. Kicking in her feline command and control system, she launched herself at top speed at her yet unseen target. At about one hundred yards to objective, a series of warning signals began howling in her brain...Abort, Abort, Abort! Looking ahead, she saw the largest by far baboon that she had ever encountered, and this particular male was showing his immense teeth and brandishing a large club-like object.

Screeching to a halt about twenty feet in front of this monster, instead of obeying her instincts and running like hell, she froze and stared. She might be able to take him, but at what cost. Clearly this was a dilemma.

Bigg, somewhat befuddled *(as usual)* by the strange behavior of this spotted cat stood open-mouthed. Fortunately for him, this provided a very clear view of his jaws and very nasty teeth and did nothing to hide his girth and the club he was holding. He was staring death in the eye and yet...it looked pretty good. In spite of the species differences, it was clear to the testosterone-besotted Baboon that this was some hot-looking cat. He searched frantically through his repertoire of "no fail" opening lines for picking up babes, but before he got one out, he heard a purring voice say, "Hi, honey, come here often?" *She* had spoken to *him*.

Flustered, the best he could come up with as a comeback was: "What's a nice kit like you doing in a place like this?"

Chita looked around. "You here alone?"

Sensing a trap, Bigg replied, "No, the rest of my troop is up there in the trees."

Chita sniffed and perked her ears – nothing and no one. This guy was clearly lying and doing it badly.

It was Bigg's turn, "How about you? You doing a solo?"

"No, my friends are in the ladies' room. They'll be right back."

"What ladies' room? I think you're alone."

(A genius!) "Oh, all right, I'm alone. I'm allergic to cats."

Standoff. Stare and counter-stare. Finally, Chita sat down on her well-formed backside and flicked her tail. "Well, I'll say this for you. You're big."

"How did you know my name?"

"What name?"

"Bigg!! With two GG's. Actually my name is Mstbitruifyuseso but I never use it.

"I can see why," she said.

"What's your name, Cheetah?"

"Right," she said, "my name is Chita – C-H-I-T-A. OK?"

The Baboon looked puzzled. "Funny way to spell Cheetah!"

"Never mind!" she growled, moving just a little closer and sizing up the situation. She had completely blown the element of surprise. Stupid of her! So, if she was going to attack, she'd have to count on her mobility and first strike capability. Against this guy, the odds didn't look too good. But he was looking pretty lecherous. Maybe she could play this to her advantage.

"Look, Bigg Boy," she purred. "The way I see it, we have two alternatives. We can attack each other and probably end up scattering large chunks of our attractive selves all over the landscape. What a waste of macho muscle on your part, and I kinda like the way I look, too. Or we could decide to trust each other for a few minutes and slowly and quietly back away. I'm not too sure I like that choice either. But make up your mind. I'm getting hungry and I need to find some food somewhere."

Before Bigg could agree that his stomach too was rumbling, a formidable voice from on high interrupted, "Oh, no, my friends. You have another alternative, and I strongly advise you to take it."

Thinking this booming voice might be a possible intercession by one of the almighty gods of the jungle; they looked up in awe and saw...a big, black duck.

Imperius – *(I know, you recognized him right away)* – flew down from the tree limb on which he had been sitting, listening to this sparkling repartee. He landed at an angle equidistant between them so he could address them both without giving either an opportunity to move.

The same thought ran through Chita's and Bigg's brain at the same time. "Oh boy, breakfast!"

But before either of them could budge, the Duck did a very strange thing. *He* laid an egg. Or at least it looked like an egg. A large egg for a Duck. A very large, black egg. Was this food a peace offering? Was it supposed to keep them from eating him? The egg rolled in between them and they both jumped at it simultaneously and...

Oh, pain supreme! The loudest, most cacophonous, raucous sound they'd ever heard pierced their eardrums and set their brains in a swirl. A seemingly endless stream of QUACK, QUACK, QUACK, QUACK reverberated throughout the forest, forcing every living thing to run for cover or at least cover their ears. Bigg and Chita weren't so lucky. They were too near the source of the torturing noise and fell over, paws and claws on their ears, writhing in pain.

As suddenly as the screaming stream of quacks began, it stopped. Were their ears playing tricks? Had the sound stopped or had they truly died of sensory overload? Imperius enlightened them.

"Now, my friends," he hissed with a slight oriental accent, "it's quiet again and if you are no longer interested in turning me into Peking Duck, perhaps we can communicate. I am Imperius Drake. This ominous black form you see me in is not my customary self, but until we have settled a few things, I will continue in this guise."

Bigg spoke first. "What is that thing?" He was staring at the shiny black ovoid now sitting silently between them on the grass. "Did you lay a big black egg? No, don't show me! Don't turn it on again."

Chita shook her head. This was going down as one of the worst days in her relatively short career. "All right, Duck, you've convinced us that you should no longer be on the menu. What do you want with us? Why don't you just fly back where you came from?"

"That would be a long trip, indeed, my dear Cat. One I do not relish making. At least not yet. No, as I say, I think I could use you two. And no, Baboon, I decidedly did NOT lay that egg. I painstakingly designed, crafted, and carefully tested that weapon until today it can be used for all manner of mayhem while being itself virtually indestructible. I alone can control it...*telekinetically*! Behold the Black Quack!"

"Catchy name, Duck," said Chita, "So what's your game, and how do we fit in?"

"The game, dear Cat, is revenge and domination, the details of which I will explain only after we have reached agreement. I am the world's greatest diabolical genius. But even geniuses have their shortcomings, which in my case are physical. While I can fly *(very well, I might add)* and have significant claws on my webbed feet, I am nevertheless usually at a disadvantage in a *mano-a-mano* dustup. I need a couple of large, swift, and agile hench-creatures to become my cadré. Some intelligence would help, too. From what I've seen of you two, you might work out quite well, if you can keep from killing each other. And don't even think of trying to kill me. I control the Black Quacks telekinetically, and I have one of them with me at all times. You'd be mindless before you even got moving. And that applies to you especially, my speedy friend. The Baboon may already be mindless. You may both follow me now, or go bonkers."

Biggs looked over at Chita. "What do you think, Chita? I'm on my own. I got kicked out of my troop. Sounds like it might work out, even though I don't like that egg."

Chita sighed. "Oh, what the hell! I wasn't doing anything important, anyway." And they walked off into the forest to the Duck's hidden headquarters,

At this point, the more astute or perhaps, quibbling reader might be wondering how it is that I, a humble Meerkat, in the service of goodness and righteousness, might have such detailed knowledge of the actions of the malevolent Black Quack gang. The answer is quite simple. Chita! She talks...to me. At least, now she does. Complex, contradictory, clever, cantankerous, and conceited as well as a bunch of other C-words, Chita gives new meaning to the word "independent." A rebellious personality superbly designed to conflict with Imperius' megalomania at every turn. But she has also developed a strong obsession for the luxuries that come with money and influence. And the "duck" as she refers to him was her current meal ticket, especially for *paté de fois gras*, champagne and her very favorite, roast boar.

Piling up her own nest egg from a series of capers, Chita's overriding ambition is to break loose from the Duck and the stupid Baboon and lead a life of luxurious freedom. She will ally herself with anyone who supports that goal...including us, but only as long as it suits her purposes. In short you can rely on Chita to be totally unreliable.

In our flashback, we left the three conspirators on their way to Imperius Drake's temporary hideaway on the African veldt where he had taken shelter after his battle with Octavius in the labs of UUI. Several years have passed, and since that time the Black Quack Gang, as it now characterized itself, became the scourge of eight continents as well as one Chicago museum.

First, they entered into their fund-raising phase, pulling off a variety of heists, scams and other lucrative capers, all aimed at providing them with the necessary wherewithal to comfortably plot and execute more arcane and daring acts of absolute atrociousness.

The pattern was pretty much the same:

- Imperius had the brainstorms, did the planning, and organized any mercenaries and assistance that might have been necessary.
- Chita was executive officer, prime perpetrator, and often chief protestor. She was convinced that Imperius was going to get them all killed or worse.
- Bigg did the heavy lifting, drove the getaway vehicle if there was one, and performed whatever strong arm activity was required. You've seen the movie.

They operated under several basic rules:

- More was better than less. Much more was much better.
- If at all possible, no one should get killed or maimed. *(Especially one of them.)* This was at Chita's insistence. Bigg liked violence, and Imperius was totally indifferent except as it applied to a certain obnoxious bear and the worldwide genetic science community– and oh, yes, his rotten Chinese aunt back in Beijing.
- Every year they would take time off to enjoy some of their spoils and, suitably disguised, live it up at some exotic location. Chita was at her best posing as the dynamite panther babe, Mlle. Catherine Catt, and Bigg was especially effective as a Latin American revolutionary, Commandante Babaloo. Imperius usually played the role of the reserved and diffident Mandarin Duck, Yu-Aul-Kum. It was easy for him, and it didn't interfere with the work he was doing during his time off. Oddly, even though he had been photographed and sketched by police artists a number of times, it was always as the dark and dreary Imperius. Yu-Aul-Kum was a disguise that had never been picked up by the police.

They had moved from Africa to France, where *La Belle Mademoiselle Catt* became the toast of the *haute couture* establishments on Rue Faubourg Ste. Honore. She sometimes appeared on the fashion house runways as a slinking black panther; sometimes in public as herself on the arm of a fabulously wealthy oil sheik or banker, always wearing her signature diamond collar and soon wearing an immense amount of expensive *bijoux* to match. She owned several apartments in the most fashionable and most stratospherically priced Parisian arrondisements and a stable of chauffeured limousines to match.

One of Chita's special talents was introducing her latest admirers to an "absolutely fah-bulous Duck, dah-ling," who could make economic predictions that were alarmingly accurate and timely, but were "much too complicated for a poor little kitty-kat like me to understand. But you must meet him. He has made so many animals too-too rich." Then she backed away and let greed take over.

Her dual persona as panther and cheetah was matched by Imperius. As Dr.Yu-Aul-Kum, noted economist and dealer in multifarious economic strategies, he could be found in the major banks and exchanges of Paris, Geneva, or Zurich, negotiating complex financial deals that all had one thing in common. They would all eventually default, well after the good doctor had disappeared, leaving the victims scratching their heads and the gang counting their assets.

Then in his guise as Dr. Imperius Drake, he would establish himself as an industrial expert who thought at levels well above and ahead of his contemporaries. In a six month period, he single-wingedly acquired and merged every European market reporting service into a single financial news outlet – The Duck Tape. If you wanted business news and advice, you got it from Imperius. This stranglehold on information resources made him a very wealthy and powerful fowl indeed. Needless to say, the money came rolling in.

Bigg, when he wasn't chasing every Parisian female who glanced at him, had discovered he had a talent for politics. In his role as an exiled Latin

American revolutionary he was honored by every left, right, and swing-wing party. He managed to lead several particularly impressive national strikes against the government, industry, the airlines, and the French Girl Scouts. He did this by simply waving his arms, jumping up and down, and uttering unintelligible shouts to his followers. Upon receiving a convenient payment sent to a nondescript postal box, the labor action ended.

Eventually, Bigg rejoined Imperius, and together they roamed the halls of the European Community in Brussels looking for international aid programs from which they could drain loose funds. Life was good, but alas, the Sureté and Interpol at last took notice when Bigg was caught trying to avoid paying VAT on a bicycle he had stolen.

They fled Europe and headed for the Indian sub-continent, where they established a major outsourcing service for call-in pizza deliveries. Their service, "Wi-Fi Pie," provided millions of famished families and hassled office workers with a reliable electronic source for ordering pepperoni and mushroom "3 for the price of 1 specials" and relieved thousands of pizza chefs from having spinning dough fall on their heads every time the phone rang. What the world did not know was they were also using this same outsource network to hack into major financial and industrial traffic, diverting money and materiel to a number of façade companies, all of which ultimately led to their unnumbered bank accounts in Switzerland, Bermuda, and the Cayman Islands.

Naturally, all this activity led to some strain among the co-conspirators. Chita was finding that she liked the high life and was becoming increasingly reluctant to take chances when she could lead an existence of luxury and comfort in any of the major capitals of the world. New York, especially, fascinated her, and she had taken to departing from Mumbai *(Bombay)* for shopping sprees in Milan, London, and the Big Apple. She didn't dare go back to Paris, at least not until she could come up with yet another knockout disguise. She had thought of becoming a Persian or Siamese cat, but none of the clothes fit her.

Shopping sprees led to longer stays, and she soon was ensconced in a multi-million dollar high rise penthouse on the upper east side of New York City. She resumed her modeling career along with an occasional MTV appearance, always in the guise of the jet set panther, Mlle. Catt. She discovered she could do more than a passable job at singing and began doing pick-up gigs with a number of heavy metal bands in Greenwich Village.

Bigg was turning to somewhat more violent activities, participating in the occasional kidnap or extortion plot in India. Unfortunately for him, after an unbroken string of capturing the wrong victims, he was tossed out by the gangs, and after trying a few capers on his own, he resorted to trying direct robbery and thefts, most of which he also botched.

Imperius had let these aberrations go unnoticed as he devoted more and more time to his laboratory, working on an improved version of his serum, a more virulent Black Quack egg, and most of all, the incomplete particle accelerator he had stolen from UUI and Octavius Bear.

His violent flight from the genetics labs at UUI after he and the bear had nearly killed each other, had left a mark on his personality second only to the loss of his beloved Lee-Li-Li. Up until that time, he had nourished an unfocused hatred for the self-important and pretentious idiots who had the unmitigated arrogance to call themselves scientists. Scientists, hah! Not one of them was fit to clean his test tubes. They had excluded him, laughed at him, and had not only deprived him of his beloved bird, but his true place in the history of disciplined knowledge. They would pay. Oh, they would pay!

But Octavius Bear was a different foe. He had physically humiliated him, tossing him out of a fourth story window in his anger. He had deprived him of access to the research facility that would have let him perfect his enhancement serum.

Thus far, he had created an elixir that would allow him to miraculously change himself into a Super-Duck at will. But as he found out tragically with Lee-Li-Li, each individual's chain of DNA demanded a modified serum. He must work to find a common denominator – one

67

treatment for all – to create a new race of ducks soaring across the cities and country-sides of the world, breeding fear in all the animals below, with himself quacking at the head of the V *(or was that geese?)*

One night, taking a brief respite in his lab, he started leafing through some of the "scientific journals" he still received. Trash! As if any of them had anything important to say. But wait, here was something of interest. A Call for Papers for the Quadrennial Convention of Genetics Experts to be held in Las Vegas early next year. Prominently displayed among the list of corporate sponsors was Universal Ursine Industries, and peering at him from ten year old photos were *Il Professore* Roberto Rabbito, that self-important, condescending hack who reviled him and his work; Ferrucio Ferreti, a small-time idiot he knew from school; and, joy sublime, Octavius Bear, who was to deliver the keynote speech.

His opportunity had come. He must finish his work on the particle beam accelerator. He must carefully plan a complex and fitting catastrophe for all of these fakes and charlatans. He must not only eradicate the noxious Bear, but he must humiliate and torture him and then watch him slowly and painfully die away. Filled with a newborn spirit of purpose, Imperius called for his two cohorts. No response! Where the hell were they?

It took him only several hours to find Bigg at an illegal taxi-dance emporium. The Baboon was putting the charm (?) on an exotic macaque. Imperius flew up and landed on his head. The female jumped back and ran screaming for the ladies room. "Where is the Cat, Baboon? The Black Quack Gang must re-establish itself. We have a date with destiny."

Bigg, as usual, was clueless. However, after searching fruitlessly in some of her usual hangouts, they finally broke into Chita's apartment and found receipts and catalogs from New York shops, a list of music clubs in Greenwich Village, a week-old copy of the *New York Times* and a discarded Mumbai to New York itinerary from *Air Cormorant*.

Even Bigg could figure that one out. "Gee, do you think she went to New York?"

Imperius raised his eyes to heaven and muttered, "Possibly, Baboon, possibly."

Next morning, taking Bigg along as potential muscle, he set off on an intercontinental jet for…you got it, New York. It took them several days of searching. They checked fashion magazines for photographs of the cat, looked at entertainment listings and even watched MTV much to Imperius' disgust. They finally spotted her one night, still disguised as a panther, doing a raucous solo in an upscale bistro on the lower east side of town. All 361 eyes in the place were on her as she wriggled and shouted and pranced and danced.

After she had finished her set, Imperius waddled up to her, with Bigg at his side, the Black Quack under his wing and quacked with all the frightening menace he could generate. "Come, Cat, you must return to the Gang, now!"

Chita sighed. "Oh what the hell, I wasn't doing anything important, anyway."

The Development of Civilization – Part 3

<u>Social Maturity</u>

(From "An Introduction to Faunapology" by Octavius Bear Ph.D.)

Tribal organization primarily based on correspondence of species formed the earliest and most powerful social forces in our world. It still prevails in many circumstances. Monkeys, wolves, felines, meerkats, and many other animal classes subscribe to the concept of an alpha leader and a pack. However, with the increase in travel, communication, and social interaction over the past five hundred years, some of these rigid structures have been softened, replaced, or supplemented by systems of trans-species cooperation.

Oddly enough, single animals, genetic loners to begin with, have found it easier to adapt to cosmopolitan living than the pack members. Cheetahs, for example, have little pack mentality. They will often socialize more easily with species other than their own.

However, some group-dependent animals have great difficulty operating on their own or in very small numbers. Even within cosmopolitan environments, we find species ghettos or barrios. It is not uncommon to find animals who live their entire lives within these confines.

Nevertheless, a growing spirit of trans-species cooperation produced the first samples of empathy in government, commerce, defense, and infrastructure. To be sure, predators are still predators and this new spirit of respectful relationships is not embraced universally. (See: The Great Inter-Species War.) Governments have emerged most often based on geographic boundaries, but there are cultural, religious, and ethnic bonds and distinctions that still survive, flourish, and influence national and international politics.

In addition to the ethnic issues another major inhibitor to growth persists. The questions of animal size, shape, weight, and required host environments such as water or forests have made standardized and common infrastructures problematic. It affects dwellings, towns, cities, and nations; transportation; communication; manufacturing, services and agriculture, to name just a few.

For example, how to design a ground, water, or aviation vehicle that will efficiently and simultaneously accommodate a rhinoceros, bear, alligator, bovine, giraffe, and rodent? Not likely! How high should ceilings be in public buildings? How can whales and dolphins with their very high intelligence share their talents with the rest of the world while confined to water? How can the land-based animals reciprocate? The list is endless and provides a steady stream of challenges to scientists, engineers, sociologists, economists and politicians.

Only recently did the International Bureau of Standards settle on and release tables describing animals as extra small, small, medium, large, and extra large. Not everyone is satisfied. Some insist weight should be the primary determinant. Witness the elephant (7,700 to 26,000 pounds); the rhinoceros (3,000 to 10,000); the hippo (circa 40,000); and most species of whales who come in wide range of sizes and weights and are of course, waterborne. Others such as the giraffe, while relatively heavy in weight (3,800 pounds) can also claim to be the tallest (18 feet) and thus want to be placed in the extra, extra large category. I should mention that my own ursine species, the Kodiak Bear, averages between 1,000 and 1,500 pounds putting us at the high end of medium.

These designations are critical to making correct decisions on many levels. Are there sufficient small rodents and reptiles to justify separate vehicle and traffic standards exclusively for them? The answer is clearly "yes" and whole industries have arisen that think and build small.

But what about elephants and giraffes? Are they doomed to be forever caught up in the custom-made category?

If not in sheer numbers, at least in variety, the medium to large category – lions, tigers, bears, wolves, kangaroos and a host of others– tends to lead in most development.

Nevertheless, with improvements in communication, reduction in language barriers, a standardized numeric and monetary system, a sense of inter-species maturity is at last descending on our world. Most foods are plentiful. Medicine is advancing. A flourishing of the arts and education is a bellwether of better things to come.

But not in all times, places and circumstances.

Chapter Eight

Meerkats often are stars on TV.

But they aren't "mere cats," don't you see.

They're mongooses (mongeese?).

Make this silliness cease.

It's just all too confusing for me.

Welcome back to the airborne stomach pump. The fact that eastern Indiana contains some of the flattest land in the country seemed to have no effect on Inspector Bruce Wallaroo as we zoomed and dived our way toward Chicago. Every time I fly with him, I swear it's the last, but Octavius usually won't take no for an answer. I owe the Great Bear a lot, but these trips are beginning to even up the score. *(Bruce, will you keep your hands on the controls and for Pete's sake, stop playing the harmonica.)*

One of the Inspector's less appealing talents is his constant playing of the mouth organ while he pilots an aircraft, especially when the only song he knows is "Waltzin' Matilda." I wish I had a nickel for every one of his harmonicas I've stolen in self defense, but he seems to have an endless supply. I'm not sure he knows I'm taking them. Among my less socially acceptable talents are my abilities as a pickpocket and thief. While we're waiting for the Chicago skyline to appear *(soon, please)* let me tell you a little about myself and why I owe Octavius so much.

Like most of my relatives, I was born and grew up in the Kalahari Desert and from my earliest recollection was part of the Menacing Mob. All tight knit meerkat colonies are called mobs, but we really meant it. We were the scourge of Southern Africa, stealing, rampaging, and generally being pains in the tail which I might add is the Meerkat's Pride. Adult meerkats

(We're not cats; we're related to the mongoose.) are only about two feet tall. But my own tail is two-thirds of my body length, and I usually carry it proudly wrapped around my arm or waist. It's also great for picking pockets. While innocently standing up at my full height and looking soooo cute with my two little praying paws in front of me, my tail was fast at work relieving the tourists of their valuables. I was a very talented kit.

My other role as a child was acting as lookout while the adults pulled off big time jobs. Since we always look like we're watching out for trouble with our alert faces and black, shadowed eyes, no one ever notices anything strange about a Meerkat standing erect, say, in front of a bank or jewelry store with his soooo cute little head bobbing from side to side.

Well, things began to get hotter than usual in the Kalahari both from the cops and the other mobs, and we had to find a new territory. One of our group proposed we get off the continent altogether and head for the islands – Madagascar, the Seychelles or Mauritius – till things cooled off. This was a very extreme solution, since we are definitely dry land animals. But nobody had a better idea, and so we voted. Since my aunt, the alpha female, had relatives in Mauritius, that was the winner.

I want you to imagine an over-water trip by forty meerkats in a leaking sloop. We were really glad we had signed up for an economy cruise. There was only a Captain and crew of four water rats, and they were drunk most of the time. The drinking water was undrinkable, and the food was inedible. Nobody was sure where we were or where we were going, including the Captain. Fights erupted! Three of my cousins fell overboard during a storm. A passenger mutiny broke out. The Captain was struck on the head with a slop bucket. There was an effort to overthrow my aunt and establish new leadership. She was having none of that, and as a result, a few more members of our clan ended up in the drink. We finally made it, much the worse for wear. I should also mention that during the trip, I graphically discovered I was very susceptible to motion sickness. *(Bruce, that's a smokestack!)*

After things settled down, pickings were pretty good on Mauritius. That's where I learned French and English to go along with my Boer Afrikaans. The tourists came by the boat and planeloads, and we helped make them welcome by relieving them of some of their more expensive baggage. And then it happened. I was standing guard outside an upscale tourist trap that sold ridiculously expensive jewelry while my uncle, and two older cousins were inside raiding the joint when out of nowhere a big furry paw grabbed me and lifted me off the ground. Octavius Bear!

Of course, I didn't know who he was at the time. All I saw was this endless expanse of brown fur topped with a very ferocious mouth, black nose, and black beady eyes. The mouth spoke or rather roared, "OK, kid, we have your relatives under arrest inside, and you seem to be the last of the bunch, so you're coming with me."

"Please, Mr. Pile-of-Fur," *(I'd never seen a bear before, much less a huge Kodiak)* I said, putting on my cutest and saddest face, "I'm just a little kid. They made me do it. Don't lock me up. They told me if I got caught, the authorities would sell me to a gourmet restaurant and make Fricassee of Meerkat out of me."

"What's your name, kid?" Lesson number one in Meerkat Crime School. Never, never, give your right name. I looked around and saw a sign hanging on a bank across the street – Le Deuxieme Mauritius Banque Nationale. "Mauritius, sir, just like this island."

"Well, Maury, you're in a lot of trouble. My name is Octavius Bear *(A bear? Oh, wow!)* and I've been hired by the island government along with my associate, Inspector Bruce Wallaroo, to end the crime spree that's been ripping through the tourist quarters. It looks like we've been successful."

"Oh, Mr. Octavius, sir! *(Irresistibly sweet expression #24 beamed across my face.)* I never wanted to lead a life of crime. Please let me go."

"Sorry, kid, can't do that, but I'll make you an offer you can't refuse. You can join me and work for the good guys, or I can turn you over to the French chefs."

I must have pondered those alternatives for at least six microseconds before I agreed to join him in whatever it was he did. Meerkat Fricassee held no attraction at all. "Just one thing," I said, "If my mob finds out, they'll dig a hole faster than you can sneeze, dump me in it, and cover it up."

"No need to worry, Maury," he said, "they'll never find you in the United States."

The United States – land of the Grand Canyon, Death Valley, and all that desert landscape, Arizona, New Mexico, Nevada – Meerkat heaven. "Wow, where in the United States?"

"Cincinnati," he replied. Suddenly Meerkat Fricassee didn't sound as bad as before. *(Bruce, I can see the Chicago skyline. No, the other way, turn us around, and lose the harmonica.)* Anyway, over I came across the pond, and I've been working for Octavius ever since. Occasionally I get to use my childhood skills *(all in the interest of truth and justice)* like removing a bad guy's weapon when he isn't looking or keeping Bruce or Octavius from being blindsided. Being with the good guys isn't bad at all, especially when the good guys live as well as Octavius does. Sometimes I miss the old mob, but on balance…

Chapter Nine

Every day she wakes up with a yawn.

She's so tired, this sweet spotted Fawn.

For she spends the long night

In the dark with no light.

Chewing everything up on my lawn.

Oh boy, here we go. The part I dread the most – the approach and landing. "Attention, passengers, this is your Captain speaking. We are now on final approach to land in Chicago. Please ensure that your mouth and barf bags are shut, and you are in the upright position for landing. Make sure your stomach and all other carry-on luggage you brought on board with you is safely stowed. We know you could have traveled on other airlines, and we appreciate your choosing *Suicide*. We hope the next time your plans call for travel, you'll consider *Suicide Airlines* as your carrier of choice."

Inspector Wallaroo felt that his position as a leading bulwark of law and order entitled him to play a little fast and loose with the rules of Air Traffic Control. Chicago Tracon thought otherwise, and to make matters worse, Bruce drifted into his most incomprehensible Strine while talking to them. Meanwhile, he was cutting across the traffic patterns for Midway Airport and heading out over the Lake, creating havoc as he went. Pulling up at the last minute, he began to hover and slowly descend.

I couldn't tell where we were. I'm only a couple of feet tall. When I'm strapped in my seat, and we're flying level, I can barely see over the instrument panel or out the windows. However, since we seldom fly level, I get to see much of our itinerary while tilted on my side or trying to scramble up the side of the bubble. We stopped descending, and he shut down the engines. I looked at the altimeter. "Bruce, are you crazy? You've cut the motors, and we're still over a thousand feet up. Get us out of here now!"

"No worries, Maury," he said and cracked open the pilot's side door and started to step out. "Bruce! Watch out!" I shrieked as I saw him drop from the cockpit but then land with his placid snout still grinning in at me as I practically strangled myself with the seat belt.

"Where are we?" I gasped.

"We've landed on top of the Aon Center Tower, two blocks horizontal and 1300 feet vertical from the Loupe Museum."

"You can't park us here. It's illegal!"

"Maury, m'bonzo jackaroo, who is going to put a parking ticket on a Chicago Police helicopter? C'mon now, time's a wastin'. Out you come."

He grabbed me and put me up on his shoulder, which is the normal way we travel together. I'm pretty fast on my feet, but trying to keep up with him by running just doesn't work. On the other hand, sitting on his shoulder as he bounds along is not much better than flying with him in the helicopter. We headed across the roof and into a utility elevator that covered the 1300-foot drop in what seemed like several seconds. Between the chopper and the elevator, I was about to send out an All Points Bulletin: Keep on the lookout for one Meerkat stomach–upset and thought to be dangerous.

"We got two stops to make. First to the Bank of Lake Michigan to collect the key transmitters for the display cases and then on to the Loupe in the Loop," he said. While we were coming in for our landing, he had called ahead to the president of the Bank of Lake Michigan and asked him to stand by for us to pick up the transmitters. It was getting into the late afternoon, and you know how bankers are about going home promptly.

We bounded *(literally)* up Michigan Avenue and into the offices of the bank. Waiting for us at the top of the longest marble staircase I had ever seen was a very attractive white-tail fawn looking at us questioningly with her big wide eyes. "Inspector Wallaroo?" she said.

"Too right, sheila," responded Bruce with his typical *savoir faire* and proceeded to leap up the stairs with me holding on for dear life.

"Mr. Moose is waiting for you. Follow me, please."

We entered the beautifully paneled office suite of Montgomery Moose III, Chairmoose and CEO of the Bank of Lake Michigan. He was standing behind his desk while another equally attractive doe polished his antlers.

"Ah, Inspector Wallaroo, Welcome, Welcome!" he trumpeted. "Thank you, Bambi, I think that should do it for the banquet tonight. Need to look good under the television lights, you know. I'm receiving the Moose of the Year Award." The deer took her kit of antler polish and quietly left the room. "And who is your companion?"

"I'm Mauritius Meerkat, Sir, associate of Inspector Wallaroo and field assistant to Octavius Bear."

"Octavius Bear? So you've called in the heavyweights, eh, Wallaroo? Quite right! Quite right! We have to get to the bottom of this mess and quickly. The reputation of this bank is at stake along, of course, with yours, the jeweler's society and the Loupe Museum. You know, The Bank of Lake Michigan is no ordinary bank. We serve clientele who have very specific and highly confidential financial needs. Security is our mania. We have never had an incident of this sort before that reflects so badly on our security. While I and my staff are absolutely certain that those transmitters are exactly where we placed them, and no one has had even the remotest access to them, the media is making us look like a bunch of negligent fools."

"We're all lookin' like a herd of drongoes, Monty. No one wants to catch that mongrel Duck more than I do."

"So, you're convinced it was the Black Quack gang, eh?"

"It sure looks like it, Mr. Moose," I intervened.

"Maury's right, MM, "said Bruce. "They left every possible signature they could. That ragin' cheetah. The note. That damn quackin' egg. "

"How did you dispose of the egg, Inspector?"

"It's sitting in the Chicago Police Lab in a soundproof room still quackin' away, as far as I know. That earbashing thing is a real screamer. We've worked on them before, and there's no stopping, analyzing or destroying the things. I don't know what powers that egg, but it never seems to wind down. Every man in that lab is gonna be ropeable before they throw in the towel. They should probably just dump it in the lake right now."

"Is this kind of theft typical of that Duck and his hench-beings. What's his name – Impertinent?" asked Montgomery Number 3.

"Imperius," I replied, "and no, lately he's been trying to upset governments or defraud companies or other antisocial types of crimes. Jewel or art theft isn't usually on his menu. Especially something like this. Unless he's trying to embarrass us all. And he sure has succeeded this time. Worst possible timing with you getting the Moose Award and all that. We all want to get our paws on him and his cheetah and baboon cronies."

The moose stared at us with his large, sincere, chocolate eyes. "Frankly, I just want to see the sapphire recovered as soon as possible. Because we sponsored the show at the museum, one of our subsidiaries wrote most of the insurance on it. Our corporate bottom line is going to take a real pounding if we have to pay off. Oh, shame about the dead peacock! Heart attack, I hear."

"Of course," he hastily added, "I also want to see that beautiful object returned to public view and the culprits brought to heel. *(Sure!)* Well, shall we go down to the vaults?"

Turning to his secretary, who had not left the room, he said, "Fawn, please call down to Security and ask the Chief and Doctor Watt to meet us in the subterranean catacombs."

He walked over to a statue of Bullwinkle and twisted its antlers. A wall panel slid back and revealed a large, ornate elevator waiting there. *(Oh, oh, another elevator. Just when I was getting my sea legs back.)*

We stepped in and sank downward at a very stately pace. "Sorry about the slow speed," said Montgomery M., "but we often use this elevator to bring our wealthier patrons down to their safe deposit boxes after a courtesy cup of coffee with me. Some of them are rather old, and we don't want to rattle them. We'll be going all the way to the bottom level."

I am still rather young, and I didn't feel like being rattled either. I said a brief prayer of thanks to the Meerkat deity for sparing me another lurch and another visit with my lunch.

We finally stopped, and the elevator door opened onto a titanium-lined room where two animals were waiting for us. One was in uniform and the other in a lab coat. My razor sharp mind instantaneously fired off a keen deduction. This was the Chief and Dr. Watt. *(Octavius has trained me well. No wonder he can't do without me.)*

"Inspector and Mr. Meerkat," intoned the Moose, "may I present our Chief of Security, Colonel Where and our Chief Technology Officer, Dr. Watt. I know you're familiar with them, Inspector. You were colleagues in setting up this end of the protection program. Colonel and Doctor, may I also present Mr. Mauritius Meerkat, Octavius Bear's primary assistant and field operative."

Paw and hoof shakes all around. The Colonel was a grizzled looking wolf who had obviously been around. It turns out he spent most of his early days in Army Intelligence and then as a mercenary in several key battle zones. He had "retired" but was called up by the Bank of Lake Michigan to help develop and manage their security system. I thought for a moment of Frau Schuylkill, the warrior wolfess. Did I have a girl for him!!

Dr. Watt, on the other hand, looked like he had just gotten his first haircut which may have been rather difficult since he was a porcupine…but a very young-looking porcupine.

For an animal his apparent age, I later found out, Watt had more degrees, citations and published papers to his name than the entire faculty of MIT. He and Octavius would have had a ball together. Some day, perhaps.

To business! The Colonel led us to a large transparent door surrounded by seals. We shooed them off to the other side of the room and approached a complex collection of ID devices, ranging from paw, voice, and face print to data card and DNA samples. The Moose and Wallaroo's images were on file. I was going to be taken in under the doctor and Colonel's escort. The final test was a photo-matched sequence of each entrant doing the Lambada. If you couldn't match each step and timing of the sequence exactly, the alarm went off.

Fortunately, everyone was very limber that afternoon and the door opened leading us into a transparent chamber and another door similar to the first – the classic animal trap. Each one of us went in separately *(Correction, I went in on the Colonel's shoulder.)* and after more gyrations, posing, and another round of DNA, we all made it safely to the other side. We seemed to be staring at a blank wall, but Montgomery Moose turned to his left and as we all followed we came face to face with a corridor interlaced with high powered cutting lasers and prominently displayed gas jets.

As he bounded around the corner Bruce bumped against the Colonel and I fell off the Colonel's shoulder right into the path of the lasers. Dr. Watt pulled me back by my tail. Before I slid backward to safety, my flight cap embroidered with "C-5A Galaxy – The *Ursa Major*," slipped from my head and rolled inside. The lasers crackled and my favorite hat was now a pile of ashes. Fortunately, the gas jets didn't open up.

"Well," said the Colonel, "we didn't mean to give you such a vivid demonstration but you can see that even something much smaller than a duck couldn't make it past the barriers. Are you OK, Mr. Meerkat?"

I had long ago been declared uninsurable by every major company in the world and today alone, I had proven their point, not once but several times. Suddenly, heading back to the island and the mob began to seem a bit more attractive.

"I'm fine," I lied. "How do you turn those things off?"

"Telekinetically!" said Dr. Watt. "Only the chief, Mr. Moose and I can do it. You stand up straight and click your heels together and say, 'There's no place like HOMES, there's no place like HOMES and...' "

The lasers winked out, and a safety light went on announcing the gas jets were no longer charged.

'Now," said the Colonel, "I waited for your arrival before I came down here. I didn't want the logs to show any unexplained access to the vault. So we're all going in for the first time, since the key transmitters were placed in the vault. Isn't that true Doctor? Mister Moose?'

Both agreed. Maybe it was the near miss on getting fried, but I was feeling a bit ornery. "Wait a minute," I said, "Are you sure no one else could have gotten in here by fooling the security system?"

Dr. Watt looked up the ceiling for a moment. "I'd calculate the odds at roughly 14,987,473,786.88 to 1 against it. And even then, there are twelve different visual, audio, weight, smell, and respiration logs all recording action in the area. They are all on different circuits and channels and they all show negative. I'll stake my quills against anyone having been here without our knowing."

With that, Inspector Wallaroo bounced over to the door of the vault and started to enter an extended alphanumeric code sequence into a keypad.

Suddenly, my near miss finally hit me with all of its implications, and I did what I always do in reaction. I sneezed.

Bruce looked over at me sharply. "Dammit, Maury, stop playin' the fruit loop. This is serious. Now I have to start all over again."

I shrugged apologetically to all and sundry and stood by as once again, Inspector Wallaroo entered the code from his prodigious memory. "Success," he bawled and swung open the door. There, glistening in their impermeable alloy sleeves were the two transmitters, seemingly untouched and, if we could believe their counters, as yet unused. Everything was set to zero.

Well, there's one theory shot to hell. No one had stolen the transmitters. On to the Loupe! As I looked around, Monsieur Mousse Troisieme was talking into the red wall phone. I guess he was telling the security guards we were on our way back out.

Bearoness Belinda
Béarnaise Bruin
(nee Black)

Chapter Ten

As I swam one hot day in the Nile,

I encountered a white Crocodile.

But it wasn't her tears

That engendered my fears.

'Twas the two hundred teeth in her smile.

Octavius was back in the den after his unscheduled bath when the Flying Aquabear hurtled up the runway to the mansion's open court. Recognizing the distinctive scream of the engines, and watching the sleek aircraft through the window, he waited with some trepidation and definitely mixed emotions, the arrival of his former love light. Damn that female, couldn't she leave him alone? But then, he really didn't want her to leave him alone.

The door chimes sounded.

"Frau Schuylkill," he sighed, "would you please get the door. I think that's Bel ringing."

"*Ja,* Herr Bear!" Strange as it may seem, given her own strong feelings for Octavius and her naturally antagonistic nature, Frau Schuylkill actually was quite fond of, even in awe of, the Bearoness. It was probably helped along by her military training and the traditional European affection for the nobility still deeply rooted in her Alpine background. Her Dutch surname, Schuylkill, resulted from a brief marriage to an Amsterdam Schweinhund who traded quite prosperously in imported dog and wolf foods. They divorced after she caught and practically killed him for having an affair with his German Shepherd secretary. Returning to lick her wounds at her

86

family's inn, the Schloss Goulasch near Breakurbach, she rescued and nursed the severely wounded Octavius back to health after his plunge over the falls with Imperius Drake. *(Who, it seems, managed to fly away.)* At his invitation, she accompanied the Bear to the U.S., where she is his gourmet cook-housekeeper-security officer-chief pilot-part time investigator and has also become a leading participant in Cincinnati's annual Oktoberfest celebrations.

She opened the door and bowing, stood aside to reveal in all her glory the Bearoness Belinda Béarnaise Bruin (nee Black).

"Thank you, Frau Schuylkill," bubbled the Bearoness, "My dear, you look lovely. What do you do to keep your coat so bright and silky?"

It is difficult for a wolf to blush, and the Frau barely managed it. Belinda swept into the room. "Tavi, my pet, you on the other hand look a bit peaked. Have you been working overtime again, you poor bear? Can't you let Maury and all of those other minions you have working for you handle all that boring business stuff and criminal nastiness? My former husband, the Bearon, made an art of doing nothing and making scads of money in the process."

It was true. Bearon Byron Bruin characterized himself as a global entrepreneur and while the fruits of his labors were seen everywhere, his actual labors were not. An international playboy, he first laid eyes on Belinda when she was swimming in the chorus at the Aquabear Review. A polar bear himself, he had romanced more than enough ditzy platinum blondes, but this one was different. Exquisite was the word. Thunderstruck, he tried to wheedle an introduction. But Belinda's mother stood in the way of all comers. She had turned out to be the stage-mother of all time. Shortly after the Bestiary Ball in Winnipeg at which Belinda, costumed as a crocodile, was a smash hit, Mother Black dropped her society pretensions and ferociously pursued a showbear career for her darling. After all, showbears met rich industrialists who could set them up in jewels and posh apartments. *(Showbears had their own furs!)*

Never one to waste time in subtle approaches, Bearon Byron took the "shock and awe" approach and bought the *Aquabears Review* outright. He immediately promoted Belinda to Star Aqueuse, giving her the stage name,

"Belinda Béarnaise, the Utopian Ursine." *(Clever names were not the Bearon's forté.)* Belinda's natural charm, beauty and astounding swimming and diving techniques took care of the rest. SHE WAS A SENSATION!!

Mother Black, realizing her mistake in giving the cold shoulder to this polar playboy, reversed her field and practically pushed Belinda into the Bearon's furry paws.

They married, and after a few years of whirlwind, worldwide travel with the Aquabear Troupe and on Bearon Byron's yacht and Concorde jet, Bearoness Belinda Béarnaise Bruin (nee Black) went into semi-retirement, preferring to avoid her mother, the paparazzi, and demands for her to chair any number of society events. She took refuge in the Bearon's palatial retreat, Bearmoral Castle, in the northernmost corner of the Shetland Islands. With the frigid North Sea to satisfy her chilly and aquatic instincts, and a huge staff and money to satisfy her every whim, Belinda led a life of leisurely luxury.

A small cloud descended on her otherwise blissful life when the playboy Bearon was killed in an avalanche while skiing downhill for a Pola-Cola commercial. However, all was not lost. In fact, nothing was lost. Belinda inherited everything. Lock, stock and ice-making machine. Today she keeps herself occupied by, among other things, reliving the great Aquabear years with former members of the troupe who all visit during the winter months. Together, they still perform in the crystal pool on the castle grounds and travel to give shows for worthy causes. The Great Bear had accidentally run into her again at a charity event where he was the sponsor. They renewed their relationship, but at a somewhat sedate and paw's length distance. Unknown to Octavius, it was another Aquabear performance that was now bringing Belinda and her friends to his mansion.

"Hello, Bel, you look lovely as usual. I'm delighted to see you. Come in, come in!" he said, wondering all the time what had prompted this visit out of the blue.

"Oh, Tavi, before I do. I have eight of the original Aquabear troupe with me and my co-pilot and flight engineer."

Bel flew the Flying Aquabear herself. The Bearon never did. He couldn't fit in the cockpit. In fact, the entire flight crew was made up of smaller polar females. They had also redesigned the passenger section of the Concorde to accommodate about sixteen polar bears of mixed genders.

"I'm sure you wouldn't mind if they came in for a bit to stretch their legs and use the facilities. It's a long flight from the Shetlands, even on an SST."

"Certainly not! Frau Schuylkill, make the ladies welcome. Bring out some champagne and a spread of fish snacks. We don't get your Scottish salmon very often, Bel, but we do have some delectable Ohio River catfish."

"Oh, don't fuss too much, Frau Schuylkill," said Belinda, "Any old delicacies will do."

"Such a lady," murmured the she-wolf, "What grandeur, what condescension. There are so few left." And she hurried off to the well-stocked larder to whip up a succulent array of *fruits de mer*.

The Bearoness, meanwhile padded back out to the mansion's forecourt and signaled the co-pilot that they'd all be welcome to come inside. Some of the *Aquabears*, put off by the spooky exterior of the rambling house held back, sniffing the air and making little grunting noises.

"Oh, come on, you silly things," cried Belinda. "This is the home of Octavius Bear, the wealthy owner of Universal Ursine Industries, among other things. He's a bit of a recluse like me, and this mansion is one of his personal oddities but he's the most darling Kodiak you'll ever meet."

Still not quite convinced, and even further disturbed when Frau Schuylkill made her appearance, *(Ohmigod, a wolf!)* the *Aquabears* and flight crew slowly made their way across the courtyard and into the house. Their amazement at the interior of the mansion and their even further amazement at the huge hunk of ursine machismo that greeted them put all their fears aside.

"Ladies, let me introduce Octavius Bear. Octavius, all these lovely bears are original members of the *Aquabear Review* – 'Some Like it Cold.' I'm sure you'll remember their magnificent performances, even if you don't remember them personally. At one point, ladies, Octavius and I were an item, but then, life goes on."

Belinda was an absolute expert at embarrassing the Great Bear, and this time she had done it in record time. Shuffling slightly, Octavius mumbled something about their being welcome and invited them to relax and enjoy the facilities and the feast.

Taking the Bearoness aside, he asked her what brought her to the U.S. at this time.

"Oh, you silly bear," she exclaimed, "you will play your undercover games, won't you? Well, as I'm sure you know, we're on our way to Las Vegas to give a reunion performance at the Quadrennial Convention of Genetic Experts, an organization I know you're familiar with, since UUI is a major sponsor, and you're giving the keynote speech. We're the closing night entertainment. I don't suppose you know who the secret sponsor was who engaged us to perform, do you? Of course you don't."

She looked at him coyly over her wrinkly black nose. "Oh, Tavi, sometimes I just want to shake you. But you go ahead and play dumb if you want to. I'll go along with your guessing games."

The puzzled expression on Octavius' face was sincere. He did *not* know who had commissioned the *Aquabears* to perform at the Convention. He did know it hadn't been him, and he was reasonably sure no one at UUI would have done so without checking with him. He wasn't about to tell Bel he was clueless, but the moment she left, he sure was going to find out. So he just smiled a little smile and started to change the subject.

The Bearoness beat him to it. "I saw Maury and that Australian policeman taking off in a helicopter as we taxied in. It looked like a Chicago police chopper. Anything exciting going on?"

90

Octavius deliberated for a moment and then thought, "What the hell! I might as well tell her. It's probably already plastered all over the news-sites, papers, radio, and TV. They couldn't keep the loss of a jewel like the Deep Blue and another 'curse' death out of the public eye for long."

So he said, "Well, it might involve some excitement, but I suspect it's just another routine jewel theft."

Nothing set the blood in Belinda's veins coursing like the word – jewel. "Oh, my! Tell all, tell all! Ladies," she shouted ever so demurely, "come and hear. Octavius is working on a jewel theft."

The thud of ten sets of polar paws coupled with the ursine equivalent of squeals of curiosity echoed throughout the mansion. Squeezing their way into the den, they stood at rapturous attention, ready to respond to his every word.

"Well," he said, "there's really not that much to tell at the moment. Our investigation has just begun, but someone has made off with the star attraction at the Global Association of Exquisite Jewelers' show at the Loupe Museum in Chicago – the Deep Blue Sapphire."

Gasps of shock, surprise, and horror!

Any showbear worth her costume was familiar with the Deep Blue Sapphire and its strange history. Largest and purest of its kind, it had belonged to royalty, the incredibly rich and an occasional movie star. Coveted by millions, it was also strongly reputed to be cursed. It was true that four or five owners met with untimely ends, but it was a bit difficult to connect the stone with two accidental deaths from overeating and skydiving. Nevertheless, the stories persisted, adding to the mystery, popularity, desirability, and price of the stone. And...the strange death of Phillipe Peacoq, Ph.D. would do nothing to banish the mystique.

The gem had recently been donated by its last mega-billionaire owner to the Loupe Museum for the upcoming show, resulting in the largest tax write-off ever recorded by the IRS. And now, it had disappeared. Needless to say, hearing this news, ten ursine jaws dropped in synchronism. *(The showbears did just about everything in synchronism.)*

Cries of, "How did it happen? Do you know who did it? Can you get it back? Why steal it, you can't sell it. You don't suppose they'll cut it up. Do you have any clues? Did the peacock really drop dead?" And the occasional, "I had a diamond bracelet stolen once, or did I lose it? I can't remember," all descended on the Great Bear's ears.

Smiling his most reassuring smile, he was cut off by Belinda who said, "Now ladies, Octavius Bear, Inspector Wallaroo, and Mauritius Meerkat have solved some of the most perplexing crimes in modern times. I'm sure they're more than up to recovering the jewel and seeing the culprits brought to justice. Well, I think the Concorde should be refueled by now, and we should be getting on our way. All of us are jet-lagged and we still have several hours before we reach Las Vegas. It's such a bother to have to fly subsonically over the United States. It's almost not worth having the world's only flying SST. Thank you for your hospitality, Octavius!"

Choruses of "thank you" and "love what you've done with place" and other felicitations flowed from the perfect polars.

As the *Aquabears* and the crew padded, out trailing the occasional catfish and bottle of champagne, Belinda took Octavius aside and said, "Two things. First, this is the third time I've flown in here when the signs, construction barrels, and bulldozers were in exactly the same place around the runway. If you're trying to stay incognito, you really ought to move things around a bit. Make it look like some building is actually going on." *(How a Concorde and a C-5A Galaxy could fly in and out on a roadway construction site without attracting attention says something about the low level of curiosity of the Great Bear's neighbors and local officials.)*

"Second, if you do recover the Deep Blue Sapphire, I don't suppose you could hold on to it for a little while. Byron always said that blue was my color, and I'd just love to see it nestled in my fur. Byron always said he just adored seeing me come out of the pool with my fur all wet and wearing just a few strategically placed jewels."

Needless to say, at this point, Octavius was having a hard time controlling his libido. It was good thing she slipped out the door when she did. *(It was also a good thing Byron was already dead.)*

"Ta, ta, Tavi," she called as she headed for the jetstairs. "You'll be in Vegas next week for the convention, won't you? Of course you will. Maybe we can take a little time out for some relaxation and gambling. Are you feeling lucky?"

"Damn that female," thought Octavius as he turned inside to get away from the screaming jets of the Concorde. "I have enough problems–but I do love wet fur."

With that, he picked up the oversize cell phone designed to fit his massive head and called UUI Corporate Headquarters. "Give me Sales Promotion! Smedley? Octavius! What imbecile booked the *Aquabears* for the genetics convention entertainment without telling me? What do you mean, we didn't book them? No entertainment at all? Cutting costs? Look, you get that overpaid staff of yours moving and find out how the *Aquabears* happen to be booked to perform on the last night of the convention. Get back to me ASAP." And, turning, he watched the Concorde leap screaming from the Interstate By-Pass. Then, he called the road crew.

He decided he needed a calming influence. The bees! Their drone would act as a soporific for his mental and emotional turmoil. Besides, it was time to check whether his honey supply could keep the meadery in raw material. Bees didn't know much about inventory management or process engineering, for that matter. But they made delightful honey, and that made for delightful mead. He loved the stuff. When he wasn't on one of his crusades against criminality or demonstrating yet another brain-stultifying device to an amazed, grateful, and money-laden world, he searched for the perfect keg of mead. This obsession had taken him around the globe many times, always seeking, sometimes coming close but never, never finding true satisfaction. Yes, his own distillations were commendable. He had won more awards than he could count– but yet, but yet. The search goes on.

He lumbered through a grove of trees and descended on the apiary. While he was adjusting his bonnet and veil to protect his large and vulnerable nose *(his fur took care of the rest),* he looked aside and sensed more than saw Frau Schuylkill. The wolf seemed capable of being in several places at once and could appear or disappear without rippling the ozone.

"May I be so bold, Herr Bear?"

"Of course, Frau Schuylkill, what's on your mind?" *(He knew she was never one to clutter up the verbal landscape with small talk or poorly thought out ideas.)*

"I know that I am not a favorite of the bouncing Inspector. He is not high on my list of animal idols, either. However, there was a time, earlier, when I first came to Zinzinnati that I, too, was honored to assist you in your investigations. Lately, I am spending most of my time in the kitchen or housekeeping or making sure the aircraft are all flight-worthy. Of course, I enjoy all this. Cooking is my hobby as well as my job. And I have been in love with flying since the first time I jumped on top of a sled full of passengers. But now Maury and the *verdammte* Inspector *(sorry)* seem to do all the looking and listening and chasing and opinioning and prodding and testing. I have been a very successful military wolf, Herr Bear. I have many commendations and medals. I miss the action."

She lowered her head and tail simultaneously. Octavius pulled off his bee bonnet and stared at her. "My dear Frau, I understand completely, and I apologize deeply. It had not occurred to me that I had stopped taking full advantage of your formidable skills, but now that I consider it, I realize that I have not been utilizing such a unique resource as yourself anywhere near your potential. That will change immediately! The problem, my dear Frau, is that you are such a damn good cook, housekeeper, pilot, and aerodrome manager that I can't imagine anyone else performing those tasks. Maury can't boil water, and I absolutely refuse to fly with that madcap marsupial. Poor Maury,

I wonder if he has found his stomach yet. Nevertheless, I guarantee you that with this nut-case Duck on the loose again, you will see action and plenty of it. As a matter of fact, I need some information and an opinion from you right now."

"Of course, Herr Bear. How may I assist?"

"Well, for starters, I don't want to pry into your secrets but everyone here at the mansion has noticed how you can seem to be in more than one place at a time…and there's that trick you do of having something we've asked for appear by itself. Now, here are my questions. Can you teleport? Have you conquered telekinesis? It's important to the case we're working on right now."

The wolf laughed…part snort, part growl, part howl. "*Ach, nein,* Herr Bear. I am not a teleporter or a telekineser, either. I don't think either of those is possible. I have studied both subjects and am convinced that it can't be done."

"Fine!! Now how do you explain what you do?"

"What I do, mein Herr, is "*Höchstgeschwindigkeit!*""

"Pardon???"

"Hyper-speed!! Through deep study, meditation, and endless hours of rigorous conditioning and practice, I have learned to move at velocities approaching light!!""

"You're physically moving faster than the eye can catch?"

"*Ja*, but only for short distances. I can traverse this property and return, but that's my limit, as of now. Of course, I'm still a novice."

"So when, a keg of mead appears out of thin air, you have actually carried it in and then run back off at hyperspeed. But sometimes you seem to anticipate what we want before we ask for it."

"A little telepathy mixed with knowing all of you very well. Nothing supernatural!"

"So, for example, you can't teleport something that is locked up without first opening whatever is enclosing it."

"*Ja, mein Herr*, I couldn't have stolen the deadly sapphire in that museum without opening the case first. That's what you were thinking, wasn't it?"

"Yes, Frau Schuylkill, I was thinking along those lines, but not about you. I was wondering whether teleportation or telekinesis was at work here. I wouldn't put it past that genius Duck to try it. But you seem to think it's impossible."

"As you always say, Herr Bear, nothing is impossible but after all my research and consultation, I would say it is extremely improbable."

"I think I agree, but tell me, why do you do your high speed act at all? It's very impressive, but surely there's no need for you to strain yourself to deliver a keg of mead."

"That's how I keep in practice, Herr Bear. You never know when I'll need it. Besides, a she-wolf's work is never done."

"One last question: You could certainly outrun a cheetah, couldn't you? They're supposed to be the fastest animals on four feet."

"Oh, Chita is a slowpoke, *mein Herr*. I assume she's the one you'd like me to outrun. But remember, only for short distances. On the other hand, she can't keep her speed up for very long either. Unless she had a very long lead on me, I could catch her. I would be delighted to try. I think a military wolf could give her a good fight, too."

"I'm sure you could. I'll keep it in mind. We may yet give you the chance. Thank you, Frau. Do you want to keep your hyperspeed talent a secret?"

"Well, it's all right if Maury knows, but I don't want that wallaroo Inspector to catch on. I enjoy keeping him confused."

"Your secret is safe until you want to reveal it. I may ask you to use it though, as this case goes forward."

"*Danke schoen*, Herr Bear. There is no need to put on your bonnet. I've already stacked all the honeycombs over there for you. The queen and I have an agreement."

Octavius watched with his huge jaws gaping as she snapped out of the landscape.

He stood there twirling his bonnet at roughly the same speed his mind was whirling and then threw it on the ground. Never one to stand when he could sit, he picked up several honeycombs, settled himself against a large elm tree, closed his eyes and mused and munched.

"Well, that was more than interesting. *(chomp)* A lot to absorb in one day! Frau Schuylkill is a speed freak! Imperius Drake and his gang are back. The Deep Blue is missing. The museum security doesn't seem to be working. Teleportation and telekinesis are real long shots as M.O.'s for the jewel's disappearance. Although you never know what that damn Duck can do. We'll just have to wait and see what Maury and the Inspector come up with. And now to add to the consternation, Belinda is back on the scene. Damn!!"

"What the hell is the matter with you, Octavius? *(munch)* Are you losing it? *(slurp)* You are usually in total command of the situation. *(crunch)* Now you can't concentrate. Even this new foray by the demon Duck hasn't gotten you up to full speed. Maybe you're getting too old for this detective stuff. Maybe you should turn the whole thing over to Maury and Wallaroo and the Frau and just sit back and suck on honeycombs.

Maybe it's time to retire altogether. You have more money than you know what to do with. UUI practically runs itself. Retire and teach! That's it. But teach what? You know so much about everything! Teach whom? Could you really stand looking at a bunch of fresh-faced cubs and juveniles whose minds were anywhere but where you wanted them? Or, worse yet, putting up with all the backbiting by over-educated academicians defending their tenure and half-baked ideas?

Maybe full-time research? Nah! Been there! Done that! How many patents and awards do I have? Don't even keep count anymore. Besides, we've got teams and equipment that does all of the really fun stuff. I haven't blown up a lab in years.

I suppose I could write. But I've done that, too. Actually Maury does it for me, if I want to be honest about it. He's already built stacks of my personal memoirs and speeches. I can't concentrate long enough to get words on paper!

There isn't even a good war going on that I could get involved with. Who am I kidding? I couldn't get out of my own way, let alone an oncoming tank."

He pawsed, shook his head and listened to the gentle drone of the bees. Restful. Was he going to have another attack? Funny how he had everyone convinced that he didn't believe he had narcolepsy. Of course he did, but he couldn't admit it in public. Talk about becoming vulnerable. "Poor Maury! I give him such a hard time about it. Kinda fun, actually. I ought to let Maury have more freedom. I doubt he wants to spend his entire life playing second oboe to a grouchy old ursine."

He picked up his bonnet and started twirling it again. Then with immense force, he sent it sailing among the trees. "Face up to it, Bear! The real problem is that damn polar sow. She's had you wound around her beautiful paw from the moment you first saw her in the Arctic. And it's only gotten worse. All this money! Even all this detecting! It was all because of her or the lack of her. Oh, for God's sake! Nothing worse than an old bruin still acting like a love struck juvenile. If the others knew, they'd laugh themselves sick. *(Munch, slurp)*

Maybe they do know. Much as I'd like to believe that I am very deep with a shell-like exterior. All business! Sometimes I'm as transparent as a...chandelier! A big, jangling chandelier! *(Snort)*

Belinda! Now she's available again and just as desirable...more so. And if I was being honest, she probably is still interested in me. She sure shows signs of it. That 'feeling lucky' exit line almost had me going up the wall. Belinda! No, not Belinda, the Bearoness! That's the problem. I love Belinda, but I'm afraid of the Bearoness. Beautiful, sophisticated, self-assured, self-sufficient, wealthy beyond her wildest needs or wants. No longer the giggling juvenile I met at Churchill. And yet, she still giggles. I heard her do it today. That same charming giggle. Belinda!"

His eyes drooped and he slipped sideways, getting sticky honey all over himself for the second time that day. Today's Score: Narcolepsy - 3, Bear - 0.

Chapter Eleven

May we now, by your leave, introduce

That spectacular animal: Moose.

Yes, his antlers are large!

Always ready to charge!

But his nose is too big and too loose.

Back at the Bank of Lake Michigan. After going through the whole exit security rigamarole again *(Have you ever tried to do the Lambada backwards?)* we finally rose in the elegant elevator to MM's offices. Inspector Wallaroo had the two transmitters locked up in his pouch. *(No, only females have built in pouches. This one was slung around his shoulder with a big leather strap.)* This time Colonel Where, Dr. Watt, and several security guards accompanied us. The elevator was taking on all the finer characteristics of a midtown bus at rush hour.

As the elevator doors opened, we were greeted by the blinding lights of several TV crews, and seven or eight microphones were shoved in our faces. That sneaky moose had used the red phone to call a press conference in his office. Pandemonium reigned as questions and cameras and spotlights and one very upset wallaroo all collided. I had to literally bring Bruce down from the wall and resist the urge to run under a desk.

Raising himself to his most majestic stature and making sure his noble profile and well-polished antlers were getting the full benefit of the lights and cameras, the traitorous moose trumpeted, "Please, please, can we have some order here. I am Montgomery Moose III, Chairmoose and CEO of the Bank of Lake Michigan, and soon to be recipient of the Moose of the Year Award. Let me introduce the bank's Chief of Security, Colonel Wyatt Where and our

Chief Technical Officer, Dr. Howard Watt. Also with us this afternoon is Mr. Mauritius Meerkat, associate and field commander for the well-known consulting detective and owner of Universal Ursine Industries, Octavius Bear. And last, but certainly not least *(insert moose equivalent of a diffident chuckle,)* may I introduce Inspector Bruce Wallaroo of the International Fine Arts and Jewelry Protective Squad? He is the designer of the museum's security system that was used to protect the now-missing Deep Blue Sapphire. After I make an initial statement, I am sure that Inspector Wallaroo will be happy to answer your questions about the theft and the mysterious death that accompanied it."

Have you ever seen an apoplectic marsupial? Not a pretty picture. I'm sure Bruce was calculating in his mind how the sight of a Wallaroo attempting to stomp a moose to death on network television would play back in Sydney. *(Aided and abetted by a ferocious meerkat, I might add.)* Montgomery the Misery had taken the precaution of having an additional number of the bank's security guards in the room. The odds of getting past the first stomp didn't look good. Bruce, professional to the last, pulled himself together, gave the Wallaroo equivalent of a teeth-gritting smile and waved listlessly at the cameras.

MMIII cleared his throat and began, "I am pleased to announce that this afternoon, we have scientifically and categorically proven that the encryption transmitters associated with the protective jewelry display cases at the Loupe Museum have been resting undisturbed in our supremely secure vaults. We have them here now, and they will be taken under heavily armed guard over to the museum to be used in *(hopefully)* solving this crime of the century. Will you please show the transmitters to the press, Inspector Wallaroo?"

Still contemplating the penalties for First Degree Aggravated Moosicide, Bruce unlocked his pouch, reached in, and with lightning speed, pulled out the two devices. With even greater speed, to the consternation of the Fourth Estate, he dropped them back in and ostentatiously went about resealing the compartment.

Struggling now to regain the crowd's attention, Montgomery trumpeted on, "No one has penetrated the bank's 'cordon sanitaire' and I am delighted to say that our unmatched reputation for security remains unsullied. I am afraid that Dr. Watt and Chief Where cannot share with you the details of our security systems, for obvious reasons, but I did want you to meet them. They are the two geniuses responsible for this impregnable environment. Since only two transmitters were created, and we have established that there has been no substitution *("Dammit, no we haven't!" I thought, almost aloud.)* we can conclude that the fault lies somewhere at the Loupe Museum. The security systems there were designed and implemented by the Inspector and his team, and I'm sure he'll be happy to take your questions as to what might have gone wrong."

(Steady, Bruce, steady!)

"But before he does, I should add that there is strong evidence to suggest that this caper, so to say, was executed by the dauntingly brilliant master criminal, Imperius Drake. In the face of this fact, I am even prouder to assert that the Bank of Lake Michigan's security systems performed to their expected level of perfection. On the other hand, if the genius Duck and his Black Quack gang are the perpetrators, I am somewhat pessimistic about the jewel's recovery until he sees fit, if ever, to return it."

"And now, I'd like to turn you over to Inspector Wallaroo for a few remarks on the nature and status of the case, and then you can feel free to accompany him and Mr. Meerkat to the museum."

"Sure, set us up and get the press out of your antlers, you two-timing bulb-nose," I thought, wondering if I could jump high enough to bite and sever his jugular vein. Probably not!

Montgomery III hadn't counted on the Aussie resourcefulness of the Inspector. His moose jaw literally dropped as Bruce cut loose with a most unintelligible spiel of deeply accented Strine intermixed with some very nasty epithets directed at Montgomery in several exotic aboriginal tongues from Down Under. Then he put me up on his shoulder and yanked my tail, a signal.

102

I got the message and said, "Well, members of the press, as the Inspector has indicated, you can see we have much work yet to do. I am sure the media relations department of the Bank of Lake Michigan will be happy to provide you with complete transcripts of Mr. Moose's and Inspector Wallaroo's remarks."

With that, Bruce bounded out of the office, down the marble stairs and out into the streets of Chicago, with the transmitters securely in his possession and with me, far less securely, hanging onto his neck for dear life.

As we pitched, bounced, sprang, and tumbled our way across Michigan Avenue and up a side street, causing at least three or four fender benders in the process, Bruce continued his tirade. I could make out very little, but I do know the moose was due for a future visit by some of the most poisonous creatures indigenous to Aussie-Land.

Leaping up the front stairs of the museum and over the crime scene tape used by the Chicago Police to seal the building, Inspector Wallaroo shouted at the police Sergeant at the door, "Sergeant Daley, no one and I mean no one, especially the press and the security guards from that mongrel bank, get through here! Ya got it?"

"Got it, Inspector. Hello Maury, long time, no see."

"Hi, Sergeant," I said. My previous life of African crime still causes me to shiver a little when I see a police uniform.

We sprang into the elevator and took it to the third floor. I dropped to my feet while Bruce caromed off the sides of the car, making it a very noisy *(and dangerous)* ride. As soon as the door began to open, he banked off a side wall and bounced off in the direction of the Deep Blue Room. I scurried along behind, arriving to see him in vehement conversation with several members of Chicago's finest. Commissioner Daley, Captain Daley, Detective Lieutenant Daley and three plain clothes officers all also named Daley, plus the Medical Examiner, Dr. Daley. Most of the Chicago police force were Irish Setters and these canines were some of the best of their breed. There were also a number of Polish Retrievers, who usually came from one breeding line, the Dzawliczas – pronounced Daley. Doctor Daley was a female whippet.

Bruce was trying furiously to control himself and speak in a Midwest American English that most of the Irish and Polish cops could understand. Breathing fire, the wallaroo told them about the infamous Roman numeral Moose and his blabbing to the media. While Commissioner Daley whined mournfully at the ceiling, wondering what to tell Mayor Daley, Captain Daley licked his chops at the number of traffic citations the Montgomery Moose limousines were going to accumulate in the next few weeks. Detective Lieutenant Daley called back to headquarters for a complete review of all files the police, FBI, Homeland Security, and Royal Canadian Mounted Police had on Montgomery Mooses I through IV. He seemed to remember the kid had been in some trouble sneaking drugs over the Canadian border. The collective Ms. Mooses would also be put under surveillance.

Finally calming down and introducing me to those members of the police hierarchy I didn't know, Bruce asked the Lieutenant what they had found during the day while he had made his round trip to Cincinnati.

"Not much, I'm afraid, Inspector," he said, "We've tried any number of ways of opening the case to see if we could duplicate the perp's M.O. No joy! We dusted for known criminal hand, paw, foot, nose, feather, and even scale prints. Clean as a whistle. Since spectators are not allowed behind the velvet ropes, and they would have set off an alarm if they did, we didn't really expect to see any stray prints. And the set-up crew says they wiped the case and plinth clean before the show opened. We dusted and came up with nothing.

We checked all the cases in other rooms. Nothing is missing, and all of the room security is intact."

We checked the walls and emergency doors to see if someone might have broken in while the cheetah took the guards for a wild ride, but everything was sealed up. We've tested the skylights, too."

There were several "special optics" glass skylights in the ceiling of the room that could become electronically opaque to keep the sun from interfering with the display lighting. In the mornings, they were set to "clear" and automatically changed to opaque as the afternoon sun rose in the sky. They went back to clear at night. High tensile steel mesh coated them internally and externally, and Bruce had installed a set of bars around each one for good measure.

Bruce looked up at the ceiling *(which was also the roof)* and asked the Lieutenant, "Any signs of tampering, breakage, jimmying, even recent prints on the outside?"

"We thought the same thing. Some kind of cat burglar entry by the cheetah or maybe the Duck and his Baboon, but there was nothing we could see. You're welcome to look for yourself in the morning, and besides, the damned case is sealed shut. It doesn't look like it's been opened and yet..."

And yet! I knew Bruce was trying to forestall the inevitable. Discovering that somewhere in the magnetic seals, the power cells, encrypted transmitters and receivers, the display case itself, or the heavyweight plinth, there was a fatal flaw that would ruin his life forever. Reluctantly, he walked over to the case, removed the velvet ropes and stared down into it. The jewel's pedestal was still there, but definitely no sapphire.

He looked at the sign that had been attached to one side of the plinth with ordinary rubber cement. "Now you see it! Now you don't!" Ornate script, vellum paper – a sure signature of Imperius Drake. He had left similar signs at many of his other crime scenes. Always some mocking, snide wisecrack to go with that maddening Black Quack egg. This one, of course, had been personalized to him and Octavius.

Bruce looked over at Dr. Daley. "Anything more on the deceased?"

"Yes, as a matter of fact, and it's weird. Nobody noticed it at first. We figured he had suffered a heart attack and staggered out into the hall, collapsed, and died. The museum Director found him all spread out beneath that wolf and pig statue."

"Not the most ordinary place to die, but what's so weird about it?" asked the Wallaroo.

"It's not where he died. It's how he died. Something that eluded me. He's a very colorful specimen. Not only his massive tail, but his entire body is covered in multi-colored feathers."

"Right," said Bruce, still waiting for the punch line, "He was a peacock. They look like that."

"But in among the colored feathers around his head, neck, and upper body were radiation burns. Even his eyes were seared."

"Radiation? How do you explain that?"

"I don't. At least not yet. I thought the perp may have used a taser on him to shut him up but the burns don't match typical taser marks. Anyway, official cause of death for the moment will be listed as cardiovascular shock induced by an unknown source of radiation."

Scratching his nose in perplexity, Inspector Wallaroo turned to the Captain. "Have your lab boys had any luck with the black egg?"

"No, but I've had to send three of them to the trauma center from getting too close to it. Even earplugs don't completely shield you. The cursed thing vibrates through your bones."

OK, nothing for it. The moment of truth. Bruce unsealed and reached into his pouch. He pulled out both transmitters. He handed one to me and the other to the Lieutenant. "I want the two of you to use these to open cases in the other rooms. Take several witnesses with you. Get a hold of Dr. Loupe and ask him to accompany you. C'mon back when you're through. "

I skittered off with the Captain and several of the plain clothes detectives into the room next door where an exquisite emerald necklace lay peacefully on a black velvet pillow. "You've already tried to force open this case without doing any damage, right?" I asked. No point in trying to break it open. The Deep Blue Sapphire's case was still intact and unscarred, so violence or breakage weren't the M.O.'s we wanted to test. "Right," said Captain Daley. "Several of us pulled and tried to lift the top but no movement at all."

Doctor Loupe came in and jumped up on the viewing platform. At last, someone smaller than I had joined the party. Introductions all around. We told the Director what we were trying to do and prove. He nodded.

"All right, let's try the transmitter." The transmitter was the size of a small TV remote with a LED counter screen still showing zero. I aimed it at the plinth, lifted a protective shield, and pressed the only button on the otherwise featureless face. The counter went to "one." Nothing happened...and then, from within the plinth, a green glow increased in intensity, and then there was a snap as the magnetic field released. I looked at the Captain. I was too small to lift the case. I nodded for him to try. He reached over and began to strain as he put his paws around the edges. The case leapt into the air and almost bounced out of his grip. The thing was feather light, and yet a minute ago, all our combined strength couldn't have budged it. Whatever transparent alloy Bruce, Octavius, and UUI had used, this stuff was something special. We all stared at it and the emerald necklace. We looked around the edges where the case and plinth came in contact. Nothing but two smooth surfaces! The plinth itself was seamless, and since it weighed close to a ton, immovable without equipment. The only access to the case's electronic innards was from under the bottom.

"Now, let's put it back," I said. The Captain slid the case back down into position and I pressed the button again. The counter went to "two." The green glow faded, and there was another snap. This time all four of us, including the plain-clothes Daley, tried to pull it back off. The spectator proximity alarm beeped but that was it. Shut and secure. The thing worked…as advertised. Damn!

We walked back into the Deep Blue Room with mixed emotions. The protection worked, yet it didn't. The obvious absence of the world's largest and most brilliant sapphire shouted that it had failed. I looked at the faces of the Lieutenant and his assistants as they walked back into the room from the other hall. I could tell without any words being exchanged that they'd had the same experience. Bruce had stayed in the Deep Blue Room with the Commissioner. He hadn't wanted to influence the tests.

Bruce looked at all of us as we nodded our heads. Both transmitters and both cases had worked as they were supposed to. A wallaroo in conflict with himself. "OK, mates, let's get it over with. There's no doubt something is wrong with this case. Let's test it." He turned to Commissioner Daley and said, "I don't want to touch any of this and the lads have done the other tests. Will you give it a burl? You're our disinterested witness, Doctor Loupe. "

The Commissioner took my transmitter and looked at Bruce. "What do I do?"

"Just like they tell you on the firing range, Commissioner. Take aim and shoot."

He did. Same green glow! Same snap! Same easy lift. We placed the case back and repeated the process several times. On-off; glow, no glow; snap, snap; lift, replace.

"That settles it," shouted Inspector Wallaroo. "That damn Duck has another transmitter. Maury, get Ocko on the horn. He and his lab helped design this system. There's a leak somewhere."

I called Octavius. I had caught him tending his bees, and one had stung him while he answered his cell phone. "What?" he roared.

"It's Maury and Bruce," I shot back. I'd had a tough day too. "We need to talk to you."

We described the entire scenario, hoping against hope that Octavius didn't choose this time to fall into a narcoleptic stupor. He stayed with us, and at the end he said, "You may be right about a rogue transmitter, but I've been thinking about this while you've been up there. There may be something else. By the way, Belinda sends her regards. She's headed off to Las Vegas. That's a subject I need to discuss with you, Maury. Stay on after this call is finished. Anyway, is there anything left in the display case?"

"There's a pedestal that the gem was laying on," Bruce replied.

"Good. Ask the police if you can bring it down here for analysis. Be very careful with it. Package it in an airtight container if you can, and come back down."

I relayed the request to Commissioner Daley, who conferred with the other Daleys and gave us a thumbs up.

"OK," said Octavius, "I'll see you in the morning. Bruce, do not under any circumstances fly down here tonight. You'll kill yourselves in that copter trying to get out of the Chicago area at night."

Rather than argue as I was sure he would, Bruce agreed. "Rightchera, Ocko. I want us to inspect the roof tomorrow morning before we fly back. Besides, the Lyric Opera is doing *Rigoletto* tonight, and I want to catch it."

I grabbed the phone and asked, "What did you want to tell me about Belinda, chief?" I was greeted by rumbling snores on the other end. Oh, well! Tomorrow is another day.

"Speaking of tomorrow, maybe you're flying back in that helicopter in the morning, Bruce, but without me. There is no way you are getting me back in that machine from hell."

Chapter Twelve

Polar bears are a dazzling sight

With their wonderful coats of pure white.

But the skin on their back

Is a deep shade of black

And their fur's just reflecting the light.

Thirty-five thousand feet above southern Illinois. "Concorde BBBB-NB, you are cleared through to Dallas Traffic Control Center. Switch to frequency 176.8. Maintain 35.000 and current speed. Have a nice day"

"BBBB-NB copies. Thank you, sir" *(or was it ma'am. Tough to tell over the radio. All controllers growled the same way.)*

Belinda pulled off her earphones, leaned back, turned, and looked at Bearnice who was sitting at the flight engineer's station. "Take the left seat, will you Bearnice! Bearyl, I'm going to take a brief rest." She unhooked her extra wide seat belt, put down her phones, passed her knee clipboard to her co-pilot, Bearyl, and clambered around her seat and past Bearnice.

"You OK, Bearoness?" asked Bearnice.

"Fine, just a bit tired."

"Just a bit?" she thought. She was exhausted. Getting older. Late nights, jet lag, and age were catching up to her. Of course, she couldn't have any of the champagne back at Octavius' lair. She was pilot in command. But a good champagne high would feel very nice right now.

She looked back at Bearyl and Bearnice as she stood in the doorway. God, they looked young and beautiful. They were identical twins who had crossed Belinda's path during some auditions for the *Aquabear Revue* in Winnipeg several years ago. Bearnice sang. She had spent several years as a struggling polaratura with the *Northern Lights Opera Company* in Manitoba. She was doing quite well. Bigger, better, and more challenging singing roles started coming her way. But the money stank.

Likewise Bearyl! Budding actress! Good! Actually better than good! She could run the range from comedy to deep drama without losing a beat. They loved her in *Ninotchka*. But good roles were few and far between and there were actresses tumbling out of every animal crate across Canada and the U.S. for that matter. And a girl had to keep herself in fish.

Belinda had taken an immediate liking to the twins. She brought them back with her to the Shetlands. She gave them small roles in the Aquabear chorus line. They weren't bad. They could dance and swim well enough, but that wasn't going to be their key to the big time. Singing and acting. That was their forté. But they needed something else to fill in the gaps.

She had an idea. She was losing one of her flight crew on the Concorde. A female wolf who had taken a job with *Air Pterodactyl*. Females held most of the professional flying jobs. They were smaller and could fit better in tight cabins. They also seemed to have faster reflexes. She tried once to woo Frau Schuylkill into joining her. The Frau was an old time jet jockey and had been sorely tempted. Octavius offered her more money and did the "loyalty above all else" routine. No Frau. But maybe she should train her own flight crew.

So she had turned to the two young polars and asked, "Can either of you handle an airplane?"

"No," said Bearyl, "but my aunt is a bush pilot."

"So is mine!" said Bearnice.

"Of course she is, you dope! We're twins."

"Well, how would you like to train to be part of my flight crew? I have a couple of twin engine Otters, two helicopters and of course the Aquabear."

"Fly the SST? Wow!!"

"Not so fast. I said 'an airplane,' not the SST. *(Down curled mouths.)* First you have to learn on the small prop jobs before you take on jets, especially supersonic passenger jets. Of course, I'll pay you while you're in training. Do you think your aunt could get you checked out on cross-country and instruments and qualified for transport licenses?? I'd pay her for your lessons. Then, I'll take it from there."

"Our aunt has flown in some of the rottenest weather all over Canada and Alaska. She's also an aerobatic champ."

"None of that! I don't want you doing barrel rolls in the Aquabear or any of my aircraft. Got that? OK, let's set it up."

And so they did. They both took to flying like birds – big, furry birds but birds nonetheless. A couple of years went by. Close to a thousand flying hours between them and there they were sitting at the controls of the last flying Concorde SST...*The Flying Aquabear*, Belinda's pride and joy. She closed the cockpit door.

Her sigh rattled the overhead compartments as she sprawled out on a couch right behind the forward galley. The rest of the *Aquabears* were sitting farther back in the plane, asleep on reclining seats or watching the entertainment system. Belinda got up, grabbed some sushi from the galley fridge, and settled back down. She was really tired, but she had to be up for this damn convention performance. *(Especially if Octavius was going to be there.)* "Never, ever give less than a perfect performance." – *The Aquabears' Creed.*

She was puzzled. Was Octavius deliberately playing dumb about being their sponsor at the convention? Could it really be someone else? Her agent said the contract came through an intermediary. A secret admirer. Wouldn't that be The Bear? She wanted it to be The Bear! Oh, hell!

She looked up! Bearyl was padding back and heading for the galley. "Want a Cola, Bearoness?"

"No thanks, Bearyl. I stopped drinking the stuff after Byron got killed doing one of their stupid downhill commercials."

She was a hypocrite, really. She didn't shed many tears for Byron's passing on. Yes, he had left her with everything, and that was a lot of everything. The castle, the staff, and loads of money to manage it. The yacht! The aircraft! This aircraft!! She was never sure where all the money came from. Byron never seemed to do any work, but they always had the best of everything.

Shortly after they had been married, things between her and the Bearon started falling apart. He was away for long periods, and she became increasingly positive that he was seeing other bears or even other species. Then he moved into a separate den. At first she was badly hurt. Or maybe it was just her ego that was hurt. Wasn't she every polar bear's dreamboat? What was wrong with her that she couldn't keep Byron for herself? Had she completely lost her sex appeal? The theater critics and the stage door dandies didn't seem to think so. She could still get a luscious champagne dinner by simply wrinkling her nose. *(Octavius loves the way she wrinkles her nose.)* And if she still happened to pad past an aurora of male polars with her fur soaking wet, she could start a small war. *(Octavius loves wet fur. He said so!)* So what was the story with Byron?

For a while she wondered if he preferred males, but she found traces of female polar scent in his bedroom after she came back from a performance. After that, the relationship turned frigid.

Her mother had pretty much stampeded her into marrying Byron. Good ole Mom. Wouldn't you know! No sooner had her daughter married into one of the wealthiest ursine families in the world *(although Octavius was probably richer now! Ironic!)* than Mom slips and falls on a half -melted iceberg and breaks her neck. So much for stage mothers and their ambitions.

She was also suspicious that much of Byron's money had come from not very honest deals but she could never get enough information out of him or his managers to prove it. Even when they read the will, her lawyers, dour Scots sheep, couldn't shed any light on the sources of funds. Everything was in off-shore accounts. She wondered why she ended up being his heiress. They were barely speaking when he went off and died. Maybe he just never got around to changing his will. *(I wonder if Octavius has a will.)* Anyway, here she was, loaded for life and fighting off the fortune hunters. *(I wonder if I'm named in Octavius' will.)* Right now, *her* will left most of what she had to the *Aquabears*, Bearyl and Bearnice, the palace staff and a large number of charities including the Glascow Theatre and the Edinbeargh Opera. With her mother dead, she had no close relatives. Byron's relatives lived at the castle, the moochers. One day she was going to let her polar fury loose and toss them all into the ocean. *(I wonder if I should leave something in my will for Octavius. He's richer than I am but maybe just a personal keepsake like some of my jewels. And something for that sweet Maury and Frau Schuylkill! What a lovely wolf.)*

Wow, was she getting morbid! Bearyl had finished raiding the fridge and flopped down next to her. "What's wrong, Boss Lady? You look pretty low for someone who's flying at 35,000 feet." She grinned.

"I don't know, Bearyl. I think I'm getting over the hill."

"Bel, if you're over the hill, I'm buried twenty feet under it. I know what you need. A good shot of audience reaction! Wait till they see you in Las Vegas. They'll be breaking down your door with show contracts, movie deals, maybe even your own TV show. Are you kidding? You're the living definition of glitz and glam."

"Maybe, but glitz and glam doesn't seem to do it any more. I just feel like I'm floating away on an iceberg."

"Could it be, my dear employer, that you need a little male attention?"

"No, thank you. Byron was quite enough for one lifetime. All polar males stray but he made a vocation out of it."

"Pardon, dear lady, but for all his money, the Bearon was a jackass. *(There's an image)* You should be glad that he's gone, and the money stayed."

"I know, but I guess I'm afraid I'll just end up with another Byron, or worse, a penniless Byron."

"Well, how about a rich Octavius? You should see the way he looks at you!"

"Octavius?? No, that's all ancient history. I have my mother to thank for that. First she breaks us up and then she practically throws me at Byron. When I didn't hear from Octavius at all, I figured he'd gone off to do his silly research, and so, I thought, well Byron's good-looking, fun, and rich. Not bad for a girl with no resources but her looks."

Bearyl laughed, "Her looks and her personality and her swimming and her dancing and her diving and her *savoir faire* and her intelligence. You're a smart fishcake, Boss Lady. Much too smart for that dope, Byron. I bet you could give Octavius, even with all his degrees, a run for his intellectual money."

"You think so? Well, I doubt if I'll ever get the chance. The Great Bear is up to his furry ears in fighting crime, inventing new marvels, researching genes, and running that megaverse, UUI. He doesn't have time for romance or for me."

"Well, if he doesn't, for all his smarts, he's a jerk. I'm going back to the cockpit."

"Yeah," she thought, "he's a jerk, but I love him."

Maury Meerkat

Chapter Thirteen

The great Lion has a menacing stare,

And a mane of such glorious hair.

Yet his cavernous jaws

Should not cause you to pause.

When he eats, he just wants his fair share.

Maury here. I headed back to the hotel, stopping long enough to buy a hat to replace my lasered flight cap. I saw it in the window. A 1930's fedora. *Film Noir* exemplified! I stared at it. What the hell! I'm a detective. Who better to wear it? I stepped into the shop. A slinky blonde Afghan inched over to me and said, "Hello, handsome. Interest you in a hat?" Her hair slipped over one eye, and she winked at me with the other.

I put on my best *Film Noir* accent and said, "Yeah, sweetheart, how much is that doggie, er, fedora, in the window?"

She reached over and placed it on my head. Rakish! I asked the price. Rakish! She sniffed at me. This one looked dangerous. Too dangerous for a two foot tall Meerkat. She sidled closer to me and asked, "Credit Card or Cash?" I said, "Cash!" I paid her. She winked and came back with my change. I didn't bother to count it. I just took the hat and walked out, bumping into a counter as I left. I thought I heard her laughing as the door closed behind me.

I had dinner by myself. I hoped Bruce was enjoying the opera. I went up to bed but I couldn't sleep. I tossed and turned, turned and tossed. Finally, I got up, got dressed, put on my fedora and went down through the hotel lobby and out into the Chicago night.

118

Midnight had come and gone. I stood on a street corner watching the fog roll up from the Lake. It was thick as vichyssoise. It suited my mood. After that catastrophe today I needed a drink and a sympathetic ear! The whole world was about three drinks behind.

I peered through the fog. On a soulless side street, I saw what I was looking for. A neon sign flickering in celadon and puce – Joe's Place – calling me in from the dark.

I started to reach for my shoulder holster. *(No holster. No shoulders.)* I pushed open the door to one of the dingiest, dirtiest, demoralizing dives I had ever seen. My kind of dump! A moth-eaten hyena looked up from the bar, squinted, and smiled, showing his false tooth.

"Well, look who's here!" he lisped. "Come on in, stranger! Always welcome! Name's Joe. I own the place." He smiled again. Ugh! I almost turned around and left. Instead I pulled my tail around my waist and bellied up to the bar.

I needed a sympathetic ear. I tugged at the brim of my fedora and looked at him, "It's quarter to three. There's no one in the place except you and me. So set 'em up, Joe. I got a little story you oughtta know." I asked for fermented coconut milk VSOP. He had it! In a joint like this! Go figure! Maybe a couple of snorts would bring some enlightenment. This damn thing with the sapphire was really pulling my tail. The idea of Imperius Drake outsmarting us didn't sit well at all.

I looked around. "Hey, we're *not* alone! Who's the scruffy cat over there at the piano?"

Joe poured me a double and looked over. "Oh, him. Of all the gin joints in all the towns in all the world, he walks into mine. He's been comin' in here every night for almost a month now. Strange mug! Shows up about nine when the house is almost full, sits down at the piano, and starts playin' for tips. When he's got enough, he shuffles over to the bar, puts his money down and takes two glasses, sticks a pint of whiskey in his pocket and heads back to the keyboard."

"What's with the bird sittin' on the music stand?"

"Oh, he comes in on the lion's shoulder, stays with him while he plays and leaves when he leaves."

"Why two glasses?"

"One's for the bird. Drinks like a fish. Don't know which one of them is worse. The lion says he's a king; down on his luck. Doesn't look like any king I've ever known."

I was about to ask Joe how many kings he'd known when the derelict, who did vaguely look like a lion, a lion who had seen much better days, hit a crashing chord on the ivories, turned, and stared in my direction. One of his bleary eyes winked.

"Good evening, dear sir, welcome to my realm. May I enquire who or what you are? Are you too, down on your luck? A female perhaps? Money troubles? Perhaps a run-in with the authorities? May I play something for you? This piano barely fits the definition, but my bartender friend refuses to get it tuned. He says it adds atmosphere if it's off-key." He ran the keyboard to prove his point. "Off-key" was a euphemism.

Cultured voice, a little worse for wear and booze. He had on a long, tattered coat, or maybe it was a robe. Couldn't tell with the dirt! Seemed to be some fur on the collar, but most of it was under his long, stringy mane. He hadn't seen a bathtub in a while, and his beard was three or four colors.

"Well," I said, "good evenin' yourself, your majesty. Joe here tells me you're a king."

"*Was*, dear boy, *was*. I am Richard the Twelfth, the Lion-Hearted, fallen, as you can see, on inopportune times.

120

"I thought Richard the First was the Lion-Hearted."

"We're all Lion-Hearted. For God's sake, we're all lions. And you are....?

I was interested but not enough to give my right name. "Name's Sam Club. I'm a private ear. People tell me things. How about you, King Richard? You want to tell me something?"

"Certainly, dear boy, certainly. Please, call me Rick! Perhaps you would care to facilitate the process with a small gratuity."

As I reached for my wallet, he pulled the bottle of rye out of his pocket and poured a shot for himself and a double for the bird. Big black thing, reminded me of the Sardinian Falcon. The bird drank the booze down with one gulp. Probably had hollow bones.

He started tinkling on the piano. I tried to recognize the tune, but it wouldn't come. Then he sang out in deep baritone. "I've got sixpence, jolly, jolly sixpence. I've got sixpence to last me all my life." Of course! I hadn't heard that song since I was a kid in the choir at Saint Farfallone's.

He turned and said, "That song quite accurately describes my current situation, Samuel, my friend. Oh, thank you, most generous of you." He put the twenty into his pocket under the close scrutiny of the bird. He downed his drink. "Here's looking at you, kid!"

He looked at my glass. "I see you have brought your own fortification or I would offer you a bit of the nectar I share with my dark-winged companion here."

The bird looked sideways, first at him, then at me, clacked his bill and made a pass at my drink. He caught a piece of my paw in the process. I went to swat him but the king held up a claw. "I wouldn't do that if I were you. There are consequences."

The bird said, "Damned right!"

I was shocked, shocked! I looked at the bird and then at King Rick, "The bird talks?"

"Only when he wants to!"

"What about you, Your Majesty? When do I get my twenty bucks worth?"

He turned to the keyboard and started to play *As Time Goes By*. "Yes, you must remember this. I had it all. A kingdom, beautiful wife, money and a world class chef who would constantly whip up new culinary delights for me. I weighed a good deal more then. That was my downfall. I got lazy, greedy, cranky…fat. One morning when I was counting my money as usual, I called for my chef. 'Laszlo, *(his name was Laszlo)* Laszlo,' I said, 'I'm bored. The queen won't talk to me anymore. Counting money is tedious. It always comes out to the same amount. I need a picker-upper. Make me a dish I've never had before. Something really special!'

"Later that afternoon, I sat alone at my table. The queen took her meals in the parlor–bread and honey. That's all I'd let her have. We had to cut costs somewhere. Laszlo entered; placed before me an absolutely immense pie and an envelope. It was from the queen. Another one of her complaints, no doubt! I'd look at it later. Right then, that pie smelled delicious. Laszlo passed me a knife, turned on his heels and left."

"I plunged the knife into the pie, and to my surprise, I heard a squawk. I opened the pie further and four and twenty blackbirds came flying out. Can you imagine, Sam?"

"Sounds like a dainty dish, Your Majesty!"

"That wasn't all. They were singing! Four-part harmony! Awful song! Something about – *I'll be glad when you are dead, you rascal, you!!*"

"Then twenty-three of them flew out the windows, leaving this one here staring at me. I tell you, I was shaken and stirred. I looked down at the envelope and tore it open. It *was* from the queen. I've kept it. Here, read it. Since you're a detective, maybe you can put it in a new perspective."

He handed me a tattered piece of paper, covered with whiskey stains and maybe a few tears. Who knows? I read it aloud. Joe leaned over the bar to listen in.

"Richard," it said, "I've had enough. You are a miserly, cruel, self-indulgent, overstuffed heap. I've run off with Laszlo. He says he loves me and will fill my days with gastronomic delights. No more bread and honey, you cheapskate. And, oh yes, don't bother going to the counting house. We took all the money. I left you a sixpence for old times' sake. Don't get too upset. We'll always have Paris. Have a nice day. *(signed)* Her Highness Queen Elsa the Lioness."

The king sniffled and looked at me with tear-filled eyes. "Read it again, Sam!"

I smiled. "You know, things are never so bad, they can't be made worse."

The king laughed. "Oh, they did get worse, much worse. I began to get reports of bird attacks throughout the kingdom. It started in the palace. The maid was in the garden, hanging out the clothes when along came a blackbird and snipped off her nose. The birds went wild. No nose was safe. You dared not go outside. Rhinoplasty clinics opened up all over the kingdom.

"Then word leaked out to the peasantry that this was all my fault. The few that still had noses got together one night and attacked the palace with burning torches, pitchforks, and stones. They burned it to the ground. I escaped with the clothes I had on, sixpence and of course, my dark-winged companion. I fled the kingdom and kept running until I ended up here. The peasants set up a bicameral, theocratic oligarchy and set a price on my head. I could never return. So here I sit, playing for drinks, watched by a bird."

123

"How come you still have your nose?"

"I don't know. Ask him. Every night when I go to sleep, I wonder if I'm going to wake up minus a muzzle." We both looked at the bird. Nothing!!

I nudged the king. "Rickie," I said, "this could be the beginning of a beautiful friendship. Move over!"

I sat down at the piano, looked over at Joe and said, "Make it one for the raven and one more for the road."

As Joe filled our glasses, I said to Rick, "If that bird doesn't leave the ground without you, you'll regret it – maybe not today, maybe not tomorrow but soon and for the rest of your life. Let's try this song. Maybe he'll get the hint and fly away." I ran the keyboard and launched into a chorus of "Bye, Bye Blackbird." Joe and Rick sang harmony.

At the end we stared at the bird, still sitting on his perch. "Well, bird," I said, "why don't you just scram?"

He fluttered his wings, but then settled back down and stared at us.

Quoth the raven, "Nevermore!"

I left feeling a lot worse than when I came in. Oh, well tomorrow is another day, and I have a feeling it's going to be a stinker.

Chapter Fourteen

Do you really think gerbils have fun

On their exercise wheels where they run?

After sprinting a race

In their circular chase,

Do they know if they've won when they're done?

"Bruce, watch out for that other chopper," I screamed. I know. You think I'm a wuss and backed down on my firm resolve to take a sensible aircraft home. I am sitting *(bouncing, caroming)* in a Chicago Police helicopter under supreme duress. I have literally been kitnapped by a representative of international law enforcement. Between screams and trying to keep breakfast down, *(fortunately, I had left my unused supply of barf bags under the seat).* I will try to bring you up to speed on this morning's events.

Bruce and I had met for breakfast at which he alternated between further grousing about the Moose and describing the Lyric Opera's ripper performance of *Rigoletto*. He was especially impressed by the fat sheila. He even remarked favorably about my new hat. I started to tell him about my encounter with the scruffy-looking lion and the bird but it was clear I didn't have his attention. It's often tough to capture Bruce's attention. The whirlwind he passes off as a mind multi-tasks and re-boots without any warning. Non-sequiturs abound. Yet the guy is brilliant and at the moment highly preoccupied. This one was really eating at him.

As we passed the gift shop, I could see some of the headlines in the morning papers – "Shocking Theft and Death at Loupe Museum" – "The Sapphire's Curse and Imperius Drake Strike Again" – "Where is the Deep Blue Sapphire?" – "International Police Stumped." I rushed Inspector

Wallaroo past the shop before he could see them and explode right there in the lobby. Once again, I called upon the Meerkat gods to bring vengeance on the head of Montgomery Moose III, although it sounded like the Chicago Police already had that situation well in hand.

He and I set out in different directions. He was heading for the top of the AON Center where the helicopter still sat. Carrying the carefully packed pedestal and the transmitters, he was going to hop over to the police heliport to refuel *(and as it turned out, see what he could do about fixing the three illegal parking citations that had been stuck on the chopper's bubble).* Then he was heading southeast to the Bear's headquarters. I had booked myself on a commercial flight at noon and would get home by late afternoon. He was using the chopper again, because he didn't want to put the evidence through airport security screening. At least, that's what he said. I think he just loved bouncing around in wild blue yonder.

I went off to the Loupe Museum to inspect the skylights over the Deep Blue Room. Lieutenant Daley and his squad had checked them yesterday for forced entry or breakage. I was looking for something different. I waved at Sergeant Daley as I skittered under the crime scene tape and bolted through the door, across the lobby and onto the service elevator heading for the roof.

Straining, slipping, and sliding, I finally got the roof door open. Being small definitely has its disadvantages. I clambered over the obstructions and pigeon detritus toward the skylights. I took out my magnifying glass *(a gift from Octavius)* and began my search. Several scratches on the frame – could have come from anything. Sleet, flying debris! The wind could get fierce up here. Nothing much else. Wait a second! Bingo!! Caught on one of the protective bars was a small patch of dark brown hair. I plucked it out and laid it in my handkerchief. Baboon hair??? I couldn't tell, but Octavius sure could back at the lab.

I pulled out my cell phone and called Bruce. He picked up while he was arguing with a desk Sergeant about the parking citations. I doubt the cop understood a word he was saying. "What?" he growled. Why does everybody get cheeky with me on the phone? It's probably because I'm little. It's been the story of my life. All the other meerkats picked on me. It stunted my growth. But I digress.

"Bruce," I shouted. "I found something on the skylight. I think they're Baboon hairs. Wait for me at the heliport, and I'll give them to you to take back to Octavius."

I raced down to the lobby and told the Sergeant I needed a police car to get me out to the heliport *toute suite*. He got on his radio, and in a few minutes we were racing through Chicago traffic, lights flashing, siren wailing, and pedestrians gaping. Near miss with a beer truck. Around corners on two wheels. Gee, I love that kind of stuff.

We hadn't yet come to a complete stop on the heliport deck when I was out of the patrol car and running over to the pilot's side of the chopper. Bruce was sitting there with the rotors slowly idling, waiting to take off. He opened the door, and as I reached up to hand him my handkerchief with the hairs in it, he suddenly grabbed my arm, flipped me over himself into the passenger seat, slammed the door, and started to take off.

"Hey, you miserable marsupial" I yelped. "What the hell do you think you're doing? You land this rattletrap right now, and let me out. I'm booked on a proper aircraft this time, and I don't intend to be 'shaken, not stirred' again."

Bruce laughed, an unsettling sound in itself, and said, "Don't be such a yobbo, Maury. Strap yourself in and settle down *(!!!???)*. We'll be back in Cincinnati before you could even board that proper plane." *(Unfortunately, he was right.)*

Doing a series of pirouettes and other ballet leaps as I tried to fasten my seat belt in the lurching cabin, I finally managed to achieve something akin to stability. After I checked to make sure my handkerchief with the hairs was still with me, I set about fishing my tail around until I found Wallaroo's latest harmonica. He had a million of 'em. Ever so slowly, I eased it out of his pocket and down between the seats and gently shoved it as far aft as my tail would reach. At least I wouldn't have to put up with Matilda and her damn waltzing.

Suddenly, Wallaroo let out a bellow that shocked me out of my fur. "What's wrong?" I shouted over the intercom, which I had just managed to get around my head.

"Nothin's wrong, ya bunyip, Don't you recognize singin' when you hear it?"

Yes, I do recognize singing. Mom told me I actually had a rather sweet voice myself. Whatever was coming out of the Wallaroo bore little resemblance to singing.

"*La donut ay mobilay!*" he bawled as I searched frantically for the volume control on my earphones. He was "singing" *Rigoletto*. Now, he switched to Gilda's death scene. Wallaroo as a soprano ranks very high in the ranks of cruel and unusual punishment. I turned off the phones, for the first time in my life grateful for the noise of the rotors and engine.

While I search with my tail to recover the harmonica, *("Waltzin' Matilda" is definitely the lesser of two evils)* let me pick up on my history of Octavius. Actually I've been telling you about everyone else, but very little about the astonishing tale of the Great Bear himself and how he came to be a crime fighter.

As I did mention, he's a Kodiak, born oddly enough near Kodiak Island in Alaska. It was apparent early on that he was a prodigy. At the age of three months while other cubs were gulping down fish as fast as they or their mothers could catch them, Octavius was dissecting the aquatic creatures, studying their structure and making entries in a series of notebooks he had set up. Yes, he could read and write at that age. His mother was a lovely bear, but hardly intellectually extraordinary. No one, including his mom, was quite sure who his father was, since many male bears tend to disappear right after mating, a trait increasingly common to males of other species.

Intent in finding out why he was so exceptional, he enrolled in Kodiak University at a time most cubs were still learning to growl correctly and was admitted into the Advanced Ursinology and Genetics program. He quickly outstripped his classmates and his professors and began a program of independent research.

It was on one of these research trips that he encountered the lovely Belinda with all of the heartbreak that went with it. After an appropriate period of mourning, he pulled himself together and decided that if it took money and fame to win Belinda, he would get money and fame. At this point, he also developed his cure for hibernation, allowing him to pursue his research year-round except for his brief dozes.

But first, he needed to be closer to major hubs of commerce and industry. He loved Alaska and the upper regions of Canada, but there wasn't much chance of a bear making his fortune up there. The Gold Rush had been years ago and trading in fur was morally repellent. Where to go? New York? Chicago? San Francisco? Los Angeles? Houston? Atlanta? None had the intense pace and bustle he was looking for. He was a bear in a hurry. Then it dawned on him. Cincinnati! Crossroads of a million up-and-coming entrepreneurs. Home of the really smart money! He set off for southern Ohio and after living in a series of one room condos in which he bearly fit, he happened upon the aforementioned riverboat Captain and his decaying mansion.

Borrowing money *(Who was going to say no to a now fully grown, nine foot, 1400 pound bear?),* he acquired the mansion and also began the construction of his laboratories out of which poured an unbroken stream of technological and chemical marvels. After repaying his original debt *(resisting the urge to dissect the loan shark he had been dealing with),* he set about investing his new found wealth in the securities markets and venture capital opportunities. This is actually the true origin of the term "Bear Market" – one that favors Octavius. It was to support his market transactions that Octavius invented the Internet.

Not content to live off the income of his patents and investments, he decided to set up Universal Ursine Industries which – like just about everything he touched – turned into an absolute gold mine.

He was now ready to go after Belinda. And then, tragedy struck. Looking through the society pages of the *Cincinnati Acquirer*, the business journal of record for all true tycoons, he saw a picture and article that flattened his fur. There staring out at him in her beautiful white wedding outfit was his Belinda. She was smiling and holding paws with a handsome *(actually, a bit too handsome)* polar male. The headline said it all. *Ursine Society Celebrates the Wedding of the Year between Billionaire Bearon Byron Bruin and Aquabear Star Belinda Béarnaise (nee Black).* Mother Black had won. What now? What good was all this wealth when he couldn't share it with his dream-bear?

He was about to try to reverse the effect of his sleep research and go into long term hibernation to get away from it all when something struck his notice on the opposite page. The headline read, *Police and FBI Stymied by National Rash of Hi-Jacked Ice Cream Trucks.*

A smile circumnavigated the Great Bear's mouth. He recognized that M.O. When he was still doing research in Alaska, a similar outbreak of ice cream thefts had become the talk of the Panhandle. The papers were full of it. It turned out to be the work of Gino Gerbil, the Juneau Gelato Junkie. Who would have ever suspected a gerbil, for Pete's sake? But Gino had an ice cream monkey on his back that could not be satisfied. He might be able to knock off a popsicle from an unsuspecting vendor or dive into a gallon drum of pistachio when no one was looking, but that was small time.

Gino wanted to play in the big leagues. One gerbil wasn't much of an operation but a hundred gerbils! Now that would be a force to be reckoned with! He set about organizing his gang. They hijacked the ice cream trucks by the simple expedient of hiding on board and then overwhelming the driver in an out the way location. They forced the driver out of the truck and drove it off to an undisclosed spot where they unloaded the ice cream, repainted and sold the truck. This worked for a while, but to the distress of the rest of the gang, Gino, instead of reselling their luscious loot, kept eating into the profits and was growing very, very fat.

Finally, in disgust, a couple of stool gerbils sent an anonymous tip to the Juneau police, and they raided the gang's lair. They rounded up most of the group, but Gino had escaped. Octavius had been fascinated by the Alaska radio, TV and newspaper reports but doubted the incident got any national coverage except maybe a short blurb in *Vanity Fair* magazine.

Now this new headline! Octavius picked up the phone and called the local office of the FBI. When the Special Agent in Charge picked up, the Great Bear rumbled, "My name is Octavius Bear. You don't know me *(yet)*, but I know who has been knocking off all those ice cream trucks. You probably won't believe me at first but I'd like to come down and spell it out for you. I am not a crank."

Something in the serious sincerity of the Bear's voice persuaded the Special Agent that he might be on to something. "Come on down, Bear. I'll be waiting for you." Two days later on national TV and radio, the FBI announced the capture of Gino and his re-established gang, giving full credit to an alert citizen, Octavius Bear. One thing led to another, and soon, Octavius was working on an informal basis with crime stoppers across the nation and then overseas.

Of course, nothing could compensate for the loss of Belinda, but the fascination of solving crimes *(as well as running UUI, making gazillions and producing an occasional startling invention)* took up his attention, and very slowly, Bearoness Belinda Béarnaise Bruin (nee Black) padded further and further into the recesses of his mind.

As for the rest of us, I've already told you how Octavius and I met and how I have become not only his assistant and number one field operative, but also his chief scribe. Of course, Frau Schuylkill literally saved his life. We all first met Inspector Wallaroo investigating the aforementioned art heist where I joined the Sore Bun alumni association. While dealing with all sorts of crime: Illegal Sports Fixing *(cf. Octavius Bear and the Hunt for the*

131

Basketballs) Extortion *(cf. Octavius Bear and Lady Windermere's Fan Mail)* and some very top secret defense work for several major governments including the U.S. *(cf. Octavius Bear Meets Clancy, the Tom Cat),* an increasing amount of the Great Bear's crime fighting energy has been devoted to one single target. The dastardly Imperius Drake, doyen of dire and dirty deeds. And the feeling has become mutual. Imperius has developed a mania about Octavius to match his mania about the scientific community.

Bruce now switched to singing "Waltzin' Matilda" in his newly found soprano. Coming close to dumping us in the Ohio River, he circled and dropped us instead on the Great Bear's helipad. Two minutes later, my stomach arrived to join me. Octavius was waiting for us in his den.

Chapter Fifteen

Oh, the howls of the Wolf are well known.

Those weird sounds can chill right to the bone.

And when they attack

They all hunt in a pack.

For they seldom will chase you alone.

The music of Frau Schuylkill's howls had alerted Octavius to the arrival of Inspector Wallaroo and, oh yeah, insignificant me. Obviously, I was feeling quite sorry for myself after our replay of *Apocalypse Now*. The only thing different was Bruce bellowing *Rigoletto* instead of the *Ride of the Valkyries*. The skies of Indiana would never be the same.

"Come in, Inspector and do sit down. No, I insist," said the Bear as he scanned the room for potential targets on which Bruce could inflict damage. Octavius looked at me. "I'm surprised to see you here, Maury. I thought you were going to use the airlines."

"So did I!" I replied, but since the Great Bear was showing no additional interest on why my travel plans changed, I just shut up. Actually, I sneezed. *(I was upset.)* In reflex action I reached for my handkerchief and almost blew my nose in the alleged Baboon hair. Wiping my nose on my sleeve, to Octavius' obvious disgust, I skittered over and put the handkerchief with the hairs on his desk.

"I found these outside on the skylight at the museum. We're not sure, but I think they belong to Bigg Baboon."

Octavius raised his vestigial eyebrows and then looked over at Bruce. "I assume you brought the sapphire's pedestal?"

"Rightchere, Ocko," and he bounded over to the desk with the sealed package.

"Well, shall we adjourn to the lab and see what we can find out?" Octavius said as he reached out and grabbed Bruce with one paw while he picked up the "specimens" with the other.

Just as we were about to leave, the phone rang.

"Damn," said Octavius. "I guess I'd better answer it. It could be Commissioner Daley." Pushing the oversized button on his speakerphone, he rumbled, "Bear here!"

It wasn't any of the Daleys. A vaguely familiar growl came over the squawkbox. "Is this Doctor Octavius Bear?" *(Good start. Hit him with the Ph.D. right away.)*

"This is he," replied GB.

"This is Colonel Wyatt Where from the Bank of Lake Michigan *(Oh sure, I couldn't forget that voice!)* and I have Doctor Howard Watt here with me."

"Colonel, Doctor. You should know that I have Inspector Bruce Wallaroo and Mr. Mauritius Meerkat in the room with me."

"Thank you, Doctor Bear. We wanted to talk to all of you. First to apologize to the Inspector and Mr. Meerkat for the abominable treatment they got from Montgomery Moose. We want you to know we had no paw in that fiasco."

"Not to worry, mates," yelled Bruce, "but yer boss is in for a bad trot, I can tell you that."

134

"That's the second thing we wanted to tell you. He's no longer our boss. We both resigned on the spot in front of the press right after you two bounded out of the room. Working for that egotistical moron has been a real circus."

Now, that was something we didn't expect. The three of us looked at each other. Bruce and I shrugged.

"And the third thing we wanted to ask you," said the voice of Doctor Howard Watt, "is whether you might have possible employment for two out-of-work security and technology specialists."

"Just a moment, please," said the Bear, pressing the mute button on the speakerphone. "What do you think? I could certainly use them if they're half as good as you have led me to believe on the phone, Inspector."

"Oh, they're good, all right. But I don't know. Maybe I'm still so ticked at the moose, I can't be objective. What do you think, Maury?"

"Bruce, I was watching them while you were getting the treatment. They were obviously outraged."

"Oh, hell! Give 'em a go, Ocko."

I heard a snuffle at the rear of the room and turned to face – Frau Schuykill. Amazing! There were very few things that could deliberately get her within yards of Wallaroo.

"Your pardon, Herr Bear, but I thought I heard the sound of another wolf."

"You did, Frau," said Octavius, "on the phone. We're talking with Colonel Wyatt Where and Doctor Howard Watt up in Chicago."

"This Colonel Where. He is a military wolf?"

"Yeah," I replied. "He's seen lots of action worldwide and was in Military Intelligence for quite a while."

The she-wolf's ears stood straight up and her eyes gleamed. She might have been salivating too, but I couldn't be sure. "Herr Bear, if I may make so bold. Another warrior wolf would be a great help."

Well, I could scratch potential matchmaking off my to-do list. Nature was already taking its course.

Octavius turned off the mute, "Colonel, Doctor are you still there?"

"Still here, Doctor Bear."

"All right, why don't we give it a trial, and see what happens. You would have to move down here to Cincinnati, however."

"That's no problem," said the Colonel. "We're both bachelors with no ties."

At this point, Frau Schuylkill could hardly control her ecstasy.

"Good. We're about to begin a project here that should take several hours. Why don't you call back, say at 2:00 PM Eastern, and we'll discuss terms. When could you be here?"

Murmurs back and forth on the other end. "We could probably make it late tomorrow. We'll have to drive down."

"Fine. By the way, Colonel, one of my associates you haven't met yet will be very interested in making your acquaintance," said the Bear as he pushed the Off button on the phone.

We all looked over and beheld one of nature's true rarities, a bright red wolf.

Down we went to the lab. Now, I am sure that you extremely discerning readers have already wondered how Octavius could control the rambunctious Wallaroo in a lab full of delicate and costly instruments when he couldn't stop him from wreaking havoc in his living quarters. No, he did not put him under sedation. Bruce and I both participated actively in the Great Bear's tests and experiments. The answer lay in keeping Bruce seated. The Bear had fitted out a highly advanced wheelchair for the Inspector. There were several problems even with this solution. One, we had to keep him in the chair. Answer: a seat belt under Octavius' control. And two, we had to keep him from driving the chair around the lab at high speed. Answer: the chair had three speeds – Slow, Very Slow, and Inert. I'm sure Bruce wasn't happy with this arrangement, but the good natured marsupial put up with it with hardly a whimper, since it was the only way Octavius would let him in the lab.

"Let's start with the hair, Maury."

"Right!"

"A spectrum analysis and DNA test should suffice."

I took the specimens over to the unbelievably well-equipped work area and set about initiating the tests. Meanwhile, Bruce and Octavius were carefully unsealing the package containing the pedestal.

"What's the big deal with the pedestal, Ocko? You looking for prints?"

"No, you or the police didn't dust it, did you?"

"Picked it up with one of the museum's specimen grippers and put it in the sterile bag you're holding. Untouched by animal paws."

"Excellent. Now, let's bring it over to the electron microscope and see what we shall see."

"Microscope – what for?"

"Inspector, I realize that patience is not part of your genetic makeup, but just give me a few moments and if I'm correct, all will be revealed. Maury, what progress with the hair?"

"It's Baboon all right!" I shouted from the other side of the lab. "I can't prove it's off that Duck's sidekick, but with all the other evidence shouting Imperius Drake, I'd take a very heavy bet on it."

"So would I," said the Bear, "but I suppose there are several other baboons in Chicago. (Several!!??) We'll have to call it circumstantial for the moment. But let's operate on the assumption that at least the Baboon and possibly the Duck were on the roof of the museum."

"So what, Ocko?" said Bruce. "Maybe they were casing the joint through the skylight, but that still doesn't tell us how they snatched the gem."

"If they snatched the gem, Inspector, if."

"Well, with that crazy cheetah running around and slapping up signs and dropping black eggs, don't you think it was them?"

"Oh, I'm positive it was them."

"Crikey, Ocko, sometimes you're as bad as that pommy Fetlock Holmes.* Quit being mysterious!"

"Just let me look into this microscope and I'll be as open as a sunlit day."

I had walked back to join them and stood next to Wallaroo, equally puzzled and equally irritated. Octavius could be a swift pain with his dime detective novel tactics.

*(The immortal Fetlock Holmes, the great Horse Detective.)

At last he looked up and said, "Maury, get the Chicago Police on the speakerphone."

Oh, boy, this was going to be a real Production Number Revelation. We couldn't gather all the suspects in the library to reveal the villain *(we already knew who it was)* but that didn't mean the Octavius Bear Drama Society wasn't going to perform at its award winning best. I should have asked Frau Schuylkill to play organ music in the background.

"Chicago Police, Daley speaking."

"Which Daley?"

"Sergeant Daley."

I turned to Octavius. "Which Daley do you want?"

The Commissioner, the Captain, *and* the Lieutenant – a Cast of Millions Production.

I turned back to the phone. "Sergeant, this is Maury Meerkat."

"I know, Maury, I recognized your distinctive bark immediately." The Sergeant was no doubt taking advanced courses in detection.

"Could you patch us through to the Commissioner, Captain, and Lieutenant?"

"Hang on!"

While three rounds of "Daley here!" echoed across the line as his soon-to-be awe-struck audience was assembling itself, I took another look at Octavius. That stone face deserved to be on Mt. Rushmore. Bruce fidgeted in his chair.

"Octavius? Commissioner Daley here. I hope you have news. Was it the Duck who swiped the Deep Blue Sapphire?"

"Most assuredly, Commissioner. It was Imperius Drake and his two minions who committed the crime."

The Captain intervened. "But how, Bear, how? Was there another transmitter?"

"I seriously doubt it, Captain. Any spurious transmitter would have to be synchronized with the encryption engines in the plinths. That synchronization was done here in our labs by the Inspector and me before they were shipped to Chicago."

"So you *were* involved in the technology," chimed in the Lieutenant.

"Strictly in a support role. This was the Inspector's program from start to finish."

"All right, Octavius," said the Commissioner, "enough is enough! *(Amen!)* Quit stalling and tell us. How was the sapphire stolen by the Duck?"

"The sapphire was not stolen by the Duck..."

A chorus of "But you just said" echoed around the room.

"I said the crime was committed by the Duck. The sapphire was not stolen. It was DESTROYED!!"

Pandemonium. Two Irish setters and a Polish Retriever howling at the Chicago end of the phone. Bruce struggling in his wheelchair and babbling Strine at lightning speed. I suspect Frau Schuylkill was eavesdropping on the other line, for she too let up a howl, and I think I gave out a couple of distressed "yips."

I recovered first. "OK, Hercule Parrot, *explainez-vous*!"

"Maury, when the improbable becomes impossible then......"

"Octavius," I screamed, "Cut the lecture and tell us how you came up with that cockeyed solution."

Voices at both ends of the line seconded the motion.

"Maury, as your employer, I expect a little more respect from you."

"Octavius, as Commissioner of Chicago Police, I expect a little more explanation from you," shouted an obviously irritated voice over the speaker.

"Well," huffed the Great Bear, miffed that his dramatics had fallen on a less than enthusiastic audience. "The electron microscopic analysis of the pedestal told me what I wanted to know. There were several minute particles of sapphire burned into its surface."

"Burned?" blurted Bruce. "Maybe the particles just flaked off."

"Inspector, please consider. Sapphires are right up there with diamonds in the hardness and ruggedness departments. Particles don't flake off sapphires."

"But," said the Captain, "how could the particles be burned? The case was undamaged, the pedestal was intact. Nothing else was disturbed. That just can't be!"

"I'm sorry, Captain but it most emphatically can be," retorted Octavius. "The weapon used was a laser powered particle beam device. It can be precisely tuned to the composition of the target and essentially ignore all intervening substances or surfaces as long as they are transparent. That's how you can aim these guns –through a series of transparent lenses. The shot was fired with amazing accuracy from the roof, through the then clear skylight *(recall it was morning, and the skylight's optics hadn't begun to shade)* through the top of the transparent-alloy case and squarely onto the sapphire. It was literally disintegrated. I think it may also go a long way toward explaining the death of Phillipe Peacoq."

"How do you know all this, Bear?" said the Commissioner.

"Because, Commissioner, the device was originally developed in UUI's laboratories under my direct supervision. I recognize the operational characteristics."

More howling, yipping, and noise-making at both ends of the conversation.

"Are you telling us, Octavius," said the Captain, "that you are responsible for the loss of this priceless gem?"

"Very indirectly, Captain, very indirectly. As you all know, I first met Doctor Imperius Drake *(we keep forgetting his scientific credentials)* when he was briefly on staff at UUI. When I found out he was doing unauthorized, and I strongly suspect, highly illegal R&D at our facility, I threw him out...bodily. But not without a fight and not without some extreme destruction on his part. One of the projects I thought he had destroyed was our experimental extreme accuracy particle beam projector. It was a highly advanced version of earlier models. The first projector was a cudgel. It would knock down walls. This device was to be a new breakthrough in precision. To be used for peaceful ends where such high accuracy work would benefit animal-kind. We have since rebuilt and further improved the prototype projector at UUI. What I didn't know was that the maniac Dr. Duck had somehow preserved enough of the design data and the original prototype to build one for himself."

"Crikey, Ocko, if that wrongo has that device of death, we have to put him out of business, pronto," shouted Bruce.

"Very true, very true, Inspector. I strongly suggest, however, that we confine this information to the six of us *(he didn't mention Frau Schuylkill)*. The longer Imperius Drake thinks he has us completely befuddled, the better.

Let's keep our knowledge to ourselves until we see what next steps the Duck takes. He may feel called upon to further point out to us how stupid we are and make a false move in the process."

"Good idea, Bear," said the Commissioner. "Although it would have been fun to watch Montgomery Moose's face when we told him that his insurance company is going to have to pay up for the missing jewel. That will just have to keep."

"Great work, Octavius," said the Captain, "although we don't look too swift. I guess our security should have accounted for that kind of attack, unimaginable as it is. We have to get that Duck and his weapon out of circulation ASAP. We'll just have to put up with the press and the mayor's office for a few more days. We'll keep it quiet on our end, and you do the same. What happened with the peacock?"

"I suspect it was reflected radiation from the jewel, but we won't know till we test it. What would you call that, Captain? Involuntary manslaughter carried out in the commission of a crime?? By the way, Inspector Wallaroo, now that we have completed our analysis, would you be kind enough to return the evidence to our friends, the Chicago Police, and give them back their helicopter in the process. Perhaps you could drive back down tomorrow with Colonel Where and Doctor Watt. You can go too, Maury, if you wish. Maury? Maury?"

I had crawled under a large CT Scanner when I first heard the word "helicopter" and I would not re-emerge until Bruce was safely *(for me)* airborne. Bruce Wallaroo was out of his chair and bouncing off the walls on his way to the helipad.

"You know, Octavius," said the Captain, "I'm still having trouble with this. We know who did it and now we know how. What I can't figure out is why."

"Indeed, Captain, indeed," growled Octavius.

Chapter Sixteen

Let's consider a bear's hibernation!

It's a subject of great fascination!

She's won't eat! She's asleep!

She won't drink! Sleep's too deep!

She wakes up with extreme constipation.

As we returned to Octavius' office, Frau Schuylkill padded into the room holding a large cordless telephone. Given his size, ordinary phones won't do for him.

"Excuse me, Herr Bear. There is a call for you."

"Get a number and tell them I'll call back."

"It is your mutter." The Frau had a very strong sense of parental respect. She held the phone directly in front of Octavius' nose and frowned.

The Bear shrugged, took the instrument, trundled over to his desk, took a swig of mead and said, "Hi Momma Bear! I was just thinking of you."

"Nonsense, Octavius! You never think of me, except of course for the monthly deposits and birthday and Christmas presents for which I thank you. I'd rather hear from you than just get presents."

"Now, Mom! You know how busy I am."

"Yes, I know. I saw on TV and in the paper today about that mess in Chicago. The media weren't being kind to you. Was it that barmy Duck again?"

"I think so! It looks like his work!"

"Doggone it, Tavi! *(Funny, only she and Belinda called him Tavi.)* Why don't you do what your father would have done and just kill him? Tear him apart with your claws!"

Octavius was shocked. Not at her bloodthirsty remarks. That was Mom. She saw herself as a backwoods bear. She still lived in a den in Alaska – an opulent den, mind you – and was very much a bear of the old school. For a sow her age, she still had all her teeth and she sharpened her claws religiously on a redwood she had installed at the entrance to the cave. Some cave! Octavius had spent millions ensuring the whole thing was *authentic primitive* –done up, of course, in the very best of modern taste. She adapted to certain civilized perks like an opulent bath cave with a walk-in stream that ran through it. She also liked her food cooked. Every week a fresh supply of salmon was delivered to the door of her den and her maid, an Arctic fox, saw to it that it was prepared to her discriminating taste.

No, what shocked the Great Bear was the reference to his father. "Mom, have you discovered who my father is?"

"No, Tavi, of course not, but it doesn't matter. Any one of them would have done the same thing. You betcha! Shredded Duck! Not my favorite but a good enough snack!"

Octavius shook his head. "I need to get that jewel back first, Mom. Killing him outright would just make it tougher to find it."

"Of course, dear! You're right, I suppose. After all, you're the one with all the degrees and honors. Doctor of this. Bachelor of that. By the way, arc you still one?"

"One what?"

"A bachelor, you silly twit!"

" 'Fraid so!"

"Sigh!! Tavi, you're not getting any younger, and neither am I. I would love to see a couple of grand cubs running around before I go into that long final hibernation. I understand that polar sow you were once so interested in is a widow. A rich widow! Not that you need her money, mind, but by golly, you two would really make an item. Polars and Kodiaks seldom mate. No one is even sure what their offspring would look like, but I am told by your old professor of Faunapology, Wallingford Penniped, wonderful walrus that he is, that cubs *are* possible."

"Mom, the Bearoness Belinda and I are a thing of the past. I see her occasionally and we are still very good friends, but that's all we are, good friends. Her mother pushed her into a marriage that didn't turn out well. Don't you start! Besides, we're too old for cubs."

"Well, you can't blame a good sow for tryin'! How's Maury and that goofy Australian?"

"Maury's fine, and so is Bruce. Inspector Bruce Wallaroo is one of the most talented investigators in the world."

"I know but he's still goofy! Frau Schuylkill *(Why she stays with you, I can't imagine!)* says you have two new associates – a wolf and a porcupine?"

"Colonel Wyatt Where and…"

"A werewolf?"

146

"No, mom, that's his name, W-h-e-r-e, he's ex-military, and he's my new security officer along with Frau Schuylkill."

"Oh, is there anything going on between the two of them?"

"No, there is not *(The great Bear sounded more assured than he really was.)* Is that all you think of?"

"Well, I watch a lot of soap operas. The other new one is a porcupine, huh? Never thought of you and a porcupine working together. All those quills!"

"Howard has perfect control over his quills, and he is a technical genius. He has multiple degrees from Stanford and MIT."

"More than you do?"

"We've never counted them up. Mom, much as I love you, I have to believe you called with more on your mind than just a chat."

"Not really, I just woke up from hibernation, and I said to myself, "Juno Bear, things have been happening while you were under. Get caught up, girl. And the minute I heard that story about you and the jewel theft, I said, Juno, call Tavi now. That's my number one priority. Flo *(the Arctic fox maid)* does such a wonderful job of keeping the place in shape while I'm asleep that all I have to do is wake up and get going. She tells me all the members of my weekly bridge group are awake. I'm having them over tonight."

"And you wanted to tell them what your wayward son is doing! Do me a favor and don't mention the jewel theft unless one of them brings it up. Then simply say, 'We're working very hard on it.' Frankly, until we get it back, it's a major embarrassment."

"Well, the last thing I would want to do is embarrass my own flesh and blood, although one of these days I'd like to get my claws on Agrippa,

147

that half-brother of yours and do a lot more than embarrass him. Has he been hitting you up for money again?"

"I get an occasional card from him telling me where he can be reached if I feel an urge to help support his wayward ways."

"And do you?"

"Sure, I never notice it."

"That's your trouble, Tavi. You're such a soft-hearted sap!"

Octavius was glad this conversation wasn't going over the speaker phone. In fact everyone had straggled out of the room while he was on the call.

"Frankly, Mom, I think he'd get into more trouble if I didn't send him money."

"Where is he now?"

"Last I heard, he was still hibernating but he gave his last mailing address as Reno. I think he deals blackjack in one of the casinos. Funny about that! I'm leaving for Las Vegas in a few days. Giving a speech at a convention. But Reno is a good distance away. I doubt if I'll run into him."

"I hope not. I've always wished your sister, Marcellina, had survived. She was a bright little cub. She would have given you a run for your money. Not like that jerk, Agrippa. I know! He's only your half brother, but what a disappointment!"

Then with her marvelous ability to change the subject in midstream she asked, "You still don't hibernate, do you?"

"No, I don't have to. That treatment I developed lets me stay active year round."

"Why haven't you packaged it? Of course, I wouldn't use it. I kinda like going for an annual beddy-bye. It's a great way to lose weight. But there are all kinds of fast track bears who would love to stay awake all year. Male and female! You could probably sell it to other species as well."

"There are still a few side effects I have to eliminate before letting it out to others."

"Nothing serious, I hope. Oops! I hear the doorbell. My bridge sows are arriving. Ta, Ta, Tavi. Call soon. Love you!"

"Goodbye, Mom!" As he reached to put down the phone, that side effect kicked in, and the Great Bear fell over into a deep sleep.

Chapter Seventeen

Beavers work very hard every day.

They cut trees and then cart them away.

But they'll block up your streams.

And in spite of your screams,

They just don't give a dam what you say.

As twilight gently shrouded the surrounding hillsides, little did the complacent beaver citizenry of Pondscum, Michigan realize that waddling into their midst was the Arch Criminal of the 21st Century. *(There has been some squabbling among crime authorities as to who holds the distinction for the 20th Century, but Imperius Drake Ph.D. is right up there with the worst of them.)*

Fresh from his assault on the Loupe Museum, he had fled with his two companions to this out-of-the-way refuge on the shore of Lake Huron. Here he could put the final steps of the termination of the wrap-up of the crescendo of the grand finale of his dastardly plan into action. It would be a Full-scale, Cast-of-Millions, Dolby Digital, Ultra High Definition, Heavy on the Special Effects Extravaganza of Gore and Destruction. This was to be his supreme act of revenge and exultation – proving to the world and especially his enemies the true extent of his iniquitous genius.

In spite of a few close calls with a persistent Coast Guard helicopter, the Black Quacks had made good their escape from Chicago in the Duck's high speed hydroplane -The Miss Lee-Li-Li. Chita piloted them up Lake Michigan, through the Straits of Mackinac to Pondscum, resisting repeated urges to wring Imperius' neck and kick Bigg overboard. She might yet, but first, she wanted explanations. Bad enough Imperius was being his usual irritating cutesy self, but that consummate idiot, the Baboon, was in on the secret, too. She was supposed to be executive officer of this band of arch-criminals. Instead she was playing the part of beautiful but dumb. No Way!!!! Answers, dammit, and soon!

The Black Quackers had docked the hydroplane at the Beaver Dam Marina. They covered it over as best they could and left it in a boat yard with a myopic yard master. They needed to find lodging, food, and workers and set up shop for the next phase of Imperius Drake's plan for domination.

They registered at a local motel *(the only motel)*. They ordered drinks and snacks at the bar next door and sat silently waiting for Imperius to break the stillness. He didn't. He seemed to be murmuring under his breath, but nothing Chita or Bigg could understand.

The bartender tried making conversation. Looking at Chita and then Bigg, he lisped through his protruding teeth, "Don't see many folks like you around here!"

Chita shot back, "Yeah and with prices like these, you won't be seeing many of us again."

The beaver stared and then got the joke. He guffawed and walked away, shaking his whiskered head. "Closing up in a few minutes, folks. Any last orders?"

Bigg started to ask for something, but Chita cut him off. "Nah, we're fine. Thanks." She paid the check. As part of Imperius' charade as an Emperor, he refused to carry any money on him. He also never paid the cat or Baboon back. Annoying!

They went back to their rooms.

A large, black, ominous, stretch SUV with steel cattle horns projecting from its hood *(bonnet, for you UK readers)* rolled into town around midnight followed by two unmarked trucks. Imperius waddled out to meet them and

151

guided them to a former bowling alley, Lowest Lanes. Originally built from old beaver dam materials, the place had been boarded up for years and all the equipment removed. It was just a large, empty shell. Bigg and Chita, full of curiosity but trying to look nonchalant, strolled up behind the Duck.

The passengers struggled out of the back doors. "Oh boy!" thought Chita, "Mr. Brutus Taurus and Mr. Belial Taurus, the Chicago Bulls, or as they like to be called in gangland circles, The Raging Bulls."

Right out of central casting for *These Horns for Hire* or *The Bullhorns*. In more polite society they represented themselves as "facilitators." They could "facilitate" the timely payment of debts, the discouragement of lawsuits, the disappearance of sensational feature articles from newspapers or TV news shows *(sometimes along with the reporters)* and of, course stage an occasional swimming meet in the Chicago River with one of the contestants being bound and assisted by concrete overshoes. They had facilitated some of the details of the Loupe Museum heist.

Imperius, while looking askance at their gangster bravado and their ludicrous attempts to appear and sound like upscale business beasts, also had a healthy respect for their special abilities and didn't hesitate to hire them as necessary. He never failed to pay them in full and on time. Chita couldn't stand them, and Bigg idolized them. It figures.

Chita looked at them out of the corner of her eye. She winced, remembering that one of the bulls had tried to make a pass at her. "Brutus, I think! He's the one with the large diamond ring in his nose to cover the scars from my claw swipes. The other guy, Belial, now has shiny stainless steel tips on his horns. I'm sure that goes over big in the Stockyards. Highly polished hooves and size fifty fedoras with cut-outs for their horns."

"Well, Doctor Drake, we're here on time and as promised. Da trucks have all the materials youse specified. You can check them if you want."

"No, Mister Taurus, I don't think that will be necessary. Ours is a relationship built on trust."

The two bulls snorted. Chita stifled a laugh. Bigg gaped!

"You remember my two associates, Ms. Catt and Mr. Baboon."

Brutus unconsciously wrinkled his scarred nose and snorted again. "Hello Ms. Chita! Hello, Mr. Bigg!" He and the Baboon both broke into chortles of laughter. Mr. Bigg! Oh, well!

"Should we leave the trucks as-is, or should we unload them?"

Imperius looked around. Pondscum was a dead as a doormat *(or something)*. "There doesn't seem to be anyone who could disturb us at the moment. Let's QUIETLY bring the materials inside." This as Bigg tripped and practically impaled himself on the SUV's horns.

As the truck doors were opened by their drivers, Chita asked first. "What are we unloading?"

"Very delicate components, Cat. I shall explain it to you in the morning while we recruit some local labor to help us assemble them. They are a critical part of the Grand Plan."

Bigg, as usual, looked befuddled. "We're going to build things?"

"Not exactly, Baboon. The good citizens of Pondscum are going to build things under our direction."

"Oh!"

It took about an hour to get everything inside the building. Imperius turned to Belial and said, "Your payment has already been transferred to your account at the Bank of Lake Michigan." He sniggered at the irony of that. Belial didn't get it.

Brutus stomped over. "I think we're finished, Doctor Drake. The boys are coming back to Chicago with us. You can keep the trucks, but I'd hide them if I were you. They're hot. We stole 'em in Illinois, but we put Michigan plates on 'em so they wouldn't be noticeable. The plates are stolen too. We'll meet you next weekend at the airport."

"Very good, Mr. Taurus. We only need the trucks for one short run. We'll handle that. You have the plane laid on and taken care of?"

"Yeah, but we had to pay for that."

"You shall be reimbursed. Drive carefully!"

Chita and Bigg had been listening to this with increasing puzzlement but knew by now that pressing the Duck was a useless exercise when he wanted to be mysterious.

Next morning, when the Pondscum townsfolk *(pop. 578)* awoke and first noticed the arrival of these three, a few of the more curious were prone to question who they were and why they had taken over the old bowling alley. But when signs went up at the neighborhood bar and grill, convenience store, lumber yard and town hall *(all the same place)* offering short-term, part-time assembly work, curiosity became enthusiasm and the entire adult population plus some teenagers attempted to sign up.

The work was easy, but it was only for a few days. After her briefing by Imperius, the project manager, a cheetah named Ms. Direction *(surely, you know who that is)* had one team taking little white plastic eggs from the trucks, cutting off the tops, and cleaning out the hollow insides. A second team would then take what looked like little computers and install them inside each egg and surround them with a sort of pliable plastic filler. A third team put a clear top back on the egg with a small LCD screen and two push buttons.

One of the brighter assemblers figured out that they were small MP3 music players, and that was the story accepted by the Pondscum authorities and leading citizens. The final team stenciled a logo: *The Genius of Genetics–2013* on each egg and carefully placed them in silver boxes imprinted with the same logo. As you might expect with beavers, it was well organized and only required

154

minor supervision by Chita and as also was to be expected, no useful effort on the part of Bigg. Imperius stayed aloof from the process, checking in periodically with his two minions to see if all was on schedule and whether quality control was being maintained. In short he was once again making himself a sporadic pain in the ass. After a few false starts when the beavers tried to use their teeth to clean out the plastic eggs, the assembly line began to hum *(actually it squeaked.)*

So much for Tuesday. *(And Wednesday for that matter. If you're really interested in Wednesday, the deluxe edition of this book contains the entire production schedule and output report for the project in Appendix 6).*

It is now Thursday. Imperius and his production crew are in their next to last day at Pondscum, making little white eggs. Inspector Wallaroo, Doctor Watt and Colonel Where are just beginning the journey southeast from Chicago to Cincinnati in the Colonel's armored Humvee and utility trailer. Frau Schuylkill and the hangar crew are beginning to check out the *Ursa Major* for its flight to Vegas for the opening of the convention. Octavius is sound asleep at his desk. And I, Maury Meerkat am talking to you. Perhaps a little more background on our nefarious "friends" would be in order.

*****

You are already well-versed in the early life and times of the Black Quack Gang. Not exactly the *Cosa Nostra* but on balance, a reasonably well-oiled criminal crew.

Then about a year ago, things began to change. Probably as a result of the constant onslaught of the brain-enhancing formula, Imperius developed delusions of extreme grandeur. He insisted that his colleagues call him Emperor Duck *(Chita seldom did)* and he increasingly left the mundane activities of theft and extortion to the cat and Baboon to handle. He was evolving his grand plot for avenging the death of his beloved Lee-Li-Li and bringing the mighty scientific, military, business, and academic communities of the world to their knees. His special targets were geneticists, biologists and members of the medical community with special emphasis on his nemesis, Octavius Bear.

155

That bombastic bear would have to suffer in a very special way – full of irony and poetic justice. The Emperor had spent more and more time in his elaborate laboratory working on several engines of destruction and mayhem, including the restoration of the partially destroyed prototype laser particle beam projector from the labs of UUI. He had purloined it in pieces and with some of the documentation.

Bigg, as usual, went about oblivious to the transformation in Imperius even as it became more intense. But Chita, her feral instincts ever on the alert, became increasingly uncomfortable with the situation. Sure, the income and the perks were great but working for a certified loon *(yes, she knew he's a Duck but he's a loony Duck)* was rubbing her feline sensitivities ever more raw. And this Deep Blue heist hadn't come off at all the way she had expected. Watching on TV last night, she was shocked to hear that the peacock had died – and possibly been killed, accidentally of course. But killed nonetheless. When she ran past him and had then collided with the pack rat museum Director, the bird was screaming, but she thought it was because the sapphire had disappeared. Now she knew better. He was having a heart attack, but there were also allusions in the media to burns on his body – radiation burns. That had the press and the *"curse kooks"* yowling that the sapphire had struck again.

So, once they had reached Pondscum, she decided to have a showdown with the Duck. Late in the evening as they sat alone at the back table of a nearby roadside inn, Chita looked at Bigg and Imperius and said, "We have to talk."

"What about, Cat?" asked Imperius. As one of his latest strokes of imperial grandeur, while insisting on being called "Emperor" and "Sire" himself, Imperius refused to call Bigg and Chita by their names. They were "Cat" and "Baboon."

"About you and us and what's going on!"

"We see nothing to discuss. *(Imperius had also adopted the imperial "we.")* The Great Plan is evolving just as we have ordained it. And you will address us as Sire"

"No, I won't, Duck. That's exactly what I'm talking about. This crazy Emperor stuff. You keeping us in the dark about the Great Plan, whatever that is. And that ridiculous stunt at the Loupe Museum. I want some answers, or I'm going to walk."

Bigg interrupted, "Don't talk to his Imperial Highness that way, Chita. It's not polite."

"You should listen to the Baboon, Cat. Therein lays wisdom. However, we are in a good mood this evening and will hear you out as long as it pleases us."

"Well, for openers. I thought we were supposed to steal the sapphire, not destroy it. Why did you go to all the trouble of having a special duplicate made if you weren't going to substitute it? My version was: After you signaled me over the radio that Bigg had cut off the top of the case with the laser, I was to switch the jewels, slap on the sign, drop the Black Quack and run like hell. Wasn't Bigg supposed to cut through the case?"

"No, Cat, he was not. He was to carefully aim the precisely tuned particle beam projector at the jewel and disintegrate it. The Baboon executed his assignment perfectly. Like the other members of his species, his five fingered hands are quite facile. We are pleased with you, Baboon."

"Thank you, Sire."

"Then what was I doing running around inside the museum with a black egg, stupid sign, and phony jewel in my paws? They almost caught me once. When I got to the case and saw it was empty, I had a cat fit."

"You were performing your part of the plan, Cat. If you had known there was no swap to be made and that we were going to destroy the jewel from the skylight, I doubt you would have shown much enthusiasm for running around while being chased by a group of museum guards and police, no matter how inept they were."

"In other words, I was conned," said Chita.

"Not a word we would use, Cat, but it will serve. You still have the duplicate jewel, we assume."

"Yes, I do, but I'm damned if I know what you are going to do with it. Any expert can tell it's a fake – a good fake – but still a fake."

"Ah, but you see, we do not plan to use it on an expert. We will use it on someone who will prove to be the ironic downfall of Octavius Bear. We have cruelly and publicly humiliated him in Chicago, but that was just a preliminary. We are on the verge of a global master stroke. A veritable *foie gras*! One that will ensure the glorious name of Imperius Drake is revered forever in the annals of criminal genius and one that will relegate the carcass and name of that despicable bear to the dustbins of history where he will no doubt molder away to nothingness. We are getting weary of this discussion. Suffice it to say that the longer the police and that ridiculous Australian believe the stone was stolen, the better. While they're searching for the fault in their protective systems, we will use the distraction to bring about their destruction. Perhaps we shall provide yet another diversion before the final masterstroke. Strictly for entertainment."

"Entertainment? Is that all we're getting out of this nutty screw-up? Half of American law enforcement is probably after us by now, and the internationals can't be far behind. And what about the peacock? They're saying he died of radiation-induced heart failure."

"Ah, yes," said the Duck, "that was most inconvenient."

"It was sure inconvenient for the peacock."

"Perhaps, but it also causes *me* some level of concern. They weren't supposed to know about that particular feature of the particle accelerator."

"What feature? Did you deliberately kill that bird?"

"Quite the contrary! I wanted him alive to increase the pressure and embarrassment on that stupid Wallaroo and that odious Bear. The peacock could have created enormous Gallic theatrical scenes that the media would have just eaten up. Instead, we have to settle for their more conventional reactions, although this curse nonsense does help heat things up. I want those two 'protectors of the peace' and the police up to their ears in embarrassing issues and distractions while we continue to pursue the true purpose of the Grand Plan."

Bigg spoke up, "What about these little white eggs we're making? Are they really music players? And what are we going to do with them?"

"Yeah," growled Chita, "what are those things? I love running an operation not knowing what I'm doing. What's this Genius of Genetics stuff?"

Ignoring Chita completely, Imperius intoned, "That too, shall unfold, Baboon. But yes, in a matter of speaking, they are music players. The sound of them carrying out their work will be like the thundering ovation of the world acknowledging our supremacy. Oh, yes, music indeed. You shall find out more when we finish our work here and move on to Las Vegas."

"Las Vegas?" shouted Bigg and Chita. "We're going to Las Vegas?"

"Quiet, both of you! Do you want these foolish Pondscummers to know what we're doing? That's another reason we seldom let you in on our monumentally diabolical strategies. You have not yet learned the value of contemplative silence. We were taught its miraculous effects at the ancient and wrinkled feet of the great Dalai Duck while we were in Nepal. You will finish the work on the souvenir eggs, and we will sneak out of town early Saturday morning before any of the locals have a chance to figure out what happened. The plane will be waiting for us and the eggs. And that is all we will say on the matter until we have left."

With that he flapped his pitch dark wings and regally proceeded out the door, with Bigg trailing behind him. Chita sat in the darkened room, snarling to herself and nervously scratching her fur. "Bartender," she yowled, "Get me another White Lightning, and make it a double."

The Development of Civilization – Part 4

The Great Inter-Species War

(From "An Introduction to Faunapology" by Octavius Bear Ph.D.)

In the closing years of the past century, a short but devastating event took place that is still affecting our lives. The Great Inter-Species War! Unexpected and in many respects, still unexplained, the War as it is popularly known stood out from our previous small and isolated conflicts in many ways. It involved almost the entire population of the world, and it came close to annihilating that entire population. It escalated at a breathtaking rate, propelled by mass hysteria and species prejudice. In only one way was it similar to all the other conflicts. It began over the stupidest of disagreements.

A crackpot professor (whose name is seldom spoken nowadays) claimed to have incontrovertible proof that animals with long tails and especially prehensile tails were endowed by nature with vastly superior characteristics: physical, mental, and spiritual. This would have ultimately been filed away to gather dust among other ridiculous theories if the media hadn't caught on to it and stirred up conflicts. Several self-styled faunapology "experts" seized the opportunity to grab the spotlight and began campaigns of hate and discrimination against the "short tails" and the "no tails."

University students and faculty members took up the war cries, aided by religious fanatics who insisted that God had a short, long, or no tail, depending on His or Her infallible revelations to the true believers. In short order, politicians entered the arena, and a frenzied group of splinter parties became a forest of biased demagogues and their followers.

And then the inevitable happened! Violence and destruction! The Parliament building in Delhi was bombed and destroyed by a hyper-radical group of long-tail felines. A semi-military band of short-tail apes and gorillas retaliated, and the entire world was suddenly caught up in a full scale riot.

Unfortunately, the riot instigators had access to deadly weaponry, transportation, sophisticated communications, and a massive reserve of disaffected animals who were itching for a fight with anyone. Individual nations took up the cause(s) and built up armaments and fighting forces to a level unknown in history. Massive campaigns were fought, lives were lost and infrastructure destroyed. But then, just as suddenly, it all collapsed.

Simultaneous outbreaks of African Horse Sickness, Contagious Bovine Pleuropneumonia, Foot and Mouth Disease, Rabies, Goat and Sheep Pox, Highly Pathogenic Avian Influenza (Fowl Plague), Hog Cholera, and Swine Vesicular Disease, among others brought the fighting and practically the entire world to a rapid end. There are strong suspicions that an attempt at using biological weapons literally backfired and uncontrollably spread these highly transmissible diseases throughout the world.

The International Association of Nations (for the first time) took control of the situation, enlisted support from the major developed countries, and gradually brought the diseases under control. Universal Ursine Industries played a major role in developing and manufacturing antidotes and medicines for curing the diseases or mitigating the symptoms.

We sincerely hope that in the few years since hostilities ceased and the world population has begun to slowly return to its former numbers, we have learned an indelible lesson about war and its impact. Some species have become extinct as a result of the epidemics. Others have been altered irretrievably and seldom for the better. Nevertheless, it is still possible to hear in speeches, television shows, on street corners, and even in churches the terms: "long tail, short tail, and no tail."

Chapter Eighteen

Wolverines have a powerful jaw

And a long, pointed, razor-sharp claw,

With a rank, nasty stink,

That's what leads me to think -

It's no wonder they all practice law.

It is late Thursday afternoon at Octavius' mansion – or as we call it when he isn't listening, the Bear Lair.

"Mraureee!!"

Ah, the Great Bear was awake. Bringing in my laptop computer and fermented coconut milk, I settled down in the easy chair opposite Octavius' desk and said, "You bellowed, sir?"

"Yes, smart aleck, I did. First ask Frau Schuylkill to come in for a minute."

Before I had a chance to get up, the she-wolf was standing in front of Octavius, wagging her tail *(a thing I had seldom seen her do.)*

"Ah, Frau Schuylkill, there you are." he said. *(How she immediately sensed he wanted her, I could never figure out. Some mysteries are better unsolved.)* "Several things: First, how are the preparations going on the *Ursa Major*? I want to be able to approach Las Vegas on Saturday night under stealth conditions."

(Now there's a trick. Try being stealthy on Saturday night in Las Vegas in an airplane originally designed for King Kong.)

"*Ja*, Herr Bear, the aircraft is undergoing full tests. I think you will be totally satisfied. This morning, one of the hangar crew walked into it without seeing it."

(For those of you unfamiliar with the C-5A Galaxy, it is almost as long as a football field and as high as a six-story building and has a cargo compartment about the size of an eight-lane bowling alley. Easy to miss!)

"As I expected Frau Schuylkill, Swiss efficiency at its finest."

"*Danke*, Herr Bear, you wished something else?"

"Yes, I think we will be having several guests this evening for dinner. Inspector Wallaroo *(choked back howl)*, Doctor Howard Watt, and Colonel Wyatt Where." *(Deep red blush.)*

"I had anticipated their arrival and have prepared rooms. Also, I have prepared a light supper for everyone."

"Excellent, nothing fancy. I want it to be a working dinner."

"As you wish, Herr Bear!"

A "light supper" later turned out to be a Lucullan Feast. It was to be served in our main dining room, a place that on a good day will give the Louvre a run for its euros. I think the Frau just might have been trying to impress someone, but of course, I can't be sure. *(Wink, wink!)* Octavius didn't seem to notice anything out of the ordinary.

"Finally, a keg of mead would be very welcome."

"As you wish, Herr Bear." She disappeared and the mead appeared. Scary!

163

"Now, Maury," rumbled Octavius, "there was something else I wanted to discuss with you, and I had forgotten it with all the hoopla. It's about the conference."

Oh boy, here it comes. Octavius hates meetings, business shows, press conferences, speech making, and public appearances in general. Unfortunately, he can only foist a very few of them off on his staff, including me. *(Although I have been told I am an excellent public speaker. A little short in stature, but excellent nonetheless.)* I'm not sure why, but the world wants to hear from the original Bear. Among his many magnificent talents, speechmaking is definitely not one. Not to put too fine a claw on it, he's lousy at it. Convention managers call him Boring Bear behind his back but because he is who he is, he keeps getting invitations. I, as you might suspect, get the dubious honor of writing his speeches for him.

There is only one thing worse than having to give a speech. It's writing one for someone else. Especially when that someone else is an arrogant, irascible and nit-picking nine-foot ursine who intimidates the audience simply by walking on the stage. The last time Octavius made a public appearance, testifying before Congress, I prepared fourteen drafts of his comments, many from scratch and carefully researched, and he was still changing them as he sat waiting his turn to speak. And then, typical Bear, he ignored the written text and attempted to ad lib. Opening joke – "Three bears walk into a Congressional hearing, a Kodiak, a grizzly, and a koala...." By this time I was under the seat and trying to scrabble out of the room. Oh well, it's a job.

I tried to anticipate. "I've already written a draft of your keynote for you," I lied, "The theme of the meeting is The Genius of Genetics and I've thrown in a lot of compliments about the immense amount of talent in the room, the glorious history of genetics, and the challenges facing the community. Not one word about the great Roberto Rabbito, Noble candidate extraordinaire."

"Good! Just as I expected. You may show me the text later. I have something else to discuss. Something peculiar."

We had just had the world's most precious sapphire disappear into thin air and a magnificent bird die of a heart attack from radiation and he wants to talk about something peculiar.

"As you know, Bel was here on Tuesday," he said.

"I saw the Flying Aquabear landing but I was too busy keeping my paws over my eyes in the chopper to notice anything else," I replied.

"She made it out to be a social call. Just a stopover on her way to Las Vegas with the Aquabear troupe."

"Now, there's a coincidence," I said. "Do you think she knows you're going to be there, too?"

"Oh, she knows all right. In fact, they're entertaining at the close of the Genetics Conference."

"They're what?" I squeaked.

"She was being her usual coy self, but she led me to believe that she was there at the behest of a mysterious, unidentified sponsor. She thinks the mysterious sponsor is me and UUI."

"Which you are not?'

"Which I most certainly am not, and neither is UUI. I checked with Corporate Sales Promotion and they said they had cut back on their show budgets and had definitely not sponsored any entertainment for the meeting."

"I may be getting paranoid but I don't like it. Who is this mysterious sponsor?"

"That, my dear Meerkat, is what I want you to find out while the rest of us struggle with this latest Duck debacle. I also have Smedley at UUI looking into it but his staff is all tied up with our part of the conference. I hate these damn things."

I was about to protest my latest assignment when the roar of an engine, definitely military, interrupted our conversation. I could hear the sound of Frau Schuylkill's paws thumping on the foyer floor as she raced for the front door. *(Normally, she is ultra-silent.)* Here we go! The reserves had arrived.

Frau Schuylkill opened the door and, I swear, curtseyed to the wolf and porcupine. I walked over and shook paws with Doctor Watt and Colonel Where and said: "Good to see both of you again! What happened to Inspector Wallaroo?"

"He's out there admiring my Humvee," replied the Colonel. "He fell in love with it on the trip down. Great for roaming the outback, he says. Gonna buy one as soon as he can, but it has to be the military version."

"Well, let me make a few introductions," I said. "Ladies first! Frau Schuylkill, may I present Doctor Howard Watt and Colonel Wyatt Where."

"Welcome, Herr Oberst. Herr Professor Doktor. We are delighted to have you with us. I am Frau Schuylkill from Switzerland. I too, was in the military, Herr Oberst. I flew jets. I am currently the housekeeper, chef and command pilot of Herr Bear's modest Luftwaffe. I would be delighted to show you our aircraft and aerodrome when you have a free moment. Your *zimmers*, sorry, rooms, are ready, and we will be serving dinner in another hour. When you wish to go up to your rooms, please let me know."

Obviously, the Frau was flustered. I hadn't heard her slip into Switzer Deutsch like that in a long while. I watched the Colonel to see if the interest was being reciprocated. It was. As Frau Schuylkill padded away, Colonel Where said, "That is indeed a lovely wolf, Mr. Meerkat, and she sounds both cultured and very capable. You have an Air Force?"

166

"Nothing fancy," I replied, "a Twin Otter, an Osprey, an F-15 Eagle, and C-5A Galaxy. They come in handy." *(I didn't mention the occasional visiting helicopter with or without Bruce.)* The Colonel's eyebrows lifted a tad but he maintained his staid military presence.

"But let me introduce you to Octavius Bear," I said. We had arrived at the bear's den. The wolf and porcupine looked around in admiration at the resplendent room and at the resplendent bear. Octavius could certainly look impressive when he wanted to, and at this moment, rising to his full nine foot height, he wanted to.

"Doctor Watt, Colonel Where! Welcome! Welcome!" he rumbled with a bass note that set the crystal chandelier to vibrating. "I regret our first meeting has to come in the middle of this sorry sapphire affair, but I'm sure we will all profit mightily from our new relationship. Maury, I think drinks all around would be appropriate."

At the word–*drinks*–Bruce Wallaroo came bounding through the door and into the room. "Beer for me, Maury. That is one bonzer vee-hicle, Colonel. A real ripper. Hullo, Ocko." *(Wolf howls from the domestic quarters.)*

"Inspector," said Octavius, his regal aplomb upset by the bounding roo's approach. "Do sit down, please. Preferably on a chair. Thank you."

I rolled over the drinks table and asked the Colonel and doctor to help themselves – Bourbon straight for the Colonel, Scotch and soda for the doctor. Octavius already had his mead keg and I refilled my coconut milk. I put a six pack of beer by Bruce's feet.

"Well," said the Bear, "I'd like to get one or two formalities out of the way first and then you can finish your drinks at your leisure and see about settling in. First, I like to operate on an informal basis here, so if you wish, please call me Octavius."

"Certainly," said the porcupine, "and Howard is fine with me."

167

"Likewise," said the Colonel. "Just call me Wyatt."

"Howard and Wyatt. Good," said the Bear.

"You can call me Bruce, Ocko.'

"Thank you, Inspector. Now Howard and Wyatt! I, of course, have had the opportunity to review your CVs *(resumés to you and me),* and I am mightily impressed, but those are just dates and data. Suppose you tell me a little more about yourselves other than what Maury and the Inspector have said to me, and of course, our brief phone interview yesterday afternoon. Howard?"

The porcupine's quills flattened for a moment, and then he said, "Well, you've seen all the degrees and publications and stuff. While I was doing post-doc work, I was given an opportunity to do some research on some new laser technology that was being developed for creating ultra-dense computer storage. It fascinated me. You know, how many angelfish can you fit on the head of pin? Stuff like that. Well, everything was fine until my father died, leaving my mother with just enough to support herself. "Howard," I said to myself. "You better get off your spine-filled ass and make some money to support Mom. Academia doesn't pay much, as you know and I was in line for a good government lab job but those damn security background checks take forever. Months, maybe a year! So, I took the Chief Scientist job at the bank as a filler. Do you know how many banks have a chief scientist? None, that I could find. Little did I know that Moose Jaw was using the job as eyewash for his customers to convince them the bank was at full state of the art in protection. I used to get paraded out to meet these old maiden ladies and officious boars who came in to count their pennies in the crypt. 'And here is our Chief Scientist, Doctor Watt. Say something scientific, Doctor!' I have to admit that working with Wyatt and then Bruce to develop the super high security vault was interesting. The lasers and gas jets were my contribution. Sorry about your cap, Maury."

I grinned and picked up my fedora. "No problem, Howard. I've got something new and better. A little more sleuth-like!" I put it on and snapped the brim. I thought Octavius would choke.

"Anyway, listening to Bruce and knowing about you and your work at UUI, I thought this might be the time to come up from the depths. I'm delighted you're willing to take me on."

"The pleasure is mine, Howard. I'd like to be able to give you substantial access to my research facilities here and at UUI, which incidentally is headquartered across the river in Kentucky. In return, of course, we would like to take full advantage of your knowledge, especially on the subjects of lasers and particle beam projectors. I looked you up on the Internet, and your publications in this area are quite impressive indeed. Is there any reason, with appropriate non-disclosure agreements and proprietary rights contracts, of course, we can't operate on that basis?"

"None that I can think of, Octavius. I have copies of the non-disclosure agreement I drew up with the bank protecting my intellectual assets. We can modify that, and I'm sure we can reach a proper NDA as far as your properties are concerned."

"Splendid. Maury, call Wolford and ask him to drive over here immediately. Tell him he can stay for dinner. That will motivate him. He's crazy about Frau Schuylkill's cooking."

Wolford Wolverine Esq. was Octavius' lawyer and UUI's chief counsel. I reached for the phone and got him on the line. "Wolford? Maury! The chief needs you right away. Dinner is included. Right. 45 minutes. Great."

Octavius turned to the wolf. I think Frau Schuylkill was listening at the door. Tough to tell. She's the original stealth-lupine. "What about you, Wyatt?"

"Well, I joined the military while I was still a pup. *(Yep, she was there at the door. I could hear her snuffling.)* You know, kid's imagination. All the glory and glamour. I joined the Air Force, but instead of being a high flying jet jockey, I got put in a close support unit flying A-10 Warthogs. It was during the Inter-Species hostilities. I gather you were in the war, too, Octavius."

The bear nodded. "The Arctic," he said. "They sent me there because I'm a Kodiak."

The Frau was also a combat pilot, but because Switzerland was neutral, she didn't see action until she transferred to the European Union Forces.

"Anyway," continued Wyatt nonchalantly, "You fly enough of those kinds of missions, and you eventually get shot down. And I was. I eventually fought my way back across the lines, and the brass thought I'd seen enough combat for a while. They transferred me to a desk job – military intelligence. Some desk job! Four months later, I was back behind enemy lines leading a group invading a secret weapons laboratory. I learned enough about physical and information security from that tour that when I got out, I had my choice of industrial spy and counter spy jobs.

"I decided I'd become a mercenary instead. That didn't last long. I got into an argument with the pack leader and practically killed him. I had to leave quick. So back I came to the counter-spy stuff, and I ended up being a security consultant. Moose gave me a contract and then offered me a permanent job. I took it. Dumbest thing I've ever done. Anyway, glad to be with you. I didn't realize you had military planes in your arsenal and a trained combat pilot, too. That's all icing on the cake."

I heard a rustling sound by the kitchen door. Clearly, the she-wolf was considering what kind of cake to put the icing on.

"Wyatt," said Octavius, "I'm not sure whether you have any professional, research or technical materials you wish to protect, but we

170

should do the same thing. On top of which, I'm sure that you'd think I was a complete idiot if I hadn't already run a complete security check on both of you. It's convenient to have friends in our country's security services. Prompt response time. Needless to say, you both passed. I will, however, need an assortment of prints, DNA and the like for our records."

"You're absolutely right, Octavius. In fact, I'd like to run a complete review of your security for you as soon as we get this Duck mess cleared up. In the meantime, I think we'd both like to settle in and get cleaned up for dinner."

Frau Schuylkill appeared from nowhere and escorted the two of them up to their rooms. When they were out of earshot, Bruce turned to Octavius and said, "Ocko, I notice you didn't mention to either of them what really happened to the sapphire. Me neither. I assume they already know about the dead peacock."

"But not how he really died, Inspector! I think we should keep that and the sapphire's destruction to ourselves for the moment. Do you agree, Maury?"

"You bet, but you'd better have a word with the Frau about it. I think she overheard our earlier discussions with the Chicago police." *(I didn't mention her listening at the door just now.)*

"Good catch, Meerkat. Some days you do indeed earn your keep. I'll speak to her alone. She won't come near you if she can help it, Bruce. Maury, right after dinner, I want you to start on that other item I asked you to pursue."

"S'okay with me if that she-wolf doesn't want to deal with me. She's a frighter, she is," said Bruce as he popped his fourth can of beer.

Meantime, Wolford Wolverine Esq. had arrived. Sniffing the air with an ecstatic sparkle in his beady eyes and just the slightest drool at the side of his mega-jaws, the wolverine said, "Good evening, all. Delighted to be back at the mansion, Octavius! Even more delighted to be invited for dinner. Frau

Schuylkill is no doubt preparing more of her culinary masterpieces. Sniff, sniff! Enough to make an underpaid *(!?)* and overworked *(?!)* officer of the court think about retiring and becoming a food critic. Not that there is anything to criticize about the Frau's cooking. No, no, she has an exquisite touch in the kitchen."

Needless to say, the Frau was standing behind the door taking this outpouring in. She wasn't very fond of Wolford. None of us was! But where flattery about her cooking was concerned, she'd take it from anyone.

Octavius grunted, "Hello, Wolford."

Bruce grunted, "Hello Wolford."

I tried to grunt and produced a cross between a burp and a sneeze.

"Ah," said the wolverine, staring at the drinks table. "A pre-prandial libation would not be amiss. Do not stir yourself, Mauritius. I shall see to my own refreshment." He walked over, unconsciously stroking his well-combed and luxurious coat as he went, and poured himself a healthy dose of sixty-year-old Napoleon Brandy. "Now, will someone introduce me to these gentlebeasts. I, of course, am Wolford Wolverine, Esquire, counselor to Doctor Bear and legal protector of his entire world-spanning empire."

I picked up the hint. God knows what Bruce would have said, and Octavius, wrinkling his nose, seemed to want to keep his conversation with Wolford at a minimum. I wasn't sure whether it was Wolford's unfortunate skunk-like smell or the heavy cologne that he used to fruitlessly cover it up. Maybe it was the reference to protecting the bear's "world spanning empire."

Anyway, I said, "Wolford, please greet Doctor Howard Watt and Colonel Wyatt Where. They are about to join the Bear's security team and some contractual work, non-disclosure agreements, terms of employment, etc., have to be completed this evening."

The Bear interjected, "Preferably before we eat, Wolford! *(How's that for motivation?)* The doctor and the Colonel will be taking up their assignments immediately, and we haven't any time to waste with prolonged legal procedures. We'll deal with the payroll and other HR administrivia tomorrow morning."

Obviously miffed but also obviously aware of where his income and tonight's dinner were coming from, the wolverine reached into his stuffed attaché case and produced a swatch of legal sized documents. Extending his paw to each of them while precariously balancing his attaché case, papers, and brandy snifter, he led them into a side room where for the next thirty minutes, the "whereases," "wherefores," and "in consideration ofs" bounced back and forth among the three. I stuck my head in once to ask about refills and was greeted with a grateful snarl by the Colonel.

The porcupine, wolf, and wolverine executed the required documentation in record time and with a self-satisfied grin on his none-too-lovable face, Wolford addressed Octavius. "The deed is done. The proceedings are completed, oh Great Employer. Signed, sealed, and air tight!"

He then headed for the kitchen in the hopes of smooth-talking the Frau into some early samples. Unnecessary, because suddenly the table was filled with great quantities of Truffles, Tyrolean Goulash, *Truite a l'Orange* and a bit later, *Sacher Torte* along with similarly great quantities of vintage wine. Wolford howled with delight. *(And we pay him, too.)* Our new associates are now, in the wolverine's words, signed, sealed and gainfully employed.

Dinner, or should I say the feast, had several effects. First, I won't eat again for a week.

Second, the Colonel Where-Frau Schuylkill Mutual Interest Index has risen a few hundred points. *("She can cook and fly, too? My Gosh!!" Little does the Colonel know she is also a crack markswolf.)*

As dinner slowed to a sluggish halt, I poured myself yet another glass of fermented coconut milk VSOP, left the room, and looked up the cell phone numbers of Professor Roberto Rabbito and his assistant, Harrison Hare. The professor is the head of the International Association for Genetic Research and the Chair for the Quadrennial Convention in Las Vegas. Harrison is the rabbit that does all the work. They had first met at the labs of the *Istituto Genetico Italiano*, where *Il Professore* was the ranking scientist, and Doctor Hare was an up-and-coming Cambridge professional on sabbatical.

I reached Harrison first. "Maury, my favorite test animal. Long time, no talk. When are you going to let me enhance your DNA, old boy?"

"When that proverbial snowball survives in hell, Harrison. Speaking of which, how the hell are you?"

"Running my cottontail off, is how I am. I'm out here in Las Vegas with the professor preparing for the convention and keeping things from spinning off into space. You know how these scientific conventions are. Every speaker is a Prima Donna. I've had requests for everything from a thousand laptop computers so every attendee could work along on an interactive experiment to housing for a school of marlins. I almost had the second one solved until I discovered the aquacade pool at the hotel was already taken over by a troupe of swimming bears."

"That's exactly what I wanted to talk to you about, Harrison.'

"What, housing a bunch of marlins? They're touchy creatures. That sharp bill will give you a nasty stab."

"No, the swimming bears – the *Aquabears*. It's a complicated story, but they have a long standing connection to Octavius and when we discovered that they had been signed on as the closing evening's entertainment, we were a bit surprised."

"So was I," replied the hare.

"You mean you didn't book them? I thought you were handling the whole works."

"*WE'RE* handling the whole works, Maury, *WE*. This one was Roberto's doing, and it took me completely unawares. When I asked him about it, he murmured something about an offer he couldn't refuse and changed the subject."

"Ouch! I guess I'd better talk directly with him, then. I have a call in to him, but I got his voice mail."

"Next time I see him, I'll ask him to call you. Is it important?"

"It seems to be getting more important as we talk," I replied

"Ok, I'll get on him, but you know *Il Professore* – absent-minded raised to the power of n. By the way, how about your boss? I haven't heard a word about his keynote address. Please don't tell me he's going to have a hundred visual aids and marching bands."

"Nope! He'll be ready. I'm on it. Sorry, just another outing for Boring Bear. No frills. No thrills."

"Well, one can always hope. Cheers, my friend."

"So long, Harrison." I hung up the phone and scratched my adorable little nose. Something didn't smell right here *(and it wasn't Wolford)*.

Chapter Nineteen

Let us turn our attention to Geese.

Oh, if only their honking would cease!

No one likes them, I guess,

For they make quite a mess

Every time their full insides release.

I reported to Octavius on my call with Harrison Hare and he shares my concern about the mysterious sponsor. We didn't mention it to Bruce. Not until I hear from *Il Professore* Roberto Rabbito, if ever.

Ostensibly going into the kitchen to congratulate her on the excellent meal, the Great Bear spoke to the Frau about the disintegrated sapphire. Mortified that she had been found eavesdropping, but reverting to her basic stalwart character, she swore on the souls of all her Helvetic ancestors that not a growl about the subject would come from her lips to anyone...not anyone! She also punctuated her oath of fealty with a series of well- chosen comments on the nature, character and family tree of that "verdammte Duck."

The phone rang and as I picked it up, a sharp voice snapped, "This is General Turmoil. Let me speak to Octavius Bear."

"Just a moment, General. I'll get him for you!" I skittered out to the kitchen, arriving just as the bear and the she-wolf were concluding their little conference.

"Octavius, phone call for you. It's General Turmoil!"

The Great Bear winced and shrugged his shoulders. "Nothing good can come from this," he snorted and lumbered into his office, shutting the door behind him.

General Turmoil is the chief of a super-secret government organization that is very seldom acknowledged as existing at all. When it is mentioned, it is referred to simply as the Business. The Business's business is an assortment of spying, clandestine exercises, and influencing governments, corporations, universities, research facilities, and important individuals. Octavius qualifies as a Business focus on several counts.

I looked at the Frau, and she looked back. Silently, we raised the receiver on the kitchen phone and listened in. If Octavius caught on, he would have me skinned and then force the Frau to cook me. What the hell! What self-respecting sidekick could resist eavesdropping on the boss especially when he's talking or more likely, listening to General Turmoil?

"You are registered as having made use of our Background Checking unit today."

If the glacially calm tone of his voice was any indication, Octavius was obviously trying to contain himself. "That is correct, General. As I understand it, I have unrestricted access to the Business's support services. That hasn't changed, has it? Your staff, as usual, were most gracious, efficient ,and effective."

"No, you still have all the privileges granted you by my predecessor, although I sometimes wonder why. You're a bit too free-wheeling for my taste, Dr. Bear!"

I almost choked. Here clearly was a textbook case of a pot calling a kettle achromatic.

The Bear continued to hold his temper. "What can I do for you, General?"

"No, it's what I can do for you. I gather you just employed a Colonel Wyatt Where."

"Yes, I did. With the approval of your Background Checking Department, I might add. Was there something faulty with their information?" *(The bear couldn't resist taking a dig!)*

"The department's information is flawless…as far as it goes."

"Meaning…"

"Meaning, I happen to have personal information about Wyatt Where that has never been recorded. Information you should probably be aware of."

"I'm waiting…"

"Not over an open phone line, Bear. Call me back on our encrypted circuit. I'll be standing by."

A click on the end of the line, and then we heard Octavius hang up. The Frau and I carefully replaced the kitchen phone receiver and waited to see if Octavius knew that we had listened in. We'd know in a moment. No roar of my name or the Frau's. He was probably getting on the cryptophone. No way we were going to eavesdrop on that call. The wolf stared at me, and I stared back. She looked extremely concerned. Obviously, she was attracted to Wyatt, but this made her wonder. So what was it with Where? We might never know.

That was last night. Octavius never let us know he was on to us, so it may well be we pulled off our little spy job. Only we were now less informed than we were before.

This morning, Howard is over at the UUI lab with Bruce to bring back our particle beam projector along with other research material on lasers. He's a bit unsure why lasers suddenly are the subject of interest but the Great Bear assured him it was a protective measure and he wanted to have the projector on board the *Ursa Major* and fully functioning before we left tomorrow night for Las Vegas and the Quadrennial Genetics Conference.

Incidentally, I should tell you about this upcoming event. I will not subject you to the agenda for this learned conclave. While I absolutely eat up discussions on *"A general framework for statistical linkage analysis in univalent quintaploids"* or *"Exploring the evolution of calicolia compatibility types: A simulation approach,"* I realize you may not share my passion. All you really need to know is that the event starts on Sunday evening with a reception. Octavius delivers his keynote first thing Monday morning. Lots of learned papers, sub conferences, group meetings, and ducking out to play blackjack and the slot machines and watching the occasional show. The event ends on Tuesday evening with, as we now know, a buffet followed by entertainment in the Aquacade – starring the irrepressible Belinda Béarnaise and the *Aquabears*.

I should also tell you where this extravaganza is being held.

Most of you are familiar with the Vegas Strip. Wall-to-wall hotels conjure up every possible motif and exotic locale you can conceive of – and some you can't. Casinos squeezed in every likely and unlikely space. 24/7/365 slot machines with their buzzes, clatters, pings, brain-numbing music and occasional clinking coins. Restaurants and showbars and showbars and restaurants. All the buffets you can consume. Luxury shops, priced to take advantage of your temporarily unbalanced sense of monetary value. AND most recently, several major art collections at some of the more upscale hotels designed to create an aura of the good life in every dimension.

The Blue Bayou Hotel, Casino and Resort *(you can guess the motif)* at which the convention is being held is out of the way in several respects. It is on the opposite side of McCarran International Airport from the fabulous Strip. This has several advantages for us and the convention planners. One: it is closer to the general aviation facilities at McCarran, and we can slip the C-5A in and out without being observed by too many members of the populace. *(In fact, you could land a space ship at McCarran, and no one would take special notice or care except perhaps, a veteran and bored air traffic controller, who has already seen and heard everything that can go aloft.)*

Secondly, from a crowd control standpoint, it's a little more difficult to get out and around Las Vegas from this hotel. What happens at the Blue Bayou, stays at the Blue Bayou! Playing hooky over on the Strip takes more than a casual effort. *(At least a cab ride!)* The hotel can hold several thousand animals. But there'll only be about a thousand at the convention. It has a couple of casinos and a number of ballrooms, but it also has an outdoor Blue Bayou Aquacade Stadium. Here, I have come to conclude, is where the *Aquabears* will be performing Tuesday night and are probably rehearsing right now.

There is one other thing about the Blue Bayou that has set my larcenous whiskers to quivering. Earlier this year, after *Monsieur Le President Foie Gras* and half the cabinet of France *(all geese, as you might guess)* had an absolutely disastrous night playing baccarat at the casino *(they didn't understand the rules),* some arrangements had to be made to pay their debts and preserve their nation's honor. A compromise was worked out and as full payment, those historic treasures, The Bayeux Tapestries, were transferred from their French coastal preserve to a specially designed room at the hotel. The Blue Bayou's Hall of the Bayeux. *Quelle finesse et elegance!* Needless to say, a few French *enfants de la patrie* were a trifle annoyed at the highhanded transfer of their patrimony and the restoration of the guillotine was proposed in the Senate. Or at least a Paris-wide gourmet banquet featuring *goose a l'orange*! Unfortunately, a jury of disinterested parties could not be assembled, and the matter went into suspended animation.

Now, here's what is tickling my antennae. If, and it's a big if, Imperius Drake is planning an embarrassing sequel or a series of sequels for Octavius after the Loupe disaster, wouldn't the theft *(or worse yet, the destruction)* of the Bayeux tapestries during the convention be typical of his warped imagination? In one swell foop, he could upset the convention, embarrass the Bear and get back at the government of France for forcing him to leave Paris. But of course he has quite a few *objets d'art* to choose from. I guess any one of them would do, just as long as the Bear is in town to be humiliated by the event. You'll recall I said that the heist in Chicago may only have been an overture. You'll also recall that Octavius had agreed with me. He and I have to chat further.

As I worked my way over to the Roman Temple hangar to see how things were going with the invisible airplane, I ran into the Colonel, er, Wyatt.

"Maury, I've been meaning to speak with you," he said.

I stood at my best Meerkat attention. "Fire away, sir."

"First, I wanted to tell you what a great stroke of luck it's been meeting up with you folks and joining this team. That damn bank was driving me nuts, and that moose is a class A horse's ass. *(Interesting image!)* Second, that Frau Schuylkill is something else. I have never met a she-wolf like her. What a combination of beauty, grace, smarts and toughness! If you could put in a good word for me, I'd appreciate it."

"Honestly, Wyatt, I don't think any intervention on my part is necessary. You have the lady's attention." *(Oh, do you ever!)*

"Hey, that is good to know. Thanks a lot. Finally, can you brief me on this Black Quack Gang? First rule of warfare: Know your enemy."

"Sure," I said, and launched into the history of Imperius and his dire and dirty deeds. Since you are already aware of all this or can go back to Chapter Seven for a refresher, I won't bore you with the dialogue that followed.

Meanwhile, Octavius had settled himself down with a keg of mead to work on his speech. I had provided him with a draft, knowing full well he'd tear it to ribbons. One of the fun things about writing drafts for him is I include a lot of stuff that he himself has written for previous speeches. Those were always the first things he cut with marginal remarks like, "Maury, when are you going to learn to write a speech that sounds like me?" I never let him in on the game but he often wonders why I'm giggling to myself while I prepare the next draft.

While he was slashing and sloshing, Frau Schuylkill *(who was also working in the hangar at the same time – you tell me how she does it!)* padded into the room and said, "Pardon Herr Bear! Herr Porcupine and the Dancing Inspector are waiting for you in the laboratory."

The Great Bear grunted, "Thank you Frau Schuylkill. I guess I'd better join them. This speech is beginning to irritate me." *(Score one for the Meerkat!)* He pressed the button under his desk and the elevator platform took him and his massive chair down to the lower level.

The Inspector and Howard Watt were waiting for him.

Octavius roared, "Inspector, please be good enough to get into your restraint chair." Dr. Watt looked on in puzzlement.

"It's embarrassing, Ocko. Howard here will think I'm a right twerp."

"You recall our agreement. If you want to play, you must sit and stay."

"Like a ruddy obedience school. All right, I'm sitting."

"Good. You must learn to control your enthusiasm."

"Actually, Bruce," said the doctor, "I think such eagerness is wonderful. Everyone is so blasé these days. It's good to see someone who's all hopped up about his work."

"Be careful what you ask for, Doctor Watt," said Octavius. "My annual furniture and equipment repair bills would furnish a good-sized research center."

I arrived just in time to hear him ask, "Now about the particle beam projector. Have you had a chance to examine it?"

"Only briefly. Your lab staff seems to have done an excellent job. I'm not sure what you want me to do."

"What I want you to do, Howard, is determine how finely we can tune the device. Can it discriminate between subtly different elements and ignore all the others as it cuts and disintegrates? Can it be used to stimulate a reaction in the target? This projector was planned to be so refined in its technology and application that it would make an ordinary laser look like a searchlight. Have we succeeded?"

"I don't know but I'll damn sure find out. When do you want my results?"

"First thing tomorrow morning!"

Doctor Howard Watt had just discovered that working for Octavius Bear was not going to be all goulash and sacher tortes.

Octavius signaled to Bruce and me to meet him up in the den as he re-ascended to his desk. The Wallaroo arrived before the Bear completed his elevation and sat on the edge of his desk. "What's up, Ocko? I don't understand what you're doing with the projector."

"What I'm trying to do without telling Dr. Watt about the disintegration of the sapphire, is determine how dangerous a weapon Imperius Drake has at his disposal. I am assuming, perhaps incorrectly, that with his accelerated brain power, he has been able to do as much if not more with his version of the projector as we have done with ours. He may not have the same fabrication facilities, but I don't want to bet on it. So, if Howard can give me an analysis of our gun's capabilities, I will have a better idea of the Duck's destructive options."

"As usual, Ocko, you don't just think outside the box. You think outside the box that the box came in."

"Thank you, Inspector, I think. Why don't you call your friends in the Chicago Police and see if they have anything new to tell us. I hope our secret is still intact. If the Duck still thinks we're doing cartwheels *(Try that one on! Octavius doing a cartwheel)* trying to figure out how he opened the case, maybe we can lull him into thinking he's completely outsmarted us."

"Well," said Bruce, "he has done a right smashing job of it so far. What do you think his next move is going to be?"

"I'm not sure, but I have this feeling and so does Maury that whatever happens next, it's going to be connected to me and our trip to Las Vegas. But maybe my ego is just working overtime."

It's difficult to think about Bruce being diplomatic, but he constrained any comments about the Great Bear's ego. He reached for the phone on Octavius' desk and rang through for Captain Daley in Chicago.

"Captain, Inspector Wallaroo, here! Fine, fine, we're all fine! Any news on our friend? You do? Just a second. I'm here with Octavius Bear and Maury. Can I put you on the speakerphone. Good. Hold on!"

Captain Daley's voice echoed over the line. "Greetings, Octavius, good to talk to you again. One of these days you'll have to bring that massive frame of yours back up here to Chicago and we'll have a real get together. Hello, Maury! But enough small talk. First, we were able to track the Duck to a marina here on the lake. He and his cohorts were seen carrying what looked like a large tube and rushing to get on a hydroplane. Then he plowed off northward in a heavy storm before we had a chance to call the Coast Guard or send up a helicopter. We've lost track of him for the moment, but we're checking tapes of satellite photos to see if we can spot his course and destination. With all the cloud cover, that may be impossible. If they survived, they probably hid out until dark. We'll be back to you as soon as we have any more news."

"Thank you, Captain. I'm willing to bet they survive. If nothing else, that cat has a reserve of lives she hasn't used up yet. Please call when you get anything." said the Bear and pressed the off key.

"Well, Ocko, that kicks a hole in your theory. I know where Las Vegas is, and it isn't north of Chicago."

"I know, Inspector, I know. Damn that Duck."

Chapter Twenty

Please be careful when near Porcupine.

He can look like he's rather benign.

But when he's upset,

In response to a threat,

He'll run backwards and plunge in a spine.

Down in the lab, Howard pushed, pulled and hauled the gun onto a test table. (*In spite of Octavius' objections, let's call it "the gun." He says it's an instrument for progress, not a weapon. Oddly enough, many instruments for progress have been weapons. But I digress. Portable endoatmospheric particle beam projector is just too long to keep repeating and PEPBP is unpronounceable. So, "the gun" it is and let the particles fall where they may.*)

To preserve the charge in the power pack, he hooked it up to a conventional power source. That in itself was remarkable. This thing could punch holes in targets with cosmic force and pin point accuracy, but it developed its clout through a power conversion pack the size of a small book. By itself, that was a major scientific breakthrough.

Add to that, the microscopic accuracy and the user's ability to expand or contract the diameter of the resulting fissure from a kilometer to an angstrom and the potential uses became mind-boggling. At least Howard's mind was boggled, an event that seldom happened. The aiming system and target control were phenomenal.

Now, on top of all that, the whole thing weighed about 7 kilograms (15 pounds). A bit heavy for animals his size, but the wolves could certainly handle it and Octavius could juggle with it.

But Octavius and the rest of the UUI team knew all that. What he wanted to know and what the UUI team had yet to test was what radiation effects a jolt from the gun could set off. He also wanted to know if the beam could hit a target after passing through transparent media. It began to dawn on the porcupine: Octavius thinks the jewel may have been disintegrated by firing the gun from *outside* the case. The sapphire wasn't stolen! It was destroyed! But why? And why was Octavius being so secretive? Not his concern for the moment!

Now Howard had to compress months of precision test and measurement into about ten hours to give the Great Bear at least some rough estimates. Talk about being tested under fire! But what the hell, he'd spent his entire academic life pulling all-nighters. Here we go again.

He had brought over a target "box" used at the UUI lab. If Octavius hadn't wanted to mount this thing on the *Ursa Major* later in the morning, it might have been easier to do these tests in the UUI labs. But Howard also had an inkling that the Great Bear didn't want the results of these tests getting around until he personally was ready to release them. Secrets, secrets!

The target box was made of transparent alloy. The same stuff used on the cases in the Loupe Museum? An airtight coupling allowed the gun's muzzle to be inserted, and then the box could be pumped out to form a vacuum. A wide range of sensors could log heat, impact, penetration depth and time and progressive strength of the burst, in addition to recording the actual event in three dimensions.

Unfortunately, the results Howard and Octavius were looking for also strongly depended on the nature of the target. The porcupine had connected a set of Geiger counters and other radiation measurement devices to the sensor array inside the box.

Now came the grunt work! Testing a broad range of target elements for radiation. He had to separate the direct effects of the gun's "blast" from any secondary emissions from the target. Strength and Timing! Strength and Timing! Octavius had made it a bit easier. One of the tests he wanted to make was to determine whether a shot at a sapphire could have produced the burns that triggered the peacock's death. He had shared his suspicions earlier in the evening with Wyatt and himself.

But first he needed to establish some baselines. Brick – Pierced like butter but no secondary radiation. Steel – a minor resulting burst, but extremely short life and no impact to speak of. Titanium and Molybdenum, ditto. A piece of the alloy used on the box and the museum cases was treated as if it wasn't there. Now, that was interesting! Glass as well! So it looked like Octavius' theory worked. The beam could have been shot unimpeded through the skylight and through the alloy case and obliterated the sapphire.

But...what happened when the sapphire was struck? Especially a humungous sapphire like the Deep Blue. Well, that test subject wasn't available, but Octavius had given him a decorative award necklace from some Eastern European country that was covered with a wild mélange of precious, semi-precious, and not-so-precious stones.

"Wore it once. Damn thing looks ridiculous, and it's too small. Almost choked me. Take it and destroy it to your heart's content. Only thing it's useful for!"

Howard had pried sample jewels out of the baroque horror and one after another ran them through the firing line. He adjusted the size of the beam from an angstrom to a hair to a finger width. He drilled holes so small they required a high-powered microscope to be seen. He disintegrated entire gems with one shot.

Some of the jewels showed little or no radioactive response. Opals just cracked and collapsed. A ruby emitted a substantial flash that excited the sensors and meters. Same with an emerald. About half of the test stones were fakes and just shattered or disappeared. Howard didn't have the heart to tell

188

Octavius his very expensive honorary necklace was a fraud. The gold may also have been gold plate. Probably all the country awarding it could afford.

A faceted diamond *(small)* set the meters off in ecstatic chattering. OK, let's try a sapphire. Nothing! Wait a second! That was a fake made of glass! Let's find a real one. Where, where, where? He came up with several, but they weren't blue. The color might make a difference. Let's see! Yellow, green, pink, ah, blue!

This time the meters went off the scale. He tried several colors. Sapphires came in a rainbow array. Chatter, chatter, chatter! There seemed to be some difference between faceted and unfaceted stones. Refraction perhaps! But essentially the radiation results were all in the same range. Diamonds and Sapphires! Did size matter? You betcha! The bigger the stone, the bigger the belt. Success!!

In the underground lab, Howard couldn't tell that the sun had already risen. He checked his watch. 7:30 AM! One more thing to do! Computer-simulate the impact of a shot to a 372 carat flawless sapphire and calculate the strength, duration, distance and pattern of the resulting radiation. Could it kill a peacock on the spot?

It was 10:00 AM as Howard spilled out the results of his calculations from the lab's computers into a memory card. He rubbed his eyes and nose. He had checked and rechecked. The dose was lethal and then some, and it could cover an immense distance in a radial pattern.

Octavius needed to know, pronto!

Chapter Twenty One

Tiger has an exotic repute.

And her cubs are exceedingly cute.

In a poem or commercial,

She's not controversial.

In person, she's really a brute.

Meanwhile back in Pondscum, a peculiar incident occurred on Friday. One of the work crew decided that these eggs would be cute things to give away at Christmas. So he decided to swipe a few. The cheetah and her foreman, an extremely unpleasant looking Baboon, descended on the culprit.

"Excuse me, Flat Tail, I believe you have purloined some of our property."

The beaver sputtered and tried to act innocent, but it wasn't working. Finally he shrugged his shoulders and said, "I was only doing a little early Christmas shopping."

They walked him over to the tool crib where he had hidden his stash and forced him to give back his supply of "music eggs." Then they got the four beaver foremen and ran a complete physical inventory on the raw material, work-in-process, and finished products and would not allow anyone to leave until they had tallied everything. When it was all done, they sent everyone home to a late dinner, shut down the production lines, and closed off the doors to the one-time bowling arena.

At about 3:00 on Saturday morning, a snoozing citizen awoke to the sound of truck engines but thinking nothing of it, rolled over in his dam and went back to sleep. At 8:00 AM when the crews showed up for what they thought would be their last day of work, the building was locked, the lights were off, the parking lot was empty, and there was no one in sight. From inside the building came the loud and persistent sound of a maniacal Duck. QUACK, QUACK, QUACK! The Black Quack gang had struck again, leaving town and taking their little white eggs with them without paying the workers or settling up at the local motel.

Naturally the agitated beavers called the Michigan State Police, but some confusion arose when they tried to give them an accurate description of the culprits. Chita was identified as a tiger, jaguar, puma, and even a lioness by the near sighted bartender. The consensus was a tiger. Bigg Baboon likewise was depicted as everything from an orangutan to a yeti. But the real problem arose when they tried to describe the Duck. Since only a few townspeople had seen him *(her?)* at all, there was a sharp disagreement as to what they had seen. Some swore they had caught sight of an ominous-looking black duck and that it was perfectly huge *(for a duck)*. Others saw an attractive multi-colored bird with a crest and iridescent stripes. And it was small to average.

They described the plastic-egg music boxes they had been working on and the logo – *Genius of Genetics 2013*. It meant nothing to the local police.

They were reluctant to set off on a wild duck chase, but they did send out an all points bulletin for two trucks and three difficult-to-describe animals. Later in the day, two deserted trucks were found next to a runway on an abandoned Air Force base. The culprits had taken to the air, and the trail had gone cold. The Chicago police also picked up on the report and knew that once again the Duck was one waddle ahead of them.

Which he was! In the early hours of that morning, at an abandoned airstrip not far from Pondscum, a DC-3 had sat with its cargo door open, waiting for its next consignment. Nearby, an oversized SUV with chrome cattle horns on its hood sat idling. Inside were *(you guessed it)* the Taurus Brothers and two husky gorillas, ready to load the plane as soon as the Black Quackers arrived.

Four headlights bounced into view at the end of the runway as two trucks skidded along the grass next to the tarmac. Bigg was driving the first truck with Imperius riding shotgun. Chita had the second. "Why the hell can't we drive on the runway?" She thought. "Is Bigg just too stupid, or is Imperius giving cockeyed directions as usual? And, oh God, where did they resurrect that crate from?" She stared at the DC-3 as it began to appear in their headlights. "We're going to Vegas in that thing? Talk about pushing your luck!"

They pulled up to the SUV and got out. The gorillas leapt out of the Taurusmobile and proceeded to maneuver the trucks next to the plane's cargo bay. They unlatched the truck doors and began to jostle the crates out onto a loading ramp.

Imperius went ballistic. "Be careful, you fools! There are very delicate instruments in those boxes."

One of the gorillas turned and said, "Sorry, but there are no 'Fragile' markings on the crates."

"We didn't have time," screamed the Duck. "We took too long loading the trucks ourselves, and Bigg got lost twice on the way up here." Turning to one of the Taurus Brothers, he hissed, "Is that the best aircraft you could find for us?"

"It's a very reliable plane, Doctor Drake! Not the fastest, I'll admit, but one of the very best in the 'No questions asked' department."

"What's the range of this airplane?" asked Chita.

"Fully loaded, about twenty-five hundred miles," said a raspy voice.

Two scraggly looking coyotes came walking over from inspecting the airplane. "Here are your pilot and co-pilot, Burt and Ernie," said Brutus. "Best in the business! Both veterans of the Great War." What they didn't tell the Duck was that Burt had served as a mess Sergeant and Ernie had been an MP.

"And what's the flying distance from here to Las Vegas?" Chita again.

"Two thousand and fifty!"

"Isn't that cutting it a bit fine?"

"Nah, we'll have fuel to spare. Besides, we don't want to make stops and let more animals see us."

Imperius shouted, "That's enough, Cat! We will arrive intact."

Chita spat back, "Oh sure, you can always open the door and fly away. What about us wingless heavyweights?"

He ignored her. He turned to Belial. "Are things taken care of at the other end?"

"Two trucks will be waiting. This time they're rented. By a pair of sheep from Las Vegas. They run a soup mission for down and outers and do things for us to raise a little more cash on the side. The trucks are legit. There will be handlers there to unload for you. The airport operator is a good friend. We use him a lot for bringing in folks who really would rather not be recognized. We're just going to abandon these trucks here. It'll take the cops weeks to discover them. Nobody uses this abandoned field anymore."

The gorillas had gotten back in the SUV. Bigg had already clambered aboard the plane and buckled in. The Duck was doing some last minute negotiations with the Bulls. Chita stared around her, gave the plane another once over, and moved slowly toward the loading ramp. She sighed. "Oh, what the hell! I wasn't doing anything important, anyway."

Imperius flew in through an open cockpit window, almost decapitating Burt. "I'll sit up here with you and help navigate."

"Suit yourself! Just don't touch anything!"

The engines started up after several tries, billowing smoke out of the exhaust stacks. The ship vibrated as the pilot ran the engines up and down and checked the magnetos and propeller pitch. "OK," yelled Ernie, setting the radios, altimeter and navigation instruments "We're good to go!" They turned the tail-dragger 180 degrees facing down the runway and if they were lucky, into the wind. They released the brakes, the engines whined at full pitch, the sound of flaps descending for takeoff shook the interior, and slowly, slowly they lumbered into the night sky. Imperius had waddled quickly back into the fuselage somewhere between the brake release and the flaps release and hid his head under his wing. *Viva Las Vegas!!*

Hours later, Chita paced up and down the fuselage, convincing herself that this was her last involvement with the demon Duck. Enough was enough! The only reason she didn't just split immediately was her curiosity. *(Which has been known to kill many a cat!)* What the hell was going on in the warped depths of his hyped-up mind? In one way, mad geniuses could be fascinating, but in this case the fascination had worn off long ago. From here on, she'd just wait for the movie version to come out.

The irony of it all was that Imperius hated to fly – in airplanes or any other form of airborne vehicle. He wouldn't go near a helicopter. And even on transcontinental jets, he had to be sedated. He could perform major aerobatic stunts and cover immense distances flying under his own power, but put him in an aerial conveyance and he fell apart. Right now, he was seated, staring glassy-eyed at nothing. Chita stopped pacing and peered out the one small window in the cargo hold. Desert, nothing but desert. Reminded her of Africa.

Suddenly the sound of the engines changed, and the plane's speed reduced. They were either in trouble, or they were getting ready to land. If this was truly Las Vegas, the oddsmakers could probably set crashing versus landing at even money. Consoling!

Swiveling through a very disconcerting desert crosswind, they bounced to a stop at a small general aviation airport somewhere outside of the city. After waking up Bigg and assuring Imperius that they were indeed on the

194

ground, she slid down the tail-dragger's cargo skids and helped a member of the ground staff open the door.

They proceeded to unload the nondescript crates from the nondescript plane into two equally nondescript trucks and prepared to move off to a remote and nondescript warehouse. Chita was definitely getting sick of nondescript, especially bowling alleys and warehouses. A few bright lights, music, and drinks would be nice. Bigg had gone looking for slot machines in the airport "terminal" the minute he scrambled off the plane. He found them and had to be dragged back to help in the unloading.

Back at the plane, as the crates filled with little white boxes were being loaded into the trucks, Imperius, in his Mandarin guise, looked sternly at the two of them and said, "We will have to remain under cover out here. No one is to know we have arrived until Monday. Then we will appear to an amazed world and show them the true might of the invincible Duck."

"We can't even go out in disguise?"

"Not even in disguise. Nothing, absolutely nothing must cause even the slightest perturbation in the Great Plan."

"When are you going to let us in on the Great Plan, Sire?"

"Soon, Baboon, soon! Meanwhile, count the boxes!"

Chita wasn't sure whether it was the high desert temperature or her current state of simmering anger, but she was definitely getting very hot under her diamond-studded collar. "Imperius," she hissed, "this plan had better be a doozey, or you may find yourself in Duck Soup."

"We are not amused, Cat," the Duck shot back and waddled off to the air-conditioned cab of one of the trucks.

They left the airport, bumping along sandy back roads and arroyos. Bigg was driving one truck. Chita the other, and Imperius was giving

195

directions as only Imperius could. Last minute turns and missed crossroads. Finally, they came to a large, but not too well-kept warehouse. The Duck opened the door with an electronic remote, and after rolling in and giving the place a quick inspection *(Chita was not impressed!),* they set about putting things in their place and stacking up one thousand boxed white eggs inside the air-conditioned warehouse. "They must not be left outside in the heat!!" This from Imperius.

"Now," intoned the Duck in his most ominous voice, "for the first part of the Grand Plan!"

"At last," thought Chita, "let's hear what the world's craziest bird has in mind!"

"We shall create a diversion."

"Isn't that what we did in Chicago, Duck?"

"Yes, Cat, but now we are closer to our true target, and the final hours of our waiting are almost over. We must put the minions of Law and Order off the scent, to say nothing of that odious bear and his fawning entourage."

"Geez, Duck…!"

"Geez, Sire!!"

"Just get on with it, will you." Chita looked over at Bigg, who was no doubt enthralled by it all, even if he didn't understand a thing that was going on. "What are we going to do?"

"Not we, Cat! You! You and the Baboon are going to steal a priceless artifact from the Golden Pagoda, one of the most opulent casinos in this god-forsaken city of sin. This time it will be a real theft. While you are creating a major disturbance, Cat, our simian friend here will make off with this *objet d'art*, run down the street to the *Aspergio Casino* and with great fanfare, dump it in the pool.

Cheetah almost choked. "Dump it in the pool? Are you crazy, Duck? What's the point of that little caper?"

"That is exactly the question I want all of our opponents to be asking themselves, Cat. Confusion! Senseless vandalism! What is the true meaning? Who did it? Why? What else did they do? Was this real or a cover up for something worse? Do you not see the beauty of it all? They will be checking their vaults and gaming tables all over this town, shutting down their ridiculous art collections, checking on their guests, running the police and security ragged, while we are free to develop and polish our Armageddon at leisure, undisturbed and unsuspected."

"Do I get to use the ray gun, Sire?"

"No, Baboon, you do not. Now, listen! On late Monday evening you two will go to the Golden Pagoda Resort owned by the fabulous Oriental billionaire, Win-Win. He has, in a carefully guarded room a collection of invaluable jade sculptures that he only permits special guests and exceptional high rollers to see. You two will be exceptional high rollers. One as a black panther, the other as a heavily robed Arabian something."

"Can I be the panther, sire?"

Imperius sighed. "No, I think not Baboon. Your tail isn't long enough. You, Cat, will create a disturbance. Someone has stolen your purse with your winnings! You, Baboon, will make off with a major antique, climbing over the walls and ceilings, hiding it under your flowing robes."

"Which one do I take?"

"I don't care. Just make sure it looks valuable. The cat will disappear and get rid of her panther costume. Then she'll go back to the gambling tables or have a drink in the bar. You, Bigg, will not lose your costume until you have dumped the statue. Then both of you sneak off and return here as soon as you can...but not together! You can work out the details. I deal in strategy, not low-level tactics."

"Duck, your brains have sprung a serious leak. That serum you take has finally pushed you over the edge. I've heard of ridiculous stunts but this one…"

"This one will succeed, Cat. If it does not, the fault will be entirely yours, and as you know, for Imperius Duck, failure is not an option! Now go and plan! You, too Baboon!"

Then Imperius did something even more peculiar. He waddled over to a long padded box and took out his particle beam projector, duck-handling it clumsily with his wings and feet. Then he set it up at one end of the warehouse. Waddling away, he took a set of small targets and set them up at the other end about 100 feet away.

Bigg walked over to Imperius, expecting to be given some kind of assignment. Firing the "ray gun" was his job. The Emperor had said he had done it very well. "What do you want me to do, Sire," he asked.

"Nothing, Baboon! Wait, perhaps you can reset the targets for us or replace the ones we hit."

"You're going to fire the ray gun?" said Bigg in disbelief.

"That should be apparent, Baboon."

"But, Sire, that's my job!"

"And so it shall continue to be, Baboon, but on one very special occasion, we are reserving to ourselves the privilege of applying the *coup de grace* to that unbearable Bear."

Chita's head snapped up. Had she heard right? Was Imperius planning to murder Octavius Bear? "He really is nuts," she thought.

"Are you planning to kill off the Bear?" she barked.

"Oh, much worse than that, my dear Cat, much worse than that."

"Look, Imperius."

"Sire!!!"

"Whatever! We already have a dead curator on our paws and claws. If you destroy Octavius Bear, you will bring law enforcement, the military and even other gangs down on our heads so fast we'll never survive. Are you trying to kill us all off, too?" howled the cat.

"All of that will be of no consequence when the Grand Plan is unfolded. Revenge…revenge is what counts, and our revenge will be sweet indeed. Now, let us get to our target practice. Bigg, help us place these grips on the ends of our wings."

Chita paced back and forth, getting more concerned with each step. "I'm sure this is a disaster of cosmic proportions but I don't know what he's going to do.

"So I don't know what I should do. Damn that Duck! I'll have to wait until his ego finally overflows and lets us in on the final secret. If it does!!!

"In Chicago, he didn't tell me what was really supposed to happen until it was all over and we were drying out in Michigan. Bigg is no help. He knows less than I do and he'd follow Imperius into an erupting volcano. This whole diversion thing is absolute madness. I've got to get to the bottom of this. Those eggs! They're important. What's that logo say? 'The Genius of Genetics' OK, that's a start. Somewhere in this town, there's something going on that's related to genetics. Let's talk to the Chamber of Commerce."

She pulled out her cell phone just as Imperius fired off the first bolt of the "ray gun," missing the target badly. "We're in for a long haul," thought the cat.

Moving outside to get away from the noise, she dialed the Chamber of Commerce and said, "Hello, this is Doctor Catt. I'm searching for a genetics conference that is supposed to take place in Las Vegas next week. Can you help me? The Blue Bayou Hotel, Casino and Resort? How long does it run? Sunday night through Tuesday evening. Can you tell me anything more about it? One thousand attendees. What's the theme? *"The Genius of Genetics."* Swell. Where is the Blue Bayou? Uh, huh, got it. Thank you so much." Contact!!

That explained the number of eggs and the logos. Chita needed to think this through. She also needed to get over to the Blue Bayou regardless of what the Duck said. "But first things first. Let's take another look at those eggs. What the hell are they supposed to do? If they're a disposable version of the Black Quack egg, they could certainly create chaos. One thousand eggs quacking in unison at an unbearable volume in one of the general sessions could send a lot of people into shock or the loony bin. Is that what he has in mind? Humiliate the genetics society! Call them all 'quacks!' But what's the part about Octavius Bear? Why does the Duck need the ray gun? No, there's more to it than just a bunch of noisy eggs. But I don't know what it is!"

She walked back into the warehouse. Imperius' aim was improving rapidly, and Bigg was beside himself in fawning adulation. "You're a big game hunter now, Sire," he said.

"Exactly, Baboon, exactly! Make the targets smaller, say about the size of one of those eggs."

"Should I use one of the eggs, Sire?"

'No, you idiot! Under no circumstances touch those eggs until the hour has come. We will tell you when and how."

"What about 'why,' Duck," said Chita. "What is this all about?"

"Curiosity, my dear, killed the cat. Let that be your watchword. Do not strive to know what you shouldn't."

200

Imperius couldn't have picked any stronger words to motivate Chita. "Don't you give me that high-and-mighty stuff, you fruitcake," she murmured to herself. "This is one cat you're not going to kill, and if I have anything to do about it, you're not going to snuff Octavius Bear either and have us hounded forever." But was the Bear even here? She had to get over to the Blue Bayou and sniff things out. "Now, Baboon," shouted the Duck in triumph, "We shall see how our aim improves when I take the enhancing serum. If a lowly Mandarin can run up a score like that, think what Imperius Drake, the scourge of the universe will be able to do."

With that he headed off to the rear of the warehouse where he had arranged for their living quarters, food, drink, and facilities to be installed. He was about to take the serum and did not like his associates to witness the transition in either direction. He slobbered a bit and said things like, "You're deshpicable!" and "Mine, mine, all mine!" as he progressed through various stages of becoming a black canard.

Taking advantage of his absence, Chita walked over to one of the egg boxes, and making sure Bigg was looking elsewhere, took it out. Smaller than the Black Quack. Lighter too. No attempt to make it seamless like the black one. And the LED face and buttons. What did they do? Holding her breath, she pressed first one button – "*O Sole Mio*" – then the other – the music stopped. But that's all. The LEDs didn't change. The egg remained inert. Something was wrong here. Imperius Drake would not have spent all that time, money, and energy to produce little Italian music boxes. These things had to have some other purpose, but the buttons just played that corny music. Or..or..or, something else was needed to activate them. Some kind of signal. Not the ray gun. You'd have to hit each egg separately, and you might demolish them in the process. Something else, something else. "What?" she howled out loud.

"What what?" said Bigg.

"What's for dinner?"

"I'll go look," he said, leaving Chita to hatch her plan on getting over to the Blue Bayou. Tomorrow. The conference will start in the late afternoon. She'll disguise herself as Doctor Catt and go join the reception. Even if she didn't find anything out, she could use a couple of free drinks and *hors d'oeuvres*. Yeah, tomorrow!

Frau Schuylkill

Chapter Twenty Two

Watch the otters swim merrily by.

They can dive in the blink of an eye.

They all eat on their back,

Giving shellfish a crack.

Did you know there's a type that can fly?

Early Saturday afternoon, in deepest, darkest southern Ohio, preparations for the great migration to Las Vegas were proceeding apace. Zapping noises emanated from the lab as Doctor Watt put the particle beam projector through its final tests. Colonel Where was sitting with Frau Schuylkill, getting checked out in the C-5A flight simulator. As a thank-you from a grateful nation, the Air Force had also thrown in the simulator as part of the *Ursa Major* package. Wyatt and the Frau *(To this day, I don't know her first name.)* were getting on famously, performing high speed virtual dives and trying not to tear the virtual wings off the virtual *Ursa Major*.

"*Ach*, Herr Oberst, you are catching on very swiftly. Not every pilot can handle an aircraft this large."

"It's your instruction, Frau Schuylkill. I probably would have run out of concrete on that last takeoff if it wasn't for you. How long have you been flying the *Ursa Major*?

"Almost from the day it arrived, two years ago. Of course, much of that time has been in the simulator. But I have taken the airplane itself to the Arctic; coast to coast in the U.S. and over the Atlantic. And please, by your leave, I would consider it a great privilege if you would call me Ilsa."

"Well, fine, Frau, er, Ilsa, and please call me Wyatt."

"*Danke*, Wyatt! Tell me, do you miss the military?"

"Sometimes, but my last hitch as a mercenary didn't turn out very well, as I told you. No, on balance, I'm just as happy to be out of uniform. How about you?"

"Not really. Her Bear's adventures keep me busy, although as I told him the other day, I would like to do more detective work."

"I'll bet you're a real bloodhound when it comes to investigations. Sorry, I didn't mean that the way it came out."

"No offense taken, but I do think those dogs are overrated. I can sniff out a suspect faster than any of them. Besides, they're all descended from wolves anyway. Stick with the original is what I say. Have you ever done any detective work?"

"Actually, search and destroy is more my style. I guess you have to be able to find and zero in on your target, but it's a bit different than whodunit. Ever thought of changing jobs?"

"*Ach, nein*! I am devoted to Herr Bear *(not too much, Wyatt hoped.)* And besides where else could I live in a mansion, cook up all sorts of *fantastiche* meals and be in charge of an Air Force? I can fly an attack jet, a slow moving prop job, and just about the biggest airplane in the world. By the way, we'd better get back to the simulator. We are about to fly the biggest airplane in the world into the ground."

Laughs, tugs on the wheel, clicking switches, whining engines, descending flaps, whirring hydraulics, and the simulated giant righted itself a little too close to the ground for comfort. More laughs and sighs of relief.

Romance seemed to be blooming militarily and aerodynamically amid the throttles and altimeters.

We use the flight simulator for most Galaxy training, because actual flights are ruinously expensive. The engines are huge, as you might expect, and eat fuel like a starving SUV. The plane also scares the natives when it flies too low. But the C-5A Galaxy is one of the few aerial conveyances that can contain the Bear, his equipment and his entourage in one unit. Octavius doesn't mind flying. He just hates trying to get aboard most airplanes, and he can barely fit into the holds of the largest of freight helicopters. Forget about the F-15 Eagle jet fighter that Frau Schuylkill has used in some of our prior adventures. *(cf. Octavius Bear and the Revenge of the Sloth.)*. He couldn't fit in it under any circumstances.

Our light cargo plane, the Twin Otter is a pretty tight squeeze, too. Last year, Octavius got stuck in the door, and the whole event was right out of Winnie-the-Pooh *(in IMAX!)* Took several hours and spraying him with soap to get him back out. We widened the door. He does manage to make it into Belinda's SST, but only after they too, widened the door. And besides, I believe there's some special additional motivation there. *(Wink, Wink!!)*

So several times a year, we take out another home equity loan to pay for the fuel and launch the *Ursa Major* into the sky. This was going to be one of those occasions. However, I was taken aback when Octavius called for it to be equipped with maximum armament.

"Are we going to land at Las Vegas or attack it?" I asked.

"The weapons may be necessary." That was all he said.

Then – "Any word from Chicago?"

I would have shrugged my shoulders if I had any, but I reached for my phone and called Captain Daley.

"We have some news," he said, and I asked him to hold on while I put him on the squawkbox and yelled for Inspector Wallaroo to get in here as well.

"Hello, Captain," roared Octavius. He never seems to be able to use a speakerphone without shouting on the top of his formidable lungs. "You have something to tell us?"

"Not much, I'm afraid, Octavius. We did track the Duck's hydroplane up the eastern shore of Lake Michigan, through the Mackinac Straits to a dock near a small Michigan village called Pondscum."

"Pondscum?" blurted Bruce. "Is that a place or a disease?" *(This from a guy whose country has towns named Gympy, Bingara, Tibooburra and Grassy Head. Oh, well, to each his own.)*

Totally ignoring the Inspector, Octavius asked, "What could possibly be the attraction in Pondscum, Michigan? Frankly, I expected him to be off on an entirely different route."

"We don't know yet, and I didn't want to reveal too much to the Michigan State Police about the sapphire, so I'm having Lieutenant Daley fly up there in one of our choppers to interview the locals. He's on his way, and we should be hearing from him later today."

"Aside from jurisdiction, why are the Michigan State Police involved?" I asked the Captain.

"Not entirely sure but it sounds like the Black Quacks created some kind of ruckus up there. We'll get back to you."

"Stranger and stranger," said Octavius as I hung up the speakerphone. "Maury, Have we heard back from *Il Professore* yet? I'd like to get to the bottom of that Aquabear thing."

"He left a message on my voicemail saying he'd see you tomorrow after you arrived, and he'd tell you the story then. He sounded perfectly normal."

"Which for him means he's on the verge of a nervous breakdown. Not only is he an absentminded genius; he's an hysterical, egotistical genius. *(Thoughts of black pots and kettles flashed through my brain. I said nothing.)*

"He's the one who thought up this theme for the convention," he went on, "*The Genius of Genetics – 2013*. Most people think it refers to the scientific essence of genetics and its profound implications for life. *Il Professore* intended it to mean him. He's trying to promote himself for a Noble Prize. Speaking of Bel, I wonder how she is."

It is difficult to follow the leaps, jumps, and u-turns the Great Bear's mind takes. The best thing to do is to just hang on for the ride.

"Have you heard from her since her visit, Ocko?" asked Bruce.

"No, being coy is her natural state. Maybe I was supposed to call her." *(Octavius makes it a point to initiate as few calls as possible. I think it's an ego thing, but I'm not sure.)* "Anyway, we will no doubt see each other tomorrow at the reception. The Bearoness can never resist free drinks and a chance to show herself off to her adoring public. What's the word, Maury? She's a Prima??"

"Diva," I said, "and they come in two genders."

He looked at me crookedly, trying to determine whether I had just shot a zinger by him or not. He let it pass.

Just then, Doctor Watt came into the den with his quills all set at twelve o'clock high and said, "I'm ready to give you my report, Octavius. That device is truly amazing. Well beyond what I expected! It's almost miraculous." *(This from a down-to-earth porcupine whiz kid who thought he knew all there was to know about lasers and particle beams.)* "Please come down with me to the lab. I want to demonstrate a few things that you may not be aware of. I'm not even sure any of your research and engineering staffs at UUI know about some of the results I've gotten. I'd like to show it to Wyatt, too, if I may."

"Certainly! Maury, ask Frau Schuylkill to come along as well. As this situation progresses, she may also have a need-to-know. *(She already knew.)* Inspector, join us but only in your wheelchair."

Bruce did an especially hard bank off the side of Octavius' desk and bounded for the elevator to take him down to the lab level. I looked at Howard, and he looked at me. "I think I'll wait for the next car," we both said simultaneously. Octavius as usual sank down below on his personal chair lift.

Once Bruce was safely belted into his wheelchair and the two wolves had joined us, Doctor Watt turned to his test table and in his best physics lecturer mode began: "I realize that some of you have far more knowledge of lasers and particle beam weapons and their behavior than others. I will try to keep this as simple and yet as meaningful as possible. I'm going to explain this device in several ways; in terms of its power, its range, its precision, its flexibility, and its destructiveness. I'll also speak to its ease of use because although it is a bit heavy – Maury, I doubt you could handle it alone – it is amazingly light for what it can do, and it is simple to operate. Octavius, you and your staffs are to be congratulated. I also think that you should take major steps to protect this unit. This is no ordinary device, and in the wrong hands it would be lethal."

(Sucking in of breath all around, especially Wallaroo, the Bear, the Frau, and me!)

"Just how lethal, Doctor?" asked Octavius. "Its predecessor could pack quite a wallop. It could exceed the punch of a lightning strike."

"It's not just the punch, Octavius. It's all of the functions combined. Let's get one thing agreed on. As I'm sure Octavius knows, this device is not a laser. It is an endoatmospheric charged particle beam weapon."

"I'm glad you're keeping it simple, Doc," said Inspector Wallaroo.

"It was not intended as a weapon, Doctor," thundered the Bear. "It was intended to be used wherever precise excitation of protons and electrons could be of benefit – mining, construction, demolition, excavation. Imagine its use in faunapology to meticulously unearth long lost tombs of great animal rulers. It can be used to stop landslides and even avalanches. It can cut through the polar ice caps. It can intercept meteors and asteroids. It is an instrument for good."

"I didn't mean to impugn your motives, Doctor Bear," said the porcupine, "and I agree that the device has many beneficial uses, but the fact remains, it can be an engine of destruction."

Octavius shook his head, "I know, I know." Visions of the Loupe Museum were no doubt running through his brain.

"I assume you want this mounted on the *Ursa Major*," said Colonel Where. Frau Schuylkill looked over expectantly.

"No, Colonel," said the Bear, "I don't want to mount it on the *Ursa Major*, but I think we have to."

"At least you can console yourself that it's the only weapon of its kind," said the porcupine.

"No, Doctor Watt, I'm afraid I can't enjoy that consolation. I have serious reason to believe that the device used by Imperius Drake to destroy the Deep Blue is every bit as deadly as our own. Perhaps more so! And I have no doubt that given a chance, he will manufacture more to accelerate his goals of world domination. That is, after all, his ultimate goal. A master race of Ducks produced through chemically induced eugenics!"

World domination!? If someone had fired off the particle weapon at that moment, the effect on the scientist and the Colonel couldn't have been more stunning. They both looked totally dumbstruck…on two counts. For Octavius had also chosen that particular moment to have another of his narcoleptic fits and fell over in a deep sleep.

"Well, Meerkat," thought I, "you have a lot of explaining to do." And I set about giving a history lesson on Octavius' narcoleptic condition and his belief that it didn't exist. I followed this immediately with a recap of the story as we currently knew it, about the destruction of the sapphire and the Black Quack Gang's activities since. I also told them that the true Deep Blue story had been limited to them and high ranking members of the Chicago Police. Everyone else, especially the press, still believes it was a theft. We didn't want Imperius Drake to know that we knew that he knew how to demolish a gem like that sapphire. The more he thought we were still chasing our tails, the better.

At the conclusion of my cheerful tale, they were even more amazed. I got the impression that the Colonel was still just as eager to be part of our merry band, but it could be that the scientist was having second thoughts.

"Maury," said Octavius, "I thought I told you to brief our associates." He'd only been out for several minutes this time, but as usual he was oblivious of the lapse.

Doctor Watt jumped in, "Actually, I'd prefer to finish my analysis of the gun for you, Octavius. Maury can bring us up to speed later."

"Smoothly done, Howard," I thought. I could get to like this guy.

"All right, Howard, go ahead," rumbled the Great Bear, obviously not in one of his better moods.

"I think I can cut it short." Grateful looks all around. "The beam of particles can travel at or near the speed of light so it will reach its target almost instantaneously. Its destructive power is a function of the power supplied to it, and that is one of the truly amazing things about this…er, device. Somehow the UUI technicians have packed an immensely potent source of energy into the housing of the gun. I was astounded with my first tests."

"Another amazing thing I discovered is its precision and selectivity. It can lock onto and disintegrate a target three inches across at a distance of at least a thousand feet and ignore all other intervening and interfering obstacles. Incredible."

"Yeah, we know," I thought. "So long, Deep Blue Sapphire!"

"One last thing that really has me fascinated is something I discovered in response to your questions, Octavius and I'm not sure your people know this either. If the projector is set to a precise and sympathetic, I'll say 'frequency', (although that's not the exact term) of the target, it can agitate its atoms to a point where they in turn begin to radiate, in *all* directions, before the target itself disintegrates. In other words, you can set off a limited chain reaction. Jewels seem to be particularly susceptible."

Now, there was something to think about. Bruce, Octavius, and I stared at each other. The explanation of the peacock's death suddenly became very clear. He was in the wrong place at the wrong time when the sapphire was zapped. Killed by a limited chain reaction. Wow, this thing is a small scale doomsday machine, although I would never say that in front of Octavius. Especially since we now know Imperius Drake has a version of it in his possession.

"Thank you, Howard," said the Bear. "You have certainly changed my priorities. Now, our number one mission is to retrieve that weapon *(he actually used the term)* from that maniac Duck before he can use it again. I do not believe the killing of the curator was deliberate. It would have had to be too finely planned and executed. So far as I know, Imperius has never deliberately killed anyone in his long years of crime, but it would be a major mistake to assume that he won't. I wish I knew where he was."

My cell phone rang. *(Convenient, huh?)* Captain Daley. I glanced over at Octavius who looked like he needed a healthy swig of mead, and said, "It's the Chicago Police. Do you want to take it?"

"No," he said wearily. "Just get the facts."

212

I listened as the Captain briefed me. The Lieutenant had arrived at Pondscum and found the hydroplane Miss Lee-Li-Li docked by the lake. He also found the townspeople in a twitter. They told him about the three sharp no-good slickers *(descriptions vary)* who had run off without paying their bills or paying them for their work.

"Work," I exclaimed. "What work?"

It turns out they had the locals assembling little white eggs that seemed to be music players. They had taken them all with them when they sneaked away about 3:00 this morning. One of the citizens had heard the trucks. When they finally broke down the door of the old bowling alley they'd been working in, there was nothing there but a black egg quacking as loud as thunder. They sealed up the building again, but you can still hear the damned egg. The Lieutenant told them to put on earplugs and dump the egg in the lake. It might kill some of the fish but they couldn't think of anything else to do with it.

"Tell me some more about the eggs," I said.

"They were white, small, in little souvenir boxes and they had a strange logo on them – *The Genius of Genetics – 2013.*

"Thanks, Captain. If you hear any more, please let us know, and we'll keep you posted."

Bingo! We now knew where the Black Quack gang was headed.

A minute later the Captain called back again to say that the Michigan State Police had found two empty trucks left by a runway at an abandoned Air Force base.

And now, we also knew how they were getting there. I relayed all this to Octavius and the assemblage.

213

The Bear went into adrenalin overload. "All right! We still don't know what he's up to, but we have a damn good idea where he is. Frau, Colonel, how soon can we leave for Las Vegas?"

"The aircraft is fueled, prepped, and checked out for stealth operation. Just as soon as we mount the particle beam weapon, we're good to go."

"How long???"

"With Howard's help, in less than an hour."

"Get on it. Maury, Inspector, collect what you need for a few days' stay in Las Vegas. You too, Howard, unless you'd rather stay here. I assume the Colonel is going to fly shotgun with Frau Schuylkill."

Howard looked up from dismounting the particle beam from the test table and said, "I wouldn't miss this for the world."

I think I could really get to like this guy.

Forty-five minutes later, the ground crew was rolling back the ersatz Roman columns that adorned the hangar doors and the road crew was checking to see there were no obstructions on the Interstate By-Pass.

Octavius was seated in his converted cargo bin, and the rest of us were sitting on reasonably comfortable seats in the cavernous fuselage. The Colonel's Humvee along with several other ground vehicles had been brought aboard, and an assortment of weapons, supplies including mead and fermented coconut milk, communications and computing gear *(in addition to the vast array already on the C-5A)* were getting last minute tie-downs.

Frau Schuylkill came down from the overhead cockpit and did a last minute inspection of the interior. She stopped by Octavius and said, "Everything is in readiness, Herr Bear."

"Thanks, Frau Schuylkill. Ready when you are."

214

"*Danke*, Herr Bear." As she walked back to the cockpit I suddenly realized for the first time, that she was wearing a sheepskin flight jacket.

The ground crew began towing the aircraft out of the hangar and into a position where the back blast of the jet engines would not pulverize something or someone. As the engines whined into a roaring crescendo, a Teutonic voice came on over the loud speakers, echoing around the huge expanse. "This is your Captain speaking. We are now number one for take off. As soon as we are airborne we will take a southwest heading direct for Las Vegas. Our flying time will be close to three hours. Since we will be flying in stealth mode, we will need to avoid the military and commercial airlanes. If we must fly above the pressurization limits of the cabin, oxygen masks will drop from above your heads. Please adjust your mask before helping any children with theirs. *(Did she mean me??)* Although the oxygen bag may not seem full, it will be flowing. Now, please make sure your seat belts are securely fastened and your tray tables and seats are in the upright position. *Danke schoen* for flying with the *Ursine Luftwaffe*. We know you had a choice."

Chapter Twenty Three

Bunny Rabbits are cute, I suppose

With long ears and a twitchable nose.

But they propagate fast

And their families are vast.

Don't look now! But their numbers just rose.

We roared off the ersatz Interstate and took a sharp right turn over the Ohio River. A flock of birds shot past us as they fled for the safety of the woods. We headed off to the Southwest and the deserts of Nevada. The C-5A slowly climbed above the clouds and we watched the sun resetting its setting. I looked over at Howard, who was working away at his laptop computer, still calculating the performance characteristics of the ray gun. Occasionally, he would slap his paw on his head, narrowly avoiding being impaled on one of his own spines.

"What's up Howard?" I shouted over the roar of the engines. This was utilitarian transport, folks. No sound deadening and in spite of space heaters, it was damn cold, especially for a desert dweller like me.

He looked up from the screen and said, "The more I simulate the gun, the scarier it gets. I really want to do a whole series of additional tests once things settle down. But, I'll tell you, Maury. We want to get that other gun out of that crazy Duck's claws as soon as we can. I shudder to think what improvements he may have made to it."

I looked over at Octavius, but inside his converted cargo bin, he snoozed, shielded from outside disturbances.

Howard continued, "Is he really as threatening as you all make him out to be?"

"Oh yes, my dear Porcupine! He is super-intelligent and even more so when he takes that damn serum of his. But that's not the real problem. We've contended with super intellects before. Octavius is one as well, and the rest of us are not exactly dopes. It's the Duck's warped personality and total unpredictability that creates the real pain. Take this situation! Do we really know why he destroyed that sapphire? Plenty of speculation and guesses, but no certainty. It may be the prelude to a diabolically subtle plan to do something catastrophic, or he may have just gone off the deep end for good. After the fact, there are plenty of capers he's pulled off that we still don't fully understand. Plus he has those two helpers of his. One is beautiful, quick, intelligent, capricious, and dangerously self-centered. The other is as dumb as a rock, but immensely strong and willing to do anything the Duck says without a moment of hesitation or argument. Just by themselves, those two are a threat. Now on top of all that, you're telling us that gun is a weapon of mass destruction. You bet we have to get it away from Imperius and those other two, as well."

Howard went back to his computing, and I went back to my despondent musing. Once again the prospect of rejoining my Mauritius mob looked more and more attractive. But whom was I kidding? Even with their larcenous capers, those meerkats would have me crawling the walls of my den from sheer boredom. I adjusted my fedora and leaned back to see if I could take a quick nap.

I was awakened by a change of pitch in the engines. The *Ursa* took a sharp turn to the left, and as I skittered over to one of the cargo windows I could see desert and a spectacular display of lights off in the distance. Las Vegas, here we come.

The Frau's voice came over the loudspeakers, "*Achtung*, excuse me, Attention please! We are approaching Las Vegas. Please return your carry-on baggage to its stowed location, return to your seats and re-fasten your seat belts. Make sure your tray tables and seats are in the upright positions. We will be coming through the cabin to collect any glasses or other service items you may still have. Turn off all electronic devices until we are safely at the gate. Tonight, after we land, we will be taxiing to the general aviation freight area. We are still in stealth mode, so we may have to make sudden stops to avoid other traffic that can't see us. Thank you again for flying with us."

Octavius let out a bellowing snore and looked around. "Are we there yet?"

*****

Sunday Noon: The Presidential Suite of the Blue Bayou Hotel – Las Vegas.

I had just gotten back from church and went looking for the Great Bear. After I had wandered through several rooms of the suite where Octavius and I were staying, I found him down on all fours *(an unusual posture for him)*. I thought he might have had another narcoleptic episode, but he was wide awake.

"What are you doing down there, Octavius?"

"I lost a contact lens," he grumbled.

I had the distinct feeling that this was not going to be a pleasant Sunday afternoon. I got down with him and scrabbled around until I found it along with several dust bunnies. *(I must have a word with housekeeping!)* Watching a nine-foot Kodiak with paws the size of volleyballs trying to place a contact lens in his eye is a sight not to be missed. I once volunteered to help him, but after poking him in the eye and being tossed halfway across the room for my trouble, I decided to simply be an amused observer.

After several gyrations you would not believe a bear could make, he succeeded and settled himself down on the floor. There wasn't a chair in the room that could hold him. Fortunately the ceilings were twelve feet high, but he kept having near misses with the chandeliers.

218

"Can you believe that room service in this fleabag doesn't stock mead?" he roared.

For obvious reasons, Octavius doesn't like hotels. Octavius doesn't like conventions or crowds. Octavius hates giving speeches, and Imperius Drake had him in a real snit. We hadn't heard from *Il Professore Roberto* and on top of that, Belinda hadn't been in when he tried to contact her. Not the makings of a good day.

"I'll call over to the plane and have one of the crew bring over a couple of kegs of mead," I said.

He grunted in return.

When we had arrived late Saturday evening, after causing a minor sensation by appearing out of nowhere, Frau Schuylkill had parked the C-5A at the extreme end of the general aviation area of the airport, right next to the last airworthy SST, Belinda's Flying Aquabear. We dwarfed the Concorde, but since our plane was so difficult to see, most people wouldn't have noticed.

The Frau, the Colonel, and the rest of the crew were staying at a motel, just yards away from the flight line where they could jump into action within minutes. One of them always stayed on board the plane, monitoring communications. Some techniques we had borrowed from Air Force One, the U.S. President's jumbo jet. The aircraft was refueled. *(If we hit it big in one of the casinos, we might be able to pay for it.)* Everyone was on standby, but on standby for what, none of us knew.

Howard Watt and Bruce Wallaroo were sharing a suite next door, and as far as I could tell, were still asleep. We had spent a good part of the night unloading and setting up at the hotel.

Now, Octavius was all business. We had about a hundred things to do before the reception:

1. Get a hold of *Il Professore* ;
2. Contact the Security Manager of the Blue Bayou and the local Police Chief and warn them of the danger to the Bayeux Tapestries *(and other Las Vegas treasures);*
3. Check out the ballroom and do a quick speech rehearsal;
4. Find out Belinda's whereabouts;
5. But, most important, start a search for the Black Quack Gang.

As we were going down the list, Bruce and Howard came through the adjoining door of the two suites. Bruce seemed somewhat subdued, although he bounces even when he is dead tired. I wondered if Howard had some kind of calming influence on him. Maybe Bruce was afraid of getting stuck with a bunch of quills.

Anyway, assignments were handed out. Bruce was off to pick up the Black Quack's trail. Howard called over for the Colonel to join him, and they were going to go through the drill with the police and hotel security. Octavius reserved the search for Bel to himself. I had to work with Octavius on his speech and look for the professor. We still needed to know who had hired the *Aquabears*. If we were lucky, we might find *Il Professore Rabbito* down in the ballroom with Harrison Hare supervising the rehearsals.

Everyone left on their missions. The great Bear and I went out in search of the freight elevator that we had used to get up to the penthouse and descended to the Grand Ballroom. When the elevator doors opened, chaos ruled. The registration desks had just opened in the Grand Foyer; hotel staffs were moving displays and booths into the Convention Center downstairs, and early arrivals were schmoozing as they checked the agenda for the next two days and compared notes on their professional triumphs.

Octavius sent me over to get us registered, and he went directly into the ballroom looking for Hare and Rabbito. As I came back with our oversized name tags *(Mine dragged on the floor when I put it on; Nobody cares about the little guy)*. I spotted the Bear in heated conversation with Harrison Hare. No *Professore*!

Harrison wasn't quite sure where the distinguished rabbit had gone, but he was positive that little or no time would pass before he came back into the ballroom, having another one of his emotional outbursts about God knows what. Harrison asked the Bear to do a quick tech review of his speech. After frightening the current occupant off the stage with his sheer bulk, Octavius trundled over to the dais, leaned on it, and promptly crushed it. Harrison, the technical producer, the hotel banquet manager, and several other functionaries all went into cardiac arrest.

"Never mind, Doctor Bear," Harrison finally gasped, "We'll get a sturdier one. There's a horse and an elephant on the program as well. I knew that dais wouldn't make it." This last remark was directed at the technical producer who was literally going back to the drawing boards along with several of the house carpenters.

"Just let us test you on the mikes, and you can run through your remarks if you wish."

Octavius didn't wish, but he was sensible enough to know that the ballroom's sound system would take a terrible beating if he unexpectedly raised his voice. In fact, he didn't really need amplification even with an audience of a thousand. They hooked him up with a wireless microphone, and he practiced a few lines while roaming around the stage.

Fortunately, the Great Bear strongly avoids using visual aids with his speeches. It's just as well. If he did, he would drive the visuals coordinators nuts by wandering away from his script, and he's usually so boring that lowering the lights in the room puts the entire audience into a trance. Speaking of which, Harrison was aware of the Bear's narcoleptic condition, although no one else on the production staff or *Il Professore* knew. If the

221

Italian self-styled Genetic Genius found out, his extreme attacks of anxiety would crescendo into total hysteria. Of course, Octavius never speaks about it, because as far as he is concerned, it doesn't happen. Public appearances are a problem. We never know whether he'll drop off at a critical moment, and the only positive step we can take is to hold our breath and keep our fingers, claws, palps, hooves, and various other appendages crossed.

Just as Octavius was finishing his brief and totally unconnected remarks, a high pitched voice squeaked from the back of the room, "Arrisone, Arrisone, *mamma mia*, catastrophe, catastrophe!"

Harrison Hare twitched his whiskers, raised an eyebrow, and looked at me. *Il Professore* had arrived with news of fresh disasters. It turned out that two of the speakers refused to appear on the same panel together, because one of them had the habit of eating members of the other's species. This happened every now and again and could usually be handled diplomatically or if necessary, by physical constraint. Harrison took off to see what he could do, and I literally cornered *Il Professore*.

"*Professore, buon giorno*," I said, "I've been searching for you"

"*Ma, Signor Mauritius, scusi, scusi*, I have been so busy. This is, how you say, a mudhouse."

I didn't correct him. My Italian is no better than his English. "I have only one brief question for you. The Aquabear Show on Tuesday night. I understood you arranged that."

"No, No, not me! *Certamente*, I agreed to it, but it is being sponsored and produced by one of our fine Italian laboratories, Genoa Genetics. Their president, Ferrucio Ferreti, is a member of the family, and he graciously volunteered to supply the program. I gather he is a great fan of the Bearonessa. Who was I to say no? But you must speak to Signor Ferreti if you want any details."

Octavius had lumbered up and had overheard the last few sentences of our conversation. He and *Il Professore* exchanged greetings, and then the white rabbit hastened off to yet another crisis, promising to catch up with us at the reception.

I looked at Octavius. "What is Genoa Genetics, and who is Ferrucio Ferreti?" I asked.

"Genoa Genetics is a two-euro shoestring operation that can hardly afford to put up a booth at this convention, let alone pay for a major theatrical extravaganza. Ferreti is a weasel. *(Actually, as his name suggests, he is a ferret but Octavius wasn't too precise about such things.)* He knows as much about genetics as I know about… *(He was at a loss. The Great Bear couldn't think of anything he didn't know a great deal about.)* Anyway, he operates on the outer edges of the profession, performing illegal cloning on contract and publishing books like *Genetics for Idiots*. A real lightweight. He's fronting for someone, and we need to find out who that is. We need to follow up on this family the professor mentioned."

Obviously "we" was "me," so I set off in search of the Genoese showman.

Meanwhile, Bruce was checking in with Las Vegas air traffic control to see whether a mysterious private aircraft had landed sometime yesterday afternoon in the Las Vegas zone. No such luck, or actually, too much luck. Many private airplanes that landed in or around Las Vegas were mysterious, and Saturday had been no exception. Wallaroo walked off with a list of fifty-seven incoming flights that might have fit the bill. But none of them had filed a flight plan from northern Michigan. But flight plans can be faked or not filed at all. He decided to work from the outside in, starting at the more remote fields and coming back toward McCarran, where it was unlikely Imperius would have wanted to land. Too much exposure!

At the same time, Wyatt Where and Howard Watt were making the acquaintance of the Blue Bayou's security officer, an eight-foot Komodo dragon whose mode of maintaining order at the hotel was quite simple – sheer intimidation. Mr. Megatunni had left his position as Chief of Police at his Indonesian island home years ago, because too many of his prisoners just seemed to be disappearing. He had migrated to Macau, where he had taken on a series of increasingly responsible security jobs at the major casinos. For reasons not entirely clear, he left Macau rather hastily and landed the job as Chief of Security at the Blue Bayou Hotel, Casino, and Resort.

When he learned that his visitors had both been engaged in security for a major Chicago bank, his reptilian eyes widened, and his tongue flicked expectantly. Perhaps this was the next step up in his career. Was the job still open in Chicago??

Colonel Where explained their concerns, mentioning the disappearance of the sapphire, but not that we knew it had been destroyed. He said that we believed that the Chicago perpetrators were here in Vegas and that they may well have a repeat performance in mind. While knocking over a casino was a possibility, the more likely scenario was the theft of another valuable piece of jewelry or art. Mr. Megatunni should certainly take extreme precautions, especially with the tapestries but he should also bring the other hotels and casinos as well as the police into the picture.

Megatunni called in his assistant, a brown caiman named Snappi, and told her to get the security officers and Las Vegas police chief on a conference call. While they were waiting, he pumped the two security mavens about their latest techniques in electronic security and the opportunities in Chicago and he gave them in turn, a picture of his impressive surveillance program. *(Maybe he wouldn't move to Chicago. The salary and perks sounded good, but it got really cold up there.)*

When everyone was on the speakerphone, Megatunni did introductions all around and then let Howard and Wyatt tell their story. As might be expected, they were received with a bit of skepticism. Several of the security chiefs said, point blank, that there was no way any Duck was going to get through their security.

Wyatt waited until they were finished, described in detail the security at the bank and at the museum, and finished with a statement that produced dead silence. "We didn't think they could get through ours, either. You might want to talk to Commissioner Daley in Chicago."

Finishing the call by describing the members of the Black Quack Gang and telling them that Inspector Wallaroo was out searching for the plane that had brought them to Las Vegas, and more important, searching for their current location, the Great Bear's two new associates left the room with the feeling that they had made their point. Certainly, the security in the Bayeux Tapestry Room was going to be enhanced. Time to report back to Octavius.

The Development of Civilization – Part 5

Other Worlds?

(From "An Introduction to Faunapology" by Octavius Bear Ph.D.)

Ever since animals first looked at the sky and the seas and created gods for themselves to explain the unknown, questions have persisted: "Where do these gods live? Can we see them? Is our world the only world? Are we alone in this universe?"

Astronomical investigations have revealed nothing, and we have had no convincing signs that alien beings have ever walked our earth. However, the belief persists that ours is not the only universe.

A very remarkable phenomenon has lent credence to this conviction although many scientists and writers dismiss it as mass, coordinated hysteria. Over the past century, a large body of reports has emerged of hibernating animals who upon re-awakening, tell a practically identical story of being conscious and aware and having lived during the hibernation period in a civilization much like our own with several major exceptions.

First, beings quite similar to our long extinct Homo Sapiens seem to have survived and become dominant. They alone seemed to have reasoning power and the ability to extensively communicate and conduct complex social relationships. Second, animals identical in almost all physical aspects to the dominant species of our world are all feral and uncultivated on this other planet. Some live in the wild in highly primitive conditions, often pursued by the Homo Sapiens. Some even seem to have been tamed and made subservient. A complex system of predation exists among the wild beasts similar to our own prior to our emergent civilization.

226

These reports have been accumulated, analyzed and published widely. Secret attempts to recreate the other world experience under controlled, scientific conditions have been minimally successful and as yet, far from conclusive. In spite of this, a highly popular and strong belief has taken hold in many circles in what has come to be called: Parallel Universes.

Supported by theories of space-time relationships by physicists and cosmologists and opposed by members of the military, governments, and other officialdom, the arguments rage on. Tabloid media keep resuscitating the theory, and not a year passes without a new batch of sensational "Now It Can Be Told!" eyewitness stories and programs being unleashed on the public. Most seem to be designed to instill panic in a world already unsettled, courtesy of the War.

The scientific jury is still out, although this world reported by "traveling hibernators" as they are popularly called, does not seem particularly favorable to our way of life. Entering it <u>deliberately</u> will probably continue to be treated as an interesting but not very desirable excursion, attractive only to our science fiction writers and a few others. The question, of course, is: If we can indeed reach them, can they reach us??

Chapter Twenty Four

If a Horse stands up fully erect,

You must treat him with greatest respect.

When they shy, snort, and rear

You must never stand near

Or your favorite neck could be wrecked.

Howard and the Colonel found Octavius alone in the suite. He was sitting on the floor without his customary keg of mead. Had he just returned from an attack of narcolepsy? Didn't look that way! Nothing was knocked over, and he had some paperwork next to him that seemed to be in order.

They gave him a detailed rundown on the session with the police and security chiefs. He growled, "They just can't take the idea of a demon Duck seriously, can they? Well, it sounds like you made believers out of some of them. They've been warned. Best we can do, I suppose."

"Howard, would you go over to the *Ursa Major* and do another checkout on the particle beam weapon?"

Howard and Wyatt both turned to leave. Wyatt, after all, was responsible for all the onboard weaponry. "Not you, Wyatt. I'd like to talk with you for a few minutes."

The wolf looked at him quizzically, but walked back and sat down on his haunches opposite the Great Bear.

"Ever heard of an organization called The Business, Wyatt?"

"Lots of businesses are called businesses, Octavius."

"Not businesses, The Business!"

"Can't say that I have!"

"I suppose you've never heard of a horse, or maybe I should say a horse's ass named General Turmoil."

The wolf tried to stifle a guffaw. It didn't work. He stared at Octavius and finally muttered, "How much do you know?"

"Noble of you to try to keep your oath of silence, Howard. There was nothing in your background check about affiliation with The Business. But when he heard I had hired you, the General took it upon himself to call and give me a highly confidential briefing on Project Sleepwalker. You have heard of that, haven't you?"

"Of course, I've heard of it. I and two other animals are, or were, Project Sleepwalker. As far as I know, the project has been aborted. It didn't work reliably enough to be worth pursuing any further."

"As the General explained it, The Business was commissioned to investigate all the stories of hibernating animals claiming they'd landed in another universe and returned only when their long sleep was over. Why would you be part of an experiment to replicate the experience? Wolves don't usually hibernate, do they?"

"No, but that was part of the experiment. To see if an artificially induced coma could substitute for hibernation and create a situation where we could determine whether these were sleep-induced hallucinations or the real thing. We used a variety of soporifics: hypnotism, drugs, electro-shock, several contemplative religious practices, even reading Tolstoy."

"But nothing worked!"

"Is that what the General told you? Well, that was either what he was told, or he's keeping that part of the project even more secret. We got results, but we couldn't control them. Or, I should say, 'They couldn't control them.'"

"Meaning?"

"Meaning, I can! I did a little bit of independent research on my own and discovered I could produce a 'personal wormhole' for traveling back and forth. Not easy, and it doesn't always work, but I've made thirty-five trips so far."

"Personal wormhole?? Wormholes are theoretical space-time phenomena. They exist, supposedly, independent of their environment. It's not even been proven that they exist at all. How did you come by your own domesticated wormhole?"

"OK. Use 'gateway' if you prefer. I didn't set out to discover or build a gateway. It just happened, and it seems, only to me."

"But you didn't report this to project management. Why?"

"As we began to come back with stories of what it was like in this other world, I could see the power players begin to strategize on how they could take over this universe or use it to take over our own. The General and his minions are very dangerous beasts, Octavius."

"I know. Our relationship is tenuous at best. I guess I believe it's better to keep a channel open than to operate in the dark, but I neither trust him nor like him and his entire agency. Why do you think he called me about you?"

"I can only guess. When they shut down the project, the three of us were subjected to all sorts of mind manipulation to determine if we knew anything more than we had reported. If they found anything, they never confronted me. Incidentally, my two fellow lab subjects are both dead. One from an accident and the other from 'natural causes.' "

"Which you doubt?"

"Let's just say I'm more than a little dubious."

"Why do you think you've been spared? For that matter you still haven't told me why you think the General called me about you."

"Octavius, let me lay it out for you in the finest tradition of conspiracy theory. The Business didn't terminate the project. They altered it. I think they know I've been successful to an extent, and they've been trying to come up with a way to pull this phoenix out of the ashes. When I took off, literally, and became a mercenary, they lost track of me for a while. Then I reappeared at the bank and they probably put me back under surveillance, but did nothing overt. Now that I'm working for you, the General thinks his fondest dreams have come true."

"Why would he think that?"

"Because he probably knows I was going to tell you this story sooner or later and that you couldn't resist organizing Sleepwalker II."

"Which you would like me to do!"

"Which I would like you to do, minus any relationship with The Business. You're probably one of the few private citizens who can stand up to that crazy horse."

A few previous rounds with the General passed through Octavius' mind. The wolf was probably right. "But wouldn't that be playing right into the General's hooves? I suppose he would find it delightful if we perfected the process on my nickel, not his, and then he commandeered it and you."

"That's why I came to you. If anyone can give The Business the business, you can!"

"All right! This conversation never happened, and you can certainly rely on my not saying anything to General Turmoil. Let me think about this. I also want you to tell me about your experiences and impressions of this other universe. We'll get back to this shortly. Right now, I can hear Maury and the Frau ready to tumble in here to wrestle me into my formal clothes for the reception. Stick around! We'll make it a tag team match.

Chapter Twenty Five

Sci-Fi stories boast ferrets galore.

Antique paintings and statues have more.

Both in future and past

Their appeal is quite vast.

Maury Meerkat just thinks they're a bore.

Bruce had rented a helicopter. He wasn't sure he could borrow one from the Las Vegas police and besides, he wanted to make this search without any of the local cops along for the ride. Consulting his maps out over the desert, he systematically searched out every smaller airport or strip that looked big enough to handle an air freighter, but small enough not to attract much attention. That narrowed the number down to a hell of a lot of runways. To make matters worse, there were few landmarks he could use for navigation.

His search didn't seem to getting anywhere. Whenever he did reach a likely looking airstrip, the locals weren't used to seeing a wallaroo *(much less a wallaroo assigned to Interpol)* and were wary of answering any questions. On top of that, his Strine accent wasn't helping any either. What we have here is a failure to communicate!

After kicking up dust on just about every taxi strip in a sixty-mile radius, he finally struck gold – well, maybe low-grade silver. At a small commercial field, the Fixed Base Operator, a coyote, told him about an ancient DC-3 *(Don't see too many of them anymore!)* that arrived yesterday and unloaded several large crates into two unmarked trucks. Right after unloading, the plane refueled and then took off again, leaving behind some kind of jungle cat, a large ape and what looked like a bird along with the trucks and the crates. Several minutes later, they took off with the trucks.

"Do you know which way they went?"

The coyote looked slyly at Bruce and said, "Can't rightly remember, Inspector, but maybe it'll come to me."

"Well," said Bruce, "we might be able to help the process along. Right now, I have to get back to the city limits, but I'll be back. Work on your memory in the meantime."

"A little stimulation might help," said the coyote with a smile.

"I read yer, mate. I'll be back with a stimulus package." The wallaroo climbed back into the chopper's bubble, started up the engines and yanked on the collective, all the while resisting the urge to flatten the coyote with his downdraft.

Back to the Blue Bayou! It was time for the reception!

*****

Male fashion took several giant steps backward as Octavius struggled to get into his dinner jacket. He had already ripped the formal shirt to shreds, and I had tried to tie his bow tie at least a dozen times. He has no patience for "male fripperies," especially after we had done a bit of investigation into high fashion counterfeiting a few years ago (cf. *Octavius Bear and the Stylish Stallion*). He came away swearing he would never take another "rag trade' assignment even if he was starving. Fat chance! The Colonel, the Frau, Howard, and Bruce wrestled him into the jacket (*a copy of the video is available for a couple of liters of fermented coconut milk VSOP*) and I finally got his bow tie around his size 62 neck. We all headed for the freight elevator and the ballroom. Meanwhile, back at McCarran, the crew had the C-5A on high alert. As Octavius and I both knew, if necessary, Frau Schuylkill could get back to the aircraft in nothing flat. For the moment, however, the Great Bear wanted his entire staff on deck at the hotel.

The reason we had all converged on the reception was simple: We didn't know where, when, or whether the Duck would strike, but even if he didn't, we still might get some answers to our questions. We each had our individual schmooze assignments for the evening. Octavius, Bruce and I headed for the freight elevator. The others descended in more genteel fashion.

The elevator door opened just in time, because Bruce had already bounced off every surface but the ceiling during our descent. Two more floors, and Octavius would have been the one on the ceiling. "Dammit, Inspector, this is a closed environment. Control yourself!" he growled.

The sounds of music, clinking glasses and an amalgam of roars, chirps, grunts, oinks, growls, yips and howls greeted us. The party was in full swing. *Il Professore*, beautifully dressed in the latest model Giorgio Armadillo suit, was holding court for a group of reporters, scientific wannabes, and genetics groupies. I could see Harrison Hare dashing in and out of the ballroom, spilling the occasional drink of one or another of the delegates as he rushed by.

Colonel Where padded over to Mr. Megatunni, who with his security group at full staff and full alert, was overseeing *(and scaring the hell out of)* the reception. "Anything unusual, Mr. Megatunni?"

The Komodo gave what was the equivalent of a laugh *(a pretty frightening sight and sound)*, and said, "Everything and nothing, Colonel. This is a very unusual bunch. Scientific meetings always turn up some rare specimens, but this one certainly ranks in the Top Ten for weirdos. Who's the gigantic bear over there with the overstretched tux?"

"That's my new employer, Octavius Bear." This produced some embarrassed tongue flicking by the dragon. "The Meerkat standing next to him is his associate and field manager, Mauritius. The marsupial that just knocked over the waiter with all the champagne bottles is Inspector Bruce

Wallaroo of the International Fine Arts and Jewelry Protective Squad – he's a klutz, but a brilliant klutz. He has a record of arrests you wouldn't believe."

"Oh, yes, I would," thought Megatunni, harking back to one of Bruce's busts in Macau. Half of the local Tongs ended up fleeing for Tibet. Megatunni decided the time had come for a major relocation and headed for the States.

"You've met Doctor Watt and you may yet meet the final member of our group, Frau Schuylkill, a veeeery unique and interesting she-wolf. She's ex-military like myself. Right now she's over there by the *hors d'oeuvre* tables scoping out the crowd. Look quickly. She can move very fast when she wants to. Normally she would be over at the airport. She is the Bear's Chief Pilot, among her many other remarkable talents.

"You have a plane?"

"Several," said the Colonel, "but the one we have here is a highly modified C-5A Galaxy, the *Ursa Major*. I'm Frau Schuykill's new co-pilot. If it's all right with Octavius, maybe I can arrange a tour for you after the convention is over. Right now, we're treating the *Ursa* as highly restricted 'no-access' territory."

"Just a thought, Colonel," said Megatunni. "Officialdom in this town gets a bit upset about unauthorized flyovers within the city limits."

"Thanks for the warning," the Colonel replied. *(Light bulb!)* "Dummy!" he thought. "So that's why we're operating in stealth mode."

Frau Schuylkill wasn't just scoping out the crowd. She was scoping out the food as well. She was not amused. "*Ach*, these Vegas hotels! Just because the canapés are free doesn't mean they have to be inedible. The sushi bar is using fish I've never tasted or heard of before. Maybe they catch them in the desert. Blah! I'll return to the plane later and whip up some goulash and schnitzel. Real food! Oh well, back to observing. These geneticists all look suspicious. I'd arrest them all and then let them talk their way out of it. If I could understand anything they're saying. I'd like to see one of them try to splice my genes."

Inspector Wallaroo was talking to a group of the security guards, "If it looks like a duck, walks like a duck, quacks like a duck, it's a Duck, and I want you to hold him or her until I get there." *(The police didn't know for certain what gender Imperius was. They treated the Black Quack crimes as equal opportunity felonies.)* The guards looked over at Megatunni, who nodded approval back to them.

I walked over to the Inspector. "Bruce, I didn't want to ask you upstairs in front of Octavius, or we would have never gotten him down here, but did you find anything on your airplane search?"

"Too many things, Maury," he replied, "This town is a bloomin' fly-in for private planes. Everybody and his dingo comes in and out, and they're all looking to slip into a high-roller suite at some hotel after making an arrival in a darkened limo straight from a remote airstrip. I found sheiks and shahs and sheilas and schmoes all looking for the big action."

"What about ducks and cheetahs and baboons?"

"Only one so far that's worth some follow-up. I'm going right out again after this rage is over. Guy at one airstrip remembers a twin engine prop job that unloaded some containers into several trucks. Nothing eventful there, but they kept having to bring one of the crew back to the ship, because he wanted to play the fruit machine in the air crew ready room. Said he looked like a funny kind of ape. Didn't get a good look at the other parties. They used local talent to unload. The ship took off again, and the trucks disappeared into the desert. Not much, but it's the best I've come up with so far, unless you're interested in a Far Eastern potentate or two."

'No thanks! That group could have been the Quackers. Did the airport operator remember which way they were headed?"

"That's why I'm going out again – to help refresh his memory with a little cash. Anything going on here?"

"I'm going to check with Wyatt. He's over there with the hotel's security chief."

"That Komodo is the chief of security?" said Bruce. "Well, I guess I see the logic, but I wouldn't want to report a lost joey to him. He might eat it."

Before I could make my way over to the Colonel, I saw Howard Watt waving his paws and his quills in my direction. He was talking to a very slick-looking member of the family *Mustela putorius furo*. Could this be Ferrucio Ferreti?

It was. Howard introduced us and Signor Ferreti oozed Latin charm, *savoir faire* and all the other stuff that made me distrust him immediately. *(The other thing I hate about ferrets is that they're cute. Cute is for puppies, kittycats, and raccoons but most of all, meerkats. We don't need no stinking ferrets cutesy-ing up the place.)*

"Signor Ferreti," I asked, "How are things progressing at Genoa Genetics?"

"*Molto bene*! Signor Maury." *(We were on a first name basis already.)* We have several major – how you say, breakaways – in the last few months. It is for that reason that I am spending so much time and money here at this convention. We want the world to know that Genoa Genetics is ready for *primo serata*."

(Oh sure, just before the 11:00 o'clock news.) I strongly suspected that this guy was lying in his sharp little teeth, but what he was saying had just a tinge of credibility.

"What kind of breakaways, er, breakthroughs, Signor?" *(You're going to have to earn first name basis with me, you weasel.)*

238

"Ah, ha, ha! Secrets! Secrets! We will make the great announcements at the convention's grand finale on Tuesday. We have a dinner and show all arranged out at the Aquastadium."

"So it's you who booked Bearoness Belinda and the *Aquabears*."

"*Si, si*, I have always admired her greatly, but how did you know?"

"The Bearoness stopped by to see us on her way out here. She is a very good friend of my employer, Octavius Bear."

Did I notice a bit of a twinge amid the genial demeanor? Just the slightest sign of nervousness?

"Ah, so you are here with the Great Bear. He is truly a unique ursine. He doesn't cut as grand a scientific *figura* as *Il Professore* but then he doesn't devote all his time to genetics."

"True, but he does dedicate a lot of his money to it," I shot back. I watched for the first signs of greed. His face lit up like the Vegas Strip.

Suddenly, a roar of excitement arose near one of the doors of the ballroom. The reporters and photographers left *Il Professore* in mid-boast and literally ran to the scene. Given my lack of height, I had to skitter up on one of tables to see what the enthusiasm was all about.

A veritable sea of white was slowly pouring into the party space. A glorious vision of snowy beauty was wending her way into the crowd followed by ten other lovely examples of the *bear-blanc*. Bearoness Belinda Béarnaise Bruin (nee Black) was making an ENTRANCE followed by the eight *Aquabears* and the two members of her flight crew, who could also have doubled as showbears. Maybe they did. Needless to say, everything stopped dead. Except for *Il Professore* who continued to explain to a nearby waiter why he alone deserved the Noble Prize.

Dressed in a white sash, diamond coronet, earrings and enough bracelets to fund the whole convention *(I'm sure they were real. Belinda is never tacky.)* she acknowledged the applause, waved at any number of delegates whether she knew them or not, posed singly and with the terrific ten for every camera in the place, and drove the security group out of their minds with concern. Suddenly she stopped, looked around and a blissful smile broke out on her lovely snout. "Octavius! Octavius Bear, fancy seeing you here!" she cried, as she advanced toward the Great Bear. Oh boy, showtime!

There is one other thing Octavius hates: The 3 P's – publicity, the press and photographs. In addition to the flashes, there were TV cameras from several of the local stations shining their floodlights on her and then on both of them. She glistened. He glowered. I'm sure he was in agony of several types. Agony over the hoopla and agony over seeing the exquisite Polar Bear again. She extended her glove-covered paw to him to be licked. She looked into the cameras and at the print media. "Now don't you bad boys and girls go telling stories about Tavi and me. There is no truth to the rumors. We are just good friends."

Octavius got control of himself and responded with as much gallantry as his species is capable of. "Bel, you look absolutely lovely, as do your companions. Ladies, it's a pleasure to see you all again."

Ursine equivalents of synchronized giggles and sighs. Clearly, they thought Octavius looked lovely too, in spite of his too-tight dinner jacket and cockeyed bow tie.

"I called you several times since we arrived. You seem to be out and about," he said.

"Well, we've been rehearsing non-stop over at the Aquacade. That nasty Harrison Hare was trying to put up a school of marlins in the pool. We stopped him but we had to be careful he didn't try to sneak them in when we weren't looking. Imagine!

"Our rehearsals are the usual madness: synchronized swimming, acrobatic diving, aqua-skis, leaping through flaming hoops and of course the ursine fashion show. It's taken a little time for the ladies to get back in the swim of things, but I think we'll be our usual sensational selves. I adore it here in Las Vegas. You know how I love to swim in the fast lane. How are you, you sweet bear? Are you all set for your big speech? Maybe I can sneak in and listen."

"No, don't bother, Bel, really. It's the same old keynote stuff. You know how I feel about speechmaking, but maybe we can see each other for a while tomorrow morning after I give my talk. I'll be free then. I guess your afternoon will be taken up with more dress rehearsals."

Belinda sighed. "This is one of the reasons I retired to the Shetlands. I couldn't take the pace any longer, but oh, Tavi, it still runs in my blood. I do so love making a big splash. Yes, meet me over at the Aquacade at ten and we can spend an hour or two and have lunch. I had some Shetland salmon flown over for just such an occasion."

This sparkling romantic repartee was still going on when I suddenly froze. A paw reached out and touched the side of my scrawny neck. "Don't move, Meerkat," growled a voice I think I remembered. "I can swat you silly with one blow, and I can run away faster than you can screech. I want to talk to you, but not here. Meet me outside in the floral alcove in thirty seconds and don't signal to anyone. Your boss's life depends on it."

Whose was that voice? On the tip of my tongue! Chita, the Black Quack moll. My first reaction was to scream for security or Wallaroo or Wyatt or Howard or Octavius, but the last thing she said stopped me dead *(lousy choice of words)*. Looking around, I skittered under a few tables and out one of the side doors. Hidden behind a huge floral arrangement was a black nose, a spotted face, a glistening diamond collar, and the fiercest eyes I'd seen in a long while.

"What do you want, Chita?" We'd had several previous encounters that ended in draws.

241

"Oh, you recognized me. That can't be helped, I suppose. I have only a minute, so shut up and listen closely. Imperius Drake is after the Bear, and this time he intends to kill him."

"What!!!"

"Shhh, the Duck has gone off the deep end and is plotting something he calls the Grand Plan. It's going to happen some time during this convention. I don't know where or when, but I do know Octavius Bear is target number one."

"How??"

'I'm not sure, but he's developed this ray gun that is pretty lethal, and he's been practicing."

The particle beam accelerator. "Why are you telling me this?"

"Because I don't mind being on that dopey Wallaroo's list of Most Wanted for art and jewel theft or on some other APB for swindling, but murder, especially the murder of Octavius Bear, is another thing altogether. I had nothing to do with that peacock keeling over, by the way. Eventually the theft cases go cold, but attempting to kill Octavius will get us all run into the ground. The Duck is nuts, but I can't stop him, because I don't know what he plans to do exactly. To be truthful, I'm not even sure where he is at the moment."

A rustle of flowers, and she started to run off. With Frau Schuylkill right behind her! The wolf had spotted Chita the moment the cat had grabbed my neck and bounded through the crowd from the opposite end of the auditorium to help defend me. She cornered the cat and snarled, baring her million or so teeth. Chita was having none of it. Growling back, she took a swipe at the wolf and rushed out of her corner. She headed up a flight of stairs, only to discover the wolf staring down at her from the top step. Turning sharply, she ran down the stairs and right into – the wolf.

"What the hell is this?" snarled Chita. "How many wolves are there? They all look the same. Is there just one? Is she moving faster than I am? That's impossible! Cheetahs are the fastest quadrupeds in existence."

Frau Schuylkill heard this soliloquy and laughed / growled. "Not any more, Chita. Turn in your Olympic Medals. You won't need them when I get through with you."

While this game of cat and wolf was taking place, I had skittered over to the spot where the two antagonists were facing off against each other. A small crowd was gathering in the hallway, and a couple of security guards were heading towards us. I didn't want Chita killed, maimed, or arrested. At least not until she could give us more information about the desperate Duck's assassination plans. "Let her go, Frau Schuylkill! I'll explain later. Let her go!"

"But Herr Maury, she is a menace!"

"I know, but at the moment she's a useful menace. Let her go!"

Still snarling, the she-wolf backed up and left Chita a clear path of escape. The cat spat in our direction, turned on her tail and did a high speed take-off out of the building, through the parking lot and into the massive gardens surrounding the complex.

Hiding amid the live oaks and fake bayous of the hotel, the panting cheetah paused to catch her breath. Suddenly she heard a voice above her. "You don't know where we are, Cat? Why, we're right here."

Then in the fine tradition of the Gang, everything went Black.

Chapter Twenty Six

When a donkey has something to say

He lets loose with a deafening bray.

But for consummate sass

The Somalian Wild Ass

Can out-stubborn a mule any day.

I stood there quivering for a moment and then took off like a Meerkat out of hell. I grabbed Bruce and Wyatt and pulled them over to a corner. *(Not easy for someone my size.)* The Frau came with me. "Look, we have to act fast. The Duck is in town, and he intends to kill Octavius."

A barrage of "What? How? When? Where? How do you know?"

I noticed nobody asked, "Why?"

"No time for argument. I just had a brief meeting with Chita..."

"Chita???"

"Chita!!! And she told me. I hate to break up that little ursine tryst over there, but we have to get him back up to the suite ASAP. Get a hold of Howard and the security chief. We all need to talk."

Somehow, Wyatt convinced Octavius that he was needed immediately. He said he had just heard from the crew. Something was wrong with the plane. The Bear needed to get on the horn and make a decision right away.

Obviously highly annoyed, the Great Bear reluctantly said *adieu* to the Bearoness, who immediately plunged back into her sea of admirers. Before we could even get him to the elevator, Octavius was besieging us with questions, ursine curses, and comments about our incompetence, lack of initiative, incomplete staff work, overreaction, and all those other swell CEO epithets.

When we finally pushed him into the room, he turned and roared Detective Story Query Number 3: "Now, what is this all about?" and then, "Why is that Komodo Dragon here?"

Twelve variously shaped eyes all focused on me. Waiting!

First, I told him nothing was wrong with the plane. Then I repeated Chita's brief warning, including the parts about the Duck being in town, having gone off the deep end and using a functioning version of the particle beam projector for target practice. I also told him about the claws-out at the OK Corral between Chita and the Frau and my letting Chita go. None of that seemed to bother Octavius, although he wasn't too happy to have his suspicions confirmed about the crazy duck having a functioning particle projector. What did bother him, naturally, was the bit about his being Target for Tonight.

"He's had a million opportunities to kill me off, and he's never done it before. In a perverse way, he seems to enjoy the continued competition. Why should he change his methods now? I grant you this is an ideal situation for a grand gesture, but he could create chaos or humiliation any time he wanted to. Those white eggs are probably some sort of disruptive devices – smaller versions of the Black Quack – but that's as far as I think he'd go. By the way, anything more about them, Inspector?"

"No joy, Ocko," said Inspector Wallaroo. "I'm going back into the desert to search for them. I have one lead that looks decent. But Maury, let's assume Ocko's right. Let's assume that spotted sheila is a red herring. Maybe they just want to scare Ocko out of making his speech in the morning. Make him look foolish."

"I am giving that speech," Octavius roared, "The delegates demand it." *(Would you care to hear a majority report??)*

The Komodo, obviously not eager to have mayhem committed on his patch, said to Octavius, "Dr. Bear, we haven't met formally. I am Bom Bey Megatunni, Chief of Blue Bayou Security. I believe it would very unwise for you to give that speech tomorrow. Up there on the stage in front of an audience of a thousand, someone your size would be a perfect target."

Nods of agreement all around! Except one!

"Mr. Megatunni," he said, "I realize that like all noble squamates, your advice is coming from a truly professional viewpoint, and I appreciate it. *(Octavius is at his most flowery rational when he is being irrational.)* But you must also understand my viewpoint. *(Here it comes!)* No scrawny little egomaniac Duck is going to tell me what to do!!! Now, you security specialists in this room as well as the Las Vegas police ought to be able to keep three beasts from knocking me off, even if one of them is using a super-weapon. And I still doubt he intends to do it. The Inspector is probably right about Chita."

The total illogic of his position seemed to elude the Great Bear, especially in view of our track record in the Chicago museum. The ironic thing is Octavius hates public speaking and here he was…oh, well. Arguments back and forth. If an eight foot Komodo Dragon wasn't going to persuade him, none of us was.

The discussion turned to protective measures. Mr. Megatunni called the Las Vegas Police Chief and asked him and several of his best officers to join us. They might have a SWAT team situation on their hands. Las Vegas, of course, is hardly a newborn when it comes to crime prevention and investigation. If the perpetrators were hiding outside the city limits, as Bruce suspected, the Nevada State Police would have to be called in as well. They were some of the cleverest mules in existence. Nevada's Finest. Most were natives except for the chief – he had come from Africa. A Somalian Wild Ass.

Needless to say, a long evening turned into an even longer night. I had the dubious distinction of telling Harrison Hare about the situation and pleaded with him not to tell *Il Professore* or any of the other delegates *(and that included the Aquabears)*. He wanted to kill the speech but realized that fully half of the convention's funding was coming from UUI. Also, about a quarter of the delegates were from UUI. If that's how Octavius wanted it, that's the way it would go. And certainly, he would not tell *Il Professore*. Operatic hysteria is not what we want at the moment, to say nothing of the white rabbit's habit of proclaiming everything to the media with inappropriate embellishment.

So, a police cordon was to be set up around the ballroom and adjacent spaces; credentials were to be checked at all entrances and exits; metal detectors were put in place, and the excuse for all this was that there had been a threat from some agitators who were opposed to all forms of genetic experimentation. *(Part or all of which may have been true.)*

In the morning, when he finally heard about the heightened security, Il Professore had an emotional supernova – not at us, but at the scoundrels who could not understand that genetics was going to create *il nuovo mondo magnifico*. Besides how would this all look for his Noble nomination?

Anyway, none of us got much sleep that night and the next morning, Monday, promptly at 8:30, the delegates began filtering into the room. Harrison had posted new delayed start times to compensate for the security efforts, but the house band started playing walk-in music, and it looked like this show was going on the road. As far as I could see, the place looked tighter than a rusted bolt. I sauntered over to Bruce, Howard, Megatunni, and Wallaroo, who were closeted together at the back of the ballroom. *(Bruce had just come in from his all night Black Quack search-and-destroy mission with no better luck, and the Frau had returned to the C-5A airplane and put it on high alert.)*

"You guys are the experts. But this place looks pretty secure to me," I said.

Megatunni grinned *(not something to see early in the morning)* and replied, "It's what you don't see that really matters," and he launched off into a chamber-of-commerce spiel on his surveillance cameras, alarms, automatic doors, and lighting controls. The parking lots were under close observation by the Las Vegas Police. Not much was being left to chance that I could see.

In fact, there was one thing that was being left to chance. In the middle of all this, it was chewing at my delicate insides. Octavius himself! He was due to arrive in the ballroom with an escort in five minutes. While everyone else on our team was afraid of his being put to sleep permanently by an assassin's weapon, I was afraid he would go to sleep temporarily in the middle of his talk, courtesy of Narcolepsy, Inc. It's a chance we always take with live performances. I often try to talk him into pre-recording his remarks and playing them back on wide-screen *(what else?)* video. He would have none of it this time. This audience was going to get the one, the only, the original, and hopefully, still alive Great Bear.

The band struck up a loud chorus of "Hey, Look Me Over," the perennial intro music for speakers and award winners and *Il Professore* hopped to the microphones. The room had four huge TV screens showing an enlarged image of the little white rabbit as he climbed up on top of the podium.

"Geneticists of the World, Unite," he shouted, "You have nothing to lose but your gene chains." And he promptly broke into hysterical laughter at his clever witticism. The audience looked bemused, bothered, and bewildered. He then launched into a barrage of self-aggrandizing patter about *The Genius of Genetics*: the progress the organization and the science had made under his direction since their last meeting and all the usual startling numbers and citations that were sure to appear as quotes in the newspapers and sound bites on the evening news. He said a brief thanks to Harrison Hare for his support in carrying out *Il Professore's* detailed plan for this event. *(Harrison was ready to spit.)* Then he thanked the speakers who would be presenting their papers over the next several days. He said not a word about the extra security, which perhaps was just as well. Finally, after what seemed to be an interminable outpouring of self congratulation, he turned and said, "Now to deliver the Keynote Speech, here is Octavius Bear of Universal Ursine Industries."

Octavius trundled toward the newly reinforced podium, almost knocking *Il Professore* off the stage in the process, and said, "Thank you, Doctor Rabbito, for that very gracious introduction. Distinguished guests, esteemed scientists, fellow fauna! Good Morning! I just flew in from Cincinnati and boy, are my arms tired."

It was going to be worse than I expected. I resisted the urge to crawl out under the chairs, but instead sat up in my seat giving Octavius the Meerkat Attention Pose Number 17. Over the next forty-five minutes, I sat worried that any minute a particle beam might zap out from somewhere and kill off my boss. I alternated that with worries that any minute, my boss might fall over in a narcoleptic seizure. At the end of the second eon of the Great Bear's drone, he suddenly wrapped up his speech. "Thank you and have a great conference." Nothing had happened!

By a remarkable reversal of nature, he hadn't fallen asleep, but the audience had. They slowly awoke to a gradual patter of applause and I felt my arm being pulled out of its socket as Octavius grabbed me and headed out the side door.

"That's over!" he grumbled. "Gather the troops!"

Back up in the suite, the troops all gathered and stared at me. "Now just a second, I squeaked, "I didn't cry wolf! *(Lousy metaphor with Colonel Wyatt in the room.)* She didn't say it would be this morning. How could we let him go up there unguarded? Maybe it didn't happen because the security worked. We scared the Duck off!"

This logic seemed to work with our own team but I'm sure Megatunni and the Police Chief were standing there totaling up their staff overtime and assorted other costs and not liking it one bit.

Bruce, bless his antipodean heart, spoke up. "Look, we've been dealing with this diabolical Duck for years. If Chita's here, he's here. If he's here, he's up to no good. I'm not sure we scared him off. He's probably picked his time and place and is just playing with us. Chita was a set-up but that doesn't mean he's going to lie doggo. He was a genetic scientist himself before he went into crime. He thinks on a whole different wavelength. He claims he's the most intelligent being on the planet, and he may well be. *(A raised eyebrow from Octavius greeted this remark.)* The only thing that keeps tripping him up is his rip-snorting ego! He's out to make a show of his own, and killing off Ocko here may just be the grand finale."

"Grand finale, grand finale," said Howard, "what happens at the Grand Finale?"

"That can't be it," said the Colonel, "Octavius isn't even on the program. It's that Genoa Genetics blowout with all the hoop-de-doo about their new announcements, and of course, there's the Aquabear show."

Bingo! We all looked at Octavius. If Bearoness Belinda Béarnaise Bruin (nee Black) was going to be performing, there was absolutely no doubt who would be sitting prominently in the audience. Octavius shook off our various entreaties to miss the Finale. Testosterone won the day.

"Speaking of *Aquabears*," Octavius growled, "I have a date with Bel in a few minutes. And no, I do not want an escort or guards."

"Well, at least take the tunnel over to the Aquacade and stay indoors. We'll accompany you that far," said Megatunni.

"OK, but this is all ridiculous. That Duck has something else up his wing feathers. I still think he's creating a distraction to get at the Bayeux Tapestries. Are they still all right, Mr. Megatunni?"

"They're hanging in there, Dr. Bear." *(A Komodo comedian!)*

"Let's go! I'm keeping Bel waiting!"

250

Chapter Twenty Seven

I've been bothered for many a moon

And the answer must come to me soon.

It's been puzzling me

How it happens to be

That this Duck is quite truly a loon.

"Oooh, my head! Where am I?" *(Sorry, but it's a union rule. Every character that has ever been knocked out has to say it.)* Chita slowly pulled herself into a sitting position and looked around. There was nothing to see. It was pitch dark. She cautiously moved around, touching, sniffing, searching out the bounds of her confinement. She was confined. Some kind of small room or container. Yes, a container! She was in a box!

Last thing she remembered was Imperius talking to her after she had spilled the beans to that jerky Meerkat and then had sparred a few rounds with that supersonic wolf. Now she had a headache and a bump that felt like a third ear in the center of her skull, and she was stuck in here. But where was here?

What the hell, let's make a little noise and see what happens. "Hey," she yowled, "let me out of here."

"Chita, is that you?" The voice was Bigg's.

"Of course, it's me. Who put me in here?"

"I did!"

"So why are you asking whether it's me...oh, never mind! Someone hit me on the head."

"I did. It was nothing personal. The Emperor told me to. He's very angry at you. He said you're a traitor, and what's more you've ruined the diversion he's planned for the Golden Pagoda."

"Well, I'm none too pleased with him, either."

"He says you will have to be dealt with."

Well, that settles that. Imperius did hear her conversation with the Meerkat. "How?"

"I don't think he's sure yet. He says you can wait to be executed until the Grand Plan is executed."

"So he hasn't done anything yet at the casino or hotel."

"No, we've been back here at the warehouse since last night. He's in his room in deep contemplation and I was having breakfast. I'm going back. I'll talk to you later."

"Wait, Bigg, how about me? I'm hungry too. How about letting me out to have a little food and water? Then you can put me back."

"I don't think I can do that, Chita. I'd have to ask the Emperor, and he said he doesn't want to be disturbed under any circumstances."

"How about unlocking this thing and giving me a drink at least?"

"I didn't need a lock. I just turned it over. You're sitting on the door."

"Interesting," thought the cat, "but that jerk is about three times more powerful than I am. How can I turn this warehouse container over while I'm stuck inside it? I can't do it without making noise. I'll have to wait until they go out somewhere or they'll stop me before I can pull it off." She sat down and started to compute forces and angles and then what she would do when she escaped, if she escaped.

Suddenly there was the sound of a high powered engine outside the warehouse, loud enough to distract her for the moment. Who was this?

Sounds of the warehouse door rolling up. Voices. Then the voices got louder as they moved back into the center of the warehouse.

"Signor Baboon, will you tell Doctor Yu that Signor Ferreti is here as we agreed," said the voice.

Chita strained to hear through the ventilation holes in the side of the container. "Ferreti? Dr. Yu? Hmmm. Imperius was doing something in the guise of his scientific, nerdy self. Who is Ferreti?"

"He's meditating, Mister Ferreti. I can't disturb him," said Bigg.

"That's all right, Baboon. I heard Signor Ferreti's car, a Ferrari *Cavallino Rampante*, The Prancing Horse. If I am not mistaken, less than four hundred were ever made." The voice was Dr. Yu Aul Kum, mild=mannered maniac.

"Eccellente, Dottore, your ear and expertise is *magnifico*. *Si*, it is Ferrucio Ferreti's Ferrari. Ah, ha, ha! My little joke. The car is my one self-indulgence."

"Oh surely, Signor Ferreti, you have others. I suspect the ladies must be very taken with a suave and experienced animal like yourself."

"Well, perhaps, a little," he simpered.

"Who is this jerk?" thought Chita. "Why is he here?"

"I assume you have come for the musical souvenirs I promised you," said the Duck. "I'd like you to be very careful with them. Each one is a marvel of Oriental technological craftsmanship and quite delicate."

"*Si*, I have brought an assistant, and if he and your Baboon could load them on your trucks, we'll take them back to the Aquacade. I will personally supervise their storage this afternoon and distribution tomorrow night."

"Certainly," said the Duck. "Then you can have your assistant come back with the Baboon in our trucks and retrieve your car."

"*Va bene*. I was hoping that I could also receive a down payment on the 250 million euros you have pledged to Genoa Genetics. I am going to make the announcement tomorrow at the Grand Finale."

Chita's eyes widened causing a twinge in the bump on her head. "What the hell is this? And where did Imperius get 250 million euros to splurge on this jerk?"

"Certainly, Signor Ferreti, the payment will be in your account tomorrow. I will instruct my bank in Bermuda to make the transfer. BUT under no circumstance are you to reveal the source of your new-found fortune. You will recall that was the first and unbreakable rule of our agreement."

"Oh, *si si*! I have created a fake foundation to cover the transaction and to satisfy the press and the regulators. But I still do not understand why you do not want to be revealed as such a benefactor."

"Signor Ferreti, Signor Ferreti, I have dedicated my life to the advancement of science, and I have been quite successful at it, but always by standing in the shadows, so to speak. I own many patents and processes that are marketed under generic names, and I always keep a low profile. If I did not, could you imagine how I would be besieged by supplicants looking for grants, investments, or just plain hand-outs. I very carefully studied a number of other worthy organizations besides Genoa Genetics and yourself, I might

254

add, before deciding to make this grant. You are just about perfect for what I have in mind."

"Wow," thought Chita, "this is classic Imperius Drake. Smooth talker. Hold on to your wallet. The only processes he owns he's stolen. As for patents…Imperius doesn't know the meaning of intellectual property. But this still doesn't make any sense. He's usually trying to part someone from their money, not give them any."

"It is also very kind of you to pay for the show tomorrow night, Dottore. We have followed your instructions to the letter. The *Aquabears* have been engaged to perform. They are very, very sexy."

"I thought you'd like them, Signore," said the Mandarin, "and how about the décor?"

"Well, we have stupendous neon signs saying 'Genius of Genetics' and 'Genoa Genetics.' This is Las Vegas, after all."

"Yes, yes, and what about the balloons?"

"Balloons?" thought Chita, "what is this? You can't release a bunch of balloons from the ceiling. The Aquacade doesn't have a ceiling."

"Well," said the ferret, "there was a little trouble about the balloons."

"What???" screamed the Duck. "The balloons are essential. The program will be ruined without them."

"Oh, no, no, no, *Dottore.* Everything is OK. The four hot-air balloons with the baskets will be in place around the pool just as you specified. They're huge. They're white and egg-shaped and have *Genius of Genetics* on them, just like the little egg giveaway models."

"Good, the musical giveaways are meaningless without the balloons. They are symbols of the progress of genetics, especially when they soar into the air at the conclusion."

"*Ma*," said Ferreti, "but that's where we had the problem. The authorities will not allow us to release the balloons. They say they'll interfere with air traffic. So we have to keep them tethered to the walls of the Aquacade."

"Hmmm," said the Duck, not at all pleased. "I suppose that will have to do. I and my associate will be down to see the show, discreetly out of the way. I assume you will be the Master of Ceremonies."

"Oh, *si si*! I had a special gold lamé dinner jacket made for me for the occasion."

Chita couldn't see the ferret, but her imagination was running wild. She had to try hard to control her laughter. Imperius may not know she was awake. She didn't think Bigg had a chance to tell him. And she certainly didn't want this Genoese jerk to hear her, either.

"Oh, one more very important thing, Signor Ferreti. I want you to meet me just for a moment behind the Aquacade near the delivery ramps at 7:30 tomorrow night, just before the evening's festivities begin. I have something I want you to give to the Bearoness."

"Ah, *La Bellissima Bearonessa*, she has caught your eye too."

"No, no, nothing like that. The Bearoness had asked me to lend her something that has been in my family for ages. A special Oriental good luck piece to help her with the show. I will keep it until tomorrow."

"Ah, ha, *Dottore*, for 250 million euros, I will be pleased to be your delivery boy. You will not forget to transfer the funds?"

"I am a Drake of my word, Signor. I shall see you tomorrow night and in the meantime, *buona fortuna.*"

"*Grazie, Dottore, grazie!*"

With that Bigg came up and said, "We have the trucks all loaded, Mr. Ferreti. You can ride down with us and leave your car here, so your assistant can get back after we return."

The sounds of the overhead door closing and the truck engines starting up were all Chita could hear.

Then suddenly, "Well, my dear Cat, we hope you enjoyed that little dialog. Oh, yes, we're sure you're awake by now and uncomfortable as well, we trust." *(Now that Ferreti was gone, he had switched back to Imperius-speak.)*

No response from the container.

"Hmm! If you feel like being unresponsive, do so. But we will not tell you about the Grand Plan. A pity! You kept asking and asking about it."

"What are you going to do with me, Imperius?"

"Oh, the punishment will more than fit your crimes, including your stubborn unwillingness to address us as 'Sire.' You've also caused us to alter our plans for stealing the statue at the Golden Pagoda. Nothing that can't be handled, but obviously, we can't let you loose now. You can't be trusted. We may have to assist the Baboon ourselves. Another annoyance, Cat! We'll let you stew about that for a while. Is it warm enough in there for you? Right now we must concentrate on every detail of our great revenge. Shall we tell you about it?'

"You can always count on this guy's ego getting the best of him," thought Chita. "He's dying for an audience to prove how brilliant he is. Oh, yeah, Duck, I want to hear it. Boy, do I want to hear it!"

'Well," she said, "since I don't seem to be going anywhere at the moment."

"This Grand Plan is the culmination of all our years of scheming and plotting against those stupid barbarians who cast us out and caused the death of our beloved Lee-Li-Li. The fools know nothing about transforming creatures into super beings. They would be awed and terrified at the progress we have made. "

Chita asked, "This serum you take. Why can't it work on everyone? Couldn't I take it and become a fabulous feline?"

"Ah, my dear Chita! That is exactly what is going to happen to you. Clever of you to guess. Unfortunately, to work properly, the serum has to be scrupulously matched to the DNA of each individual. In your case, using serum that was designed for ourselves will turn you into a very dead cat, no matter how many lives you think you have. It will be very painful, too. Just the way our beloved Lee-Li-Li died when she tried to save us from ourselves. Poor little bird! How loving but how wrong-minded! But that's a thought for later. Let us lay out the scenario for you.

"Ever since we escaped from the UUI laboratories with pieces of the Bear's particle beam accelerator, we have been calculating and planning for one great crescendo of revenge to descend on all of our enemies, especially that accursed Bear.

"It started with the Deep Blue Sapphire. That is the symbol of this whole chain of events. You will no doubt see the sheer poetry in all of this as we relate it to you. The reason we didn't steal the sapphire is very simple. We couldn't get it out of the case. The security the Bear and that intolerable Wallaroo had designed was too much for a quick hit. We would have needed at least a week in our lab to defeat their controls. But we wanted to give them the impression that we had succeeded in the heist and thus trigger off the media circus about the curse. Botheration, distraction, and embarrassment. We wanted the Bear and the Wallaroo's attention to be elsewhere as we made our final preparations for the *Grand Guignol of the Genius of Genetics*."

258

"So we chose the perfect alternative to stealing the sapphire. We vaporized it. A pity to destroy something so beautiful, but we had to make them think this was just another jewel theft, not the prelude to an act of mass destruction. Even though the accidental side effect on the peacock may have given them pause, we believe they still think that somehow we defeated their security and made off with the gem. That's what we want them to think. It will keep them from surmising our real methods and purpose."

"And what is that, Duck?"

"Patience, Cat, patience. We knew this genetics convention would be the best opportunity we would have in many years to get almost everyone we hated in one place and to construct a fate for Octavius Bear that will either kill him or better yet, leave him bereft of all he values and wants, overwhelmed by guilt for the rest of his ugly life."

"In one single stroke, we will dispose of those genetic geniuses who expelled us from their temples; we will destroy the cream of the intellects at Universal Ursine Industries; we will eliminate that loudmouth lepus, Professor Roberto Rabbito and that imbecile, Ferreti. He'll never see a cent of that money we promised him. But most of all, we will crush Octavius Bear and his ridiculous minions. AND the instrument of his catastrophic annihilation will be none other than the beautiful and brainless Bearoness Belinda Béarnaise Bruin (nee Black)."

"What are you talking about, you crazy Duck?" Chita was getting panic-stricken.

"Do you not see, Cat? The little white eggs are not music-makers nor are they annoying quackers. They are bombs! One thousand personally delivered bombs to obliterate the entire Aquacade and everyone in it."

Reality flashed at Chita. "Oh, no," she thought, "it's the plastic filler in the eggs. It's an explosive compound. I just thought it was there to keep the electronics from being jarred."

"Yes, Cat, the plastic filler!" *(Is he reading her mind?)* "And the electronic music makers that produce such sweet Italian Opera are also the triggers and detonators.

"But here is the most delicious part. We couldn't trust electronic timers to work that closely together and set off the satanic eggs all at once. We do so want it to be a beautifully coordinated performance, so we developed a trigger that is both effective and foolproof and oh, so diabolically cruel. The particle beam weapon."

"But," said Chita, trying to keep from going beserk in the hot and dark container, "How are you going to do that? You can't hit a thousand eggs simultaneously. Even Bigg isn't that good a shot. I assume since you've been practicing, that you're going to be the executioner."

"True, Cat, true! But there is so much more to this weapon than meets the eye. Even if he has developed another one after we stole the original plans and the prototype, Octavius Bear couldn't possibly know one very peculiar but lovely aspect of the particle beam weapon. We discovered it by accident, but we have honed it into the most potent feature of the gun. If it is tuned to the correct frequency of the target, it can induce that target to radiate in all directions before destroying it. That's what killed that stupid bird. Some targets radiate weakly or hardly at all, but oh, my dear Cat, jewels, especially sapphires – they are the supreme radiators. One gem the size of the Deep Blue will radiate enough energy to trigger every one of the detonators in all the eggs in that stadium."

"But you destroyed the Deep Blue...oh my God, the sapphire I was supposed to leave as a substitute. It's real!"

"Not in all respects, Cat, but it has that one absolutely essential characteristic necessary to our plan. Tomorrow evening, when the Bearoness goes up to the diving board to begin her act with a swan dive, she will be wearing the sapphire sent to her by her admiring, loving bear."

"The package you want Ferreti to deliver."

"Yes, Cat, she'll think he's recovered the Deep Blue and is letting her wear it for the show before turning it back to the museum."

"But Octavius will be there," said Chita.

"Yessss! That's essential to the plan. But he will not know what to make of the jewel – or if he does figure it out, he will be too late to stop the carnage. We will have fired the gun at the jewel at light speed. The jewel, the Bearoness and immediately after, everyone in the Aquacade will be disintegrated. Even if the Bear escapes, he will live his life in torture and guilt."

"But how about you and Bigg?" she said. 'Don't tell me you plan a joint suicide."

"No, no, Cat, we wish to live and savor our triumph, and we also want to deal with your death at leisure after we tell you in detail how magnificent the apocalypse was. You are our captive audience."

"Duck, that is the most complicated exercise I have ever heard. Practically anything could go wrong. Why can't you ever do something simple?"

"Because," he screamed, "we are a genius, Cat, and geniuses never do anything simple when they can do it the hard way. But the Grand Plan is foolproof. We haven't told you everything. We must keep some secrets, even though we're sure you can't get out of there. We won't tell you how we will fire the weapon or how we will escape, but it has all been planned out. Do not get your hopes up. We will not be killed. Now, a quick flight to the Aquacade would seem to be in order to make sure things are going the way they should. We don't know who is stupider, Bigg or Ferreti. Then I also must review Plan B for tonight's diversion. We'll do it without you. You see, I want the police crawling all over The Strip hotels tomorrow and not the Blue Bayou. Bigg and I have preparations to make at the Aquacade, and I don't wish to be interrupted. It's a shame you betrayed us, Cat. You are a great criminal, and it's so hard to get good help nowadays. Bye, Bye! Don't go away."

261

Chapter Twenty Eight

Salmon act like they haven't a care.

They jump rapids like climbing a stair.

But when that's all through

It's quite sad but it's true.

They end up in the mouth of a bear.

"Tavi! I wasn't sure you were coming. You're late, you naughty bear. *(It was two minutes past ten.)* Rule number one: The lady is the one who keeps the male waiting, not the other way around."

"Sorry. Good morning, Bel, you look lovely as usual."

"Only as usual? Oh, dear, I must be slipping. I was trying to look especially lovely today. We haven't really had any time together for ever so long, and I did so want to impress you."

"You've succeeded, my dear, beyond your dreams."

"Oh, Tavi, how gallant! Under that big, brown furry exterior beats the heart of a true romantic."

"And under that sparkling white fur, beats the heart of a dangerous flirt."

She laughed. A sound that would frighten many animals, but was music to his ursine ears. To top it off, she had just finished a morning rehearsal, and her fur was still wet. He loved wet fur.

They were sitting inside her dressing room at the Aquacade out of sight of any possible particle beam snipers. *(About which Belinda knew absolutely nothing.)* Megatunni had agreed to leave Octavius unguarded when he discovered where the two were meeting. He and the Colonel had been trying in vain to get the bear to wear a protective vest, but Howard put the kibosh on that when he pointed out that the ray could just zap right through it. Octavius resolved to keep all thoughts of Imperius Drake out of his mind for the next few hours. His staff, hotel security, and the combined police forces of Las Vegas and the State of Nevada were on the job.

"What can I get for you, Tavi? I assume it's not too early for a little mead. I called Maury and asked him to have some sent over. He's such a dear little animal. As for me, I'll stick to champagne and salmon. This is my last meal for a while. I can't eat or drink at all tomorrow before a performance. My tummy always goes fluttery."

This could be the Great Bear's last meal, too, courtesy of the Duck. And his stomach was fluttery too, but for an entirely different reason. He really had forgotten how desirable this bear was. He had to be careful. Fortunately, it wasn't the mating season but since he had cured his need to hibernate, a few things had also changed in that department, too.

"Relax," he thought, "Enjoy this while you can. That Duck just might get lucky."

"Would you like some salmon? I told you I had it brought in from my castle in the Shetlands."

"Thanks, Bel, you're a marvelous hostess."

"I got a lot of training living with Byron. Parties, dinners, weekend guests. It got to be such a bore. State occasions. Meeting royalty. Although I do admit I like to dress up and have an audience."

"What's next on your schedule after this appearance?"

"Why, do you know, Tavi, I have no idea. I have to fly some of the girls back to their homes or at least to an airport where they can easily get back. They come from all over. Each year we have a reunion at the Bearmoral Castle. But after that, I am at a loss. How about you?"

"I'm not sure, either. I just took on two more assistants – Colonel Wyatt Where, a wolf and Doctor Howard Watt, a porcupine. They're both great security and science experts and, of course, there's Maury and the Frau with the occasional drop in from Inspector Wallaroo. With all that help, I'm thinking about taking a little time off."

"Well, that would be something new. When was the last time you took a vacation? You look positively pooped."

He didn't want to tell her that the reason he looked so tired had nothing to do with lack of vacations. It had everything to do with a surfeit of Diabolical Ducks. In fact, he was trying to skirt around the whole assassination issue.

"Well, who knows?" he said, "Maybe on Wednesday, I'll think of something. We moved a whole planeload of stuff and weapons *(ooops!)* down here, and they have to go back to the mansion."

"Weapons? I saw or I should say, I bearly saw the *Ursa Major* parked next to the Aquabear. Why did you have to bring weapons?"

Think fast, Octavius! Aloud he said, "Oh, the Colonel, Frau Schuylkill and Dr. Watt wanted to use the opportunity to test out several of our new armaments. Can you think of a better place than the Nevada desert?"

She looked a bit skeptical but didn't press the point. It sounded lame to him, too. "Is that why the *Ursa Major* is in stealth mode?" she asked.

He kept forgetting that this gorgeous polar bear also piloted the last remaining SST and was light years away in intellect from the ditzy diva image she kept projecting. He'd have to be much more careful. If she got wind of what was going on, she'd want to be in the thick of it, possibly getting her pretty head vaporized. Not that she wouldn't be a major plus. This could be one tough, smart, agile female. But old habits died hard and Octavius still thought fighting was for males. He asked for more mead and salmon.

"Oh, by the way," said Belinda, "I've been meaning to ask you. Have you made any progress on the jewel theft? You know me. I never read the papers or watch TV news except for Variety and the show biz gossip programs. I do read the *Shetland Pony* when I'm home, but that's all about farmers and sheep and fisheries and annual caber tosses. Last year a local bull heaved the caber a full kilometer. He was disqualified, though. It broke a stained glass window in a church." She giggled. "Oh, Tavi, you must think I'm just a bubble headed, over-the-hill showbear!"

"No, Bel, that is not at all what I think," he said, meaning it quite sincerely. "We have made a little progress on the sapphire theft. We think we know who the culprits are."*(Second ooops! Don't mention Imperius. She knew what a threat he was from previous occasions.)*

"Really, who???"

"It's a new gang. Technically sophisticated. Doing some grandstanding to raise their ratings in the Guiness Book of Gangs."

"Do you have the sapphire?"

"Sorry to disappoint you, Bel, but you're going to have to wear some other gem in the show. Besides, you don't need any help. You look marvelous just the way you are."

"You've been practicing, Tavi," she said. "I remember in Churchill, you couldn't get a compliment out to save yourself." She pawsed. "Do you remember Churchill? Those days were so lovely. I was just a silly little juvenile, and you were a very serious graduate student intent on figuring out what made polar bears tick. Did you ever answer that question – what does make polar bears tick?"

"I think I figured out what makes polar bears tick in general, but I've been having trouble figuring out what makes a particular polar bear tick."

"Why, Octavius Bear, are you saying I am an ursine of mystery? Nothing could be further from the truth. I am as transparent as an ice floe!"

"Sure," thought the Bear, "and I'm the Cowardly Lion."

"Will you be at the show tomorrow night?"

"I wouldn't miss it for anything, Bel, although I have to tell you that Ferrucio Ferreti really gets on my nerves."

"Isn't he the sleaziest creep? He's been trying to hit on all of the girls since we got here. I had to tell him that while we really appreciated his sponsorship, romance wasn't in our contracts. By the way, I was so disappointed. I thought for sure that you were our sponsor. Imagine when we got here, and we all discovered that instead of a big rugged Kodiak, we owed our jobs to a little Latin lothario. The ladies all think you're such a hunk."

Octavius started to blush *(really)* when his cell phone rang.

"Oh, Tavi," she said, "How tiresome. Do you have to answer it?"

"I'd better."

"Well, go ahead. Saved from Bel by the bell." She giggled again. That Churchill giggle.

"Bear, here!"

"Octavius, this is Wyatt. Howard's here with me. Two trucks pulled up about fifteen minutes ago at the Aquacade storage rooms. Ferreti was in one of them, and there are two drivers. They're unloading several crates. I can't tell what's in them, and there's no printing on the outside of the crates or on the trucks. Megatunni asked Ferreti what was in the crates, and he said

266

more decorations for the show tomorrow night. It may be true, but one of the drivers looks a little like those pictures you showed us of Bigg Baboon. Whoa, Ferreti's still here, but the trucks just left and they're going pretty fast. Do you want us to follow them?"

"No, I doubt you could catch them." said Octavius, "but get on the horn with Inspector Wallaroo. I think he's out in a helicopter searching again for the gang's hideout. Tell him to be on the lookout for the trucks, and see where they go. Do you think you can find out what's really in the crates?"

"I'll try, but Megatunni is a bit of a stiff about the privacy of guests. He'd probably take a chunk out of one of us just for suggesting it."

"Well, see what you can do, Colonel. This whole thing has got me confused, to tell the truth. I'll see you shortly."

Belinda's ears could pick up a swishing salmon at a thousand yards, so it was no surprise when she turned to Octavius and said, "What's this about Inspector Wallaroo chasing some trucks? Are you still on this sapphire case while you're down here? And for that matter, why was the hotel overloaded with police and security this morning?"

Octavius looked at her. "She's guessing," he thought, "and she's getting too close. Much as I hate to, I have to get out of here."

"My dear Bearoness, I shall answer your questions in the order in which they were posed. We are not on the sapphire case right now *(crossed claws behind his back)* and Wallaroo is helping the local police in a helicopter sweep. There have been some anti-genetic agitators on the Web threatening to disrupt the conference. That's what this morning was all about."

"Do you think they'll try tomorrow night?" she asked. Belinda was torn. On the one hand, she disliked agitators – especially agitators who threatened to interrupt her performances. She had lived through one or two protests about equal rights for food fish. On the other hand, if something did happen *(right after the show, of course)* think about all the publicity.

267

Naturally, she wouldn't want anyone to get hurt. Oh. Maybe that creep Ferreti, but no one else. She'd have to tell the *Aquabears* to be careful.

"I think they have security well under control, Bel. Just relax and be your usual spectacular self. I'll be in the audience. I'm sure you're going to be exhausted after the show and surrounded by your public, but how about on Wednesday morning, maybe the whole group of us – including the *Aquabears* and my staff – could get together in one of the Bayou's party cabanas and have a celebratory brunch."

"That would be wonderful, Tavi. You have yourself a date."

"Yeah," thought Octavius, "I hope I get a chance to keep it."

Chapter Twenty Nine

Poker playing can be an addiction

And result in a lifelong affliction.

But it's not just the cost

Of the money you've lost.

High stakes betting can lead to real friction.

As Octavius emerged from the connecting tunnel onto the casino floor, the incessant clatter of the slot machines and rinky-tink music further jangled his already irritated nerves. Passing the Black Jack tables on his way to the freight elevator, he stopped short. He looked back, turned away and started to move a bit faster, when he heard an affected British voice call out, "Octavius, old boy! I say, what a coincidence! I've been searching for you, and here you are! Who says I'm not lucky. Just a tick!"

Agrippa! Octavius was staring at a somewhat smaller carbon copy of himself dressed in a bow tie with dealer's cuffs on his forepaws. Agrippa called over to the pit boss and asked to be relieved. The boss nodded. Paying off his last hand and turning the decks over to an attractive desert fox; he trundled out from behind his table and extended his paw to the Great Bear. Octavius pretended not to notice it.

"Agrippa *(They never addressed each other with nicknames. It wasn't that kind of relationship),* I thought you were in Reno. What are you doing here? You never could stand the desert heat."

"Let's just say Reno has gotten a little too hot lately, old boy. I have come seeking refuge from a few misunderstandings."

"And seeking me out for a handout, no doubt."

"No need to be snide, old boy. A few spare simoleons might indeed help me to re-establish myself up north in the cooler climes and make relationships more cordial. But I had seen your picture on TV and in the Las Vegas papers and decided to come over here on my day off at Caesar's to see if I could find you. I'm just dealing here today at the Blue Bayou to pick up the price of a meal or two. It's you I want to see."

"You could have always called or sent me an e-mail, Agrippa. When you need to, you certainly know how to reach me or even my accountant, Herbert."

"True, old boy, true, but I really do have to have a *tete-a-tete* with you."

"So, it's more than money, this time."

"In a manner of speaking, yes! I say, shall we sit over here in this cocktail lounge and have a nip. I'll pay!"

"OK, but I only have a few minutes."

The offer to pay in itself was enough to pique the Great Bear's interest. It would be interesting to see if he really did. They trundled into the darkened space and a bored looking waitress asked the traditional, "What'll it be?"

Agrippa looked at her and said, "Two meads. Mine on the rocks, his straight up!" He looked at Octavius and grinned, "See, I remembered."

'No mead," said the jenny, "We don't stock the stuff!"

"What a dive," said Agrippa. Octavius nodded. For the first time in either of their memories, they agreed on something. Agrippa settled for single malt scotch. Octavius had a cola.

"Cheers, old boy, cheers!"

"Agrippa, why don't you knock off that phony British accent and fake aristocratic drawl. The closest you've been to the UK is London Bridge on Lake Havasu. Hey, Are you trying to grow a mustache? You are!! What, no monocle? This is your half-brother you're talking to. Not some unsuspecting mark for your latest con game. Although the way I give you money, I'm probably the biggest patsy you work over."

"Not true, old boy, not true! You certainly are big, of course! Heh, heh! But I have adopted the accent for so long now, I can't shake it. Plus, it does have its uses when communing with rich widows. I employ it all the time now just to keep in practice. And yes to the moustache and no to the monocle. Could never keep it stuck in my eye without blindin' myself."

"Well, Agrippa, what do you want?"

"Well, a small contribution to the cause would certainly help, old boy."

"How much?"

"Would ten thousand dent the piggy bank?"

"Probably not, but one of these days I'm not going to be around to pull your paws out of the brambles."

"I know, old boy, I know. It's just that I have a gambler's streak in my blood. Probably from my own late lamented and unknown father. Not in your bloodstream, of course. You don't gamble, and Mater never goes beyond a rubber or two of bridge. Have you spoken to the old fruit lately? I haven't talked to her in a turtle's age."

"Just the other day, in fact. She sends her regards!"

271

"I'll bet. The old crone would like nothing better than to see me stretched out as a bearskin rug."

"With good cause, I should say. You haven't exactly endeared yourself to her."

"Always so bossy! 'Make something of yourself, Agrippa!' Never willing to part with a farthing of her hoard!"

"She has no hoard. She gets most of her livelihood from me."

"Ever the dutiful son!"

"One more snide remark like that, Agrippa, and that ten thousand will just be another desert mirage. I'll tell Herbert to expect your call. Is there anything else?"

"Yes, old bean, ectually there is. The real reason I wanted to talk to you in the fur, as it were. It seems I have accidentally gotten myself into a bit of a quandary. A rather dangerous quandary, I might add."

"That seems to be a lifetime situation with you!"

"True, perhaps! But this one requires the skills of a great detective and scientist like yourself. You see, I have been the witness to a murder."

"Well, report it to the police. You didn't have a hand in it, did you?"

"You know how I feel about the police, Octavius! Besides, there are a few details that would make that difficult. And no, I did not. Murder is well beyond the pale for me."

"Will you stop being so damn coy and just tell me what the hell happened! When did this take place?"

"A few weeks ago!"

"Didn't you tell me in one of your recent e-mails that you would be hibernating in Reno?"

"I was! I was! Anyway, I was engaged in dealing a high stakes poker game. Hundreds of thousands per hand. Real cash! No chips! Flowed back and forth like champagne. All very cordial! Then things changed. One of the players accused one of the others of cheating. It started getting nasty. Threats back and forth. Finally the suspected cheat pulled out a gun and shot his accuser dead. Pandemonium! More shots! Everyone headed for the doors. I scooped up the pot and ran for my life. Now I'm sure they're looking for me."

"As I said, tell the story to the Reno police. Hand the pot over to them and let them track down the killer. They can protect you until they have him (or them) in custody."

"Can't do that, old bean. You see, we were playing the game in another universe and the players were all *Homo Sapiens*!"

Chapter Thirty

Most Baboons live together in troops.

They're the liveliest, noisiest groups.

Their demeanor's dramatic,

And they're so acrobatic,

They do back-flips while jumping through hoops.

Chita kept her ear to the ventilation holes. It sounded like the Duck had flown off, but it also sounded like he had closed the overhead door behind him, probably with the remote control. OK, it wouldn't take too long for them to get down to the hotel, unload and come back. Imperius would probably ride back with Bigg. Having to fly in the desert heat didn't appeal to him. He'd want the air conditioning in the truck. This was the only chance she would have. Thank heaven the Duck was overconfident, and the baboon was stupid.

"Let's see if my geometry and physics are right here," she thought. "I have to strike a top corner of the container keeping my back feet in the air so the force can knock it over on its side. Then the door will be on the side instead of underneath me. And I have to do this in the dark. Swell!"

She leapt and fell back. She leapt again from one side wall, trying to push the top of the other side wall away from her. The box teetered a bit but re-stabilized itself. "Got to do this faster. Get it teetering and then hit again and again before it settles down." The sounds inside the warehouse were like thunderous bass drums echoing every time she hit. She was getting tired, but she was also getting furious. She didn't have much time left. She wasn't going to let that pipsqueak Duck fill her full of super serum.

Boom! She was getting the rhythm now. One more sequence and yes, it was teetering in the right direction. She jumped on the far wall and felt it go down under her feet. She turned back, and sure enough, the door was on the side, and it could be pushed open. "Oh, Bigg, you stupid ape. I am so glad you are so dumb."

"Now let's see if I can get the warehouse door open," she thought, pausing just long enough to get a drink of water. She had been hyperventilating the whole time she was in that box and this last round of exercise hadn't helped a bit. Her eyes were wide and even her very few sweat glands were overworking. She definitely didn't feel good. At least it was a bit cooler in the warehouse. But the thought of having to run any distance in that desert even if she could get the door open didn't sit very well. She padded over to the door. It was locked in place by the overhead mechanism. She looked out through a slit in the door and spotted….the car. Ferreti's Ferrari. She had to get to that car. She called on all the cat gods of Egypt, Mesopotamia, Assyria, and North Hollywood to command the keys to still be in the car. He had to have left them! The little jerk! He just had to! She wouldn't know how to start it otherwise. You don't get too many opportunities to hot wire a muscle car in the African veldt.

"Now, where is the button to open the overhead door?" It should have been right next to the door, but it wasn't. Had the Duck removed it and just used the remote, so he could be the only one who could open and close it? "Damn that Duck!"

While she was pacing back and forth, she heard the sound of truck engines increasing in volume. They were back! Bigg and Ferreti's driver and probably Imperius, too. Only one thing to do, but she was good at it. Surprise! The second the door opened, she would be out like a shot and into the car before any of them knew what happened. This is Vegas! Go for broke!! But they had to open the overhead door. If they decided to have a conversation, or if Ferreti's driver took the car before the door opened, she was dead. Literally.

She heard voices. It was Ferreti's driver. He was on his cell phone, probably to Ferreti. Telling him he was coming back.

"C'mon, Imperius, open the door. Open the damn door!" she thought. After at least two eternities, the overhead rumbled into action. "Yeesss!" It had opened no more than a foot when Chita scrambled out and headed like a rocket for the Ferrari. She grabbed the door. The keys were in it. She jumped in and started it up. The car was hot as hell. Where's the air conditioning? Let's go!!! Oh no, this thing isn't an automatic. I've never driven a stick shift! Where's the stick? Paddles? Where's the clutch? Step on the gas, and slap the shift paddle. The car started to move and then stalled. "Crap!" Do it again. This time she got the sequence right, and she roared off.

For the first few seconds, Imperius, Bigg and the driver were paralyzed. Then the driver shouted, "Hey, that's Signor Ferrari's Ferreti. Where you going? You can't do that!" He jumped into the truck and sped off after her.

Now, a truck catching a Ferrari isn't as ridiculous as you might think, because so far, Chita was afraid to shift out of first gear and stall. She had pushed it all the way to eighty, but she had the engine and transmission whining unmercifully. She needed to get some breathing room, so she could shift without bucking all over the road. Speaking of breathing room, "How the hell do you turn on the air conditioner or open the windows?"

Imperius shouted, "Baboon, get her!" Bigg jumped into the other truck and was about to set off after the cat when Imperius flew into the cab and said, "Wait! Stop! Either Ferreti's driver will get her, or she'll kill herself or...Ferreti will probably report it to the police."

Bigg's jaw dropped. "The police!"

"Yes, our first priority is to get out of here before they arrive. Get out of the truck and start loading it with our stuff. Thank badness we've gotten rid of the eggs. Hurry, we have to go and leave no clues."

"Where are we going?" asked the Baboon.

"There is always a plan B, Baboon. Always a plan B." And he flew into the warehouse and set about getting his contemplation rug and other essentials gathered up.

Meanwhile, Ferreti's driver was losing to the Ferrari. Chita had to stay off the main roads, and she was taking hairpin curves at incredible speeds. The driver was still on the phone to Ferreti. "I'm losing her, *signore*. I can't keep up with the car."

Oddly, the ferret was not upset. He said, "*Va bene*. Don't worry about it. It's a rental. I'll call the police. Bring the truck back to *Dottore* Yu and take a cab back here."

Imperius and Bigg were loading the other truck and getting ready for a fast getaway. Twilight was setting in, and they could use the darkness. If the police were coming at all, it would take them a while to arrive at the crime scene. But who knew where Ferreti's driver was? They had to leave...now.

Bigg finished loading the few things they needed, including the weapon. Imperius flew into the cab holding the box with the fake sapphire and said, "Let's go!"

"Where?"

"Baboon, where do trucks go when it's night time?"

"To beddy-bye?"

"No, you imbecile. They pull off onto rest areas on highways. Get on Interstate 15, and go north. We'll get off at the first siding and stay there until it's time for us to execute the diversion. I will not allow that infernal cat to ruin my plans, but wait, just wait until I get my claws in her." He chuckled, "What I meant was get my serum in her."

They sped off.

Chita wasn't having too much luck with the car. But she could no longer see the truck in her rear view mirror. Had she lost him? She seemed to be the only one on this two-lane road, so she slowed down and tried to shift into second. The car bucked and roared, but she finally got it. Now, let's try third. Whoa, horsey! Yes! She'd stay in third. The hell with the twenty-seven other gears this monster seemed to have. As long as she didn't hit a busy intersection and that was very unlikely out here, she'd be OK."

"Right, Chita," she thought, "here you are in the middle of the Nevada desert in a car you can't handle and that sticks out like a sore paw." Red was not her color.

"What do I do now? I'll have to switch cars as soon as I can find one I can steal. There'll be a town along here somewhere. Imperius and Bigg may or may not come after me. It's too close to Grand Plan time for them to divert their attention for long, but I can't take that chance. I might be able to get out of Nevada altogether, head for Los Angeles and fly out of the country. Yeah, that's the plan…the Grand Chita Plan!"

"The Grand Plan! Should I call the Meerkat and tell him what's going to happen? They'd never believe me, especially when this morning's assassination didn't come off. Besides, that would just set more of them off after me. Right now, saving my lovely, black spotted hide is job #1. Now, which way am I headed? This powerhouse doesn't have GPS."

Ferreti had called the rental agency, who in turn called the highway patrol. In any other state in the union *(except southern California)* it should be easy to spot a Ferrari. Out here, they're a silver dollar a dozen. The police issued an All Points Bulletin but did not set off in hot pursuit. It was getting dark, and they'd catch the car and the driver when it crossed the border to California, Arizona, or Utah, depending on which direction it was going.

*****

Bigg and Imperius had reached the Interstate and were moving along at a "reasonable and proper" speed *(75 mph)*. They did not want to attract

278

attention. "Now, pay attention, Baboon. This event has caused us to alter the Grand Plan a bit, but it is still flawless. We shall add this inconvenience to the list of Chita's sins for which she will have to atone."

"Yes, Sire."

"Tonight, you and we will go to the Gold Pagoda and ask to see the billionaire Panda, Win-Win. You will still be dressed as an Arab as we planned, but we will be your assistant."

"You as my assistant! That's a good one, Sire!"

"No, it's not! Shut up and listen. When we get there, we will identify you as a rich oil sheik who wishes to play with the Golden Pagoda's high rollers. Then, very subtly *(The thought of Bigg being subtle tested even his sense of the ridiculous. Nevertheless...)*, very subtly, we will suggest that you would like to see the fabulous jade collection in his special room. After that, we will proceed as planned by stealing and then ditching the statue."

"Are you going to dress up like a panther and scream that someone stole your purse with all your winnings, Sire?"

"No, Baboon, I definitely am not." *(He had to get some better help.)*

"In the mass confusion, we will return to the truck, drive it back to the highway rest area, and sleep. Tomorrow, at about mid-morning, we will casually drive over to the Aquacade and you will join in with the workmen putting up the signs and the balloons."

"Oh good, I love balloons."

"This is the hot air kind, Baboon. They are about forty feet high, and they operate on propane gas. There is a basket tied below each one. In the early evening, you will climb up into the one nearest the diving board and hide with the ray gun. We will join you just before the show starts. We have a short errand to perform first."

279

"Can I go for a ride??"

"That is the one kink in the plan that must be compensated for. The authorities have insisted that the balloons remain tethered to the walls of the Aquacade. It was our original intention to escape by floating away after we have exploded the bombs. We may yet be able to. You must try to re-rig the balloon you're hiding in so it can be released from the tether. If you can't, you will have to quickly climb down the tether. We, of course, can simply fly away on our own power."

"What's a tether?"

This was going to be more difficult than the Duck thought. "We'll draw you a picture at the Truck Plaza,' he said.

"Did you say 'bombs,' Sire?"

"Yes, Baboon, bombs. All those pretty little white eggs you assembled up in Michigan are not just music boxes. They are exquisitely lethal carriers of death. One thousand animals will simultaneously disintegrate into tiny particles with one shot of the ray gun. Does that bother you?"

"No, just curious!"

"The centerpiece of our marvelous mayhem is the jewel. We will send the fake sapphire via our stupid friend Ferreti to the Bearoness Belinda Béarnaise Bruin (nee Black) with a forged note from her beloved Octavius asking her to wear the gem during her performance. We have watched her at rehearsal. After she is introduced, she poses on the high diving board and then executes a swan dive into the pool. She will never get a chance to dive off that board. Instead, I, that is, we will, with unerring accuracy, use the particle beam projector to zap the sapphire hanging around her neck, and that in turn will radiate in all directions, setting off the egg-bombs. No one will be spared. No one! Like the Chicago peacock, the Bearoness will be a victim of collateral damage. Octavius Bear will either be killed outright or will lie dying, bereft of his Belinda Bear. Then while chaos reigns, we, my dear Baboon, will escape in the balloon that you have rigged for quick release."

"Wow,' said Bigg, "that sounds complicated."

"As we told that treacherous cat, complexity is the sign of true genius...oh, never mind. You would never understand. Understand?"

"Sure, I get to ride in the balloon," said Bigg.

*****

Meanwhile, on the back roads, Chita was still trying to show the Ferrari who was boss. So far, the car was winning by quite a few lengths. "I have to get off this thrill ride and find a more rational form of transportation. It's getting dark! I'd better turn on the lights. No, that's the windshield washers. This one! No, I don't want the emergency flashers. Ah, here we go! What's that?? Supercharger engaged??? Yipe, I don't want to go any faster in this thing. I'm going to kill myself as it is. Slow down, you monstrosity. Slow down!!"

She stomped on the brakes. Bad move!!! The car fishtailed, skidded and ran off the side of the road and down into a ravine at 90 miles an hour. Holding on for dear life, she hung helplessly as the Ferrari spun around several times and then...flipped. Over...and over...and over...and over... finally settling on its roof in a dried out creek bed.

Chita now had a second bump on her head to match the clubbing she had taken from Bigg. She was tangled in the steering wheel, deployed air bags, seat belts, and collapsed seats. Trying to stay conscious, she looked around. She was upside down. The top of the car was crushed inward. There was no way she could open the gull-wing doors. The windows were cracked and caved in, and the openings were too small for her to get out. Out of one cage and into another!

It was getting darker and colder. Maybe she should stay inside the wreck until morning. Then she could see better and figure out how she could escape. Yes, that's what she would do. Pain did a fandango up and down her limbs. Then she passed out.

Chapter Thirty One

All the world loves the Panda, it's true.

Whether wild or ensconced in a zoo.

They are great entertainers

But not food abstainers.

They devour tons and tons of bamboo.

They had dozed off. The hum of the passing traffic had been hypnotic. A huge semi unleashed its air horn as it sped by, jarring Imperius into consciousness. He looked at the clock on the truck's dash – 8:00 PM.

"Baboon," he squawked, "wake up! It is getting late. It is time for the Plan B diversion. While you get into your Arab costume, I will drive."

"No, Sire, It'll only take me a minute." *(Bigg had been on board the last time Imperius had tried to drive a vehicle. His adrenalin bubbled just at the thought.)*

"Very well, but hurry!"

Bigg started the engine even as he was struggling to get into his robes. His *keffiyeh* kept falling off his head and down on his long snout and he got tangled a few times in his flowing robes. The fact that Imperius was shouting at him didn't help much. They swerved out onto the Interstate, cutting into traffic amid a symphony of blaring horns and headed for the Strip and *The Golden Pagoda*.

Bigg had never been to Vegas before, and he stared dumbstruck as they rumbled up Las Vegas Boulevard – the Strip. They had passed through the

Fremont Street area first, and his initial reaction was "been there, done that, seen better neon signs." But now...this was more like it.

In a city where the word "opulent" had lost most of its meaning, *The Golden Pagoda* did much to restore its impact. As the name suggested, the huge Oriental complex was topped off by a soaring pagoda covered in, you guessed it, gold. Rumor hath it *(or was it PR hype?)* that the roof was actually sheathed in *pure* gold. A number of potential thieves had fallen to their deaths trying to find out. The roof was electrified with one hundred thousand volts. Even the Las Vegas pigeons *(the winged variety)* avoided settling down on it.

Sitting or more properly, towering over the gaudy landscape of the Strip, *the Golden Pagoda Hotel-Casino* out-glitzed the "grandeur" of the other architectural floozies surrounding it. Lights reflected off the gold sheathing creating a wonderland aura. Animated dragons hissed steam into the atmosphere and created a golden fog surrounding the tower. The pagoda itself was a masterpiece of ersatz Oriental, dripping with glittering ornaments and sinuous shapes.

Opposite the pagoda was *The Aspergio* where Bigg was to dump the statue. With its fountains gushing in the evening twilight, ably abetted by a million spotlights, *The Aspergio* looked like someone had started a collection of spritzers and didn't know when to stop. Versailles was a puddle by comparison. The fountain's spray drifted with the evening wind and combined with the steam from *The Golden Pagoda* to form a full-spectrum fog.

Down the block *(way down the block – The Golden Pagoda was huge)* stood *The Venusian*, someone's idea of gaming on a planet deeply buried under super hot carbon dioxide and sulphuric acid. Definitely for the outer fringe. It was, no doubt, an acquired taste.

From all directions, blinking neon, chaser lamps, spots, LEDs, and halogen lights bombarded the senses. Huge infra-red and ultra violet displays for animals with different visual ranges glared, if you could see them. Imperius and Bigg, still adjusting his Arab costume, walked out of the parking

284

lot toward the entrance of *The Golden Pagoda*. The fading traffic noise, ersatz Oriental music and the pinging-ponging of an insane slot machine orchestra splattered on their ears as they entered the huge pseudo-wood doors *(replicas of the Forbidden City)*.

Two Fu Lions, real ones, supposedly direct descendants of the fabled Imperial Guardian Lions, roared a greeting and bowed as they passed through. Inside, inscrutable chaos! *Shar Pei* card dealers dealt Black Tong games *(a variant of Twenty One.)* The ominous pit bosses were *(aw, you're ahead of me on this one)* pit bulls. Animals from the Chinese Zodiac, females, scantily clad, strolled, thumped, hopped or slithered through the crowds bearing trays of drinks. And the slot machines, oh, the slot machines!!

Sidling *(as best he could with webbed feet)* up to a panda in a fur tuxedo, Imperius hopped on a game table and whispered in his ear. The panda bowed, led them to an alcove, held up his paw in the traditional signal for "Wait here!" called over a dragon and ordered drinks for Imperius and Bigg. The dragon angrily snorted *(maybe it wasn't her year or maybe they were all like that),* and asked, "What'll it be?"

Bigg was about to order a *Cuba Libre*, when Imperius poked him with his wing. "His Highness speaks only Arabic. In the tradition of his country, he will have orange juice. I will have a Singapore Sling."

As the dragon stomped off, the Duck hissed at the Baboon. "Remember who you are supposed to be, a rich oil sheik from Saudi Arabia. The only English you know is poker talk. 'I'm in; three spades; I'll see you and raise you two thousand!' Things like that. Got it? I am your Oriental assistant. Arabs are not supposed to drink hard stuff. At least not in public. Be careful!"

The panda came back and gestured for them to follow him. "Mr. Win will be pleased to meet with you." As he said that, the dragon arrived with the drinks. Imperius thought the Singapore Sling looked a bit Indonesian, but he wouldn't complain. The orange juice looked orange. Bigg wrinkled his snout, but said nothing. The panda took their drinks from the dragon's tray and led them to a private elevator hidden behind a large bamboo tree. There was hardly room for the three of them and the drinks. They whisked skyward, probably climbing the pagoda. The elevator doors whispered open and they found themselves in a room expensively furnished in Swedish Modern. The sounds of a jazz quartet were coming from somewhere in the walls. Bigg wondered if it was a recording, or if there were musicians trapped behind the wallboard.

They looked across the room at the largest Panda they had ever seen, staring out the window at the skyline. They were at the top of the pagoda. He turned, walked toward them on his hind legs, gestured at the floor manager and said, "Thank you Stan-Lee, that will be all." The smaller panda looked like a toy compared to his boss. He bowed and left on all fours. The elevator door whooshed open and closed and they were left facing…

"I am Win-Win. Welcome, gentlebeasts! In what way may we serve you? I understand from Stan-Lee that you are looking for some high-powered action. The Golden Pagoda can provide that…for the right people. We have a very exclusive private club for sensitive, serious and of course, very wealthy clients. Such may be ideal for your needs. No matter what your game – *chemin-de-fer*; baccarat; twenty varieties of poker. Your pleasure is our pleasure."

Bigg stared at Win-Win and then Imperius. He didn't know baccarat from a sewer rat. He knew a little about cards, although he sometimes mixed up spades with clubs. They all looked black to him. He hoped that the Emperor could carry this off.

Imperius spoke. "Thank you Mr. Win. May I present His Highness, the *Sultan of El Mirajj*. He has come from his Saudi Arabian home for a little rest and relaxation away from his oil wells and currency exchanges. The Sultan speaks some English. Only enough to hold his own in a card game or to order an assassination."

The Panda smiled a teddy bear smile, bowed and said, "You are most welcome, Your Highness. I do hope we can be of service."

286

Bigg grinned a stupid grin, which was the only one in his repertoire.

Win continued, "And may I know who you are, sir?"

"A thousand pardons. I am his Highness' *aide-de-camp*, *major domo*, adjutant, Lieutenant and chief of staff. Colonel Ding Wing Dong at your service."

"Ah, you are a military man?"

"Not really, His Highness just likes us to dress up in uniforms and wear medals. Of, course we are both in *mufti* while we are here. He in the robes of the desert. I in a simple."

"Aren't we in Las Vegas," wondered Bigg to himself. "Where's Mufti??"

"You are Oriental like myself, Colonel Ding?" Win asked in rustic Cantonese.

"Yes," Imperius answered in the same dialect, "but as you can see, I am a Mandarin Duck. Do you perhaps speak my language, too?" *(The Duck had decided to appear in his non-threatening guise.)*

"I do indeed, and fourteen other dialects as well," he said, switching effortlessly into perfect Mandarin. "How is it that a foreign person such as yourself has come by such a powerful and prestigious job in an Arab kingdom?"

"Luck!!"

"Oh come, Colonel, you are far too modest."

"No, I inherited the job from my grandfather, Luck-Yee-Mi. The *El Mirajj* family has important connections in China, and my family has served them for centuries. Shall we return to English out of respect for His Highness?"

"Ah yes, back to English and back to business." Win-Win rolled himself into a large chrome and leather desk chair and motioned for them to be seated as well. Bigg slipped over backwards as he sat down in a large leather recliner and then crawled around and began to remount the offending furniture. Imperius stared at the ceiling.

As he tried to reseat himself, Bigg struggled with his robes, his slipping *keffiyeh* and his orange juice, most of which he had spilled. Imperius thought he had better continue the small talk for a moment longer. "I notice that while your entire premises, a glorious place incidentally, is outfitted in the most luxurious and authentic Orientalia, your office has, forgive me, stark but very comfortable modern western furnishings."

"Right," said the Panda, laughing. "Absolutely detest oriental art, food, furniture, music, costumes, Noh plays, the works. The customers expect it though, and who am I to deprive them. The *Golden Pagoda* has to be a...golden pagoda. Speaking of food, how about a nice fresh piece of bamboo? That's one Oriental dish I do eat." He took a tender shoot from a silver plate on his desk and chomped.

"Thank you, no."

Bigg also shook his head in the negative.

"But, Mr. Win, surely you are not entirely a modernist. I have heard you have a fabulous collection of ancient jade artifacts here in the casino. Surely you collect them for aesthetic pleasure."

"Nope, hate the things, but they're a major tax dodge. More laundered money tied up in that room than anywhere else in Vegas. I suppose you'd like to see the collection."

"His Highness is most anxious to see them. In fact, it is in part because of the collection that he instructed me to arrange accommodations here."

"Well, he certainly shall see them then, but first, before we arrange your membership in the Platinum Pagoda Club, I must ask for some demonstration of your earnestness, so to speak."

Bigg looked blank *(what else?),* but Imperius picked up on it smoothly. "I have here, made out to His Highness a letter of credit from the Royal Bank of Riyadh for one million riyals – that's about 250,000 American dollars. He would like you to hold it as a guarantee against any losses he might incur. This, of course, is just his traveling pocket money. Much more is available if necessary. Let me suggest that while your office checks out the validity of the letter and the contents of the account against which it is drawn, we go and see the jade artifacts."

Win-Win picked up his phone and summoned Stan-Lee to return to his office. Bigg leaned over to Imperius and mumbled, "When do we get out of here??"

Imperius turned to the Panda. "His highness has just asked me to inquire if you might be interested in a mid-eastern partner for your enterprise. He finds the business of gaming fascinating!" Bigg choked on the remainder of his orange juice.

"Please tell His Highness that I am most grateful for the offer, but at this moment such an arrangement would be most difficult due to strict regulations by my native country as well as this one. Ah, here is Stan Lee."

He handed the letter of credit to him and said, "Please open a credit account for His Highness for the amount stated here. Although we are perfectly willing to accept his letter on face value, he insists that we check his bank account and the validity of the letter. Please do so, and come to see us in the Jade Room when you have finished. Meantime, let us proceed to the home of the precious jade collection on the second floor."

Stan Lee bowed and once again down on all fours, stood aside while the three of them squeezed into the elevator. Win-Win chuckled. "This elevator was made for my mother who built and ran this facility for years. You can tell that she was somewhat smaller than I am. However, Colonel, you should have no problem. Feel free to stand on my shoulder, if you wish."

"Thank you, no, I have become used to tight places, ha ha!"

They were still laughing as they reached the gallery. Another guardian Fu Lion stood in front of the door. He bowed to Win-Win and his companions and stood aside as the panda entered a set of codes into an electronic lock. Imperius didn't like the looks of that lock and door but said nothing. When they got inside, he turned and saw it opened back out by simply pushing a crash bar. Fire regulations. Let's hear it for safety! He turned and stood in awe. Bigg too, was slack-jawed, but with him, it was usual. Jade and more jade, sparkling greens, ebony black, and almost crystalline white, grey, yellow, pink, orange, and delicate violet. The statues gleamed with a soft luster. It seemed you could reach inside them and stir up the colors. A spectacular violet statue of a lady of the court dominated the room. Not very large, but delicate and intricately carved. Oddly, she stood in the open without any sort of glass or compound covering. No doubt there was a pressure-sensitive alarm under the base just waiting for someone to make a wrong move. "Overconfident," thought the Duck. "We will teach them some humility."

He walked over to Bigg and took a large black ovoid from him. He turned to Win-Win and said, "His Highness has asked me to present this to you as a token of gratitude for allowing him to view this wonderful collection. Perhaps it will find a favorable place in your Spartan (?) office. It is natural, not fabricated. It looks like an egg but is in fact a solid piece of some as yet unidentified element found at the bottom of the Arabian Sea. Special divers search for them. Only two or three a decade are found. It would please him greatly if you would accept it."

The Panda was overwhelmed. Finally, something he could enjoy looking at. He didn't notice both of them slipping electronic plugs into their ears. He looked up from the "egg" just in time to see Bigg grab the violet statue and start running for the door. The pressure alarm went off, but so too did the Black Quack that was under Imperius telekinetic control. It was unbearably loud. Win-Win sank to the floor. As the Fu Lion ran into the room past the exiting Bigg and Imperius, he too fell over in agony.

They took the stairs to the ground floor. The Duck threw off his costume as they ran. They emerged on the gaming floor, where the blinking lights and machine cacophony were now joined by blue alarm lights and sirens. As they strolled through the front door about to be closed by one of the guardian lions, Bigg turned back and tossed two more Black Quacks that Imperius immediately triggered. The sounds of the games and alarms were drowned out by an incessant and excruciating, QUACK, QUACK, QUACK!

"Now, Bigg, you must run across the street to the Aspergio, jump briefly into the fountains, grab one of the flagpoles, and screech. When you have the onlookers' attention, shinny up the pole and drop the statue into the water. They'll think it's a bomb and scatter. Then, get the truck out of the Pagoda parking lot and meet me back at the Interstate service area. Got that? Good. I'll take a cab."

The police joined the security officers at the casino, trying to deal with the squawking eggs. Security checks were being set up at all the Strip locations. Stan-Lee come up to a frazzled Win-Win and said, "That letter of credit was a phony."

"So were they! Shut up and get me a drink!!"

Chapter Thirty Two

Dragons all have such threatening looks

And their claws are like well sharpened hooks.

They set hundreds of fires.

They're really high fliers.

They reside in most fantasy books.

Bigg pulled up to the rest area just in time to see Imperius waddle out of a Las Vegas taxi. The Duck flew the last few yards and dropped into the cab of the truck.

"Quickly, Baboon, we must leave here as soon as that taxi pulls away. That driver is suspicious. He couldn't understand why we wanted to be dropped off at this rest area, and he was asking us what all the fuss was about at *The Golden Pagoda*. He probably has a description of this truck and the license number. When he finds out about our little caper, he will put two and two together."

"That makes four, Sire!"

"Yes, thank you, Baboon. Much as we dislike the idea, we must return to the warehouse, change trucks and then lose this one somewhere. I trust you followed our instructions to the letter."

"You didn't send me a letter, Sire. You just told me." Bigg started up the truck and raced out onto the Interstate traffic once more to a clamor of horns and screeches.

"Not too fast, Baboon. We don't want to get caught speeding. Now did you or did you not follow our instructions?"

"To the letter, Sire. Splash, splash, crash, and dash! Ha, ha, ha, ha, ha!" Bigg had been thinking up that reply for the last hour and was convinced it was hilarious. He couldn't understand why the Emperor wasn't laughing. But then, the Emperor never laughed unless he was committing some kind of mayhem. That was a big word – mayhem. A Bigg word! Ha! And he fell into another round of giggles, almost hitting a car in the process.

"Be careful, you ridiculous ape! You'll kill us both before the Grand Plan can unfold in its full glory."

"Sire, why did we do that?"

"Do what?"

"Steal the pretty statue and then dump it in the water. It was a lot of fun, especially being dressed up like an Arab prince, but I still don't get it."

"As usual, Baboon, our subtle mind is far ahead of yours. But let me try one more time. We were creating a diversion. We wanted the Las Vegas and Nevada State police, every last mule of them, and all the security guards as well, very, very busy trying to figure out what we had done and why and trying to prevent still another theft. We need a clear field at the Blue Bayou for the next twenty four hours to set up for the climactic last act of the Grand Plan."

"But, we didn't really steal it. That's what I don't understand."

"And that's what the police and that ridiculous Panda won't be able to understand. We want them confused. Theft they understand. Our vandalism won't make any sense. Understand?"

"Not really! That pretty jade statue was worth a lot of money. Why didn't we keep it and sell it?"

293

"Baboon, there isn't a fence in the world who would touch that statue, especially after the word got out."

"Then why didn't we just keep it? It's pretty."

Imperius was getting to the end of his normally short temper. ***"Because we hate jade statues, that's why!!!*** They remind me of my stepmother. She was a real dragon."

"She couldn't have been that bad!"

"No, we mean she was really a dragon!"

"But you're a bird!"

"Exactly, but my stepmother could never understand that. Our egg got mixed up with all of hers in the hatchery. When we all came out, she thought we, I, was, were just a wyrd-looking dragon. She kept trying to stretch our tail. She was disgusted when we couldn't learn to breathe fire. All of my hatch mates made fun. They called us Old Frozen Breath! We couldn't stand it any longer, and we finally flew away, but not before we broke every one of her jade statues. Most dragons have a massive stash of treasure they sleep on. Not Ma! She collected jade. Said it was the right thing for an Oriental dragon to guard. She'd been doing it for thousands of years."

"Wow!"

"Yes, wow! But we showed her and those stupid brats. They had all gone out for flying lessons. Left us behind. Said we couldn't fly right. We flapped, and they whooshed. While they were gone, we broke every piece of jade we could handle. Then we flew away, leaving her with a garbage heap. Ha, Ha, Ha!"

"See," thought Bigg. "Now he laughs."

"We wandered around until we met up with a flock of Mandarin Ducks. They said we looked just like them. We didn't know what we looked like. The dragon never kept mirrors. They took us in and it was great stroke of luck. You see, the chief Duck of the flock was a real Mandarin. The royal kind. We grew up in luxury and privilege and went to university after university where our intelligence outshone all the others. We became confident and self-assured after all that humiliation with the dragons. We hate dragons. We wanted to attack that cocktail waitress. Then we devoted ourselves to science, and you know the rest. To this day, jade makes us itch. We were glad to get out of that stupid casino. We couldn't touch that statue. That's why you had to be part of the job."

"Too bad Chita wasn't with us. She would have enjoyed it. I wonder where she is."

"After Chicago, we doubt she'd enjoy any kind of museum theft. She is probably in Arizona. We don't care as long as she keeps her mouth shut. She won't call the police. They have warrants for her arrest. That's why she always poses as a panther. She might call that idiot Meerkat but we'll have to take that chance. We will still have our revenge on her. Someday! We hope she is dead. That car probably did her in. She never got her driver's license. Always used chauffeured limousines or ran. Boats! She was good at boats. Funny, when she hated water. Baboon, we are here! Quickly, we must switch trucks and find some flea-bag motel to sleep in until morning."

"I didn't know fleas ran motels!"

Chapter Thirty Three

The Prairie Dog's hardly a mutt.

He is cute and extremely clean-cut.

Though he's usually nice,

If he's "rutting," think twice!

Then he's tough and can really kick butt.

A mule from the Nevada Mounted Desert Patrol was working his way across the bleak landscape looking for problems, stranded tourists or thirst-maddened prospectors. *(Although what they were prospecting for, he could never figure out. The place was a desert, for gosh sakes.)*

The mule had a search light strapped between his ears, along with a radio headset down the side of his face. Mounted across his back were two saddle bags filled with water bottles, food, a back-up radio, GPS, blankets, and two prairie dogs armed with sawed-off shotguns and stun darts. Together they formed the patrol team. The dogs with their sharp, color-sensitive eyesight, amplified by binoculars and an exquisite sense of smell could spot problems or predators miles away and give a warning to the mule and to each other.

Once they'd identified whether the subject was friend, foe, or neutral, they would go into an assessment drill. They would decide whether to pursue and attack or simply let the status stay quo. If they did attack, the team was a formidable war machine. The mule could bite, kick, or fatally stomp most opponents. Venomous, antisocial snakes were their most common foes, but the occasional wild puma or worse yet, an armed and dangerous criminal running from Las Vegas could also liven up an afternoon or night. In those events, the prairie dogs, agile and well armed, turned the saddle bags into gun turrets and protected the mule as well as getting in a few good shots, themselves.

This particular team, Henry the Mule and Ozzie and Izzie, had been working together for years. They called themselves Operation Desert Storm. They seldom needed to talk to communicate. The dogs squeaked, the mule brayed, and between them they understood perfectly. However, they were hardly speechless or illiterate. They had to talk to HQ, the other patrol teams, and of course, anyone they came upon as they covered their waterfront. *(Rotten simile)* But generally, they were typical desert folk. Terse in speech, swift in action! Henry provided transportation. Izzie handled the stun darts and the rescue gear. Ozzie was the team sharpshooter. For entertainment, Henry would kick a rock into the air, and Ozzie would shoot it to pieces.

However, right now the dogs were in their annual "rut." Personality change! Irritable, short tempered, quick on the draw. Henry was never comfortable when they were like this, but all the prairie dogs went through it for a couple of months each year. Usually they took a leave of absence, but this year there had been budget cuts, and the Patrol was short staffed. All hands had to be available, ruts or no ruts. So the mule just put up with it. What he especially didn't like was the number of false alarms the dogs called when they were in this state. This tour had been an exception. They were coming to the end of their 24-hour shift and were heading back to the road where a truck would arrive to pick them up and unload their relief team. Maybe they could get through this round without incident.

No such luck! Ozzie gave out with a couple of complex high pitched squeaks. Izzie popped his head out of his saddle bag and stared across Henry's back at his partner. Henry didn't even turn. He brayed, but the meaning was very clear. "This isn't another one of your desert mirages, is it Ozzie?"

The prairie dog squeaked again and threw a rock at the back of the mule's head. He kept rocks in his bag as auxiliary weapons. Henry stopped in his tracks and almost dumped the dogs on the ground. Izzie barked, "No Henry! I see it too."

297

"You're just as bad as he is, you pipsqueak. OK, show me!"

"Over there, in the *arroyo*. Something red and black. Could be a vehicle or a downed plane."

The mule, whose eyes were nowhere near as sensitive, stared into the early morning sun as it rose over the hills. "I don't see anything."

"To your right, about ten degrees! Keep walking! Keep walking! Now do you see it?"

"My sainted Grandpa Francis, you're right! Sorry, guys, I owe you one." He picked up the pace, and they slid down the side of the *arroyo*.

"I think it's a car. Upside down! Yup, see the wheels?

"OK," said Henry. "Let's approach this one cautiously. Cars don't always overturn accidentally. See any sign of a driver?"

"Not yet, but I don't see any footprints leading to or from the car either. Someone may have tossed it over the hill, or there may be a driver still stuck in there. Let us down and we'll sneak up on it."

Henry sat on his hindquarters, and the two prairie dogs, well armed and cautious, skittered out of their saddle bags and crept up on the car. "There's someone in the car. It looks like some kind of spotted cat. Not native to anywhere around here, though. Can't tell whether it's alive or dead. It's certainly not conscious. Henry, can you get your hind hooves under the car and see if you can roll it over and kick it back upright? The roof looks pretty badly smashed in, and the windows are shattered. Snazzy car! A Ferrari!"

The two prairie dogs swiftly dug the sand out from under one side of the roof so the mule could get a footing and some purchase to push the car up and over.

Henry backed up against the side of the overturned car, slid his hooves underneath, and gave it a mighty kick. The Ferrari rolled up on its side, teetered but then fell back on its roof. The mule and prairie dogs just missed getting squashed as it fell back. Izzie shouted, "Careful! It may be leaking gasoline. I can smell it! Oh, hell! It fell back in a different position. We'll have to dig again."

Digging, of course is a prairie dog's vocation, avocation, and recreation. They have been known to undermine cattle pasture land overnight with their incessant tunnel building. Back they went for another shot at the ground under the Ferrari, this time digging the hole a bit deeper, so the mule's kick would have maximum leverage. Henry tried again. This time the car, after teetering precariously for a few seconds, rolled all the way over and landed on its wheels. They were about to congratulate each other when they heard a god-awful shriek from within the smashed speedster. There was another speedster inside, not quite smashed, but hurting and damned upset about the way she had been awakened. Chita!!

She had drifted in and out of consciousness during the first rollover attempt, and by the time Henry unleashed the second kick, she was awake, raging and ready for a fight. She lashed out with her paws. and the crumpled gull wing door on the driver's side sprang open. Scrambling out as fast as her battered body would allow, she saw the mule and the two prairie dogs each wearing deputy stars on their neck collars and screamed, "All right, coppers! Come and get me!" *(She was obviously temporarily deranged because her normal reaction would have been to just run like hell.)*

Wrong thing to yell at two prairie dogs who had been up over twenty-four hours and were well and truly in the middle of their rut season. Ozzie pulled his sawed-off shot gun and swung around toward the cat, but Henry gave him a slight kick and ruined his aim. Not so Izzie. He shot several sedation darts point blank at the cat and they all three watched as she crumpled down next to the wreck. Out cold and then some!!

"What did you hit her with, Izzie?" asked Henry.

"Everything I had. I'm not gonna let some consarned cat give me and my brother a hard time after trying to rescue her. What kind of cat is she?"

"Don't rightly know," brayed Henry. "Never seen one like that before with the spots all over her body and the streaks on her face. Look at the legs on her. She ain't local."

Ozzie had put down his shotgun and had skittered over to get a better look. "I'm no expert but I think that's a diamond collar around her neck, and she's been driving a Ferrari. This cat is somethin' special! We better call this one in, pronto!"

Henry wasn't quite convinced she was special. He had seen some pretty cheap show girls flaunting diamonds or what looked like diamonds and driving around in fancy cars until their boyfriends got tired of them. This was probably just another one of those. And that "come and get me, coppers!" routine wasn't the height of elite sophistication. Nevertheless, procedures were procedures!

He got on the radio to Headquarters, reported their position and described the situation. The minute he described the cat, the Lieutenant on the other end shouted in his ear. "That's Chita! We've been searching for that cat and her gang for a couple of days. Don't let her get away."

"She isn't going anywhere. She'll be out for hours. Izzie got a little trigger happy with the sedative darts."

"Just as well," said the Lieutenant, "so long as she doesn't die on you. We need her alive." *(Henry shot a sideways glance at the shotgun totin' Ozzie and shook his head.)* Was there anyone else with her in the car?"

"Nope, and there were no footprints coming or going! She was doing a solo!"

"OK," said the Lieutenant. "Just stand by. We'll have a medevac helicopter and a tow truck out there right away. Your relief truck will be coming along, but you guys hang on till we get there. You can come back with us after we're finished. We need to get an accurate description of the scene before you flipped the car upright and zonked the cat. Nice work!"

Oh, swell," thought the mule, "stuck out here waiting in the desert with two rutty prairie dogs, a wrecked sports car and a very unconscious spotted cat. Then we get grilled by the brass. Well, I guess it beats pulling a wagon."

The prairie dogs had dug themselves a couple of holes and curled up in them to take a nap. Henry shook his head, let out an irate bray and sat down on his haunches to watch the sun rise further over the horizon. His legs hurt!

Chapter Thirty Four

Yes, the Fox is as smart as can be.

But you don't have to take it from me.

She will make you aware

Of her savvy and flair

On Fox cable and broadcast TV.

Maury here! I had gotten up early Tuesday morning and decided to have breakfast down in one of the hotel's dining rooms instead of ordering room service. Octavius was up but in no mood to go public. Howard skittered into the room just as I was leaving and I invited him to join me. Bruce was already out scouring the landscape with a Las Vegas Police helicopter. We took the normal-sized elevator down to the main floor. Elevators were the bane of my existence. Not the elevator itself, but the usual occupants who shared it with me. This time it felt great not to be nearly smothered by the Humungous Bear or stomped to death by Bouncing Bruce. Of course, I didn't want to get too close to Howard's quills, either. Story of my life! Threatened by all – a threat to no one! I was always moody before my first cup of coffee.

The conventioneers were all filing into one of the ballrooms to snarf up a continental breakfast. "Continental" meaning enough food to fill a small-to-medium size continent. Europe or Australia, maybe! We steered around the raucous mob and headed for a small show lounge that doubled as a breakfast room in the morning. Almost empty! A meal in peace? No such luck. We had just gotten our orders off to the waitress, a cute jenny with a ring of flowers curled around each of her ears, when I looked up right into the lens of a TV camera. The lights were blinding. So was the phony smile on a well made-up female fox face. She pushed a microphone at me causing me to spill coffee all over myself and the table.

"Mr. Meerkat? You are Mauritius Meerkat, Octavius Bear's number one operative in his startling anti-crime exploits?" Turning to Howard, "And you, sir, I don't know your name."

Howard thought quickly and said, "Polyphemus Porcupine, Mr. Meerkat's stock- broker and financial adviser."

A quick flash of disappointment swept across her face, but she quickly recovered. She wasn't interested in stock quotes or my portfolio. Oh, well, one victim was better than none. She became all teeth again as she flourished her beautifully coiffed tail and turned her attention back to me. Her cameraman and producer, two scruffy looking desert rats, got into position. The producer was trying to mop up the coffee I had spilled. Wouldn't look good on hi-definition, 60-inch screens. Coming to think of it, neither would I. I wanted to clobber Howard for confirming my identity, but what the hell. This Meerkat was out of the bag.

I tried to push the producer away as she dabbed and mopped at me. "Please, ma'am, I hardly know you." She didn't take the hint.

Then, I heard Foxy say, "I'm Vera Vulpine of KRAP-TV News, Channel Sixteen. There are a lot of rumors going around town about your boss having threats made against him." The camera's red light had gone on, and the producer was listening over earphones to a portable recorder.

"I'm not sure I understand the question, if it was a question."

Putting on her most breathless and annoying, breaking-news-from-the-seat-of- the-action voice, she rattled out, "KRAP-TV has learned exclusively that attempts are being made on Octavius Bear, multi-billionaire business bear, scientist, intellectual and international crime-fighter. It's apparent from the increased security that the police and this hotel are very much concerned about his well-being. Now what can you tell our audience about the situation, Mr. Meerkat, since you two have such a close relationship."

"It's not true, we're just good friends," I quipped. She was not amused.

"Maury! May I call you Maury?"

"No!"

"Maury, we have it from several reliable sources that security is being further tightened here through the remainder of this convention. Rumor hath it that the reason is threats against Octavius Bear."

Giving me her you're-not-getting-away-without-a-comment stare, she wielded the mike like a weapon, and the camera lens zoomed in, taking a clear shot of my left nostril. I'm less than two feet tall, and obviously, resistance was futile. So I gave her Innocent Meerkat smile #5.

"Oh that…no, no, no, no! I have heard thru a back channel *(whatever the hell that was)* that the convention managers had received several threatening text messages, e-mails, phone calls, and smoke signals vowing to disrupt and close down the convention. Genetics is a touchy subject, as you probably know, and there are many animals *(including me)* who feel that their DNA is their private property and who are willing to sustain arrest and bodily harm to make their point *(not including me).* It happens every time a group like this gets together. No matter how much the scientists try to explain the benefits of their research and development, the extremists refuse to listen. But no, it has nothing to do directly with Mr. Bear. I suggest you track down Il Professore Roberto Rabbito, the chair beast of this colloquium and query him about the threats. I'm sure he'll be happy to share his views with you." *(Immediately after emerging from the cardiology intensive care unit he's bound for after meeting up with you.)*

"And now," looking at my watch, "it seems I am late for my next appointment. These conventions are so hectic. Polyphemus, please send me an e-mail with your investment recommendations. I'll have to get back to you by phone. It was a pleasure meeting you, Miss Vulpine, and your charming

crew. Be sure and give the *Professore* my best regards when you see him."
(And I hope you do. The two of you were meant for each other.)

I bowed, tossed my tail around my neck and strode off, looking briefly over my shoulder at a deadpan Howard and a confused waitress who had just arrived with our breakfasts. No doubt, Howard would polish both of them off. He owes me big time.

Chapter Thirty Five

The Komōdo is built to astound

Stretching eight feet or more on the ground

He's a frightening sight.

Sixty teeth in his bite!

I don't think I would like him around

Octavius, Howard, Megatunni, and I were to meet in the lobby of the Blue Bayou at 10:00 AM. The din from the conventioneers was incredible. Two moose got into an argument, trumpeting across the hall at each other, and a Malamute was doing its "Woo, woo, woo" call. Noise and more noise. The Great Bear had been playing hooky from the convention proceedings at the insistence of security and the police. Octavius was standing, trying to make himself heard by the Indonesian Komodo as I came up. He could have roared the whole lobby into silence but he was trying not to draw too much attention to himself, although he was standing erect nine or so feet high. Ah, well! Paradoxes! Paradoxes!

Howard arrived a few minutes later, wiping egg off his whiskers. I never did get breakfast. He and I proceeded to tell Megatunni and Bear about the TV reporter. "Damn, Mr. Megatunni, there's a leak somewhere in the security system," growled Octavius.

The Dragon looked from side to side, flicked his tongue several times, and roared for his assistant, Snappi. The caiman came bustling over from talking to a cop and said, "Yessir, what's wrong, sir?"

"Snappi, someone in this protection operation has a big mouth. *(Coming from a Komodo, that was quite a statement. Eight feet long with jaws to match, to say nothing of a maw full of venomous saliva.)* Get on it!! Then leave the culprit to me."

Megatunni wasn't very happy about our standing there in the lobby, either. He ushered us off to a room behind the main desk. At least, it was quieter.

Then he proceeded to tell us about the incident last night over at *The Golden Pagoda*. Was it Imperius and Bigg?? No doubt about it! But what were they doing? The police had fished the damaged, dripping jade statue out of the *Aspergio* pool around six this morning after one of the guards at the hotel said he thought he saw the Arabian Baboon drop something. They were still trying to get the screaming eggs under control and had evacuated the entire Golden Pagoda in the process. Guests weren't happy. Gamblers weren't happy. Win-Win wasn't happy. No one in authority on the Strip was happy.

"AND," said Megatunni, "I just got off the phone with the state police before you arrived. Chita has been picked up."

Expectant looks.

"Yeah, they found her in a wrecked car in a ravine about thirty miles north of town. Your Inspector Wallaroo is up there with them."

"Maury," said the Bear, "use that speakerphone and see if you can reach the Inspector. What do you suppose she was doing alone in a wrecked car? Do you think she was on some kind of mission? Or perhaps Imperius had found out about her talking to you, Maury, and she was trying to get away."

The sound of a helicopter rotor thwup-thwupped over the speakerphone. "G'day mates. Bruce Wallaroo, here."

The sound of a Kodiak Bear roared back. "Good morning, Inspector. This is Octavius and I have Maury, Howard, and Mr. Megatunni with me."

"Mornin' all. I have just landed at the scene of the accident. It seems a desert patrol found a wreck, and the state police arrived to find a cheetah. She was trapped inside an overturned Ferrari."

"A Ferrari?" I thought. "Why does that ring a bell?"

"Are you sure it's Chita?" asked Howard.

"Oh yeah, right down to the diamond collar!"

"What kind of shape is she in? Can she talk? Will she talk?"

"Not likely for a few hours. They had to use sedative darts to subdue her. She's out for the count. I'm following the medevac chopper back to the hospital."

"Did you find out where the Duck has been hiding out?" asked Megatunni.

"We thought we had a pretty good lead on a warehouse not too far from that small airport we investigated. But by the time we got there, it was completely empty except for an overturned cargo container. There were vehicle tracks all over the place including some recent rubber burns on the roadway outside."

"Caused by the Ferrari? Chita? The Gang?" I asked.

"Could be, Maury! We're checking. But even if it was them, they're long since gone."

"Yeah, we know. They pulled some bizarre job off over at the Golden Pagoda last night. Well, at least we've got her. Unless he's hired some additional help, that just leaves Imperius and Bigg."

"What did that damn Duck do now?" yelled Bruce.

"Weird. They go into the casino pretending to be rich Arabs. They con the casino owner into letting them see the hotel's collection of priceless jade. Then they steal one piece, throw out a bunch of Black Quacks, escape, and finally, Bigg is seen hauling himself up a flagpole at *The Aspergio* and dumping something into the fountains. Turns out it was the jade statue. Wet and broken!"

"Shades of Chicago. Senseless destruction of valuable gems. Well, Maury, still think he's trying to prove something, or has he just gone off the deep end?"

"Don't know, Bruce. He's certainly created a massive response over at the Strip. Every cop and his mother-in-law are over there checking all the hotels and casinos. All we've got is a skeleton security crew left over here."

"I don't like that very much!"

"Neither do we, but Octavius insists he can take care of himself. I've asked Wyatt and the Frau to come here from the plane. A little more defense never hurt."

"Not necessary!" grumbled the Bear.

Bruce asked, "I wonder if he got more help now that Chita's out of action!"

Octavius interrupted, "I doubt if he'd let anyone else in on his scheme, whatever it is. Those musical eggs they were making up in Michigan hold some kind of clue, but I can't put it together with the rest of the threats, like the particle beam projector. Thanks, Inspector, please call me the minute you have anything from that infernal cat."

"Roger, Ocko!" And the connection was cut.

Frustrated stares. OK, I'd be the one to say it. "Now what??"

"Let's head over to the Aquacade," said Octavius. "I want to see what they're doing and maybe we can talk to Signor Ferreti again."

"Ferreti, Ferrari! I knew there was something. I've seen that little creep zooming away from the hotel in a bright red overpowered muscle car. I wouldn't know a Ferrari from a freight car, but maybe that wreck out there in the desert belongs to him."

"Good catch, Maury. Mr. Megatunni, will you call the state police and check the registration on that wreck? Meanwhile, let's see if we can find our little friend, Ferreti. He should be busy with all the final arrangements for the show."

Indeed he was. In fact he was rushing around, giving orders, changing his mind, clapping his paws to his head and generally, having a grand old time playing frustrated impresario. As we arrived, he was supervising the installation of two huge neon signs that said: *The Genius of Genetics – 2013* and *Genoa Genetics Welcomes You. (What else?)* He came close to having one of the signs dropped on him while he was having an argument with the crane operator.

Along the Aquacade walls, crews were setting up four white, hot air balloons, two flanking the stage and two in the rear of the horseshoe-shaped arena. They were tying the baskets securely to the walls with heavy cables. One crew was testing to make sure they would inflate properly. When one of the balloons was almost fully inflated, I almost lost the breakfast I hadn't had. There, staring down at me from the side of a pulsing, forty-foot white egg was a full color portrait of *Il Professore* and Ferrucio Ferreti, smiling idiotically and embracing in a congratulatory hug. Each one had a paw held up in triumph. Underneath this masterpiece were the words: "*Viva Italia!*" So much for subtlety and international amity.

The *Aquabears* were going through their paces in the pool, and media technicians were testing microphones and video projection screens. Yes, this was going to be an extravaganza, even by Las Vegas standards. Yet another group was setting up a laser light show.

Howard looked at me, and I looked back. "A laser show," he said. "That would be a perfect cover for the particle beam projector, if it's here."

I replied, "If the Duck is here, the particle projector is here and we know the Duck is somewhere in Vegas or even closer."

I didn't know it at the time, but I was absolutely right. Helping to set up the balloon at stage right was Bigg Baboon disguised as a rigger. Hiding up in a light tower was a harmless looking Mandarin Duck, looking out at the proceedings. Bigg, like several of the riggers wore a head set, but unlike the other riggers, he was getting directions from Imperius Drake.

Octavius padded over with Megatunni. "I don't like that laser show being here but I don't suppose we could get it cancelled."

"Not without causing a strike of all the technicians, riggers, actors, waiters, ticket handlers, sweepers…"

"All right, Mr. Megatunni, I get the picture. Howard, you're the expert. Go on over and start up a conversation with the laser crew. See if there's anything unusual about them, their equipment or their show plans."

The porcupine went off, armed with his quills and his laser jargon, and the three of us moved off to see if we could get Ferrucio Ferreti to talk calmly and sensibly for a few minutes. Unfortunately, by the time we got there, he had been joined by *Il Professore*. Frenzy at Warp 9.5! They were shouting and gesticulating at each other and anyone else in sight. All they needed was a soccer ball to start a World Cup riot.

"Buon giorno, Signore," rumbled Octavius. *"Va Bene???"*

"Not so *bene*! Signor Bear," said the ferret, "All of these last minute things and we're behind schedule and *Il Professore* here doesn't like his picture on the balloons," *(Why was I not surprised?)* "Scusi, Signore," and he turned to the Rabbit and there followed a rapid-fire explosion of Italian squeaks and yips. *Il Professore* stalked off.

311

Making a world-recognized sign with his paw at the departing rabbit, the ferret turned to us. "I do not mean to be rude, but I have so many things to oversee."

Megatunni jumped in. "We won't bother you, Signor Ferreti, except to tell you that I plan to have maximum security around the Aquacade tonight, if I can get them back here. We still haven't caught up with those anti-genetic agitators, and your little party could make a great target."

Have you ever seen a pure white ferret? Ferreti had just turned albino at the thought of his cast-of-millions production being turned into a massive protest. *"Santa Orechietta!* I think I have a heart attack! You know this is going to happen?"

The Komodo smiled a consoling smile. *(Which was just the same as a threatening smile.)* "No, no, no. We just want to be very cautious. You just do what you're doing. Those balloons can't get loose, can they?"

"Absolutely not. I personally guarantee. You are all coming to the show this evening? *Bene, bene.* I have a great announcement about Genoa Genetics and of course, Signor Bear, I am sure you will enjoy seeing the *Bellisime Aquabears*, especially *La Squisita Bearonessa."*

I'm not sure which was worse, a scared stiff ferret or a leering ferret. As I said, I don't like ferrets.

We were just about to turn away when Octavius casually dropped a nonchalant query. "Oh. By the way, Signor Ferreti, among my few diversions, I am something of an automobile enthusiast. Unfortunately, I can't fit into most of them, but I do like to admire them. Was that a Ferrari I saw you driving the other day?"

Short intake of breath. "No, no signore. I drive a Lamborghini, although they are both fine Italian motorcars. Unfortunately, it is in the shop. They are like beautiful females, no? They must be pampered and tended to."

Yuck! What a sleaze! I had a sensation in my whiskers that he was lying about the car, but I couldn't figure out why.

Just then, Belinda came up on the diving board, saw Octavius and waved furiously. Then she took off with a full gainer and slid into the water like a fur-covered sword. Octavius just stared. When she surfaced, she waved again and we all waved back.

"Let's go back to the suite," he said. "The Frau and the Colonel should be there by now. We need to strategize about tonight." I called the plane. They had left twenty minutes ago.

Up on the Aquacade light tower a pair of beady eyes was following us. In the basket of a stage-side balloon, a brown-haired rigger was slipping a long object under a pile of ropes and a tank of propane.

Down below, a porcupine was running back to meet us. "What have you found out about the laser show, Howard?" asked the Great Bear.

"I'm happy to report that they are your standard showcase laser jockeys, Octavius. They do a lot of the rock concerts and special effects around town and they've been here for years. I'm sure you know most of them, Mr. Megatunni."

The Komodo nodded.

Howard went on. "The low power lasers are aimed at the stage area and are triggered by a high speed, computer-based firing system. Latest technology. Complex software of their own design. I don't see them as being the source of a particle beam, but all the light and sound could mask a shot from the ray gun."

"So I fall over, and nobody even notices." said the Bear. "I may even be disintegrated."

I swear, sometimes his ego is tough to figure out. Here we are, trying to stop a possible assassination, and all he's worried about is whether his death will be sensational. I could use some coconut milk.

"Let's head back to the hotel," I said.

When I got back to the rooms, I raised the Inspector again. He told me they had taken Chita to a well-guarded hospital room and that a preliminary examination of her unconscious body showed some scratches and bruises, some dehydration but nothing else serious. Of course, they'd have to wait till she came to. That would still be a couple of hours from now.

"For gosh sakes, Bruce, what did they pump into her with those darts?"

"I think they gave her the raging elephant dose. She gave them quite a scrap, did that spotted sheila." He sounded almost admiring.

"Can you get back over here for a meeting with all of us at the suite? Nothing much else you can do over at the hospital, is there?'

"Gotcher, sport. Be there in a spot."

When I hung up, Megatunni was on his cell phone. He was nodding and writing something down. He looked at Octavius and me. Nodded again and hung up.

"That was the state police. The Ferrari is a rental."

Chorus of voices: "A rental??"

"This is Vegas, boys. You can rent anything."

"Who was it rented to?" I asked.

He was enjoying this. His tongue flicked several times and he said. "Signor Ferrucio Ferreti."

314

"That perjuring pervert! 'Oh, no signore, I have a Lamborghini.' Well, he just might, now that his Ferrari is scattered all over a ravine. Why would he lie?"

"Reflex action, Maury," said Octavius, using his calming voice #42 that annoyed the hell out of me. "He knew it had been stolen, and he wasn't sure whether it was involved in a crime or a major accident. I agree. He's a real shyster, but I don't think he's in on any of Imperius' plots. For one thing, Imperius probably would have had Bigg strangle him by now."

"Wait a second, Octavius," said Howard. "That doesn't compute. If he wasn't involved with Imperius, what was Chita doing in his car?"

"Good question, Howard. One we should ask the ferret as soon as we get finished here. It's getting late, and we haven't had any lunch *(or mead)*. Maury, order up some room service. Oh, and get enough for the Frau and the Colonel."

Speaking of whom, they walked in the door, I swear, wagging their tails in unison with silly grins on their faces. What was happening over at that airplane?

"Herr Bear," growled the she-wolf, now all business, "Here we are. We brought a keg of mead with us. Is there to be a battle plan?"

"Thank you," he said, brightening considerably. "Battle Plan?? Perhaps, Frau Schuylkill, perhaps! We definitely believe that Imperius Drake is here with a version of the particle beam projector and that I may well be his target tonight."

She cut loose a spate of Switzer Deutsch swear words, and even the Colonel looked amazed. She finished with, "We must stop that verdammte Duck, no matter what."

"Yes, we must. I've planned a festive get together for all of us tomorrow and I'd like to be there with you to enjoy it."

315

"Frau and Colonel, the show begins at 8:00 o'clock tonight. At 7:45, I want the *Ursa Major* aloft, fully armed and on station over the western desert. I want you to be able to get in over the Aquacade at any time in less than sixty seconds. Needless to say, you use full stealth and watch out for other air traffic."

The wolves looked slightly annoyed. "We are competent combat pilots, Herr Bear."

"I apologize, Frau Schuylkill and to you too, Colonel. I guess this thing is getting on my nerves. I have the utmost trust in you."

"We understand. But what will be our targets, Octavius?" asked the Colonel.

"I hate to admit it but I'm not sure. I'm not even sure there will be any targets. And believe me, it pains me to be using up all that fuel on what may turn out to be a wild duck chase."

"You've got it, Octavius," he said, "You call in the fire. We'll be on it." Frau Schuylkill nodded her assent.

"Thanks, Colonel. Now let's go around the room. Mr. Megatunni!"

"We will have the entrances and all the exits as well as the shipping docks covered. Back stage and the corridors will be manned. Same drill as the keynote session. Show your credentials, or no admittance. The convention name tags have pictures on them, but I have to tell you, all you mammals look about the same to me. The police will have cars at the main entrance and the rear to block any escape."

Octavius nodded, "What about those balloons? I wish they weren't there." *(Me too! The twenty-foot pictures of those two frauds on the sides of the balloons were more than I could take.)*

316

Megatunni said, "Sorry, so do I, but the balloons were part of the hotel's contract with Ferreti and the professor. I'm sure they'd sue management for every silver dollar we have if we made them take them down. There's just not enough evidence of an imminent threat originating from the balloons."

(I guess he's right, but he had never met Imperius.)

"Anyway," he continued, "they are firmly tethered to the walls of the Aquacade and once they are fully inflated, no one will be allowed inside the baskets. They'll stay up until the propane runs out."

"We've checked the stage crews, and they look OK. This Imperius Drake is going to have to be pretty clever to pull anything off."

Bruce bounced through the door. "Oh, if there's one thing that ruddy Duck is, it's clever. Just thinkin' of him gets me spewin'."

(I looked over at Frau Schuylkill. No howling. No upset at the Wallaroo being there. Of course! It wasn't her hotel room, so she didn't care.)

"Hello, Bruce," said Octavius.

"G'day Ocko! G'day all! Is this a council of war?"

"You could say that. It's more like a civil defense program."

The Bear turned back to the group. "For everyone's information, Doctor Watt has checked out the laser show and it looks above board to him. Correct, Doctor?"

Howard nodded.

"Maury, what about you? Any thoughts?"

"I'm going crazy trying to figure out those damned plastic eggs. We're almost certain he brought them down here from Michigan, but no one has seen them. They weren't at the desert warehouse, if he was ever at that warehouse. We don't really know what they are, except what the Pondscummers told us. Music players, my Aunt Matilda *(sweet lady)*! If Chita ever comes to, we may be able to get it out of her. That is, if we can persuade her to talk at all. I don't like those egg things one bit but I can't tell you why, except the Duck is behind them. We don't even know if they're going to appear tonight. I didn't see anything when we were down at the Aquacade. How about you, Mr. Megatunni?"

"Not a thing. There's lot of stuff stored down there, but it all belongs to the hotel or Genoa Genetics. The ferret says it all checks out. I don't like him much, either, but I don't think Ferreti would be involved in an assassination. He's afraid of his own tail."

Octavius, as usual, had the final word. "*IF* he knows he's involved, Mr. Megatunni. *IF* he knows!"

Chapter Thirty Six

Poodles often are dressed up like toys.

So you can't tell the girls from the boys.

But beneath all the glitz

A strong canine still sits

Who can bite and make plenty of noise.

At 7:30 that evening, at the reception in the ballroom, the delegates were munching one last shrimp or spinach roll and inhaling one last slurp of champagne before they trickled over to the Aquacade for the Grand Finale.

Backstage, the cast and crew were going through last-minute checkups. The *Aquabears* were warming up, doing tumbles and stretches.

Ferrucio Ferreti, glistening in his gold tuxedo, made his way down to the below-stage storage areas. "Ferrucio," he thought, "This is your hour of *bona fortuna. Molto bene!* No more clandestine cloning. Genoa Genetics will be in the big time. Genes, RNA, DNA! Science awards. Maybe he'd get the Noble Prize like *Il Professore*. A global corporation. He would sell stock, do mergers, borrow more money! He would have money! Lots of money! No more stealing copyrights and patents. Although why should having money keep him from continuing to steal patents and copyrights? All the big guys do it!"

He reached the back of the loading docks. "Yoo hoo, *Dottore* Yu, I am here."

A mandarin Duck waddled out from behind a large piece of scenery and said, "Shhhh, Signor Ferreti. No one must know we are meeting. Our relationship is very hush-hush. Is it not?"

"Oh, *si, si.* You have the package for *la Bearonessa? Grazie.* I will deliver it myself."

The Duck had handed over a beautifully wrapped box the size of a jewel necklace.

"Yes, please make sure she gets it right away, but don't mention me. She'll know who it's from. It's that family heirloom I told you about."

"I will do it right now. But before I go. I do not like to mention this but I checked with my bank several times today. The 250,000,000 euros had not arrived at the account."

"I am so sorry, Signore. Today is a bank holiday in Bermuda. I didn't realize. The money will be there first thing tomorrow."

A sigh of relief. "*Grazie!* As you can see from this show, I already have a few bills to pay."

"Ah, but it will be worth it, Ferrucio, it will be worth it!"

"One more thing. The police found my Ferrari. It was wrecked in a ravine. They said they found a cheetah inside."

"Oh, I am so sorry again. That cheetah was a warehouse hand I had hired on to assist me. Recovering drug addict, down on her luck. I thought I'd give her a chance. See how she repaid us. I will compensate you for the car if the insurance doesn't cover it."

"Oh, no worry. Between us, it was a rental!"

"Ah, but tell me, this cheetah. Was she alive or dead when they found her?"

"I don't know, *Dottore*. Now I had better get up to the *Bearonessa*."

"Yes, please do! But wait one more moment. I wonder if I could impose on you for one more favor. Would you please have this envelope delivered immediately to Professore Rabbito. It is essential he gets it before the start of the show. Here is some money to tip the belldog. "

The ferret skittered off with package and envelope whistling, "Money for Nothing." Little did he know!

Inside the envelope was a single sheet of high quality vellum with the blue imprint of the Noble Prize Selection Committee, along with a tastefully emblazoned facsimile of the gold medal conferred on each winner: The profile of Nils Noble, progenitor of the red fox population in Sweden. On the page was typed this sparse message:

"To whom it may concern: The Committee is pleased to announce that the winner of the 2013 Noble Prize for Genetics is Doctor Yu-Aul-Kum for his breakthrough studies in enhancing the brains and developmental capabilities of the avian species. We congratulate him and will welcome him to the ranks of the prize-winners at the next Noble convocation." Signed Sven Moose - Secretary General of the Noble Association.

"That should finish off that little white rabbit charlatan," chortled Imperius. "I want to see him at the Grand Finale, if he shows up. Maybe he'll jump off the diving board and drown himself in the pool. Or maybe he'll have that heart attack he was always claiming he was about to have. More likely a nervous breakdown. But enough fun and games! The Grand Plan must proceed as it was so brilliantly designed."

"There is one stone in the birdseed," he thought. "Chita may still be alive. Perhaps she will betray us again. Well, she has less than an hour to do it. Nothing will stand in our way. We must prepare." With that, he took out a glass vial from under his wing and waddled behind the scenery.

The Aquacade glowed with neon and spotlights. The band was tuning up. Each balloon was washed in light and the faces of Ferreti and Rabbito smiled inanely from their inflated sides. The guards had just checked to make sure no one was in the baskets. Suddenly, one of the spotlights shattered *(as planned by the Duck)* and everyone turned to see what had caused the "boom." Everyone that is, except Bigg, still dressed as a rigger. He took the opportunity to shinny up the cable and jump into the stage-right balloon. He ducked down below the side of the basket and began to assemble the particle ray gun.

"Let's see! Put tab A in slot A. Turn holding screw one quarter to the right and insert barrel in housing. DO NOT TURN ON POWER SUPPLY." He had practiced and practiced at the warehouse. He liked the ray gun. He loved to hear it zap.

There was a flap of wings, and a black Duck flew into the basket from out of the increasing darkness. Imperius!

"Oh, hello Sire! The exploding lamp worked like a charm. I didn't recognize you. You've been in your other costume for so long."

"Ah, but tonight is a very special occasion, Baboon. We must appear at our very best. Let us inspect the projector. Have you assembled it correctly?"

"Just like you taught me, Sire. Put tab A in slot A. Turn holding screw one quarter to the right and insert barrel in housing. DO NOT TURN ON POWER SUPPLY."

"Yes, yes, fine, Baboon, fine." He tested the power supply. All green. He calibrated the sight and chortled to himself as he struggled to put his special grip gloves on the end of his wings. "Help us with these gloves, Baboon. We must be properly dressed in every detail."

322

*****

Up in a penthouse suite within the hotel, a buzzer sounded and a hotel belldog presented an impressive envelope to a young cottontail graduate student who was serving as secretary and go-fer for *Il Professore* Roberto Rabbito *(who, at the moment, was checking his dress in every detail in front of a floor to ceiling mirror.)* "*Scusi, Professore,* this envelope just came for you. It looks like it may be important."

"Bah, always the botheration when I am so overloaded with responsibilities. Check and see if my tail is properly powdered while I look at this. It is probably yet one more invitation to dinner or cocktails from some ambitious young scientist. They should know it takes more than dinner to influence *Il Professore Magnifico*."

Then he saw the seal on the back of the envelope – The Noble Committee. Paws shaking, he attempted to open the flap but dropped it instead. "Giulio, pick that up and open it for me. And be careful! You have my life in your hands."

The student gaped at the scientist and then used his teeth to pry open the sealed flap. The professor went into a rage, "Not with your teeth, idiot. That is almost certainly the most important communication I have ever received. I am too excited! You may have the privilege of reading it to me."

The cottontail unfolded the paper and began to examine the text.

"What does it say, Giulio? What does it say?"

He read! Before he finished the second sentence, unmerciful screams assaulted his long and sensitive ears. Rabbito snatched the letter from his paws and stared at the print, willing it to be otherwise. He tore the letter into pieces, pushed Giulio out of the way and raced toward the open balcony of the suite. Just as he was about to climb over the guardrail, the graduate student grabbed him by his ears and dragged him back inside, slamming the sliding doors shut as he went.

Rabbito screamed, "Yu-Aul-Kum! Yu-Aul-Kum! Yu-Aul-Kum!"

"Who should come, *Professore*?" the cottontail unwisely asked.

"The idiots! That Oriental trickster! That fraud! They gave him the prize! I should have had him assassinated when I had the chance. No one would have ever noticed. Now, I am disgraced, disgraced!"

He fell over in a dead faint. Giulio hopped to the nearest table, picked up the phone and shouted, "Emergency! Suite 3100! Professore Roberto Rabbito! Send medical help immediately. I think he's having a heart attack!"

*****

Down in the Aquacade stadium, an argument was going on involving Octavius and Howard, Mr. Megatunni, and me. We were trying to persuade the Bear to go back up to the suite and watch the show with a pair of binoculars. He was having none of it.

"As you have pointed out so many times, we don't know what is going to happen, if anything. We don't know whether I am a target. We have no assurances that anything is going to take place at all. I just heard the *Ursa Major* taking off. I hate to deploy that airplane for no reason. We are extrapolating all these dire events from a warning given us by a definitely unreliable source. Speaking of whom, is she awake yet? Has she talked?"

"I'll see if I can reach Bruce," I said. "I believe he's at the hospital."

The audience was taking their seats, and the band started playing walk-in music.

*****

Backstage, Belinda had just returned from a trip to the ladies' room and padded into her dressing room. There on her make-up table was a beautifully wrapped package. Could it be from him? She tore open the

324

wrapping, snapped open the box and gasped. There glowing out at her was the Deep Blue Sapphire, and it was attached to a long gold chain. She put it around her neck and preened. The chain disappeared in her fur but the sapphire, oh, the sapphire just sat there and glowed and glowed and glowed. Oh, that darling bear. She reached for her cell phone.

*****

Just about everyone had taken their seats in the stadium. We were sitting in the center section next to an aisle and right on top of an exit. We could get Octavius out of there in a few seconds if we had to. I was on his right side, Howard was on his left and Mr. Megatunni was sitting directly behind him.

The lights lowered, except for the ones shining on those stupid faces on the balloons. The band hit a tremendous fanfare. Out onto the stage, paw-in-paw with two beautiful show-poodles *(who were a foot or more taller than he was),* ran the Ferret. His gold tux glistened in the spotlight that followed him and the two drop-dead gorgeous canines. They had on spectacular headdresses making him look even more insignificant. There was some applause. I believe it was for the poodles. They strutted back offstage.

He was wearing a wireless mike. "*Buona sera*, fellow scientists. I am Ferrucio Ferreti, president of Genoa Genetics and your genial host for this evening's spectacolo. Welcome to the Blue Bayou Aquacade – or tonight maybe we should call it the Gene Pool. Ha, Ha! *(He broke up. No one else did. This was going to be a tough crowd. Bring on the Aquabears!)*

"I am delighted to be with you here tonight as is my great friend and colleague, *Il Professore* Roberto Rabbito." He pointed into the audience and a spotlight caught *Il Professore* in the front row dressed in white tie, tails, sash and an array of medals that would make a cub scout green with envy. Il Professore, surrounded by a doctor and a nurse, waved to the rather tepid applause without standing up and began shaking. Was he sobbing?

"Before we begin the show this evening I have a few announcements to make." *(Muffled groans. They're even tougher than I thought.)* "*Primo*, you are probably wondering how a relatively small laboratory like Genoa Genetics could afford to present this show. Well, I'll tell you. We are small no longer." *(Fanfare!)* "I am happy to announce that through the good offices of the newly organized Genius of Genetics Foundation, we have received a grant of 250 million euros to expand our research and our world renowned publishing programs." *(Shocked silence. What the hell was the Genius of Genetics Foundation? And of all the labs, institutes, and gin joints in all the world why would they give such an immense grant to a sixth rate schlock shop? Murmurs throughout the audience.)*

The band picked up with "A Pretty Dog is like a Melody." Down each of the aisles pranced a fully costumed Show-Poodle followed by a Great Dane in a tuxedo. The Dane was carrying a large container filled with little boxes. They were the entire chorus line from the hotel's nightly shows.

Ferrucio squeaked, "And to commemorate this magnificent evening, I have a gift for each one of you. A music player shaped like the conference's egg logo. Enjoy them."

The poodles reached into the containers held by the great Danes and passed the little white boxes out to row after row of the audience. Lots of noise and pandemonium and an occasional yip from a poodle who had gotten within pinching range. As individual members of the audience opened the boxes and pressed the buttons, fragments of Italian opera, totally out of sync, filled the Aquacade. In short, Ferrucio had lost control of his show, the jerk.

A Poodle-Dane duo strutted down the aisle near our seats.

"Howard," said the Great Bear, "get one of those boxes!"

Howard reached out. "Ouch, watch those quills, buddy," barked the chorine. The Dane growled menacingly. "Here, there's enough for everyone."

At last, we had several of the eggs to examine. Howard started to disassemble one. I was about to call Bruce again. I hadn't been able to reach him since Octavius asked me to call. Suddenly, Octavius' cell phone rang.

"Bear here!"

A definitely feminine ursine voice squealed with delight on the other end. "Oh, you sly darling! You did get it back. I know I can't keep it, but I'll wear it tonight. I'm going to do a special dive just for you. Thank you, thank you, thank you. Gotta go. Bye."

It was Bel, and her voice on the phone was so loud, we could all hear it. "What was she babbling about, Octavius?"

"I'm not sure, but I think she believes I sent her the Deep Blue Sapphire to wear during the show."

"The Deep Blue? But that's impossible. That jewel was destroyed. "

"Bel doesn't know that. I never told her."

"But," said Megatunni, "who would send her a jewel to wear tonight if it wasn't you?"

Silence and then… "Imperius!! Is Bel a target? Is he going to try to kill her to avenge his lost sweetheart? Is that how he's going to get back at me? But why the jewelry?"

Octavius turned to Howard and asked, "You *did* say the projector could set off secondary radiation from a target?"

"Right!"

"And not all elements radiate at the same level?"

"No, some of them are almost inert."

"What are the strongest radiators?"

"Oh, diamonds, other faceted gems, sapphires especially..."

My phone rang. It was Wallaroo. "That damned cat has escaped."

"Escaped?" I repeated for the others. "How? When?"

"Just a few minutes ago. She woke up and said she had to go to the bathroom. They uncuffed her, and she went into the loo. Then she banged open the door, caught the guards wrong footed and took off like a shot. They're looking for her now."

"There goes our chance to learn anything."

"No, she left a message scrawled on the wall in iodine. It says, 'The eggs are bombs.' " I repeated it for Octavius.

"Oh, God," roared the Bear. "It's not just me or Bel he's targeting. He's trying to destroy the whole convention. Howard, is there some kind of timer in that egg?"

"Not that I can see. There's just a circuit board with a processor and memory chip and all the plastic holding it in. I guess there could be a timer in the processor, but I don't know how you would set it."

"That's it. The plastic is the explosive, but if the trigger isn't self-contained, what sets it off? Could a radiating sapphire really do it?" He stared at Howard who nodded vigorously.

"Good God, Mr. Megatunni, we'd better get those bombs away from this crowd and get everyone out of the stadium. Call backstage and make sure Belinda doesn't make an entrance. "

Megatunni got to his feet just as the band struck up a gigantic fanfare. Ferreti shouted, "And now the moment you have been waiting for –

328

Bearoness Belinda Béarnaise Bruin (nee Black) and the *Aquabears*." Cheers and applause. The *Aquabears* plunged into the pool in unison and slowly moving up to the high diving board strode Belinda

"Too late," I yelled. "Roar at her, Octavius."

"Bel, get down from there. Get down!!!"

The Bearoness recognizing the stentorian voice but obviously not understanding what he was saying, smiled out at the audience. With spotlights shining on her she couldn't see us, and even if she did, she would have thought we were just being overly enthusiastic about her appearance.

Octavius searched the crowd furiously. "If we can't stop her, we have to stop him. Where the hell is he?"

Scanning around, I spotted a black head peering over the top of the basket in the stage-right balloon. "There," I shouted.

Octavius picked up the headset that connected us to the *Ursa Major* and shouted, "Colonel, there are four hot air balloons at the stadium. Take them out, now."

"We see them. Four heat-seeking missiles are on their way."

Belinda had reached the end of the diving board, and bowing, turned away from the audience.

In the basket, Imperius went berserk. "What is she doing, she's facing the wrong way. This isn't in the script. I can't get a clear shot at the jewel."

"Octavius roared out, "Dive, Bel, Dive!"

She did a backward somersault in the pike position ending with a twist and recovery. Imperius fired at her in sheer frustration and missed just as four missiles screamed into the propane gas jets on the balloons, adding substantially to their heat and blowing them to atoms.

The crowd was on its feet cheering. They thought the balloons were timed to blow up just as Belinda hit the water. They'd never seen anything like that. Only in Las Vegas!

But enough was enough. The exits were sealed, and Megatunni had the guards and the police racing up and down, confiscating the eggs. They told the audience they were contaminated. No one seemed to want to keep them anyway. The band kept playing and the *Aquabears* continued cavorting until order could be restored. Megatunni himself grabbed Ferrucio Ferreti. Howard and I ran over to where the balloon had been. No trace of the Duck or Baboon – but wait – stuck in a shrub was a shining tube. The projector! It had probably been blown out with the blast.

"Is it intact, Howard?"

"Not really, but I can still get an idea of how far he's taken its development. This thing was super lethal."

"Any sign of those two?"

"Not a shred!"

Octavius had given the Colonel and Frau a "well done" over the radio and told them to stand down. As he was doing this he was trundling to poolside to reach Belinda.

"Bel," he shouted, "Are you all right?"

"Of course I'm all right, you silly bear," shaking the water off herself. *(Oh, how he loved wet fur.)* "But what has happened to the show, and what were those explosions?" Tavi? Tavi? Octavius??"

The Great Bear had rolled over into a deep sleep.

330

Chapter Thirty Seven

Homo Sapiens? I must insist

That those creatures no longer exist.

We have proof that's succinct.

They are clearly extinct.

Yet the rumors still seem to persist.

Wednesday started out just like any other morning after an attempted mass assassination. There was no way we could keep the story quiet, although we did manage to keep the particle beam weapon under reasonable wraps by telling the press that the eggs were radio-controlled from one of the balloons.

With a contingent of the Nevada State Police, Frau Schuylkill and Dr. Watt went out into the deep desert, and after carefully taking an inventory, exploded the eggs. *(along with the phony sapphire we'd sneaked into one of the boxes).* The police kept a couple of eggs as evidence, but since there didn't seem to be anyone left to charge at the moment, they filed a number of reports and left the case open.

Bruce Wallaroo, Mr. Megatunni, and I had to persuade the Nevada Police that Ferrucio Ferreti was just the victim of a carefully complex scam, contrived by the deadly Duck. He was released from jail only to be slapped right back in again when he attempted to leave town without paying the hotel. No sign of Chita and no remains of Imperius or Bigg. Not surprising, considering the explosive impact of the missiles.

That missile attack may have been a bit foolhardy in retrospect, but the alternative was infinitely worse. We took some flak from the local authorities for taking matters into our own hands, but they had to admit that

Imperius Drake might have just succeeded if we hadn't. *(Not really true. Bel unwittingly foiled him when she switched her dive, but we weren't going to admit that to the constabulary.)* Thank goodness, only the bad guys got hurt in the explosions. One member of the audience was flattened by an irate chorus dog, but that didn't count.

This morning, the delegates were leaving the hotel as fast as they could. The media were having a field day, and the hotel authorities were doing a major survey to see how much damage had been done at the Aquacade. Recovered from his bouts of hysteria, *Il Professore* Roberto Rabbito wandered around the halls, searching for something he couldn't find. Someone suggested it might be the Noble Prize. *(It turns out the prize wasn't going to be awarded this year.)*

Octavius took advantage of the fact that no one was around and called his mother.

A voice growled, "Kodiak 465789. Please leave a message after the beep."

"Florence, this is Octavius Bear!"

The Arctic Fox picked up after the beep and said, "Oh, good morning, Doctor Octavius. Sorry about that, but we've been getting some weird phone calls lately. Heavy panting on the other end of the line."

"I understand. The world is getting stranger and stranger. Speaking of that, is my mother there?"

The fox twitched her ears and then said, "Yes she is. She's just finishing breakfast. Some salmon I poached for her. Just a minute,"

The Great Bear wondered what would happen if Florence and Frau Schuylkill were to compare culinary notes. Sounded like a win-win situation. Provided lupine and vulpine egos didn't get in the way. Something for another day. He heard his mother's voice in the background.

"Octavius? What a surprise! How are you?"

He decided not to tell her about last night, the near miss on his and everybody else's life and the probable demise of the dastardly Duck. That would have taken up most of the morning. He needed some information, and he needed it quickly before he got together again with Wyatt Where.

"Mom, I have a question for you!"

"Fine, thank you!"

"Oh, I'm sorry. How are you?" He almost said, "What's new?" but that would have set off a torrent of Kodiak Island gossip in which he had absolutely no interest.

"As I said, fine, thank you!" A bit frosty. "But I'm sure that isn't what you wanted to ask me."

This wasn't going to be easy. She was in a mood, no doubt set off by his clumsiness. She had always told him, "Brawn 10; Bravery 10; Brains 10++; Social Skills Zip!" Oh well.

"We had some interesting developments here in Las Vegas. It's a long story. I'll call you back later, and we can have a nice chat, but right now, I need to know something. You've been hibernating over the past few years, haven't you?"

"Of course I have. Beats dieting every time!"

"Do you dream while you hibernate?"

"Now, that's odd that you should ask that. Usually I don't. At least, not that I can remember. Except for this year. It was very strange. It was like I was awake while I was still asleep. I was outside. It looked like the Kodiak woods, but some things were different."

"Like what?"

"Well, for one thing, I couldn't find my den, and Florence wasn't anywhere about. And then I saw some other bears, but they were different too. They looked like normal bears, but they acted strange. None of them talked! They growled at each other and snuffled around the ground and bushes. I walked over to one and said, 'Hello!' She snarled and ran right at me. I turned to run, but she caught me in the hindquarter with her claw. I yelped, turned, and snarled back and then limped off. I think I passed out. It was not too long after that, I guess, when I woke from hibernation. But then, as you know, all bears can wake up and go back to sleep while they're hibernating. But maybe you don't know. You don't hibernate anymore!"

"Sounds to me like you just had a nightmare!"

"I thought so too, but I don't know how to explain the deep gash I have in my hindquarter."

Long pause. "Thanks, Mom. That helps a lot. Is your leg OK?"

"Fine, thank you!"

More silence, then, "I'll call back later. Bye!"

*****

Later the same morning, Octavius and Wyatt Where were closeted somewhere within the hotel.

"Wyatt, I've given your proposal a lot of thought, but before I make any commitments, I want to know more about this alternative universe. If we succeeded in developing a reliable transfer process, what sort of chaos might we unleash on both worlds?"

"A good question, Octavius. One I've mulled over for a good long while. It's probably the major reason I don't want this to fall into General

Turmoil's hands. Ideally, what I'd like to see happen is for us to make contact with individuals in this 'Alter-Earth' who can demonstrate their stability, wisdom, and good-will. I know that sounds Utopian, especially after what I'm about to tell you."

"Before you start, do you have any reason to believe that they have a similar capability and may indeed, be among us now?"

"It's certainly possible, I suppose, but if they did come here they would stick out like a sore paw. You see, Octavius, the dominant species by far on Alter-Earth is…"

"No, no! Let me guess. No, not reptiles, not felines, not even ursines! I've got it –*Homo Sapiens*!!!

"How did you know?"

"It just came to me *(via Agrippa)*. The same *Homo Sapiens* that supposedly went extinct here over a 100,000 years ago?"

"Sure looks that way to me."

"OK," the Great Bear thought, "At least two confirmed sightings by reliable *(semi-reliable in Agrippa's case)* witnesses. I'll have to take this seriously, at least for the time being."

He said, "Well, that puts quite a spin on things. I guess you got away without being discovered, because there are other wolves on Alter-Earth."

"Yes, but they are not what we'd call intelligent life, as I found out the first time I tried to communicate with them."

"Just like Mom," thought the Bear.

"But if I was extremely careful, I could make my way around certain portions of their world. Unfortunately, wolves are considered wild and dangerous beasts by h.saps and you won't find them in any built up, civilized corner of their world, except in zoos."

"Zoos??"

"Places where wild animals are kept on display for the h.saps' amusement.!"

"But we're self-aware. We communicate. We are civilized. They wouldn't try any of that with us."

"Don't be too sure, Octavius. They'd need evidence of all of that, and even then it may not click. I had a terrible time making any sense out of their language. I should say languages. Each group seems to have its own way of talking. There are a few dominant languages but no real consistency."

"Were you able to converse with anyone at all?"

"Not directly. I did manage to find an empty cage in one of their zoos and got to listen to the gawkers talking to each other. There were a lot of *h.sap* kits and cubs so much of what I was hearing was probably not very useful. I did manage to travel around a bit by sneaking onto freight trains and even a plane – a freighter."

"Planes, trains? They're that far advanced?"

"Even more than that. They've been out in space! Octavius, the real shocker is not just that they're advanced, but how extremely similar everything is to our world. At first, I thought I was having a highly creative nightmare. When you see cities with the same names, streets that look almost the same as ours. Their infrastructure is a lot more uniform because all *h.sap* adults are between five and seven feet tall. They don't have to accommodate the wide range of shapes and sizes that we do. But much, much more is the same than different. They have the same continents, same countries, more or less. They look like smooth-skinned apes. They walk erect, and they wear clothes all the time, not just on special occasions. And not just for decoration.

336

They need to. They have no fur to speak of and they have weather extremes just like here on Earth. By the way, they don't have tails."

Shades of the Great War! Octavius peered at the wolf. "Does that matter to you, Wyatt?"

"Er, no. At least I don't think so!" Embarrassed cough, bark, growl. Time to change the subject.

"I got a chance to watch some of their television. While I couldn't really understand what was being said, the pictures told a story. They seem bent on self-destruction. Bombs, guns, crashes, death – day in and day out. At first, I thought it might have been made-up dramas, but the more I watched, the more I was convinced it was real. Now, do you begin to see why I'm so reluctant to let someone like General Turmoil near them? He'd have us in a conflict in nothing flat. Although if he did go there, one of the *h.saps* might try to put a saddle on him and ride him." He broke into laughter at the prospect, and so did the Great Bear.

"So tell me again, Wyatt, why we should reinvigorate this project? Sounds like the only thing we would end up doing is putting ourselves in peril, starting with you. You said you've made thirty-five visits?"

"Yes! Of course some of them were for less than five minutes. The longest was for six days."

"Can you do it at will?"

"Not entirely, but I'm getting better at setting up the conditions. I keep trying to 'world jump' without having to be dead to the world. So far, no joy! But I've learned to induce the sleep on demand. I'm not entirely comfortable with having to be asleep when I go. I want to do a last minute review of the terrain and situation before leaving."

"How did you survive?"

"They're omnivores, and it wasn't too difficult to cadge a bite or a drink here and there. And I found shelter in a variety of places, including with a pack of friendly stray dogs. Unfortunately we couldn't converse, but they sensed that I was one of them."

"Do you think there are friendly members of *h.sap*? I mean potentially friendly to us?"

"In spite of all of their destructiveness, for the most part they do seem to live in a cooperative mode. They have common meetings! They buy and sell things! They travel to each other's places. They treat their kits and cubs well in some countries. Others seem to leave them to starve to death. They are civilized and uncivilized at the same time. Rational and irrational. If we do nothing else in restarting this project, I would want to bring back more of their books, recordings, television shows, news media for analysis. "

"More?? Does that mean you have some already?"

"Quite a bit! I found I could take things back with me. They ended up sitting on the floor next to me when I woke up. Are you up for some real irony?"

"Fire away!!"

"Everything I took is stashed in a vault at the Bank of Lake Michigan under the name of Imperius Drake." He broke into hysterical laughter. Octavius snorted.

"It might be a bit tough to get them out," said the wolf. "I wouldn't put it past Montgomery Moose to try to block their recovery."

"If he does, we'll just have Commissioner Daly subpoena them. We'll say they're top secret evidence of some of the Duck's most heinous international misdeeds. By the way, does Howard know about any of this?"

"I never told him anything, but Howard is no dope. He may know that something strange has been happening in my life."

"Do you think you can bring anyone else with you?"

"I haven't tried yet. I'm not interested in putting anyone else in jeopardy."

"Even the Frau," thought Octavius, "Or perhaps especially the Frau. That relationship needed a little more scrutiny. Romance was all fine and good but those two could set off an accidental catastrophe if they couldn't keep their libidos separate from their foolhardiness."

He also wondered if he could convert his own narcoleptic seizures into opportunities for other-world exploration. Trouble was, he couldn't control the damn things at all. Then again, he hadn't really tried to do anything except prevent them. He had been remarkably unsuccessful at that. Maybe he could exploit them. Step One! Need more information!

He looked at the wolf. "OK! Here's what we'll do. As soon as we're all back at the mansion, I'll contact the Commissioner and tell him that the Duck has been trading in exotic and dangerous materials. Given the Duck's mad sense of humor, he deposited them in a vault in the Bank of Lake Michigan. You know the number and the combination. We want to get them out and search for additional criminal activities Imperius may be involved in. It's a little lame, but the Commissioner owes me quite a few and he knows I'm always doing something a little bit over the top or outside the box. Then we can look at this material and decide whether we want to let sleeping h.saps lie or stir things up."

"We may also be able to get some clues on whether they're doing the same thing. I guess that's what has me most worried. If they've gone out to space, what's to stop them from invading alternate worlds once they find out they exist" said Wyatt.

"Well, let's not get too anxious. Do you actually believe there might be multiple worlds out there?"

"Sure, why should the count stop at two?"

"Do you always end up in the same Alter-World?"

"I really don't know. It always looks and seems the same."

"By the way, when was the last time you made a slumber trip?"

"Three days ago!!"

Octavius closed his eyes, threw up his paws and laughed, causing the fire alarms to go off throughout the hotel.

Chapter Thirty Eight

With his feathers an ominous black,

And his wings poised to stage an attack,

Was our villain blown up?

Should I really own up?

Like the Phoenix, he just may come back.

So, now it's Wednesday at about 2:00 in the afternoon. The Bearoness and the *Aquabears* were splashing around in one of the hotel's many swimming pools, giving us a private showing of last night's performance that never came off.

I had taken Belinda aside last night and explained about Octavius' narcolepsy. She hadn't known. He'd developed his hibernation cure after they had broken up. She was both shocked and amused. After the uproar it had taken him about half an hour to wake up again, and she was clever enough to pick up the conversation right where it had left off.

We had all gathered at a large party cabana. Megatunni and several of the police had dropped by. Bruce was doing leaps and cannonballs into the water, splashing the bears. Belinda was trying with no success to get Octavius into the pool. Howard was sitting off in a corner with a large drink and a big bowl of tree bark, working on some diagrams. I was sitting comfortably with a large fermented coconut milk VSOP. *(We'll have to leave tomorrow. The Frau told me confidentially that we were down to our last three kegs of mead.)* She and the Colonel were lying in the sun and occasionally growling at each other.

Megatunni looked over at Octavius and asked, "So this all began in a museum in Chicago?"

"Yes," said the Bear, "and we can't really tell that story completely because it would reveal that the jewel was disintegrated by the ray gun. We need to keep a lid on both those weapons."

"Oh," said Megatunni. "There are two?"

"Actually, one and a half. We developed the first one, and that's the one Imperius stole from UUI in pieces. We never knew whether he had made it operational. Obviously, he had. Once again, it's a ruin, but this time we have it. The other one belongs to UUI and is kept under major wraps at the insistence of the government. I think you'll find yourself in some trouble if you talk about either, Mr. Megatunni."

The Komodo nodded and flicked his tongue several times.

Bruce bounced over and said, "I'm heading back to Ozzie Land for some R &R, Ocko. Want to come along?"

"Thanks for the invitation, Inspector, but I think I'll pass."

Belinda had gotten out of the pool and was drying herself off. Octavius was right. Wet fur is sexy. "I think I have Tavi talked into spending a little time with me, haven't I, dear? We're going to fly up to Churchill and watch the polar bear migration and possibly renew a few memories."

The Great Bear harrumphed.

"Bearoness," I said, "I guess you and the *Aquabears* will never see any of the money you were supposed to be paid for last night's performance."

"Oh, Maury, you sweet little naïve Meerkat, one of the first things my late husband, the Bearon, taught me about show biz was always get the money up front. I'm sure Ferrucio and probably the professor are in major financial pickles, but we are doing fine."

"I guess we'll have to concoct some story that Montgomery Moose's insurance subsidiary will believe so they'll pay up for the loss of the Deep Blue Sapphire," I said. I thought Bruce would have a stroke from laughing at that prospect. Howard and Wyatt were enjoying themselves, too. "I'd love to see his face and listen to him trumpet," said the Colonel.

The Colonel looked over at Octavius and said, "Ilsa and I are planning to take a little time off too, especially if you're not going to be at the mansion for a while."

(Ilsa!? I've known the Frau for years and never knew her first name. Something serious going on here.)

"Ja, Herr Bear, by your leave. We are planning to hike around Transylvania for a few weeks."

"Transylvania, Colonel?"

"And perhaps a few other places, Octavius!" *(Meaningful stares!)*

Certainly, Frau Schuylkill, (*you're not going to catch Octavius calling her Ilsa.*) You deserve a vacation. Just make sure you come back. *(A sideways look at the Colonel.)* I'm sure Maury and Howard can take care of themselves in the meantime." *(Nobody asked Howard or Maury. I felt a pout coming on.)*

"Bel, I'm sorry you couldn't keep that 'sapphire' but we weren't even sure what it was. The Duck had obviously manufactured it but we didn't know how or with what. We felt it was better to destroy it along with the eggs. "

"Don't worry about it, Tavi. It certainly was beautiful but when I found out what it was supposed to be used for, I didn't want to touch it ever again. As far as I'm concerned: "Diamonds are a Bear's Best Friends."

*****

At a boarding ramp at Los Angeles International Airport (LAX) a gate agent was returning a carefully forged passport and taking the boarding pass of an extremely attractive black panther. She was wearing a very distinctive diamond collar. "Are you taking anything aboard with you, Ms. Catt?" he asked. "Oh, just some carrion," she said as she strode into the plane.

In a casino in Reno, Nevada, a rambunctious, hairy and bandaged Latin American revolutionary who arrived in the middle of the night was shouting from his seat at a Big Jackpot slot machine. "I want three plums. I want three plums."

And hidden in the dense foliage of a live oak tree overlooking a cabana party at the Blue Lagoon Hotel, Casino and Resort, Las Vegas, Nevada, a Mandarin Duck sat staring, staring, staring.

About the Author

Harry DeMaio is a nom de plume of Harry B. DeMaio, successful author of several books on Information Security and Business Networks. A retired business executive, consultant, information security specialist, former pilot and graduate school adjunct professor, he whiles away his time traveling and writing preposterous articles and stories.

He has appeared on many radio and TV shows and is an accomplished, frequent public speaker.

Former New York City natives, he and his extremely patient and helpful wife, Virginia, and their Bichon Frisé, Woof, live in Cincinnati (and several other parallel universes.) They have two sons, living in Scottsdale, Arizona and Cortlandt Manor, New York, both of whom are quite successful and quite normal, thus putting the lie to the theory that insanity is hereditary.

Also from MX Publishing

MX Publishing is the world's largest specialist Sherlock Holmes publisher, with over a hundred titles and fifty authors creating the latest in Sherlock Holmes fiction and non-fiction.

From traditional short stories and novels to travel guides and quiz books, MX Publishing cater for all Holmes fans.

The collection includes leading titles such as *Benedict Cumberbatch In Transition* and *The Norwood Author* which won the 2011 Howlett Award (Sherlock Holmes Book of the Year).

MX Publishing also has one of the largest communities of Holmes fans on Facebook with regular contributions from dozens of authors.

www.mxpublishing.com

Also from MX Publishing

Sherlock Holmes Short Story Collections

Sherlock Holmes and the Murder at the Savoy

Sherlock Holmes and the Skull of Kohada Koheiji

Look out for the new novel from Mike Hogan – *The Scottish Question*.

www.mxpublishing.com

348

Also from MX Publishing

Our bestselling books are our short story collections – of which we have several;

'Lost Stories of Sherlock Holmes' , 'The Outstanding Mysteries of Sherlock Holmes', The Papers of Sherlock Holmes Volume 1 and 2, 'Untold Adventures of Sherlock Holmes' (and the sequel 'Studies in Legacy) and 'Sherlock Holmes in Pursuit', 'The Cotswold Werewolf and Other Stories of Sherlock Holmes' – and many more……

www.mxpublishing.com

Also From MX Publishing

London, 1920: Boston-bred Enoch Hale, working as a reporter for the Central News Syndicate, arrives on the scene shortly after a music hall escape artist is found hanging from the ceiling in his dressing room. What at first appears to be a suicide turns out to be murder.

Also coming in 2014 the second in the Enoch Hale series –
'The Poisoned Penman'.

www.mxpublishing.com

Also from MX Publishing

"Phil Growick's, 'The Secret Journal of Dr Watson', is an adventure which takes place in the latter part of Holmes and Watson's lives. They are entrusted by HM Government (although not officially) and the King no less to undertake a rescue mission to save the Romanovs, Russia's Royal family from a grisly end at the hand of the Bolsheviks. There is a wealth of detail in the story but not so much as would detract us from the enjoyment of the story. Espionage, counter-espionage, the ace of spies himself, double-agents, double-crossers...all these flit across the pages in a realistic and exciting way. All the characters are extremely well-drawn and Mr Growick, most importantly, does not falter with a very good ear for Holmesian dialogue indeed. Highly recommended. A five-star effort."
The Baker Street Society

Also published in Italian, Russian, and audio versions and the sequel 'The Revenge of Sherlock Holmes' is released in spring 2014.

www.mxpublishing.com